THE DEVIL
YOU KNOW

Praise for the Cain Casey Saga

The Devil's Due

"A Night Owl Reviews Top Pick: Cain Casey is the kind of person you aspire to be even though some consider her a criminal. She's loyal, very protective of those she loves, honorable, big on preserving her family legacy and loves her family greatly. *The Devil's Due* is a book I highly recommend and well worth the wait we all suffered through. I cannot wait for the next book in the series to come out."
—*Night Owl Reviews*

The Devil Be Damned

"Ali Vali excels at creating strong, romantic characters along with her fast-paced, sophisticated plots. Her setting, New Orleans, provides just the right blend of immigrants from Mexico, South America, and Cuba, along with a city steeped in traditions."—*Just About Write*

Deal with the Devil

"Ali Vali has given her fans another thick, rich thriller...*Deal With the Devil* has wonderful love stories, great sex, and an ample supply of humor. It is an exciting, page-turning read that leaves her readers eagerly awaiting the next book in the series."—*Just About Write*

The Devil Unleashed

"Fast-paced action scenes, intriguing character revelations, and a refreshing approach to the romance thriller genre all make for an enjoyable reading experience in the Big Easy...*The Devil Unleashed* is an engrossing reading experience."—*Midwest Book Review*

The Devil Inside

"*The Devil Inside* is the first of what promises to be a very exciting series...While telling an exciting story that grips the reader, Vali has also fully fleshed out her heroes and villains. *The Devil Inside* is that rarity: a fascinating crime novel which includes a tender love story and leaves the reader with a cliffhanger ending."—*MegaScene*

Praise for Ali Vali

Writer's Block

"Absolutely great! A totally unexpected story filled with a touch of erotica, a hidden gem, and a scenario so brilliant I had no idea what would happen or how the story would turn out. I was so excited to read this, then when I started I couldn't believe how addictive it was, nor how clever it was all going to be. A fantastic story that I couldn't put down and cannot recommend enough!"—*Lesbireviewed*

One More Chance

"This was an amazing book by Vali…complex and multi-layered (both characters and plot)."—*Danielle Kimerer, Librarian (Nevins Memorial Library, Massachusetts)*

Face the Music

"This is a typical Ali Vali romance with strong characters, a beautiful setting (Nashville, Tennessee), and an enemies-to-lovers style tale. The two main characters are beautiful, strong-willed, and easy to fall in love with. The romance between them is steamy, and so are the sex scenes."—*Rainbow Reflections*

The Inheritance

"I love a good story that makes me laugh and cry, and this one did that a lot for me. I would step back into this world any time."—*Kat Adams, Bookseller (QBD Books, Australia)*

Double-Crossed

"[T]here aren't too many lesfic books like *Double-Crossed* and it is refreshing to see an author like Vali continue to churn out books like these. Excellent crime thriller."—*Colleen Corgel, Librarian, Queens Borough Public Library*

Stormy Seas

Stormy Seas "is one book that adventure lovers must read."—*Rainbow Reflections*

Answering the Call

Answering the Call "is a brilliant cop-and-killer story…The crime story is tight and the love story is fantastic."—*Best Lesbian Erotica*

Lammy Finalist *Calling the Dead*

"So many writers set stories in New Orleans, but Ali Vali's mystery novels have the authenticity that only a real Big Easy resident could bring. Set six months after Hurricane Katrina has devastated the city, a lesbian detective is still battling demons when a body turns up behind one of the city's famous eateries. What follows makes for a classic lesbian murder yarn."—*Curve Magazine*

Beauty and the Boss

"The story gripped me from the first page…Vali's writing style is lovely—it's clean, sharp, no wasted words, and it flows beautifully as a result. Highly recommended!"—*Rainbow Book Reviews*

Balance of Forces: Toujours Ici

"A stunning addition to the vampire legend, *Balance of Forces: Toujours Ici* is one that stands apart from the rest."—*Bibliophilic Book Blog*

Beneath the Waves

"The premise…was brilliantly constructed…skillfully written and the imagination that went into it was fantastic…A wonderful passionate love story with a great mystery."—*Inked Rainbow Reads*

Second Season

"The issues are realistic and center around the universal factors of love, jealousy, betrayal, and doing the right thing and are constantly woven into the fabric of the story. We rated this well written social commentary through the use of fiction our max five hearts."—*Heartland Reviews*

Carly's Sound

"*Carly's Sound* is a great romance, with some wonderfully hot sex, but it is more than that. It is also the tale of a woman rising from the ashes of grief and finding new love and a new life. Vali has surrounded Julia and Poppy with a cast of great supporting characters, making this an extremely satisfying read."—*Just About Write*

By the Author

Carly's Sound

Second Season

Love Match

The Dragon Tree Legacy

The Romance Vote

Hell Fire Club
in Girls with Guns

Beauty and the Boss

Blue Skies

Stormy Seas

The Inheritance

Face the Music

On the Rocks
in Still Not Over You

A Woman to Treasure

Calumet

Writer's Block

One More Chance

A Good Chance

Never Kiss a Cowgirl

Rivals for Love

The Cain Casey Saga

The Devil Inside

The Devil Unleashed

Deal with the Devil

The Devil Be Damned

The Devil's Orchard

The Devil's Due

Heart of the Devil

The Devil Incarnate

The Devil You Know

Call Series

Calling the Dead

Answering the Call

Waves Series

Beneath the Waves

Turbulent Waves

Forces Series

Balance of Forces: Toujours Ici

Battle of Forces: Sera Toujours

Force of Fire: Toujours a Vous

Vegas Nights
Double-Crossed

Visit us at www.boldstrokesbooks.com

THE DEVIL YOU KNOW

by

Ali Vali

2024

ISBN 13: 978-1-63679-471-6

THIS TRADE PAPERBACK ORIGINAL IS PUBLISHED BY
BOLD STROKES BOOKS, INC.
P.O. BOX 249
VALLEY FALLS, NY 12185

FIRST EDITION: JULY 2024

CREDITS
EDITOR: RUTH STERNGLANTZ
PRODUCTION DESIGN: STACIA SEAMAN
COVER DESIGN BY TAMMY SEIDICK

Acknowledgments

Thank you, Radclyffe, for bringing me into the fold all those years ago. Thank you, Sandy, for all you do to keep me on track, and for all the great titles you come up with. To my BSB family, you keep me grounded and teach me what real family is about. You all have been a blessing.

Thank you to my editor, Ruth Sternglantz. Ruth, thank you for all the lessons and fun along the way. I'd also like to thank Tammy Seidick for the great cover. You always capture the essence of every book.

Thank you to you, the reader. It's good to know y'all are as bloodthirsty as I am and wanted more of Cain, Emma, and company. Writing is a solitary exercise, but the emails and texts I get from some of you are what keeps me going. I appreciate you all.

Thank you, C, for getting me back on my feet, literally. Knee replacement was no fun. I'm ready for all the new adventures we can think of. Verdad.

For C
Always

CHAPTER ONE

This one, Mom." Hannah Casey had her face pressed against a glass case in Tiffany's and pointed to a bracelet with sapphires and diamonds. If the FBI needed a full set of the child's finger and nose prints, now would be a perfect opportunity to collect them. "Mama loves blue."

Derby Cain Casey watched as Hannah demolished the clean surface of yet another case while they shopped for her wife Emma's birthday present. She had to smile at the young sales associates who followed her children discreetly, with a bottle of glass cleaner. Everyone in the store seemed smart enough not to tell Hannah anything that might lessen the exuberance she showed in getting her mother the perfect gift. Hayden picked his little sister up so they could both see what Hannah had picked out, and the top of the case got a fresh set of smudges.

"Excellent choice, Miss Hannah," the saleswoman said, unlocking the case. She rattled off the information about the piece as she handed it to Hannah.

"It's beautiful," Hannah whispered, and Hayden kissed her temple.

"What do you think, Mom?" Hayden glanced her way as Hannah held her arm out for the woman to put the bracelet on her. Cain took a picture of both of them while holding Billy, who was still too young to give an opinion on his mama's birthday gift.

"Your mama does love blue." Both Hannah and Hayden had inherited her own blue eyes, which was why Emma always said it was her favorite. Billy, though, had inherited Emma's green eyes, and Cain had been thrilled from the first sight of them. "We'll take it if you can replace one of the stones with an emerald."

"Certainly, Ms. Casey. We'll have it done within the hour." The young woman handed the piece to one of the waiting staff before facing

Hannah and Hayden again. "Is there anything else you'd like to look at?"

"Do you think we should get the matching earrings, Mom?" Hayden asked.

"We can replace a diamond in each with an emerald if you like," the woman said.

Cain nodded as Billy chewed on her shoulder, leaving a line of drool on her suit jacket. This was Emma's second birthday since coming home, and their children had loved the first shopping trip so much she thought they'd turn it into a tradition—a tradition the saleswoman had been schooled on by her guard Lou before they'd arrived. This was the kids' gift for Emma, so they'd participate in the payment.

"Let's have lunch, guys, and we'll come back and pick it up." Hannah clapped her hands and appeared thrilled with her world.

"Will you be paying cash?"

"Yes, ma'am," the kids answered together.

Hayden put his sister on her feet so she could open the bag she'd carried, and he could fish out his wallet. He counted out the couple of hundred he'd made doing odd jobs for her, and Hannah had spent quite a few hours helping Emma with the baby. The little girl handed Hayden her money so he could help her count, and she happily handed over her share. The saleswoman sighed with her hand over her chest, as if all the cute in the room was too much to handle.

"Thank you, and I promise to wrap it for you. Your mama's a lucky woman."

Cain and the kids filed out into the mall with more guards than they normally traveled with, and as usual it drew attention to them. She wasn't taking any chances with anything, though. Their businesses were doing well, and that success was supposed to bring peace. It had—until some wrinkles in that plan derailed what she had in mind.

The Russian mob along with an unknown factor in the FBI were giving her some long afternoons of thinking and worrying. She prided herself on putting puzzles together, but so far, the pieces were elusive. That alone was aggravating, which only made it harder to think about all this rationally. Finding the *who* of all the problems was the first step in eliminating the threat, but so far they were well hidden.

They headed for Saks to find Emma. Her birthday was the next day, and they'd celebrate with the family at home, but Saturday she was hosting a dinner at Blanchard's followed by a party at their club, Emma's. The private affair would be the first event at Emma's since the renovations, made necessary by the gun spray that destroyed the club that carried her wife's name. Emma wasn't someone who enjoyed the limelight, but Saturday was her day.

"Mom, do you think Mama's going to love our present?" Hannah skipped next to her holding Hayden's hand.

"She is, and you'll have to tell her why you picked it." Lou led them to the escalator, and she was surprised to find Tracy Stegal—Colombian cartel boss Hector Delarosa's girlfriend—standing on the second-floor landing. Hector's little pet's hatred ran deep, and Cain was sure that if she could get away with it, Tracy would slit her throat with no remorse. That's what she'd ordered for Tracy's sister, and in Tracy's eyes, it was unforgivable. It was her fear of the consequences of that move that kept Tracy on Hector's short leash. "Ms. Stegal."

"Ms. Casey." Tracy bowed her head slightly, but it appeared to be a move to study the children. "Family outing?"

"A bit of shopping," she said. She didn't like this woman any more than she did her sister, and that hadn't ended well. Kim Stegal had played a dangerous game and ended up on the floor of a warehouse in a pool of her own blood.

"It's my mama's birthday," Hannah said, loud enough to alert the entire second floor.

"Tell her happy birthday for me." Tracy smiled at Hannah, and Cain could see a bit of heart shining through. "Enjoy your shopping."

"Take care, Tracy. It's become an interesting world." The baby babbled in her ear, grabbed a lock of her hair, and pulled harder than she thought a baby could.

"Is that a threat?" Tracy lost her smile, and her wariness was back. It was like paranoia ran deep in the Stegal family.

"It's just advice. We aren't friends, but we don't have to be enemies." Hayden glanced between them and stepped beside her. She loved his instincts when it came to the family. He'd not only come to her side, but put Hannah behind him. "If only you and Hector would get that small fact through your heads, we could all live in harmony."

"Have a good day, and I'll see you sooner than you think." Tracy smiled but it gave her more of a predatory look. The death of her sister had hit her hard, and Cain understood that kind of pain. It was the only reason she hadn't done something about the disrespect Tracy liked to dish out in heaps.

"Do you ever think before you let words spill out of you like vomit?" Cain placed her hand on Hayden's shoulder when he inhaled deeply. "You threaten as if you have the power to do something about it."

"Perhaps I do." Tracy didn't lower her head, but she did break eye contact first. "You should watch what you say around me."

"Then we *will* see each other soon," she said with the same scowl before laughing. "You talk to me like you want to kill me, but we both know there's only one way that's going to happen. Killing Hector will give you your shot, so he might need a heads-up."

"You have children with you, so let's stop there."

Tracy glanced back a few times as she walked to the other escalator. It was a sign of weakness, which telegraphed Tracy's inexperience. The woman might've been indispensable to Hector, but she was still a guppy trying to swim with sharks. Billy pulled her hair again, interrupting her wasting time thinking about Tracy, so she started walking in search of Emma. She put odds on getting a call that afternoon.

"Are you causing trouble?" Emma asked, taking the baby from her.

"I was enjoying the morning with our beautiful kids, pretty lady. We missed you, though, so we came to invite you to lunch." She kissed Emma before giving the kids a chance to hug her. "Let's eat, and we'll come back and help you pick something."

"Best offer I've gotten today." Emma handed Billy to Hayden and took Hannah's hand. "The restaurant upstairs should be good. You used to love it as a toddler," Emma said to Hayden. "You would bang on the windows until you were exhausted. I was always thankful they didn't open, or we would've had to fish you out of the Mississippi."

Cain laughed at Hayden's slight blush, which could only be put there by his mother. Her phone buzzed, and she shook her head at Hector's name. The cartel boss was still swimming in problems, which was why it surprised her Tracy was so disrespectful. Hector's call meant Tracy was smart enough to tell him what happened.

She understood the position Hector was in. When there were enemies at every gate, making more was an amateur move. Hector owed her for delivering Jerome Rhodes and his father to him. Jerome—really FBI Agent Anthony Curtis—along with his father had destroyed Hector's fields and business. Cain had also wanted Anthony dead, but sometimes it was better to make friends than to pull the trigger herself. Eliminating Hector's main threat should've bought her some goodwill for months to come. But Tracy hadn't gotten that message.

"Why is he calling?" Emma asked.

"The kids and I were lucky enough to run into Tracy and her threatening ways right before we found you."

"Do you think that woman was dropped on her head as a child?" Emma asked when the kids followed the host to their table. "She stopped me too and had the burning need to tell me Hector was thinking of going back to Colombia."

"We'll throw him a farewell party if that's true." She pulled out Emma's chair and silenced her phone. Across from them, the agents assigned to her sat with their menus high enough she couldn't see their faces. It was comical to see these guys intently watching when she had her family with her. What could be nefarious about that? "Right now, enjoy the day."

❖

Special Agent Shelby Phillips sat in the van and listened to Hannah Casey tell a story about her dog that was making her mind wander. These were the only times Cain turned off the jammers, and it was almost as obnoxious as the music Cain subjected them to. She was stuck in the van today because of a chipped bone in her foot that'd landed her in a boot. That was the last time she'd believe anyone who said rollerblading was a great form of exercise.

"She's the cutest kid, but she knows every word in the English language," Special Agent Joe Simmons said.

"It's better than listening to 'Chopsticks,'" their IT specialist Lionel Jones said. "Any more of that, and I'm going to need therapy before I go postal on someone."

"It gives me a good reason to press the snooze button on my biological clock." Shelby went back to her search for Drew and Taylor Kennison and their daughter Lucy.

Cain and Emma had told her—and Annabel Hicks, her boss—about the family that seemed to have disappeared. Cain was right. They didn't exist beyond the few months they were in the city. Whoever had created their cover story had done an excellent job of burying them deep enough to make them invisible, but not good enough to make it nonobvious they were fictitious.

"Are we still on for tonight?" Lionel asked.

Their original team had been working on the case of the Kennisons and their young daughter who'd tried to talk Hannah Casey into bugging Cain's home office. Emma's first instinct had been to blame

Shelby and the team, but no one in the FBI who wasn't a total moron or totally dirty would've set up a kid like that. Their problem now was that the Kennison family were ghosts. The adults she could understand, but disappearing a kid brought up questions she didn't necessarily want to find the answers to because of what those answers could be.

"Yes," Shelby replied, "so mention it to Claire," she said of their other IT specialist, Claire Lansing. "The search hasn't panned out so far, but we'll talk about it later." She laughed as Hannah kept up her story, and then she and Lionel cut their mikes so Joe and the others couldn't hear them. "I don't know if I'm paranoid, but I don't want to talk in here."

"I sweep every day, not that I'm not paranoid too, but there's too much weird shit going on. You were right about Gardner." Dylan Gardner was the newest agent on their team, and Shelby had pegged her as trouble. Lionel put his finger up as they listened to Joe's commentary. The Casey family had only included their personal guards at lunch, with the rest of them in the lobby as a backup, Joe guessed.

Shelby had covered as many bases as she could without giving away they were watching more than Cain. There was something off about the whole day, and she couldn't figure out what. When Cain was this relaxed and open, there had to be something big working, and they'd only find out about it once she was done. Granted, Cain had offered to work with them, but she wasn't naive enough to think she'd be totally forthcoming.

"Did she make any phone calls while she was in the jewelry store?" Shelby asked Joe.

"Not one, but the day of shopping and lunch with the family smells like she's setting up for an alibi. If we ever get her in a courtroom, we'll be her best defense." Joe sounded calm, but Shelby could hear the frustration bleeding through.

"Lionel checked, and it really is Emma Casey's birthday," Shelby said.

"You would take up for her?" Dylan said, sounding like a sarcastic Valley Girl. Their new team member had mentioned more than once that they were too close to Cain, too chummy. "She could probably shoot one of the waiters while we're here, and all of you would miss it."

"Agent Gardner, if you'd like to file a complaint against me or anyone else on the team, go ahead. Your comments are getting old and are not appreciated." Shelby'd had enough of this bitch, but Annabel wasn't ready to transfer her, so she'd asked for patience. That was in short supply for all of them when it came to Dylan Gardner.

"Noted," Dylan said and nothing more.

"They're done and splitting up again. Casey's taking the kids," Joe said. "Gardner will stick to Emma."

"We should switch for a new perspective." Dylan wasn't someone made for the background. Shelby was convinced Dylan had Wonder Woman pajamas to fit the superhero persona she liked to exude, after a few arrests of low-level players in California.

"Sure, Covington will back you up," Joe said, as if not in the mood to argue. "Remember, *do not* approach her."

Shelby dialed Joe's cell after telling Lionel to cut their mikes. "Thanks for putting that idea into her head. I hope you don't have plans for—oh, say—the next month when we're all filling out paperwork."

"I know what Annabel told us, but I've had an ass full of surfer girl." Joe sounded like he was walking, and she heard mellow music playing in the background. Saks liked to relax you so you never noticed how much money you were spending.

"We'll talk about it later, but I had an idea about that." She heard chatter from Dylan's end, so she had to hang up. "See if there's any good sales, but I have to go." She got out of the van and put a jacket on as she headed for the front door. "Lionel, keep the line open and make sure Joe can hear in case I need backup." Thankfully Tiffany's was close to the main entrance since her foot was killing her. "Fuck me, man. Joe," she said into her wrist mike as she took in the situation, "I need you down here *now*."

Dylan was jamming her finger in Cain's direction, and Hannah and the baby were crying all while Covington sat back and watched. Right when Shelby walked up, Hayden stepped in front of Cain, and Dylan jammed him in the chest with the palm of her hand in front of witnesses. The store employees appeared riveted, as did the gathering crowd.

"Ms. Casey, a moment please." Shelby grabbed Dylan and shoved her back. "Get in the car now." Dylan didn't move. "Now, Gardner, or there will be consequences."

"Ms. Phillips, what the hell?" Cain spoke through clenched teeth, but she still understood her.

"Agent Gardner," Joe said. Leaving your post was unacceptable, but this had the potential to have major blowback, so Shelby was grateful he'd come down. "There's a car en route to escort you back to the office."

"I don't get the same courtesy she does?" Dylan asked so loudly it startled the baby into kicking his crying up a few notches.

"Here's the security footage," a woman with a silver *T* pin on the lapel of her great suit said, handing Cain a Jumpdrive. Shelby was convinced Tiffany had the best security in the business, so there'd be no denying what happened when they watched it in high definition. "Ms. Casey was simply picking up a purchase and told this woman hello."

"Fucking great," Dylan said but did comply by taking a few steps back.

"Cain, I'm sorry." Shelby spoke up so Cain would hear her over the screaming kids. "We'll deal with this internally if you agree. You're also within your rights to file a complaint."

"The line of hostility in that one worries me. Let Agent Hicks know a slap on the wrist will not be acceptable in this case. Not when it has to do with my children." Cain winked at her as Dylan lingered to the side. "Agent Gardner, I expect a heartfelt apology with a generous donation to my favorite charity."

"Would that be your pocket?" The way Dylan sneered made Cain smile, and Shelby wanted to groan. This would not go well if Dylan couldn't keep her mouth shut. Cain had a doctorate in goading people.

"That would be illegal, but I'm no legal scholar. The Community Children's Fund through the St. Louis Cathedral Foundation does great work. They have sports and art programs for underprivileged children that are very successful. My wife introduced me to it, so I'm a big fan." Cain lost her smile, and Shelby couldn't decipher her expression.

"Ms. Casey, I'll be in touch." Shelby pointed to the door and expected Dylan to follow.

There was no way to predict what some people were capable of, but Shelby wasn't fast enough to stop Dylan from tackling Cain to the ground, probably not a career-ending move had Cain not been holding a six-month-old baby. A cute baby who was screaming loud enough for the entire shopping center to hear.

The only person who sprang to help Cain and her son was the saleswoman, who then turned and yelled at someone behind her for a first-aid kit. Dylan stood with an expression of shock. Shelby only imagined the string of curses going through her head. She didn't have time for that, especially when she noticed the blood under Cain's head.

"What in the hell?" Emma Casey yelled as she ran toward Cain. "Someone explain."

"She came at me." Dylan pointed at Cain, making a bad situation worse.

Emma appeared ready to kill someone, especially when Cain sat up and her collar was soaked with blood and there was a stain on the tile where her head had hit. "I hope you enjoyed that, because life as you know it is over. Lou, call an ambulance."

"Shit," Shelby said when she saw Cain's collar. The white shirt was wet, and the stain was growing. She noticed Joe jogging in and slowed when he took in the scene. He made eye contact with her as he made a call.

"You have twenty minutes before Agent Hicks arrives, so try to come up with something good. What were you thinking?" He shook his head at Gardner, and Shelby understood his frustration. Dylan-the-wonder had made their jobs that much harder.

"She came at me, or I thought she was. I had no choice but to protect myself." Dylan rubbed her head hard enough to peel off her skin. "You have to back me up." For some reason Dylan glanced at Angus Covington, and he shook his head. That was another mystery Shelby had no time for.

"Even if we're stupid enough to do that, the security footage will never support your story. Start using your head and keep your mouth shut." She ran her hand through her hair and had to hold back the scream that wanted out.

"You only want to get rid of me, but it's not going to be that easy." Dylan tried that finger-jabbing motion with her, and Shelby only laughed. "Come on, you have to help me."

Gardner wasn't used to the surveillance they conducted—out of sight and quiet. Her job in California had been to interact with the guys selling drugs, and it had gotten results. It had also almost gotten her killed, so her transfer here hadn't been voluntary. "Agent Hicks is going to be pissed, so silence is the best way out of this. That's the only help I can give you. That and you should start praying Cain made even a step toward you."

"Hicks has to understand why I did it. There's no way I'm going down because of that bitch." Dylan spoke loud enough for Emma to hear her, and Joe seemed to want to shove a rag in her mouth if only he could find one.

Two EMTs entered with a gurney and carefully lifted Cain onto it. The bleeding didn't appear to have stopped, and Cain appeared dazed. "*That* bitch isn't the one who should concern you," Emma said, bouncing the baby since he was still screaming. Hannah was louder than him, and Shelby noticed there were people recording with their phones. "Agent Phillips, be ready to take everyone's statement. We're pressing charges."

"For what?" Dylan did indignant well, and the question disregarded everything she'd just told her.

A man came out of Tiffany's with Lou and handed Emma another Jumpdrive. "I gave Mr. Romero a list of everyone who witnessed what happened, with their phone numbers. Our security team apologizes for not acting sooner, Mrs. Casey."

"Of course," Shelby said closing her eyes. How a day could go so bad so fast would take an investigation on its own, but she took a breath before heading to the gurney. "Cain, are you okay?"

"Agent Phillips, step away from her and remember what I said. You've done enough damage today, so we'll be waiting at the hospital or the house, but we're not backing down."

"Mrs. Casey." Annabel Hicks pushed Shelby aside and held her hand out to Emma. "Trust me, I'll handle this myself. Make sure Cain's okay, and I'll come by the house with Shelby."

Emma nodded but stayed quiet. The Casey security detail closed ranks and followed Emma and her children out. "That's going to play well on the six o'clock news," Shelby said when Annabel pinched the bridge of her nose.

"The only way forward is through all this shit." Annabel exhaled and opened and closed her hands into fists. "See if you can get a copy of the security tape for us."

"Maybe Emma will share her copy." That comment got Dylan to glare at her. "Angus, start getting everyone's number and see if they'll turn over the information on their phones. We need every angle of this before Muriel Casey gets involved and we all end up writing tickets on cars parked illegally on Canal for the rest of our careers."

CHAPTER TWO

Remi Jatibon walked two paces behind her actress wife Dallas Montgomery and her sister-in-law Kristen, who was still at Tulane and dating Muriel Casey. They'd been back from their honeymoon in the Keys for a couple of weeks, and the wedding frenzy had switched to home renovations.

Remi and Dallas had been working for months on the house they'd purchased, and they were getting close to moving in. It was the only reason she'd joined Dallas and Kristen shopping for appliances. Her younger self was laughing hysterically at that unlikely move, but she was looking forward to finishing with all this. Their new neighbors would be the Casey family since they'd purchased the house Cain had grown up in. She wanted her family to grow up like her and her twin brother Mano, with the Casey kids as their friends. Cain wasn't only her oldest and closest friend, but also her business partner.

"Honey, try not to fall asleep. We're almost done," Dallas said, holding her hand out to her. "Do you want stainless or black?"

"Which one do you want?"

"You ask that every time we have to make a decision, then you agree with what I want. Try to remember it's *our* house, or I'm painting our bedroom pink and violet." Dallas raised an eyebrow and smiled.

"How about a compromise?" She took Dallas's hand and stepped closer. "The black stainless will show less fingerprints and look good with the paint and tile we agreed on. The fingerprint thing is a happy bonus in our business," she said and winked.

"See"—Dallas stood on her toes and kissed her—"you didn't break into hives, and no one jumped out and took your butch card away." Dallas bit her earlobe next. "Are you all shopped out, or would you like to come and pick out the last of the furniture we need?"

"You don't play fair, querida." She made arrangements for delivery and took the woman's card. "Remember who I am, so keep in mind what condition I want all this delivered in. Any extras as far as electronics and I'll be back."

"Don't worry, Ms. Jatibon. All this will process under another name. The delivery and install guys will only know who it's for when they arrive at the house."

They were on their way to the next stop when her main guard Simon took a call, then handed her the phone. "It's Lou."

"Hey, Lou," she said and Dallas leaned against her. "What can I do for you?"

"Just wanted to give you a call and tell you we're in the emergency room with Cain." Lou told her what happened in the most generic way possible.

"We're on our way. Do you need me to send some extra guys?" She covered the phone and gave Simon the new address.

"They're about to toss some of our people out—I've got too many, they said, so we're good. Thanks, Remi. Cain wanted to give you a heads-up because of the end of the quarter stuff."

"Mano will be happy to take that over, so tell her to stop thinking until we get there." She tapped the phone against her chin until Dallas tugged her hand down. "One of the guards went off the rails and tackled Cain while she was holding Billy. They're all at the emergency room. Sounds like she got hurt enough to warrant a trip." Dallas and Kristen seemed as surprised as she was at the news.

"Who would take a chance of hurting a baby?" Kristen asked.

"There's a small number of agents who don't mind cutting corners when it comes to the rules, so they justify the results they're after." Remi hadn't run into many problematic agents, but the reality of the life they'd chosen was that they were always there. The actuality was as real as seeing your shadow on the sidewalk on a sunny day. "We've lived our lives by rules people like the feds don't approve of, so it's a gamble."

"The problem isn't the gamble, my love. It's that you're playing with a stacked deck, and Cain's counting cards. A steady diet of losing can make some people, even the feds, crazy." Dallas slipped her hand into Remi's shirt and scratched over her navel. "That they would go after someone and take the chance of hurting their child doesn't make them the good guys."

"I agree with you," she said, threading her fingers with Dallas's as they headed out of the store. "We'll finish picking out stuff later if that's okay."

"Of course. I want to check on Emma," Dallas said.

The hospital was a ten-minute ride, and they all sat quietly as they headed down the oak covered streets. The drive gave Remi a chance to think about how closely their businesses were connected with Cain's now and what that meant for their safety going forward. She wouldn't change it, but it wouldn't hurt to put extra security in place. They needed protection from the people paid by the government to uphold law and order. What a joke.

"Lou's sending some people down, so I'll drop you off and meet you inside." Simon stopped on the ambulance ramp that led to the ER.

The ever-present van was across the street, but she ignored it as she helped Kristen and Dallas out of the car. Muriel Casey opened the door for them, and Kristen immediately put her arms around her and pressed the side of her face to Muriel's chest. This relationship was the best-case scenario—they'd never have to worry about Kristen stepping away from them.

Some might've thought that notion as preposterous as arranging a marriage, but Kristen was now her family, and she took her safety seriously. With Muriel she'd be as protected as she was with her, and Cain would take a bullet before she'd let anything happen to Dallas's only living relative. Also having a Casey in her family would only enhance their years of friendship.

"Is she okay?" she asked Muriel. Cain's cousin was an attorney who specialized in burying things that should never be found. All Cain's businesses were buried under so many layers of subterfuge, it would take a lucky archaeologist to find them.

"She will be after the rage burns out, but it's minor compared to Emma's. I don't know if Lou told you, but the baby was in Cain's arms when she was pushed to the ground." Muriel appeared calmer now that her arms were around Kristen. "You know Cain, though. She fell so Billy would be okay. It just makes us all angry that Hayden and Hannah had to see that."

"Do we need to take the kids?" Dallas asked. Her compassion was one of the many things Remi loved about her wife.

Muriel walked them to the waiting room, and Remi knelt when Hannah ran to her crying. "Aunt Remi, Mom got hurt and we didn't get Mama's presents."

"Let's check on Mom and Mama, then Aunt Dallas and I will

take you to get Mama's presents. Do you want to sit with Kristen and Muriel?" She stood with Hannah and kissed her cheeks. Dallas seemed to understand and took the little girl and sat so Remi could talk to Hayden. "You okay, buddy?"

"I'm pissed—I should've knocked that bitch out." Hayden spoke loud enough to alert anyone listening in, and the feds were always listening in.

The tone and anger that radiated off him reminded her of Cain's brother Billy. They'd grown up together, and she knew Billy was a standup guy, but he also was careless at times. It had always happened when his temper overrode his good sense. The only reason he'd never gone to jail was that his sister never let her emotions get out of hand, and she had been smart enough to pull him out of every jam.

She and Cain had talked about Hayden and his future. Cain was no different than any concerned parent. Hayden was Cain's heir, but her first job was to put a leash on his Casey temper, and teach him to start with his head and not his fists. To rule, you needed that rage to stay on top, but it had to be tempered with patience. Hayden would be fine, but youth was the passage they all had to make it through to learn those lessons about balance. Not a single one of them had made it through without mistakes.

"You don't need me to preach, but think about your mom. First you handled it perfectly, so don't start backsliding now. Anger will bring you down faster than a bullet." She placed her hands on the sides of his face and brought his head forward so his ear was close to her mouth. "The day will come when you can unleash all that rage until the job is done, but that day is not today." That was easy to say, but harder to live especially now that she was married. When someone touched family, her first instinct was to burn the world to the ground, but that's not what Hayden needed to hear.

"I want it to be now. Fuck, I felt like an asshole who stood by while that happened to her." He tried to pull away, but she hung on to him.

"Do you think your mom is going to share that sentiment? Don't lie as an excuse to go out and prove to them everything they believe about all of us." She knew the feds thought of them all as a pack of psychopaths, but even the Bible preached an eye for an eye. Her job now was to temper that out of Hayden because he wasn't ready to mete out that kind of punishment.

"No, but I should've done something."

"You did everything she expected of you. Billy and Hannah are fine, as is your mother—*both* of them. Let all that go for now, and concentrate on the job ahead until she's home. Your family needs you to stay calm. The other thing is to not let your mother hear you cursing. Emma doesn't need that on top of everything else. Loyalty *and* respect will be the cornerstones of your life. Your mother deserves that in spades, no matter the situation."

"You just sit and take it?" He seemed to lose himself again, so she tried to think of what Cain would do to handle this.

She grabbed him by the bicep and dragged him somewhere more private, the men's room, and she motioned for Simon to keep everyone out. "Stop talking before I put my boot up your ass." He opened his mouth when they were alone, but she put a finger in his face. "Do you want to be the first clan leader to go away before you even get the position?"

He hesitated and she pushed him against the wall. "No, ma'am."

"Then get yourself under control. You do that, and you never forget. The bitch did that today for only one reason—to get a reaction. From the way you're acting, she's winning. And you're smart enough to know that lashing out will not only get her off the hook for what she did, but land you somewhere you don't want to be."

"I'm just mad." Hayden sounded like it hurt to admit it.

"I've been there, but you can't go off on these people. You get locked up, and Cain will have no choice but to trade something to get you out. Neither of us wants that, so cool it." She softened her hold and her voice. "Give yourself time, Hayden, and do your job right now. Take care of your mother and siblings while your mom gets treated." She hugged him, and he returned the gesture.

"Thanks, Aunt Remi. I felt like a loser just standing there." Hayden was going through what she had at his age. The biggest task in her life was filling her father's place in the business. Her dad was still the head of their family, and God willing, Hayden would have that kind of time with Cain. Dalton Casey's death had dropped all that responsibility on Cain in an instant, and she admired how Cain had carved her own path. "Remember this when you have your own family and are counseling your oldest. Your time will come, and when it does, Derby Cain Casey will have poured every bit of herself in you."

"Her first lesson will be there's a time for everything." He laughed, making her relax. There wasn't a chance now he'd do something stupid.

"That's the first thing we all learn, kid, but sometimes that's the hardest lesson of all." They came out as Annabel Hicks and a few agents entered the waiting room.

"Muriel," Annabel said with her hand out. "We wanted to come and check on Cain."

Muriel took Annabel's hand and held it. Everyone's temperature was off the leash, it seemed. "Eventually you're going to have to get control of your office. You've put my cousin in the hospital more often than if she wrestled bears for a living. Why are we here, considering my cousin was shopping for a gift for her wife's birthday?"

"I'd like to speak to Cain, not make the situation worse." Annabel had gotten this far in her career, Remi guessed, because she controlled her fear well.

"Agent Hicks," Emma said, seeming to surprise all of them, "Muriel has a valid question. What exactly are you doing here? It's like you won't be happy until you kill her. Once you do, do you all get a Christmas bonus?"

Annabel took a breath and held it for a bit. "You won't believe me, but I came to make sure she's okay. I'm never going to condone that kind of behavior."

"That's a joke." Emma sounded venomous, and Remi couldn't blame her. If it was Dallas in the hospital, she'd have thrown all these guys in a pit, consequences be damned. "You weren't up nights afraid a seizure would kill her if I fell asleep—terrified one more would erase me and her children from her head. Cain had them for weeks because another one of your hardworking agents used her like a punching bag, so I don't exactly believe your concern."

"The agent today will be dealt with. You have my word."

"Our patience won't last forever, Special Agent Hicks," Muriel said. "Depending on how this goes down, I'll have no choice but to take drastic measures."

Annabel made a fist before she opened her mouth. "Threatening a federal agent won't ever go over well."

"Cain's right. You're easy and single-minded. Our threats will take place in a courtroom where we'll show all the videos we found online." Emma's voice was low but chilling. She'd been right about how the feds had treated Cain. Hell, she had a scar from the agent who shot her at the order of another family head.

"You're trending." Dallas held up her phone. "Don't believe the lie that all press is good press no matter what."

Remi had to laugh at that. "Agent Hicks, read the room. Now isn't the time." Some people needed a prod to stop swimming before they lost a limb in the shark-infested waters. "Take the kids in, Emma, and I'll take care of this."

"Ms. Jatibon, we'll need to talk to her eventually. There's nothing I can do to Agent Gardner unless Cain speaks to me and my agents."

"Special Agent Hicks," she said, sighing, "right now, Cain's getting staples put in her head because of an unprovoked attack from one of your people. An attack I understand this Agent Gardner carried out while my friend was holding her baby. Who do you think is going to win the media war that kind of headline will cause?"

"Our aim is justice, not publicity."

She shook her head at Annabel's shortsightedness. "I run a studio, so everything is wrapped in public perception, whether we want it to be or not. Right now, the smart play is to go, bide your time, and talk to Cain when she and Emma have had a chance not only to rest, but to assure their children after what they saw today."

"Thank you, and please let Mrs. Casey know we'll be happy to help with whatever they need."

They all watched Annabel walk out with as much dignity as she could, and the only good thing was that Hayden had stayed quiet and followed Emma out of the room. Remi sat and took Dallas's hand and closed her eyes for a moment. "These people are something."

"There isn't any excuse for this behavior," Dallas said. "Sometimes *sorry* doesn't cut it."

"True, but that's a discussion for another day. Right now let's concentrate on taking care of our friends."

"Can we take the kids to get their gifts? I doubt Cain will be in the mood for a party this weekend."

"Cain's resilient, especially when it comes to her wife. It's something we have in common, and we can do our part by taking the kids." Her visit would have to wait, as would any plans for the agent who'd done this. Left unchecked, the FBI could become problematic.

"Remi," Lou said, "Cain would like to see you before you go."

She followed him out and laughed when she caught Cain and Emma kissing. "You must be feeling better."

"Sometimes you have to go through the motions, my friend. I enhanced this round by getting staples in my head, which will back up my claim when we head to court. Agent Gardner is about to learn the meaning of getting taught a lesson on self-sabotage and how that can destroy her life." Cain kissed the side of Emma's head, and they looked at each other before Emma left. "Thanks for stopping by. I have to talk to you about something, but there's a better place for that."

"We're heading to your place after we take the kids to pick up Emma's gifts. Hannah was upset you guys didn't get to finish." It was never smart to talk in the open, especially when something had to be done to reset the relationship with the feds. "We'll drop them off and pick up dinner unless they're going to keep you overnight for observation."

"I vetoed that idea, so the doctor wanted to wait another hour to make sure my brain didn't get scrambled, so thanks. My kid loves a party and her mama, so we don't want to disappoint her." Cain shook hands with her. "Thanks for coming by, and I'll send some of my guys with you."

"I'll watch over them, don't worry." Dallas had been talking babies from the time they got together, and watching Cain with her children made her wonder what kind of parent she'd be.

"You ready for what comes next?" Cain smiled and winked at her. "It's the best thing you can do with your life, even on days like today. You found the right girl, so give her what we both know she wants."

"You sound like my mother, so cut it out. Just make sure your head's screwed on right and don't worry about the rest."

She found Dallas holding Billy and talking quietly with Emma. There was plenty left to do work-wise, but she knew Cain's comment was the most logical next step when it came to her own relationship. For the longest time she'd thought she hadn't been ready, but one look at her wife holding that baby was the only thing she needed. It was time to give Dallas everything she wanted, making them both happy.

❖

The sound and sight of the rolling waves were relaxing and mesmerizing to some, but Nicola Antakov wasn't just anyone. Today the Atlantic was pounding because of the storm just offshore, but it was of no interest to her. It had been two months since someone had taken a shot at her that had walked her as close to the brink of death as anything ever had. The bullet had done so much damage to her kidney, the doctor had removed it along with the bottom lobe of her lung.

Nicola didn't know who shot her, but she knew the order came from Cain Casey. That she'd bet her life on, and Casey had done it to keep Abigail and their children away from her. Her ex-wife was now with someone named Finley Abbott, but Abigail was under the protection of Casey and her partners. Abigail's lies had cost her not only her position in the Antakov family but her parents as well. She was her father's heir, but no one in their family would follow the weakling she'd become.

There was only one member of her family left who she trusted, so she'd come to recover in Miami with her twin brother Fredrick. That hadn't gone so well, since infections and other complications from having their doctor perform all the procedures in the house had left her depleted and in pain. They'd both survived a plane crash, but the agony she was in now surpassed even that. It had a way of twisting her mind to the point she'd do anything to get it to stop, despite the fact she hated painkillers. This whole thing had left her humiliated and angry.

"Any word from Nina?" Fredrick maneuvered his chair next to her and spoke in that soft, almost feminine voice the plane crash had left him with, along with a broken back.

Nina Garin had been her personal guard and hadn't been by her side the day she'd been gunned down like a dog in the street. She wanted to blame Nina, but there was no way Nina would've come back with her to beg Fredrick to let her find and bring her children to her. That Nina had gotten her immediate medical help and transportation to their house in Miami had saved her life. The same would not be true of Nina once she got her hands on her.

"Wherever she fucked off to," she said, holding her side, where the wounds had healed but the agony persisted, "she's gone and she's not coming back. The only one still loyal to us is Svetlana." Svetlana Dudko was the woman she'd been training to take Nina's place. "Our dear cousin Sacha has received the blessing of the family to take over. That he gladly did since he thinks both of us are dead."

"Think of the phoenix, Nicky. If we weren't meant to rule, we'd be dead." He was shirtless and it hurt to look at him. Fredrick was her twin, the mirror image of her in a male body. The crash had reduced him to this small pathetic creature who had naked women fawning over him all day. The only thing she could think was it reminded him of who he was before their lives came close to going up in flames. "You have to get stronger, so you can kill Sacha. Once his head is on a plate, the rest of the family will have no choice but to bow to you."

"We concentrate on what we can concentrate on." She was

disgusted that she was tired since all she'd done was look at the surf from the moment she woke up. "Our plans haven't changed. It'll just take time." The thought of letting someone else do what she'd been planning for a few years made her want to kill something, but that's what it might come down to if she couldn't fully recover.

"You have Volkov blood in your veins," someone said from behind them. Volkov was her mother's maiden name, and her mother's family had fronted the cash for her father's business. Granted, her father's business expertise had built an empire that surpassed the Volkovs', but they'd been expected to pay respects to her grandfather until the fucker dropped dead. That day had yet to come, and it pissed her off her father hadn't lived to see it.

It'd been years since she'd seen her mother's sister, Kira, and she wasn't sure why she was here now. "My mother forbade you from talking about my father like that. Death hasn't changed what she wanted."

"Valerie was proud, and your father more so," Kira said, shrugging. "That pride led to blindness and to ignoring the danger so close to them. The price for that stupidity was death."

"Do *you* have a death wish?" Fredrick asked, as loudly as she'd ever heard him. "Our mother saw the best way forward was with our father. She wanted something more than living in the gutter, so careful how you speak of our dead."

"My dear nephew, you barely have enough men to keep your women in line, so don't threaten me. It's laughable. Both of you are hiding here, licking your wounds, hoping no one will find you. You do this because you know once they do, you'll be as easy to pick off as a pair of wounded gazelles in the middle of a pride of lions." Kira laughed, and Nicola wished she had the strength to strangle her. "Am I wrong?"

"What do you want?" Nicola stayed seated and cocked her head to the empty chair across from Fredrick. "Or is your visit only to insult us to make yourself feel better?"

"Your father, Yury, wasn't my father's choice, but Valerie loved him. He took what my father gave him and did build an impressive business."

"It was an empire. One that has left all the Volkovs far behind," Fredrick said with heat.

"Of course." It was impossible not to detect Kira's sarcasm. The talent to slice with words must've been something her grandfather Ivan taught well. Her mother was a master with cutting words, and her father had hated it. "The great Antakov empire. Is that why you're here and not in New York in the palace your father built? No." Keira tapped her chin. "Sacha lives in the shrine Yury erected to himself and runs the *Oblonsky* empire. He understands something Yury never did."

This conversation was as tedious as it was aggravating, yet she had no choice but to listen. The men watching them from right inside belonged to Kira, which meant her men were smart enough to stand down because of the numbers. Kira had played this well. "What's that?" She bled the anger from her voice, but she wasn't defeated.

"You keep an eye on the business and those close to you. That Yury allowed your cousin Linda to keep the ledgers and then take those and her brothers and disappear into the mist was, to us, unbelievable. Yury was successful, as you say, but in the end, he used it for his own sick sexual needs." Kira put her hand up when Fredrick took a breath. "He thought with his dick like a dog in heat, and he died in the street like a mutt."

"What do you know what a man needs?" Fredrick asked, his hands clinched in fists. Shit, even Nicola found him pathetic enough, and she loved him.

"A man has a wife, a family, a business, and needs. The needs come last, Fredrick, and they should be enjoyed in moderation. I look around here and see that it's something Yury passed down." Kira snapped her fingers, and a woman handed her an envelope. "Hate me all you want. The truth is inconvenient when it doesn't fit the story you tell yourself and want desperately to believe. Sometimes, though, we have no choice but to listen to the truth from the voices of our ghosts."

"What voices?" She could see from how Kira held the envelope, that it was important to her.

Kira handed it to her. "I'll never part with the original since it's the last I have of your mother. She wrote me a week before she was killed, and you both deserve to read it. How you respond to her words will decide if I leave you here for your enemies to finish off, or not."

Nicola took the page out and unfolded it. The stationery was her mother's, and she recognized the handwriting. "Read it," Fredrick demanded.

Sister,

I hope you, father, and the family are well. Our search for the grandchildren continues, but it's like Abigail has melted into a hole. Yury doesn't seem to understand the importance of finding them, and he ignores my desperation. The children are all I have left, and once they're back with me, they will be raised in the Volkov family. My loving husband doesn't want to face it, but everything he's accomplished is turning to ash, and there'll be nothing left.

You and Father were right. With the loss of Nicola and Fredrick, Yury has become cruel and absent. It's no secret he spends most of his time at the Hellfire Club, so we no longer have a relationship outside of the business. I understand grief—the loss of my children has nearly destroyed what's left of my life—but it's still no excuse to sleep his way through the club. He's made me someone I detest since I'm nothing more than a joke.

I've grown to hate Yury, but also come to fear him. He's planning something, and I assume it includes getting rid of me. All I want is my grandchildren, so I can give them a good life. My only wish is that Nicola had spent more time with them, so they'd know what their place is in the world, but family life isn't something that ever interested her, like her father when they were children. That Abigail was her choice has only made this more difficult, and it'll continue to be so once the children are back with me.

The shooting Yury ordered to fix his screwups was so close to Abigail and the kids that they're afraid. My last conversation with Abigail before they disappeared confirms that they want to leave the city and not come back. It will take a lot from all of us to assure them that this is where they belong.

I'll keep you informed, and if something happens to me, know that Yury has led me to my death. If I'm right about that, find my grandchildren and protect them. They are all that'll leave proof of my existence and deserve to know their family.

With love,
Valerie

"Wait for me to call you," Nicola said, her fingers white on the paper. It had to all be a lie.

"There's more," Kira said.

"Wait for me to call," she said in a low menacing voice. One glance at Fredrick, and she knew she was right. "Whatever else there is will have to wait."

CHAPTER THREE

Marisol Delarosa studied the signs in the Bogotá airport and tried to ignore the kids running around after being cooped up on the long flight. Her argument with her father meant she was no longer his heir, and she was also without a home. She'd been trying for weeks to talk some of the men into joining her, but that hadn't worked well. One of the fools had come back and told her Hector would give no more warnings. It was time to go.

The blame for all this lay on Tracy's head, but doing something about it would take time. She wanted revenge more than anything, but she wasn't suicidal. Her father had become weak after inviting Tracy into his bed, but he also wasn't the sentimental type. No more warnings meant a bullet to the head if she kept pushing.

Her only recourse now was to come home to her mother and figure out what the best next step would be. Hector had paraded her mother out every so often as a way of showing her how lucky she was he'd been kind enough to take her in. His wife hadn't been horrible, but Marisol wasn't her daughter, and she hadn't been interested in mothering her. In the years since, they'd made their peace and had a friendship that revolved around their mutual hatred of Hector. But her stepmother would go only so far in defying Hector for fear of losing the lifestyle he provided in exchange for not having to deal with her.

"Señora Delarosa?" a man asked once she cleared customs. "Your mother sent me."

Compared to New Orleans, Bogotá was a different world. The streets were crowded, and the buildings were plastered together for as far as she could see. There was more poverty and crime here, but it was home, and it was nice to be back. Her mother's business was in an upscale neighborhood, walled off and protected from the dangers of the city. She was successful enough now that she had guards posted around the clock and the richest men in the city coming to fulfill their needs. Here the streets weren't crowded and the walls were topped with razor wire to keep the scum out.

The gates opened, and the courtyard where the driver stopped was beautifully landscaped. A man waved to the driver, and she heard the trunk pop open. "I'll get your bags, and Señora Zapata is waiting for you upstairs. Don't keep her waiting." She wasn't going to forget the disrespectful way he'd spoken to her. Those days were over.

The main room of the house had clients even at this early hour, and they barely glanced at her as she made her way up to her mother's rooms. "Mija," Catalina Zapata said, throwing her arms around Marisol. "I missed you so much." Her mother was still a young, beautiful woman who continued to entertain her elite clientele even though she could've retired to a good life. Hector's explanation had been that once a whore, always a whore. It was all her mother knew.

"Mami." It was all she could say as she clung to her mother. This was the only place she'd ever felt safe enough to show emotion. "He threw me away."

"Sit and let's talk." Her mother poured her a cup of tea and sat close to her. "Drink that, and it'll make you feel better." Catalina helped her lift the cup and didn't let go until she took a sip. "I know you thought you knew your father, but now that you've seen a different side of him, you know who Hector Delarosa really is. I'm a prostitute, but he was one of the only men I've ever loved, and he repaid me by taking the one person I love above all others. It was either hand you over or die."

"He's a bastard, and after everything I've done, he took that bitch Tracy's side over mine." Her tears dried at the return of her anger, and her mother simply held her hand. "I killed for him, and I'm the one on the street."

"Stop and breathe, mija. What you should think about is the position Hector's in." Her mother's smile was almost mysterious.

"Are you saying I should forgive him?" If this was her mother's answer, she'd really be alone in the world. "Fuck if that's going to happen. If he can throw me away, then the protection he provides you here is not going to last. What are you going to do if he comes after both of us?"

"Stop and listen. There's no reason to yell and curse—I'm your mother, and I'll always be on your side." Her mother pointed to the cup, and it prompted her to take another sip. "What I'm saying is the mighty Hector isn't so powerful that someone wasn't afraid to attack him. It happened, then it happened again, and what did he do about it? Nothing. He's done nothing because he can't without looking even weaker to the world. He's like a wounded animal waiting for a jackal to come along and devour him."

"You know who took a shot at him?" Hector was weak, but his organization was still intact. Maybe all it needed was someone new at the helm.

"No, but you have to start thinking of this as having left a dying thing to start a new life with someone who'll give you the respect you deserve." Catalina put her arm around her and kissed her cheek. "Get some rest, and tonight I'll introduce you to Cesar Kalina. It won't take much time before he'll be the new head of the cartel, and he's got a place for you."

"I was supposed to take over for Hector." What her mother was suggesting would put her right back at the end of the line, taking orders from someone else.

"Kalina is giving you the chance to run his operation from Texas to Florida. You'd be the boss, and you already know the landscape there. I had a long talk with him about you after you called me. This is so much better than what your father was willing to give you."

"He told you that, or are you guessing?" Sometimes her mother couldn't tell the difference between what a man told her to get her in bed, or if he really meant it. "Taking over for Hector means I'm a boss in the US as well as here. I can protect you with that kind of power, and you can leave all this behind."

Her mother patted her cheek as if she didn't understand how the world worked, but it wasn't the time to talk about all that. "Tonight, all you have to say is yes, and it's yours. Cesar is a friend who's come here to relax, and the girls love him. If you listen to the deal he's offering, it's one step closer to getting everything you want. Once you take over, I'll help you get what is rightfully yours. This is where we start, though, so what do you want?"

"I want it all."

Catalina smiled and pressed her hands together. "Good, and once you have it, there's nothing stopping you from whatever you like."

"I want Tracy's head as well as Hector's. They both have to pay for their betrayal." She couldn't wait to see his face right before she killed him. A gun to the head would be Hector's lesson in what a mistake he'd made letting her go.

"Never be afraid to ask for the things you really want," Catalina said, kissing her cheek again.

"If Cesar asks, my answer will be yes."

❖

Cain opened her eyes when the car stopped, and she saw Emma's expression of worry. "Lass, I'm fine. You know I wouldn't lie to you about something that important."

"What's wrong with these people?" Emma held Cain's hand to her chest.

Cain leaned over and kissed her. "Come with me."

They went inside, and Cain greeted her cousin, Finley Abbott, who was sitting in her kitchen with her fiancée Abigail Eaton's three children. Sadie, Victoria, and Liam Eaton loved Finley and would soon take her name, but they'd also gotten close to her and Emma. Victoria and Liam ran over and wrapped their arms around her legs. Cain gazed down at them and vowed silently that she wouldn't let anything happen to any of them. Abigail and the kids were still in play as far as Nicola Antakov was concerned, but they all were *her* family now.

"Aunt Cain, where's Hannah?" Victoria asked.

"She's picking something up for her mama with her brothers." Cain sat and they scrambled up on her lap. "How about we surprise them with a cookout tonight, followed by ice cream?" She smiled at the yells and clapping. "Great, go tell Miss Carmen and Mr. Ross."

Finley seemed to notice the blood on her collar and didn't say anything for a long moment. "What the hell?"

"That was my question too," Emma said.

"Let's talk in the office." She took Emma's hand. "But give me a minute to change and shower."

No one stopped them on the way to their bedroom, and Emma now stood in front of her and started unbuttoning her shirt. The way her fingers shook meant she was upset. Cain covered her hands and pulled her closer. Emma's zipper came down easily, and she shimmied her shoulders to get her dress to come off and pool at her feet. Cain's shirt went into the trash, and she took a shuddering breath. She lowered her head to reach Emma's lips.

"You are the woman who fuels my imagination and fires my heart." She wiped Emma's tears and unfastened Emma's bra. "I'm a little beat-up, lass, but I'm okay." She pulled Emma closer by putting her fingers in the sides of her panties. "Do you know the only thing that'll take me away from you?"

"What?" Emma took a deep breath and Cain bit her earlobe.

"Years from now when we've put our great-grandchildren to bed, I'll drift off in your arms. I'll be well over a hundred, and I'll still chase you around the house with my walker." She moved her hands to squeeze Emma's ass.

"Mobster, we have someone waiting."

"You think Finley's going to complain?" She kissed Emma with more intent. "Sometimes I want you, no matter what's happening."

Emma stepped back and unbuckled her belt. Once Cain's pants hit the floor, Emma pulled her blue panties down and they followed Cain's underwear to the floor. "Remember one thing, honey. Wherever you go, I'll be right behind you, so plan to live to be at least a hundred and fifty." Emma helped her off with her boots so she could finish pulling her underwear away. "You know what?"

Her headache disappeared when Emma gazed up at her, and she wanted all of her. This beautiful woman loved her, and she had, at times, wondered why. "What?" she asked when Emma pressed her naked body to hers.

"I want you like that too." Emma kissed her chest before pressing her chin right under her collarbone. "What are you thinking about?"

"I'm thinking about a girl who poured beer on me and changed my life. I know my mother loved you, but I wish you'd known my parents together. They were true partners in every aspect of their lives, and they loved each other in a way I didn't think I'd find." She felt a ball of emotion in her chest, and she didn't hide it. She'd made promises to Emma to never keep anything from her, even her fears and vulnerability.

"Your mom told me their story and told me the important part." Emma turned her head and pressed her ear to Cain's chest again. "You're mine, Derby Cain Casey. You're mine like your da belonged to your mum, and they did share a relationship she treasured. When she saw us, though, she told me ours would surpass theirs only because we'd share more years together." Emma placed her hand over Cain's heart. "You made promises to me, that you'd never let anything happen to me, so now promise me you'll stay safe, so you won't steal my happiness."

"I do love you, lass, and there's nothing that would ever make me stop, so I promise." She led Emma into the shower and pressed her to the wall. "And my mum was right. All of me, and who I am, belongs to you."

She ran her hand down Emma's back down to her butt.

"Then show me," Emma said.

There was no need for a big buildup when she put her hand between Emma's legs and groaned at how wet she was. From the first time she'd touched Emma, she knew she'd never be able to stop. "What do you want, lass?"

"You." Emma gripped her forearm with one hand and pulled her head down with the other. "I want you."

She slid her fingers in slowly and smiled when Emma moaned. The position made her bend down a bit, and Emma took advantage by kissing her. It was the type of kiss that spoke of belonging, want, and familiarity, the kind of familiarity that assured both of them that this fire between them couldn't ever die or fade. Her mom was right—with Emma, her life was complete. There wasn't room for anyone else.

"Like that, honey, don't stop." Emma sounded close.

She sped her strokes, wanting to prolong this but not wanting to torture her wife. "Come for me, lass."

Emma squeezed her shoulders hard enough to bruise, but she didn't mind. "I'm so close, please don't stop." Emma's hips kept up stroke for stroke, and she swallowed every moan with a long kiss. "Yes," Emma said, her head pressed back into the tile. "I'm…" It was like she couldn't finish and let out a moan Cain totally understood, just by the way Emma intimately squeezed her fingers.

Cain held her up and swayed with Emma to give her time to find her sea legs again. "You okay?"

"You have a way of loving me that makes me want to shut out the world. It's such a gift." Emma's soft voice and the way she kissed over her heart made her want to take the day just for them. Hell, she had staples in her head, but she had children to reassure and family waiting.

"You are my gift, lassie, and tonight you and me have a date to pick up right here. But right now, I need you to wash my hair."

"The doctor said not to get it wet." Emma reached for the shampoo anyway.

"That guy doesn't have kids who watched some freak accident that ended with me bleeding like that idiot shot me." She knelt and kissed Emma's nipples. "I love you, and it's a chore sometimes when we have to be responsible adults, but that's what's waiting for us."

She watched as blood circled the drain and tried to ignore it. Emma was being gentle, and the way she massaged her scalp made her relax, easing the headache that was radiating from the center of her skull. This time was different from the time then-Special Agent Brent Cehan had slammed her head against the car and then hit her with a closed fist a few times. The seizures were disconcerting, and it'd taken time for them to stop.

"I know you need to sit Hayden down and calm the anger out of him, but can you talk to Hannah first?" This was the first time Hannah was old enough to understand what had happened.

"I'll be happy to, but our Hannah girl is resilient. Your birthday and the party we have planned will knock all that out of her head."

"True, but I want you to talk to her anyway. Then you can share with me what you're planning to do."

"Today, I'm going to calm all our kids down and see what Fin has. Tomorrow, we talk to Annabel and see how desperate we can make Agent Gardner." What she wanted was to cut Gardner from the FBI's herd. Once Gardner was alone and vulnerable, she was going to have a conversation with her that would give the asshole no option but to spill her secrets. After that, Gardner could die with them.

They got dressed in casual clothes since they weren't planning to go out again, and Hannah started crying again when she walked into the room where the kids sat with Dallas and Remi. Hayden wasn't in tears, but he was upset, so Cain took them both into her office.

"What happened today was scary," she said for Hannah's benefit. "But I'm proud of both of you for how brave you were. You watched over me until Mama got there, and you took care of your little brother." She lifted Hannah into her lap and placed her hand on Hayden's knee. "All you need to know is that I'm going to be okay. What that lady did was wrong, and we'll deal with it."

"Are you going to punish her?" Hannah said, and Hayden finally smiled.

"I'm going to get her boss to do that, but I don't need either of you to worry about anything. It's over, and your mama's party is coming up, so we want to celebrate with her."

"Yes," Hannah said with her fist in the air. "Can I go tell her we picked up her presents?"

"Sure, but don't ruin the surprise," Hayden said. "You don't have to say anything else. Aunt Remi talked to me, and I understand what has to happen. I was mad that happened to you and I couldn't do anything but stand there and watch it happen, but I promise I won't do anything stupid."

"That's the last thing I'm worried about. Your time is coming, son, but I'm glad you understand that instant action isn't always the smart play. Today you used your head, and the day will come when you understand the gratification of dealing with problems the way we have to sometimes."

"I know, Mom, and I promise I can wait. Just don't take this shit lying down."

She laughed and slapped the back of his head gently. "Don't let your mama hear you talking like that. And you have to know taking shit from people like Dylan Gardner isn't a hobby of mine."

❖

Nicola read the letter over and over for the next three days. She'd never considered anything from her mother's perspective, and Fredrick's argument was that she shouldn't start. They were told by their father that the world was destined to bow at their feet, and they shouldn't accept anything but that. Whatever and whoever they wanted was theirs, and anyone who questioned it was eliminated. That had been the blueprint of her life.

The club in New Orleans had been hers to run and enjoy, and she'd done that plenty. Her regular girls had been happy to fulfill her every desire. But now with time to reflect, she wondered—had Abigail known, like her mother had with her father? She and Abigail hadn't been intimate for months before her accident, but the why wasn't something she'd worried about. Her wife was a decent mother, but a boring lover. No, there was no way in hell Abigail would ever think about cheating on her.

It was true that once Abigail had given birth to her heirs, she'd only needed her to take care of them until they were old enough to be introduced to the business. She'd come home only to keep an eye on their development, and whenever Abigail informed her of a school event. There hadn't been many of those, and when she found out about them after the fact, Abigail's excuse had always been she didn't want to disrupt her busy schedule. Had the little bitch known she was using the club to bed as many women as she wanted? Did it really matter if she did?

Abigail Eaton belonged to her, just like the children. It wasn't Abigail's place to dictate how she conducted her business or who she had in her bed, no more than it had been her mother's. The only difference was her mother understood her place. Or so Nicola had believed, until she'd read this goddamn letter. Her mother's loyalties lay with the Volkovs, and she would've raised her children as such. The only blessing was she was dead.

"Stop reading that fucking thing and burn it already," Fredrick said. He appeared freshly bathed, and one of the women sat on his lap. "We don't need Kira or the old man to get back what we own."

Her grandfather, Ivan, was ruthless, but his lack of imagination led him only to be a thug, a low-class drug runner and pimp. "We're going to take their help, then walk away. Our mother might've been happy to go back to Ivan, but we're Antakovs. We'll never be happy with scraps."

She crumpled the paper and tossed it on the ground. "Call Oleg and Larissa, and have them come to the house." Once she'd regained consciousness, she'd relocated and renamed the club here as well as the others they owned. Her father and his love of paper had given their cousin Linda too much power, so she'd changed the system and was able to monitor it from here. She'd ordered all the managers killed and promoted from within. Oleg Balakin and Larissa Vassiliev had been there for the opening and had done a good job of rebranding.

"You want them to come here?" Fredrick gave a woman on his lap the vial he kept in the chair's cup holder. All of his helpers had a stoned look about them, and she mostly ignored these strange proclivities of his.

The house was guarded, she'd always made sure of that, but her brother lived in fear of an attack he couldn't run away from. He wanted no one here he wasn't expecting, so it'd surprised her that Kira's appearance hadn't freaked him out. Ivan's children weren't the smartest, but she couldn't discount their violent streak.

She saw the physical therapist she'd hired had arrived, and Nicola nodded. Up to now she hadn't wanted to push past the pain, but that was over. "It'll be fine, but it's time to start working toward all we need not only to survive, but eventually to rule. Survival is paramount, and the rest will come."

"All these things *you* want, you mean?" Fredrick sounded petulant. "What the shit do I have?"

"You have me, and soon the children. Both of us have to work together to ease them into the changes in their lives. If we do that, they'll be strong for us when we're old." She took his hand and smiled at him. Her father had made her promise to take care of him, so her honor wouldn't allow her to put him out of his misery.

"What do you want with Oleg and Larissa?" Fredrick seemed appeased by her holding his hand.

"We need men, soldiers, and they're going to recruit for me." She needed muscle to start her moves against Sacha and the rest of the family, and the clubs were the perfect starting places.

"You're going back to New Orleans?" Fredrick sounded concerned.

"Abigail and my children are on my list of things to deal with, but we start with Sacha." Her cousin would crack under what she planned for him. She needed to know who had shot her to make them and their family sorry for trying to kill her. "That'll get us to New York, making the rest easy."

CHAPTER FOUR

Cain sat as Emma tied her bow tie. Their night was starting in the upstairs seating area at Blanchard's, for the dinner with friends and family to celebrate Emma's birthday. After that, she'd prepared Emma's for the night to continue the party. The club was about a week from the grand reopening, and she thought this would be a good dry run.

"I've always loved you in a tux," Emma said as she straightened her work. "You're handsome to me all the time, but damn." She laughed when Emma squeezed her shoulders.

"You're good at flattery, my love, and no one's ever looking at *me* when you're standing next to me."

Emma smiled and kissed her temple. "You're a sweet talker yourself, and everyone can look all they want. I'm all yours, and I just put a bow on you. That means I get to unwrap you later."

"That you do." She turned and slid her hands to Emma's waist, liking the feel of the silk robe. "Happy birthday, lass. I hope you enjoy your night."

Someone knocked, so she kissed Emma before opening the door to Hannah, Dallas, Kristen, and Abigail with her girls. She kissed everyone's cheeks before waving at her wife and leaving to join her friends downstairs. From the day she'd come home from the hospital, Finley had been digging into Agent Gardner to see what motivated her. She'd put off a meeting with Annabel until she had more answers.

"My report's almost done," Finley said, but Cain waved her off.

"No shoptalk tonight. It's Emma's birthday, and we're going to celebrate that." She accepted a drink from Muriel and sat in the den.

"Then let's talk about when Muriel's going to propose to my sister-in-law," Remi said, pointing a finger at Cain's cousin. "You're about to meet snake eyes if it's not soon." Remi didn't refer to the nickname she and her brother Mano used when they had to take care of problems permanently very often, and it made Cain laugh.

"If you're getting ready to use the excuse of her graduation, I might join them," she said, nodding to Remi. "This time go with your heart, cousin, and not your head. We're already united in business—I'd like to cement it in family."

Hayden came in with Billy in his arms, both wearing tuxedos, and everyone stopped talking. For everything they'd all done to consolidate power, the baby still brought out a softness no one on the streets would ever imagine. Cain always believed that's why they were so successful. Family always trumped everything else, and that was especially true when it came to *their* children.

"Cain and Remi are right," Ross said, as Billy reached for him. Emma's father had taken to retirement better than she and Emma expected. "And look at what you have to look forward to. The Casey family makes beautiful babies."

"They do, even when they're adopted," Siobhan Abbott said as she entered. Cain stood and put her arms around her father's younger sister and held her for a long moment before allowing Muriel to do the same. "They grow up to be good looking as well." Her aunt placed a hand on both her and Muriel's cheeks. "I've missed you both so much, but what you've done for my Fin, I could never repay you for."

"There are no debts in families, Aunt Siobhan." She hugged her aunt again and waved Hayden over. "These are my sons, Hayden and Billy. It's been a while since you've seen them."

"Emma's good about sending pictures, but it's not the same." Siobhan took the baby and kissed Hayden's cheek. "Your da and mum are smiling in heaven, Derby. What a gorgeous brood you have."

"Fin's working on her own," Muriel said.

"Those kids are gorgeous, but she's not done," her uncle Shaun said. "It's taken Siobhan two days to spoil the three of them rotten, so think of a way to plan Finley's coming out party. There's no way Siobhan's coming home with me." He made everyone laugh because they knew it was the truth. "I see a move in our future."

"The cameras will catch a glimpse of Finley and Abigail tonight, and Fin's old boss has been in touch," Cain said.

"They'll come for her if you do that. First for lying, and then she'll be blamed for the Eatons," Siobhan said.

"Not now, Mum," Finley said.

"Fin, your mum knows how these things work, and she's right. Russell Welsh, though, is a man who understands reason." She handed her uncle a drink and took Siobhan's hand. "He'll be a peacemaker, or risk losing the best chance he has at bringing the Russian mob under control."

"How do you know that?" Her aunt was persistent.

Russell was Fin's boss in New York, and he was still working through the information Finley had gathered for him on the Eaton family business built on drugs, prostitution, and sex trafficking. "We met with him two days ago, and he's satisfied Fin's no killer when it comes to the Eaton family, and the feds know I was home that night. My run-in with the local branch a few days ago also gives us leverage over how this plays out."

"You promise me Fin, Abigail, and the kids will be fine?" Siobhan asked Cain.

"On the soul of my da. Our family has been separated, so Finley could do good in the job she wanted, but she's home now and under my protection." She put her hands on Siobhan's shoulders when Hayden took the baby back. It was a blessing her aunt would be a part of her children's lives going forward. "Tonight's Emma's night, though, so let's celebrate and we'll work all that out, you have my word."

Hannah led the girls down, and she figured they didn't have much time before her kid would demand they open Emma's gifts, so she signaled one of Carmen's helpers for the champagne and sparkling juice. She took Emma's hands and whistled when she saw the dark blue dress. It was gorgeous and highlighted Emma's blond hair and green eyes.

"You're beautiful, my love." She kissed Emma and waited for the glasses to go around. "To my wife"—she lifted her glass in Emma's direction—"you're the heart of our family and deserve all the happiness we can give you. Happy birthday, lass." She lifted her glass higher and toasted Emma. "To Emma." Everyone in the room repeated and drank.

Hannah and Hayden came up and held out the gift bags the jewelers had put together and encouraged their mother to open them. Jewelry was something Emma loved, but she'd gone in a different direction and wanted to wait until the party was over to surprise Emma, wanting to celebrate with her alone.

"Did you like it, Mama?" Hannah asked from Hayden's arms as she helped Emma on with the bracelet.

"We picked it out, and Mom had the idea of putting the green stones in," Hayden said. He was much taller than Emma now, but Cain doubted her wife would ever see him as anything but her little boy. "Did you really like it?"

"It's all beautiful." Emma stood on her toes and kissed Hayden's and Hannah's cheeks. "You guys did a great job. I'll treasure them forever."

They mingled a little before they left for Blanchard's in a caravan of cars. The nondescript vans were out in force as they arrived, but considering their invitation list, she understood their interest. She'd picked the location tonight to limit access. Their time lately had been spent spinning their wheels and not getting anywhere, so it was time to bloody the water. Who knew it would be this literal, she thought, as she felt the staples in her head.

She helped Emma and Hannah out of the car, leaving Hayden to get his little brother out of his car seat. "Guys, go in with your grandparents, and I'll get your mama upstairs." Ross and Carmen were in the next car, and their longtime housekeeper was still getting used to being included as one of their guests. Carmen had always been family, and now Ross was waiting for his divorce to be finalized to make that true in a legal sense.

Their group of friends headed up, and she guided Emma through the kitchen and into the office. "Are you okay?" Annabel asked when Cain closed the door.

"I'll be fine, and I promise Gardner isn't in my crosshairs. The move at the mall went like we thought it would—well, like I thought it would. My only surprise was the trip to the emergency room."

"What'd you say to provoke her?" Shelby asked. "We watched the video, and she lost her mind for no reason."

"Gardner reminds me of Barney Kyle. He was quick to temper, and he thought he was always the smartest person in every room." Emma had experience with the lead agent in charge of bringing Cain down. Kyle and his scheming had stolen years from them—years from Hannah and Hayden they couldn't get back. "He did everything he could to destroy Cain and our family."

"That's a dead subject," Annabel said, gazing at her.

"It is, and I'm sure Bracato is so sorry about that. And to answer your question, Agent Phillips, all it took was a wink." She put an arm around Emma's waist and kissed the side of her neck. "It's Emma's birthday, but we have a gift for you." She took an envelope from her coat pocket and held it up. "Emma's right that Gardner's quick-tempered, and she's not worried about curbing or hiding it. That's what it seems like to me."

"What's that?" Shelby asked, seeming nervous.

"Patience, Agent Phillips. Answer the question first." Annabel waved her on. "Why do you think an agent isn't afraid to express not only her anger but her disapproval?" She waited for an answer, and Annabel seemed to catch on faster than Shelby.

"They have a safety net that's rock-solid. A rabbi who she thinks is untouchable."

"Exactly," she said. "She transferred here, and you need to start asking questions as to why that is."

"The bureau doesn't give you much choice sometimes," Annabel said. "Besides, the bureau didn't give me a choice when it came to Gardner."

"That's true, so there had to be someone who's tried to change your landscape and failed. Someone who's also going after me, which, let's face it, is all of you. Some of you, though, are more dedicated than others." Emma laughed and pinched the top of her hand. "That someone is also after you, Agent Hicks, at least your job. If that's not motivation enough, I don't know what is."

"Ronald Chapman," Shelby said. Special Agent Ronald Chapman had arrived in New Orleans loaded for bear when it came to Cain and her family and had done everything he could to bring her down. His methods had been very public and didn't exactly track the letter of the rules he was supposed to follow, so she'd found his weakness and used it like a sledgehammer to the side of his head. Ronald was gone, but Gardner was his advocate.

"We don't know that," Annabel said.

"You're right, we don't. Whether it's him or not, my life won't change much, but can you say the same? Tonight's a family celebration, and I haven't forgotten about our deal, so trust me and take a look at your gift, and I'll be in touch."

"This has to do with Ronald?" Annabel asked. Her expression flashed that it was the last thing she wanted to hear.

"Why ruin the surprise for you? That's a copy, but you can trust it. Shelby will tell you how I work when motivated enough." She handed Annabel the envelope and glanced at Shelby. "I have plenty more than that, so this is a starting place."

"Happy birthday, Mrs. Casey," Annabel said, shaking hands with both of them before leaving through the back door with Shelby.

"I'd love to be in the room when they watch that." Emma stepped into her arms and smiled at her. "This should be interesting once they pick up the scent."

"There's always a chance I'm wrong," she said and winked. Emma's reaction to that was quite different than Dylan Gardner's, and that made her laugh.

❖

Dallas watched Emma enter with Cain and envied her friend's confidence. She was still working on ridding herself of the place in her head where that pathetic kid who was waiting to be thrown out on the street lived. Remi had accepted her, but she couldn't let go of all those old fears.

The only thing she was happy about was Kristen, who appeared just as confident as Emma as she stood with Muriel. Her younger sister was happy and in love, and Remi enjoyed telling her it was all because she'd taken a chance. That she had, but life had taught her an important lesson, one that'd kept her alive. Letting her defenses down, no matter how many protective layers Remi had put between them and her old life, would be a mistake.

"Is there a reason you look like you have a dead fish rotting under your nose?" Emma's question broke her out of her thoughts and forced her lungs to expand. "It's dinner, my friend, not a firing squad."

"Sorry, I still have the occasional wormhole in my head." She hugged Emma, glad that life had not only given her Remi, but the friends who'd come with her.

"We haven't had a girls' night in a while, so that's what I want for my birthday." Emma pointed at her as Abigail, Kristen, and Linda Bender walked up.

Linda was still an unknown entity, but Cain had Nicola's cousin and her brothers living in their pool house, and Remi had given her a job at the studio. The job was in research, but really the only research she was doing had to do with finding Nicola. It was that research that worried Dallas.

"We do need that," Abigail said. "And you look beautiful, my friend."

"We all do, which makes our partners lucky women," Emma said and laughed. "Keep everyone entertained, and we'll be right back." Dallas followed Emma to the bathroom and sighed when Emma turned and stared at her. "You don't have to tell me, but you haven't looked like this since we first met."

"It's your birthday, Em. You should be out there enjoying it." God, she didn't need to cry now.

"You can't have forgotten what you mean to me. You're the first person I could trust with all my secrets, worries, and hopes. The first person outside of Cain." Emma put her arms around her. "You don't have to tell me, but talk to Remi. I hate seeing you like this."

"You're the best friend I've ever had, and I don't want to ruin your night. How about lunch tomorrow?" She dabbed a tissue to the sides of her eyes. "We're in postproduction, so I can come over."

"Good," Emma said, handing her another tissue. "Are you sure there isn't anything I can do for you tonight?"

"I'm sure it's nothing but my past," she said and shivered. Her life had consisted of running, or trying to outrun who she'd been. It was like a hungry beast she could feel breathing on her neck, its teeth grazing her skin every so often. They were sharp and a reminder that, given the chance, the beast of her past life would tear her peace to shreds. "It's something I can't really bury so it stays dead."

"I can't imagine the shit you went through to make it here, but the thing to remember is you made it here." Emma put her arms around her again and kissed her cheek. "I'm on your side, sweetie. If you need to talk about it tonight, we'll head downstairs and do that."

"No, I'm here to celebrate you, not dredge up old bullshit." She was glad for the cover of Emma's embrace. The last thing she wanted was for Remi to see her crying. "I promise we'll talk about it tomorrow. Come on, let's get a drink."

They rejoined the party, and Cain smiled when Emma stepped closer, stopping when she seemed to notice Dallas was upset. "Hey," she said to Emma, "my aunt wants to show you off to some old friend she invited. Abigail's eyes are starting to glaze over, so go over and rescue her." Emma hesitated but Cain's head cock got her walking. Cain turned to Dallas. "Let me show you something interesting about this place." Cain offered her arm, and Dallas noticed Remi talking to her brother and his family, so she let Cain lead her away. Any escape was welcome at this point.

They stopped at the two matching carvings affixed to the wall in the dining room closest to the top of the stairs. "Della Blanchard, the restaurant's owner, told me hurricane Katrina demolished the upstairs of this place to the point it had to be gutted. These ladies, though, got dinged a little but came through fine." Cain put her hand on the wooden woman's hip. Both statues would've been at home in the front of an old ship. "You should compare these guys to me and Remi. The storms come, but we come through just fine. Maybe a little ding here and there, but no real damage."

"Why are you telling me all this?" While she and Emma were good friends, Dallas couldn't remember a time she'd ever had a conversation alone with Cain. "Not that I mind. Remi found me, but you had a lot to do with saving me and my sister. You were who Remi trusted with that because she told me you were good at finding things, but even better at burying things."

"Remi's someone I've known since I have memory of anything. She and Mano grew up with me and my siblings, so I consider her family." Cain pulled out a chair for her, and she noticed Simon hovering close to the door, ensuring their privacy. "Her family got here when we were tots, and her dad and my da became the best of friends."

"She tells me stories about your family's old home as we work on it. All of them make her laugh, and she talks about our kids growing up with yours. That you share that bond is something she treasures."

Cain smiled and Dallas saw nothing but kindness in her eyes. "I'm looking forward to that myself."

She nodded but was still confused. "Is that what you wanted to talk about?"

Cain's smile widened. "You're my wife's best friend, and my closest friend's wife, so talking about our families will be a lifetime thing between all of us. Tonight, though, I wanted to discuss what's upsetting you. It's Emma's birthday, but let me give *you* a gift. It's an old Irish tradition."

"Really?" It was different, going from no one caring for her to all these people lining up to do so.

"If you'd met my mum, you'd know the answer is yes, really, and she expected me to do it whether it was my wife's birthday or not." Cain gazed at her, but it wasn't uncomfortable. "I know you have Kristen, but let me fill the role of big sister in your life. It's a part I miss."

"It's so embarrassing." She blinked, hoping to keep the tears from falling.

"Sometimes it's easier to talk to someone who isn't your spouse, and if I'm overstepping, we can go back to the party and forget this." Cain kept her voice light. "Eventually, though, you'll see that Remi will never think anything that upsets you is silly or embarrassing. The friend

I've known all my life won't ever judge, either—not when it's someone she loves. That goes for me too. If you tell me, it'll stay between us like I'm your priest."

There was a boulder of acid in her stomach, and the longer she kept it in, the bigger it got. It was starting to eat away at her joy. "All the stuff I did, it's going to haunt me forever."

Cain sat back and crossed her legs tapping her fingers in a random pattern on her knee. "The past is a bastard that needs to be wrestled to the ground sometimes, and you've done that. You did that without any of our help, so don't knock yourself because you went to the right guy."

"Not very well since you found me and my guy right off." The cadence of Cain's voice was soothing in the same way Remi's was. It made her feel safe even if she really wasn't.

"Like I said, what you accomplished for you and your little sister is something you should be proud of. And I found you because I went specifically looking. We're talking about the past and what solutions we need to put in place to keep it buried. There's one more step you need to consider."

She stared at Cain, but there was no sign of impatience on her face. "What's that?"

"Sometimes the only solution is to put a bullet in the bastard's head, and the only way for me to do that is knowing what's upsetting you." The logic Cain had was calm and straightforward, and another trait she shared with Remi. "Or you can wait and talk to Remi or Emma."

"When you sent someone to my old agent Bob's house to get all the copies and the master of the film I made, it was a start."

Cain nodded and opened her mouth momentarily like she'd gotten an idea. "We tried to erase as much as we could, but from your demeanor, there's more. You can trust me, Dallas. I'll be the last person who's going to throw stones. Whatever you tell me is never going to come back to haunt you."

"The people I got mixed up with had me do more than one of those films. Bob was lucky and somehow got his hands on the one film I was front and center."

"You have a specific concern? Give me a starting point."

"It's Linda." Blurting it out maybe wasn't the way to go, gauging by Cain's expression. Her calm was replaced with wariness. Cain had invited Linda Bender, Nicola Antakov's cousin, into her home with her brothers.

"Has she given you a problem?" Cain leaned forward. The concern on Cain's face was welcoming. "You're important to me, so please be honest. I'll believe you no matter what you tell me."

"It's not Linda specifically, more like what she's doing. You have her digging to find Nicola, but it's everything else she'll find that scares me." She should've said something before now. That she hadn't made her feel horrible. "If I'd told you and forgotten about my fears, you might be closer to finding Nicola."

"Hey, you're the only thing that matters. What scares you about Linda's search? She's concentrating on the clubs. The Hell Fire chain is dead, but I'm sure Remi told you Nicola opened new spots. One was a block from our club, Emma's, but that place is closed. If it's opened somewhere else, we haven't found it yet. I need to know where those are to have a starting point for dealing with that multitude of problems."

"I don't know if Nicola's family is involved in that kind of film, but the company I worked for was Russian run." The fear of someone like Nicola finding her history was making her lose sleep. She glanced at the door and saw Remi. Her spouse wouldn't come in unless she gave her a sign, so she lifted her hand and gave her one. Cain rose to leave, but Dallas shook her head.

"You know I love you, right?" Remi asked when she sat next to her. Dallas nodded, and Remi took her hand. "Then you need to keep an eye on this reprobate."

Cain laughed and pointed at Remi. "I'm happily married, thank you, but I'd like to ask Dallas out on a date. You can come if you want."

"When and where?" Remi asked as if understanding what she was talking about.

"If you're okay with coming by the house, how about we set something up so whatever we say stays private?"

"Emma invited me for lunch tomorrow, so I can bring Remi," Dallas said. Cain nodded and knocked on the table before leaving. She turned to Remi. "I'm sorry I didn't talk to you first."

"Don't apologize, querida. However you can get over a bad time is okay with me." Remi kissed her, and she could tell Remi was sincere. "There's something you should know, though."

She combed Remi's hair back, and the fear in her chest dissolved a little bit. That this wonderful person loved her was the best thing to ever happen to her. "What's that, my love?"

"You're my wife, and I love you. Whatever you're carrying, you can trust me to carry it for you. At least I'll share the load." Remi put her arm around her and kissed her. "Believe with everything in your heart that there isn't one thing that'll make me stop loving you. We don't talk about it, but I know you—all of you. There isn't anything in your past or going forward that's going to make me leave you."

"I know you get upset when I say you deserve someone better," Dallas said, "but it's true. If your mom ever knew the truth—about me, I mean—I'd never be able to face her." She needed to get Remi back in the other room before anyone missed them and came looking. Despite her job, being the center of attention for any reason wasn't something she was ever comfortable with.

"I didn't marry my mother, and she loves you just like my father and my brother do. After fifty years or so, you'll come to believe me." Remi held her hand and pulled her closer. "And you need to think of one important thing."

"What?"

"Let's say that someone does find out about your past." Remi held her against her chest when she began to pull away. "Hear me out."

"If that happened, I'd disappear. I'd never embarrass your family like that—you have to believe me."

"No, you stood before the bishop and promised to love me no matter the circumstance. The vow we said to each other was in good times and bad." Remi put her fingers under her chin. "Think about who you married, and I mean the unvarnished truth of me. I'm going to run all of my family's businesses eventually, and I'm also snake eyes. Knowing those two things, who do you think will have the guts to break the news about you? I don't want you to think any less of *me*, but you know the truth of who I am, and yet you married me."

"I love you, so of course I did." Remi was sweet, but the real problem in their marriage was her. Even if Remi wanted to ignore that, it didn't make it any less true.

"Then believe me when I tell you the same thing. My sins will always outweigh yours."

She put her arms around Remi's neck and shook her head. "You are to me perfection, and you're mine."

Remi stood and helped her up and hugged her so pretty much every inch of them was touching. "Then let's have a baby."

She inhaled and held it, thinking she'd heard wrong. "Are you sure? I thought you wanted to wait."

"I wanted to give you time to get used to this new life, not because I had doubts about you or us."

They'd talked about it, but there'd been so many things in the works since they'd met, including their wedding planning. A family with Remi was something she'd wanted from the first time Remi had touched her. "You don't have to convince me." Remi held her tight enough to lift her off the ground. "I'm all in."

CHAPTER FIVE

Cesar Kalina was short. It was the first thing Marisol noticed about him, and she couldn't notice anything else. That anyone would follow this guy's orders was hard to believe, but from what she knew about him, he'd built a profitable business. He wasn't in Hector's league, but with her help, he could be.

"Why are you here?" He poured a tequila for himself and waved at the bottle as if it would be an insult to his manhood to pour her one. "From what Hector's always said and bragged about, you were taking over for him. His other children only seem interested in spending money and doing nothing."

She hesitated and thought about what her mother had coached her to say. Humility, her mother had warned, was the way to everything she wanted. If Cesar could trust what she was saying, it would crack him open and give her the first rung of power she sought. Her mother hadn't been very present in her life, but she did know how to get anything she wanted from men.

"Hector decided to believe a bitch he'd just met over me. He had his fields torched, and his street dealers killed, and it all happened because his faith in this woman is unshakeable. I tried to take more responsibility, starting with killing Tracy, the one who made him ignore everything else, and he repaid that with throwing *me* out."

"He threw you away?" Cesar's emotion surprised her, so she only nodded. "That's Hector's mistake, but I know your mother, and she talks about you with such pride. Why don't you spend more time with her?"

"Hector's my father, and he never let me forget who my mother is—*what* she is, I mean." She'd always resented Hector for that. After what he'd done, she'd never call him Papa again. "I come from a whore, so that's tainted me in his eyes even if I'm his."

"My father did the same thing, so I made him pay. My mama now lives in a big house and has people working for her." He poured them both a drink now, as if they'd bonded over crappy parents. "Your mother still works, but she tells me that you help because Hector does nothing for her. He should remember she gave him the best of what children he has. You are the only one capable of taking over once he's dead."

She took a very small sip of the drink, not wanting to lose her head. "I grew up with Hector's wife, but I was alone. She only cared for her own children. That's not something I blame her for." The emotions that came from confession were so out of her norm she wanted to leave, but she could bury her pride for the night to get what she wanted. "When I was old enough, I tried to make Hector proud, but all he wanted was Tracy."

The way Cesar was nodding made her want to laugh. He was close to salivating over getting her to work for him. Adding her to his organization meant gaining what he wanted most. She was someone who understood Hector's business and also knew all his secrets. "You have to understand one thing. The only thing I have in common with Hector is where we started." He steepled his fingers and tapped them together. "We both clawed our way to the top. I don't plan to go back to the gutter."

"Give me a chance, and I'll give you the crown."

He smiled and tapped his fingers together again as he shook his head. "Slow will get us there, and it'll keep us from the kind of mistakes that land you in jail or killed. Do you think you can do that if I send you to start in New Orleans?"

At this point she'd say anything to do just that. Now that Hector had thrown her away like trash, he'd never have to think of her again because he thought she was stupid. Now, though, Tracy, Cain, and her loving father were all fair game. Maybe Hector would see what a mistake it'd been to choose Tracy over her when she had a gun pressed to his forehead. The only child he had who was equipped to run the business and have it survive was the one he didn't want. The only payment for that mistake was death—it was a lesson he'd taught her well.

"There's plenty of room in New Orleans for you to expand," she said. "Hector controls some, Cain's two idiots control some, and the rest are small players. The city is perfect to use as a base of operations because of what surrounds it."

"What do you mean?" Cesar leaned forward and placed his elbows on his knees.

"Miles of unpatrolled coastline, which makes it easy to get product in and disperse it in every direction. If we concentrate on that, you'll move under the radar until you're ready to show some muscle."

"Good." Cesar looked pleased, and she let him enjoy his moment. Once the chance came, she was taking it, and Cesar would join the others in the grave.

"You can trust me, and we'll start in Biloxi. It'll give me a chance to put everything in place before we start to build the network we need to cover from Arizona to Florida, and then we move north." Then she'd crush all the competition and take Hector's place like he'd wanted, once upon a time, only not how he'd planned for her move to the top spot. "There might be some pushback, but I'll take care of it." That she definitely would.

When they arrived at Emma's, Cain watched Emma laugh as everyone took turns toasting her. Dinner had been nice, and she'd been happy to see Dallas had lost her expression of hopelessness. The music started, and as she'd requested, it was the same slow song that Emma loved enough to dance to it at their wedding. Emma gladly took her hand and smiled when she led her to the dance floor.

"Does the day we first made love ever cross your mind?" Emma didn't lose eye contact with her, and it was like they were alone in the room.

"I'd wanted you for so many reasons, but touching you was and still is an honor. What I remember about that day was that I would've waited if you'd wanted me to." She tapped the end of Emma's nose and remembered how her mother had laughed at her Emma-imposed celibacy for an entire year. "That's when I knew I'd marry you if I could get you to say yes. You're the only woman who taught me patience as well as love for someone outside my family."

"That seems like a million years ago, and it wasn't until recently that I've felt like I'm living up to being your partner." Emma shrugged when she must've read the incredulity in Cain's expression. "You aren't going to agree with me, but I want you to have what you give me."

The song ended and she didn't let Emma go. "What?"

"A safe place for you to be yourself—a place that's yours alone. That sounds crazy, but that's what I want to be for you." Emma kissed her chin and squeezed her hand. "You do so much for me, and I love you for it, so you deserve no less. Thank you for tonight."

"You're welcome, and if you're thinking you're falling short, cut it out." She followed Emma to the table where they sat so Emma could feed the baby. "The night I got shot in that warehouse, I'd taken Hayden out to dinner before I left. He was mad with both of us, but I told him something I wanted him to remember no matter what happened."

Lou stood with his back to them giving Emma the privacy she needed to lower the front of her dress. "He was angry, and I couldn't blame him."

"We agreed to bury all that, lass. I told him that night he needed a safe haven, and for that moment, his had to be the one I'd had for years." She wrapped her arms around Emma and smiled at the way Billy held Emma's breast. "You've been the one person I can show all the parts of me and know you'll keep them all safe, so don't think you're not being a good spouse. You're my partner for life, and the woman I love."

"You really told him that?" Emma kissed the side of her head and sighed.

"I did, so smile and keep having a good time. No one's having more fun than your father, but we can give it a shot." There'd been such a change from when Ross first arrived in New Orleans, but Carmen had been the one who'd dragged him out of his shell and given him something to be happy about. He deserved it after living under Carol's thumb for so long.

"Did Mary tell you when the divorce will be final? I'd like a lot of warning if my mother's coming to town." Judge Mary Buchanan had fast-tracked Ross's divorce, and once it was final, Carol Verde would be out of their lives forever.

"Give it another couple months, and we'll be done with that. Once he's free to marry again, we'll build them a small house on the property if they want privacy."

"That'll give him another project to hover over, so thank you, my love. Now burp this big guy, and dance with me again." Emma handed over the baby and got her clothes in order.

They stayed until midnight, and Ross and Carmen promised to get the kids home. She walked Emma out the back door to get her into the SUV Lou had left parked in the loading dock. With luck, she could avoid having anyone follow them so they could be alone for what came next.

"What are you up to, mobster?" Emma turned in her seat as if to study her for clues.

"It's your birthday, and I haven't given you your gift." She headed into the Quarter, which was just revving up for the night. They turned on one of the short side streets on the right of the cathedral with only four of the homes the area was famous for, and it was a quiet oasis free of pedestrians.

The almost nondescript front opened to a beautiful courtyard to the side of the small garage she pulled into. There were four sets of French doors that led to the den and small kitchen, which she wasn't wild about, but a call to the glazier would take care of that. She didn't want anyone to be able to spy on them.

"Are we spending the night?" Emma was taking in the courtyard that was lit by the garden lights in the flower beds.

"Our house is full of family and permanent guests lately, but I love having you all to myself. Don't get me wrong, I love everyone under our roof, so I came up with a plan to give us some privacy every so often. Happy birthday, lass." She handed Emma a small box and closed her fingers over it. Inside were the keys to the place on a sterling Tiffany keychain with a globe on it. "If I could give you the world, you'd already own it."

"What did you do?" Emma appeared shocked, gazing at her, then outside.

"It's yours, lass, and the only thing I put in for now is the bed. You can make it your own because it is yours."

"*What?*" Emma asked in a way that sounded like she wasn't computing what she was saying.

"Like I said, I love our family, but it'll be nice to have a place where we can head into the kitchen naked, and no one is waiting for answers and solutions to problems. It can also be a great spot for your buddies to come over and raid the wine fridge that has yet to go in."

"You did this for me?"

She opened the door and came to Emma's side. The place was perfect because it came with the small carriage house across the street, so there was a spot for their security to keep an eye out without being underfoot. "I know it sounds schmaltzy, but I'd do anything for you. The privacy gives us a chance to practice that whole newlywed thing."

"Thank you, love." Emma took the keys and unlocked the side door when Cain pointed it out. She kicked her heels off and stepped into the middle of the room.

The place was old, but all the previous owners had done excellent maintenance. Unless Emma wanted to change what was already there, all it needed was to be furnished. She stood back and let Emma explore. The running commentary her wife gave kept her mind off everything she had going on, and she wasn't wasting energy thinking about it.

"Let's see the upstairs." Emma took her hand and pressed against her. "Show me."

She picked Emma up and walked to the foyer where the staircase was. It sounded like every single one creaked on the way up, but that was a good thing. No one could ever make it up unannounced. The rooms appeared as empty as the downstairs, but the large room at the end had a converted antique bed her friend had found for her.

"You've given me plenty of great birthdays, but this one is the best." Emma started with her tie, then the buttons of her shirt. "You loving me is the answer to every prayer I ever offered to God when I was growing up and dreaming of who I'd marry. The dominoes that fell because of that are only a great bonus." Emma stopped on her belt, and Cain raised her eyebrows in question. "My father found his true happiness, Dallas is my best friend—the list is long, and all because you love me."

"Of course I love you, lass." She combed her fingers through Emma's hair, liking the feel of it. "All that's true, and I love the family we've built. Don't think of this gift as me wanting to escape from all that, but as a place for you to enjoy—hopefully with me sometimes. You could lend it out to your father, Abigail and Finn, or whoever you like. I only want to make you happy."

"You've done that." Emma unbuckled her and let her pants drop. "I'm looking forward to you making me even happier."

They'd been together long enough to know what touch drove the other crazy, and any shyness about what she wanted had been something Emma had gotten over years before. That was something Cain worried about at first, but now, Emma was the one who initiated these moments, and she did because Emma was her partner in all things. Being intimate and enjoying each other was an important aspect of their relationship they both reveled in.

Emma put her hand between her legs, and it made her stop thinking. "It's your birthday, lass. Let me make you feel good."

"Then make love to me."

She took her time getting them both naked and laid Emma down. The room was dark, but she didn't need to see to touch all the skin she'd memorized, as she had the distinctive color of Emma's eyes.

Emma was wet, and Cain moaned when she slid her thigh between her legs. Tonight, she wanted to be close, so she squeezed her hand between them and entered Emma as Emma kissed her. The moan reverberated in her head and reminded her how lucky she'd been in her life—how blessed.

"Honey, faster." Emma lifted her hips and squeezed Cain's ass. "So good. Don't stop." She did as Emma asked, and it didn't take too long to bring her to the orgasm she wanted to give her. "Yes…yes," Emma said loudly, and she kept going until Emma stopped moving.

"I love you," she whispered, holding herself up by the elbows. "Happy birthday."

"Hmm." Emma didn't open her eyes but reached up and touched her face. The way she ran her fingers along her jawline made Cain want to repeat the process. "You're like fine wine, mobster. You get better with age."

"With you I always want to improve my skills." She rolled to her back and opened her arms to Emma. The place was quiet, and she enjoyed not hearing little girls running up and down the hall, or the baby crying, at least for the night. "I didn't want you to toss me out for someone who's going to try harder."

"Get serious, mobster. You were a keeper from the day I met you, and you're stuck with me. I think I'll go crazy if you ever decide to get rid of me."

"Neither of us have to worry, then." She reached for her shorts and sat up on the side of the bed. "How about a snack and something to drink?"

"You want to get up now?" Emma pressed herself against her back and flattened her hands over her abdomen. "If you stay, I promise I'll be nice to you," she teased.

"I'm sure you will, but tonight is all about you." She stood with Emma still pressed to her back. "Let's go down. I had Carmen stock the fridge with all your favorites, and there's a smaller version of your cake down there."

"It's not my birthday any longer, honey." Emma wrapped her legs around Cain's waist and hung on for the ride. "I have to admit that going down to the kitchen naked in the middle of the night makes this place perfect."

"Once it's done and we've furnished it, we could spend a few nights a month here, and lend it out to the family. Silent lovemaking isn't fun for months at a time." She sat Emma on the small island and laughed when she squirmed on the cool stone. If she'd wished for a perfect person for her, Emma would be it.

"What are you thinking about, mobster?" Emma traced her eyebrows with the tips of her index fingers, then kissed her.

"You," she said, wanting to forget why they'd come down and carry her back upstairs. "I love you, and I don't say it enough."

"You tell me and show me every day. Don't worry about that." Emma trapped her by wrapping her legs around her waist again and tugged her closer so her sex was pressed against Cain's abdomen. "Take me back to bed." It was like Emma had read her mind.

"The cake and everything else can wait. All I want is you." She put her hands under Emma's butt and headed back to the stairs. It'd been a few months since they'd been totally alone, and she was planning to enjoy it. She sat on the side of the bed with Emma straddling her lap, and the kiss they shared made her hard.

"Touch me," Emma commanded, and she squeezed her hand between Emma's legs. "And keep touching me."

They fell asleep at four in the morning, so the light streaming through the large windows in the room—waking her earlier than she would've liked—made her want to moan. The room was different than their bedroom at home, but she liked the old appeal of the place. It was, according to the real estate agent, one of the oldest in the Quarter, and one of the few that'd been in the same family for generations. That this generation wanted to sell surprised her, but then family fortunes didn't always stretch to eternity if all you did was spend it and not add to it.

Her phone buzzed in her pants on the floor, which was hard to miss in the quiet. Whoever it was would have to wait until Emma woke up on her own. The most pressing thing she was concentrating on was finding Nicola, so she could remove the threat to her family and the menagerie of people she'd picked up along the way. That was important, but she'd never lost sight of her FBI problem. Gardner was toward the top of her list, but she hadn't forgotten about Hannah's little friend Lucy.

The small girl had been, in her opinion, starved for affection, and that didn't compute if she had parents who loved her enough to fight over her. She often thought of what Hannah had said when she finally told them why she and Lucy weren't friends anymore. *I had to do it, Lucy said, or they'll send me back to live with bad people.* She'd rolled that around her head and had come to only one disturbing conclusion.

"All that thinking is waking me up way sooner than I'd like." Emma slid up and stared at her with a bad case of bed head. "And you reek of sex." The phone buzzed again, and Emma groaned. "Go ahead and tell whoever that is you're not getting up until noon. It's the day after my birthday, and I want at least the morning."

She reached down for her pants, not surprised to see Fin's name. Her cousin's persistence had made her a highly successful field agent and was making it difficult for her to adjust to a different kind of schedule that wasn't so regimented. "Good morning." She watched Emma walk naked to the bathroom and hoped Fin didn't have anything major going on.

"Hey, will you be here this afternoon?"

"I don't know what time yet, but yes. Carmen was planning a family dinner, and we'll be there. Is there a problem?"

Emma walked back toward the bed and wrinkled her nose when Cain said that but took the breast pump out as a signal she had more time.

"Linda might've found something." That Fin sounded optimistic might've been too strong a word. "She wanted to review it with us."

"Set that up for tomorrow, but I'd like to talk to her tonight." The conversation she'd had with Dallas the night before popped into her head.

"Is something else up?"

"I wanted to talk to her about an unrelated matter. Any luck on the other search?" She placed her hand on Emma's abdomen when she leaned against her to pump. Emma usually breastfed for eight months, so they had a ways to go, and pumping allowed Cain to sit with their son and feed him. That was especially good when he woke up screaming his head off in the middle of the night, and she could give Emma a break.

"I'm having lunch with her, so I'll let her know." Fin didn't sound freaked out, so she relaxed and rubbed Emma's stomach in small circles. "And I'll let you know about what we found, later. It can keep."

"Thanks, and just so you know, Emma will punch you in the nose if you call back." She ended the call and kissed the top of Emma's head.

"Did Dallas tell you what was bothering her? She seemed so upset last night." Emma took her hand and threaded their fingers together.

"She did, and I promised to help her. I know how important she is to you, so I'll try my best."

Emma turned her head and smiled. "I'm going to have to call her and cancel lunch, and I know you will."

"Maybe don't cancel." Dallas was, it seemed to her, working herself into a dark hole. "Let's invite them to lunch, probably at their house, and we can talk." She combed Emma's hair back and kissed her cheek. "I'm guessing she hasn't talked to you yet, and a bit of privacy will give us the opportunity to do that."

"That doesn't matter to me as long as she talks to *someone*. I doubt Dallas will have much of an appetite, but hopefully sharing what she's kept to herself all this time will allow her to breathe."

She waited for Emma to finish removing the pump and ran downstairs with the bags to give Emma a chance to put everything away. Emma was in bed when she made it back.

"To finish what we were talking about," Cain said, "Dallas said she'd share it with you, and she talked to Remi last night. Remi must've put her at ease enough that she enjoyed the party."

Before they got lost in themselves, Emma called Vincent and ordered food to be delivered to Dallas and Remi's new place, after one.

Cain felt for Dallas and Kristen for all they've been through, but Dallas seemed like a fighter. Even if any of her secrets came to light, Cain would do everything she could to make sure her friend would survive the attack. She wanted to do that not only for Emma and Dallas, but also for Remi. Her old friend deserved a life with the woman she loved without the judgment.

They took a shower and dressed in the clothes Cain had packed, and Cain texted Lou a grocery list of random things. It was a signal to follow them out.

"Can you do me a favor?" Emma asked when she started the car.

"Anything."

"When it comes to Dallas"—Emma maintained eye contact— "don't hold anything back. I know you worry about it sometimes, but she deserves to let all of that worry go. You and Remi have been planning to give her that, but it sounds like there's more on her mind. Don't worry about doing what needs to be done when it comes to these people."

"You have my word, lass. Some problems are easier to deal with than others, but there's always a solution. This time, I'm hoping the key is living in our pool house." She leaned over and kissed Emma, placing her hand on the side of her neck. "As for the rest, don't worry. When I'm done, we'll be done."

❖

Dallas studied Remi as she unbuttoned her shirt and pulled it from her pants. Their talk before dinner seemed like ages ago, and she wondered if now, in the quiet of the condo, Remi was starting to question her choices when it came to her. She couldn't blame Remi if she wanted her out or changed her mind about the kind of commitment she'd made.

Someone like Remi was proud, strong, and in control of her life. Having a wife her friends knew had done things no woman should ever have to admit to had to be an embarrassment. Leaving she'd understand, because she was damaged, and there was no changing that.

She'd done so many demeaning things in an effort to stay ahead of any danger so she could keep Kristen safe. In her gut, though, she knew all that was about to come back and swallow her whole. Granted, now she had money, enough that she didn't have to work again, but she'd miss the friends she'd made here. Emma, Abigail, and the rest of the family were people she'd come to love and trust, especially Emma. Having Emma to confide in had given her a sense of place that'd made her relationship with Remi that much better, but it couldn't last forever.

"What are you thinking about?" Remi asked, dropping her shirt on the chair closer to her side of the bed. "It has to be something if it's making that wrinkle in the middle of your forehead." The pants went next, and Remi sat on the bed and faced her. "Is it about earlier tonight?"

She reached over and stroked Remi's thigh as a way to not only connect to her, but to calm herself down. "Do you want me to leave?"

"What? Leave?" Remi said loudly but not in anger. "What gave you that idea?"

"You never want to know everything about my past, but there's more, and it's only a matter of time before it comes out. You and the family deserve better." Thinking of Remi's parents having to read about all the disgusting things she'd done made her want to disappear.

"You dwell on that, but think of the most important thing that's happened so far since we've met," Remi said in a calmer tone.

"What?"

"That first day, you had a successful career, a home, and Bob.

You had all that without me, and the only problem in that equation was Bob." They'd first met in the airport in Key West when Bob, her abusive ex-manager, had mistaken Remi and her friends for flunkies with the studio. Bob had blackmailed Dallas for years, and there'd been no getting away from him until Remi had a persuasive conversation with him. She nodded, and Remi continued. "We eliminated that threat as well as all the information he had. What makes you think we can't do it again?"

"I don't know, but I'm scared. Linda is trying to find Nicola, and if she has any information on me, you're not going to be able to stop it. If I leave now, it'll save you and your parents the humiliation of all that becoming public."

"I thought we'd decided a few things like kids, moving into the house, and making a life?" Remi put her hand over hers and stared at her as if trying to figure out if she was serious. "I mean, we already started on that life, but there's so much more to look forward to."

"I'm giving you an out."

"That's nice of you," Remi said, shaking her head. "Why in the world would I want an out when I've found the one person that's perfect for me? Let's make a deal, you and me." Remi held her hand out and waited.

"Remi, I'm serious. You shouldn't take a chance, not when the outcome could be this bad." She'd been hopeful a few hours ago, but now with time to think about it, there was no escaping what she had coming to her. Never mind that all she'd done wrong was to be born to Johnny and his sadistic streak, but it didn't matter. She loved Remi and her family, so one more sacrifice was worth it.

"I know you've had this conversation with Emma, and you don't have to tell me the details, but you know who you married. Just like Emma, you have to know the parts of me that got me to where I am." Remi turned so the tattoo on her upper arm was visible.

Dallas traced her finger along the edges and kissed over the eye of the snake. It was half of a hooded cobra with a blue eye in the form of a die that matched Remi's right eye. Mano's tattoo was the other half of the snake with a green eye that matched Remi's left eye. The two mismatched eyes were a trait the twins shared, in mirror image. When they stood shoulder to shoulder the tattoo made sense, and it was their symbol, snake eyes. On the streets, they were not only known but feared.

Her lover was a contrast of strong and gentle, and she loved the way Remi was with her. "Are you saying that to make me fear you?" She leaned in and kissed Remi, loving how she responded to her. "I have talked to Emma, and her one lesson in all she told me was to not repeat her mistakes. Your sense of justice is what made me fall in love with you, honey, and I never want you to change that about yourself. I'd hate to think where I'd be if you hadn't helped me escape my crappy life."

"Then why would you want to leave now?" Remi touched her cheek and wiped away the few tears that'd fallen. "When we met, I knew you were special, and I would've done everything I did even if you hadn't ended up with me." Remi rubbed her back when she rolled over and stretched out over Remi's body.

"That I know, and it's one of the reasons I love you so much. You gave me my freedom, and I'll never regret giving myself to you." She lifted herself up a little to look Remi in the eye. "You've never scared me, and you don't have it in you to hurt me. I'm telling you I want to leave because you gave me my total freedom back, and I want to repay what you've given me."

"I didn't ask you about Emma because I want something from you, love. Emma left Cain because she misunderstood a situation that should've been handled in a more permanent way. Cain's love for Emma let that problem fester until it cost her Marie, her one living sibling. Those types of mistakes are hard to come back from, but they forgave each other," Remi said, stretching up and kissing her.

"She still carries a lot of guilt over that." Emma had cried when she'd told her about Marie and what had happened to her. She'd warned her to not hold the darker side of what Remi had to do at times against her.

"Cain forgave her, so she should put that boulder down. What I'm trying to tell you is I handle problems the same way. Anyone who dares print anything about you isn't going to have the payday they think will come of it. But really, I'm going to do whatever it takes to take care of whatever's left of your previous life before it comes to that. All you have to do is trust me, and trust Cain with the truth." Remi rolled them over so they faced each other, side by side.

"I'd do it all over again if it meant I ended up here," Dallas said, "but my God, it's so embarrassing." That's what it boiled down to. Facing the people who cared for her and seeing that shame in their eyes when they knew all her secrets. Shame was hard to shed, and it lived inside her like a parasite eating away at her happiness whenever she tried to forget it.

Remi framed her face with her hands, not letting her glance away. "Before you, I had women from all kinds of backgrounds. Getting someone in my bed was never a problem."

Remi's declaration was something she also knew from her talks with Emma. It's why she'd told her to set herself apart if she wanted a future with the confirmed serial dater. Hearing it from Remi, though, made her irrationally jealous. "I know that." Her words came out soft and slow, like they were frozen in her mouth.

"I'm not bragging, querida." Remi put her hand between her legs. There'd been so many degrading jobs, not to mention everything her father had done to her, but Remi's touch washed her soul clean. "I know you. Even those parts of you that you keep hidden from me. I know you, and I love all of you. I'm going to as long as you allow me in your heart and in your bed. I'm going to fight for you, for Kristen, and for us for the rest of my life. Why do you think I stopped worrying about your little sister only after she picked Muriel?"

"You're not listening to me," she said, but Remi's fingers were making her lose concentration.

"I think it's the other way around."

"That was sneaky," she said when she opened her eyes and tried not to rub herself along those long fingers.

"Sneaky?" Remi said, rolling them over. "I could stop and wait for an invitation. Now answer my question."

"No way," she said, laughing. "You made your move, so you'd better finish." She had to stop talking when Remi's fingers entered her slowly as her thumb massaged her clit. The touch where she most wanted her was maddeningly soft, and Remi eased up when she lifted her hips to make better contact. "Why did you stop worrying?" The last thing she wanted was to continue their conversation, but she wanted Remi to understand her position.

"Do you have any idea just how beautiful you are?" Remi asked as she brought her fingers out and pushed them back in. "I stopped worrying because she'll be as protected as she would be if she'd stayed with us for the rest of her life. She and you deserve a life, though. A life that's of your choosing and one that makes you happy."

"You do that, and you also make me feel beautiful, my love. You just make me want you." She had to stop talking when Remi gave her what she wanted, and the strokes became firmer and faster. "Yes," she said, opening her legs wider.

"You want me?" Remi said softly.

She turned her head from side to side, trying her best to hang on and make it last. It was hard, though, since Remi made her insane whenever she touched her. All the things she whispered in her ear as she touched her made her believe she did deserve all the joy Remi gave her, and that'd been something she thought would never be true. Now, though, she didn't have to wait any longer.

"Yes, please, lover, harder." She grabbed Remi's ass and brought her hips up to meet her hand, and it was driving her crazy. "Oh yes, don't stop, don't stop." Remi stopped moving when she went rigid and kissed over her eyelids. "My God, your powers of persuasion are truly legendary."

"You inspire me, and I'm not letting you go." Remi rolled off her and opened her arms so she could move closer. "If you go, I'll have no choice but to follow you."

"You're making it hard for me to explain my side of things." Dallas sat up slightly so she was leaning over Remi and smiled down at her.

"If your side of things is to leave so I can't stick by you if things about you come out, then no. When I said my vows, I meant them. Every word," Remi said, tapping the end of her nose.

"The truth is, I don't think I could survive you changing your mind. This way I can prepare myself for the media onslaught if it comes." She ran her hand up and down Remi's abdomen but kept her eyes on her expression. Saying all that was harder than being on the front page of every entertainment magazine in history.

"Do you not have any faith in me?" Remi's expression was hard to see. If there was one thing that separated Remi from anyone else in her life, past and present, it was her selflessness. Remi put aside her own wants if she thought it wouldn't be good for her.

"I have every faith in you, my love. It's the rest of the world that worries me." Dallas skimmed her hand down Remi's thigh.

"Then let's talk to Cain, and then we'll talk to Mano. If you're serious about not wanting to wait, then we'll get started on my mother's future grandchildren."

"We already talked to Mano and Sylvia about him helping us, like Billy did with Emma and Cain, so there's no reason to put it off. As for my career, it'll either be there or it won't if something is reported. All I care about is you and that you love me. I've made enough money to be comfortable if I have to start over."

"I think between the two of us we'll be okay when it comes to anything we have to face. As for your career, just remember—we own the studio." Remi stopped talking for a moment when Dallas cupped her sex. "Do you think our partners, Cain and Emma, will turn you down for a role you want?"

"You're hard to argue with." She moved her fingers over Remi's clit and pressed down.

"Then stop trying." Remi laughed, then closed her eyes when Dallas got more serious in how she was touching her. "Shit," Remi said, sounding short of breath.

"What?" She smiled when Remi opened her eyes and raised her eyebrows. "God, you're sexy."

She moved lower as Remi's breathing became more pronounced with her touch. If there was something Remi enjoyed, it was having Dallas's mouth on her, and she loved making Remi happy. Remi groaned when she teased her with the tip of her tongue, and Dallas wanted to hear more. She increased the pressure until Remi wrapped her hand in her hair and pulled a little harder than usual. "Shit, querida," Remi said as she tilted her hips forward.

She sucked harder and slipped her fingers in, making Remi moan louder. The sound made her feel both powerful and happy. That she could please Remi to the point she always wanted more was the best gift for their future. It really was a gift that Remi had never held where she'd started against her.

"Fuck," Remi said as she tightened her hold on her hair as she tensed, then pulled away when she seemed too sensitive to Dallas's touch. "I love you," Remi said when she lay over her again and kissed her.

"I love you, and I love touching you." She laughed when Remi slapped her gently on the butt.

"That's a good thing for me, but I love reciprocating." Remi combed her fingers through her hair and scratched the back of her head. "Trust me, love, everything is going to be okay. I can't keep you from worrying, but I won't let anything hurt you if it's in my power to do so."

"That I know and believe like knowing the sun will rise every day." She kissed Remi again and pressed her hand to the side of her neck. "I'm so lucky I found you."

"We can argue that point as well, but it's late. Let's get some sleep, and we'll deal with all this in the morning."

She rested her head on Remi's shoulder and flattened her hand over her heart. Admitting that she did worry was something she had a hard time admitting since she'd conditioned herself to expect the worst. Accepting that there was nothing to fear, and that she wasn't going to be thrown away because there was nothing to love about her, was unbelievable. The last person who'd believed she was worthy of something was her mother, and she barely had a tangible memory of her. Now she felt like she was betraying Remi for not believing what she was saying.

"What?" Remi said softly, as if sensing the turmoil in her.

The tears came, and she stayed quiet hoping Remi wouldn't notice. Hell, there hadn't been anything to hint someone was plotting against her, but her brain had a way of digging holes that were at times totally unnecessary. "I'm sorry," she said and closed her eyes, hoping to curb her emotions.

"Did you see Kristen and Muriel tonight?" Remi's change of subject made her take a deep breath. "Are you ready for what comes next with those two? I don't think there's anyone more excited about a potential wedding than my father. Joining our family to Cain's in a way that goes beyond the partnership we have now would make him a happy man."

She nodded, glad to have the reprieve Remi was offering. "I wasn't sure that was a good idea until I saw them together. Kristen's young, but she found what we have a lot sooner than we did, and Muriel makes her happy." She felt Remi tighten her hold on her, and it made her let go of her demons for a bit.

"Muriel does do that, and we gave her some stuff to think about tonight when it comes to their future. I take my job as Kristen's protector seriously."

"Thank you, honey," she said, and she kissed Remi's neck. Sleep came after that, and she woke, startled, five hours later. Their room in the condo was flooded with sunlight, and with it came the same sense of dread she'd had for a couple of days, that had started when Remi had told her Linda was researching Nicola's businesses.

"Do you trust me?" Remi spoke softly as she pressed up behind her.

"With everything I am."

Remi reached for her phone and dialed Cain's number and asked her to lunch. They were close enough for Dallas to hear everything Cain said, and it made her stomach ache. Surviving bad stuff was one thing, but reliving it all was another. "This might be hard, but you're not alone. The only way to make you believe you're safe is to face it—together."

"I believe you, and this reminds me of one of the first things Emma ever told me." She turned around and kissed Remi after studying those brilliant unique eyes. "She warned me that sometimes the answer lies in the ugliness of life. The way to make sure you sweep away what needs to be erased is by not hating you when you have to do what's necessary."

"Do you know what she was talking about?" Remi held her like she was precious. "The ugliness of life makes me a terrible person in the eyes of some people."

"You'll never be a monster to me, so don't hold back ever." Emma was right—some people deserved killing. Living and exploiting people for power and personal gain made some people hard to bring down, but Remi and Cain had never shied away from trying. "You're mine, and I love you no matter what needs to be done."

CHAPTER SIX

The flight into Biloxi had been bumpy enough to make Marisol ill, so she got off and glanced around for her contact. She was anxious to lay down how things were going to go and get these idiots to respect her. Her mother had warned her about taking chances and not following Cesar's instructions, but her mother had no idea how things were done. The little guy had enough people in the States to eliminate her if she became a problem. His strategy was sound, but she had no patience for methodical. The man standing outside the terminal smoking put his hand up when she walked out.

"Did you call everyone?" She followed him to the car, and he drove her to the casino where he'd made a reservation for her. Finding a place to live was the last thing on her list. She waited until they were in the suite before getting to business and being clear about what she expected. If she was going to be the boss here, she had to live up to the image.

"They're coming to the meeting you wanted tomorrow," her contact said. "We've got a shipment arriving today, so I wanted them to concentrate on that first." He opened the minibar and took out a small bottle of Jack without asking. Like Cesar, he wasn't tall, but he was also skinny enough that she thought there might be something wrong with him. He had a smirk when he talked that made her think he looked at her like a punchline he had to put up with, but not work with.

"What's your name?" She sat with her back to the sun streaming through the wall of windows, making him have to squint to look at her.

"Oscar Lopez." He went to sit and stopped when she shook her finger.

"The next time I give you an order, Oscar, I expect you to carry it out. You don't, and I'm going to cut off a finger for every time you disrespect me." She had to establish authority and eliminate any problems.

"Cesar likes all his captains there when the big shipments come in." Oscar glared at her with what she considered defiance—she could hear it in his tone. Unless something changed, Oscar was going to serve nicely as her sacrifice. "We're the only ones operating in the area, so we like keeping the supply safe."

"Who the fuck do you think sent me here?" She decided to channel her father and kept her voice low. "Are you confused about that?"

The smile died on Oscar's lips, and he slowly shook his head. "I didn't know we were changing everything we do even if it works."

"Think about what it's going to cost you when all the six of you are babysitting the boxes we're expecting, instead of trying to get ahead." She hoped he got how disgusted she was. "Are you all a pack of old women who need that much backup? Get out, and I'll see you at the cut house at nine." She leaned back and closed her eyes, expecting him to leave. This was a good chance to not only show who was boss, but to go out and start her plans.

She smiled when the door closed and her thoughts turned to Nicolette Blanc. The Frenchwoman who'd arrived in New Orleans to do business with Cain Casey had sought her out when that didn't work out. She'd learned the story of what Nicolette had wanted from Luce Fournier, Nicolette's old lover. Cain had been Nicolette's target, and that had gotten her killed. It was the only explanation for her disappearance.

The Gulf view from her room gave her an excellent vantage point to see the storm offshore. It reminded her of what Nicolette was like when they'd been together. Behind that beautiful face was a dark attitude full of bluster and passion mixed with the type of anger that exploded when she couldn't get what she wanted. In Nicolette's mind, Cain had been the one who got away, and she was back to claim what was hers. It didn't matter to her that Cain had married.

Nicolette needed to get what she wanted so she'd come to Marisol and offered a partnership, but she wasn't stupid enough to think she'd been Nicolette's first choice. That'd been her role until now. Everyone had dismissed her and knocked her to the back of the line all her life, and those people were going to be sorry. She wasn't willing to play second choice for anyone no matter how beautiful they were.

She waited an hour before going out through the casino and saw

Oscar on the phone. No doubt he was on the line complaining to Cesar about what a bitch she was. He was glancing around and looked right past her because of the blond wig she wore and a change of clothes. That's what she was going for.

The drive to the safe house Hector used didn't take long. The neighbors would have been shocked to learn what was going on inside. The place was full of women in their underwear cutting coke. It was Sunday, so while the good folks went off to church, Hector had the old women who transported his product make their deliveries.

Marisol slid down in the car she'd rented and waited. The women were never that punctual, but reliable enough that they showed up before two in the afternoon. Hector's process worked because everyone around here dismissed them as the maids. She sat up when a large black SUV pulled into the drive and three white guys got out with duffel bags. This was different, and it was way too much product. Had someone already beaten her to derailing Hector?

"There's no way you get away from me." She drove to the condo building where Miguel Gonzalez, the old boss Hector had put in charge here, had lived. Miguel had been sleeping with Tracy until Hector had taken her—along with Miguel's head—for the mistakes of his brother. The condo still belonged to the business, but Navarro Ingles was the new tenant, and the new boss. His brother Ernesto ran everything for Hector in Colombia.

She adjusted the blond wig and sunglasses before getting out and walking to the elevator while trying not to engage with anyone. The top floor had only two apartments, and Navarro's condo faced the Gulf. Hector had sent her here a few times to keep this fool in line, since he was new to the business and made enough mistakes that she figured that was his hobby.

The doorbell echoed through the space, and she heard him talking, his voice getting louder as he headed toward the door. If he was on the phone, she'd have to wait him out in case he said her name out loud. She moved to the alcove of his neighbor's door and pressed her back so she'd be out of his view. He stopped talking when he opened the door, then stood there.

"What the fuck?" she heard him say and almost laughed. That he didn't study the security feed before opening up without knowing who it was made him a moron deserving of a bullet to the brain. "Let me call you back, but we're okay. The stuff got here, and it'll be to you by tomorrow night. I talked to the new service, and everything is under control." Marisol guessed he was talking to Hector. "You have my word."

The call ended, and she moved fast before he could close the door. His expression was comical when she pressed the gun to his forehead and ordered him to drop the phone. He fumbled with it since he had a drink in the other hand. She pushed him to the chair next to the sofa, which cut them off from the security measures he had access to. This would be a long conversation, and any wrong answers would be costly.

"Navarro," she said smiling at his jeans and polo shirt. He'd never looked the part of someone in charge, but Hector had excused it by saying he was still young. Youth, though, had nothing to do with his sense of loyalty. It was the one thing that'd gotten him this job. He and his brother would die for Hector, and she was about to test that theory.

"Mari," he said staring at her and smiling. It had to do with the wig she assumed. "Do you need money already?"

She wanted to smash the butt of her gun across his face, but she didn't want to get that close to him, especially now that his hands were empty. Navarro wasn't only young, but big and much stronger than her. He faced her with no fear. "Be careful, Navarro, before I put a bullet through those pretty teeth."

"You want to do that—go ahead. My brother told me it's the price we pay sometimes for this life, but the cameras will make it easy to figure out who killed me." He pointed up, and she noticed the blinking light on the ceiling in the corner. "You wanted out, so get out. Just don't think you'll start your business off your father's back. Security will be much harder to crack if you try."

"The safe house is still on the same schedule, asshole. How hard will it be to get inside?" She should've thought this through, but it was too late to back out now. "Hector keeps playing the same tired game."

"Tracy beefed up the security after what happened, with everything that went wrong. The old safe house is nothing more than a place to sleep for the guys making deliveries to other cities." He crossed his legs and cocked his head as if trying to figure something out about her. "What can I do for you?"

"How are the deliveries different?" she asked, lifting the gun and pointing it at his forehead. "And you're full of shit about Tracy, so tell me."

She heard the glass shatter when her shot went wide, and she would've taken another one, but she'd fallen to the ground when Navarro's bullet went through her bicep. The force of it had knocked her off balance, and the pain was instant. He was over her with his bare foot on her hand. The bastard appeared smug as he brought his weight down enough to make her drop her gun.

"Pepe, come up here and bring some guys with you," Navarro said into his phone. "Mari, do you want me to kill you and save you the embarrassment? Hector told us you're no longer under his protection, so this won't go the way you think."

The pain was making her nauseous, so she swallowed repeatedly to keep from embarrassing herself. "I'm his daughter, asshole, and that still means something to him."

"Okay." He lifted the phone again and waited after asking for Hector. Navarro told Hector what'd happened and then listened for a long while. The men he'd called for tied a towel around her arm and waited for orders. "Here"—he handed the phone over—"Papa wants to talk to you."

"Fuck you." She refused to take the phone, so Navarro put it on speaker.

"Marisol." Hector said her name with enough contempt to make his displeasure known. "Listen to me."

"You told me to leave, *Hector*." She said his name with the same inflection he'd used. "That means you lost the right to tell me anything."

"The thought you're mine makes me want to kick my own ass." Hector sounded like he was talking through his teeth. "You've had every chance, and you've fucked every one of them up. Now you take a job with Cesar, and your first move's against me?" He was screaming by the end.

"My life has nothing to do with you." She hated sounding pathetic, but she was panting from the pain.

"Navarro's guys are going to drive you to the hospital and dump you in the parking lot. Once you get treated, you're going to disappear." Hector sounded serious, and that meant no negotiation. "If you're brain-dead and decide not to take that advice, the next bullet goes in your head. Once you're dead, I'll have your mother dropped in a hole where no one will find her, much less look for her."

"I work for Cesar and only wanted to talk to Navarro."

"Navarro," Hector said, and Navarro shot her in the upper thigh opposite her arm wound. "Cesar's my next call, so disappear, Marisol, and stay gone. Go back to your mother, only this time don't believe everything she tells you. She might think you're a genius, but up to now, that's been very wrong."

She yelled when the two guys picked her up and headed for the elevator. Hopefully Hector wasn't lying about the hospital. Once she got treated, she'd have to call her mother so she could send her some security. One guy tossed her roughly into the back seat and held her down until they slowed. "Shit," she said as the guy pushed her out. The shouts were the last thing she heard before she passed out. Complete blackness was bliss.

❖

Emma gazed out the window as they headed home, thinking of last night and the morning. Cain's gift had been a surprise and was going to be a lot of work. That part made her laugh, and it was loud enough to make Cain take her hand. She turned and faced the one person in the world who saw her and loved the sight.

"What are you laughing at, hayseed?" That was the nickname Cain had given her in the beginning.

"I'm just happy." She squeezed Cain's hand and sighed. "And you're the reason why." That morning no one was knocking on their door demanding entrance, no one was calling with a problem, and the baby wasn't crying down the hall. She loved her family, but they, along with the kids, were a handful. "We woke up late, and it was so quiet."

"I know how much you do to keep us going, so you deserve to take a break every once in a while." Cain smiled and threaded their fingers together. They were headed back to the club to get a ride home to throw the FBI off, since they were led to believe they'd headed home last night.

Her wife was successful as the head of their clan because she wasn't only smart but had enough stamina to make the right decisions even when she was exhausted. Cain was a whirlwind, and that energy that drove her had been passed to the next generation. Their three kids were very seldom still, especially Hannah.

"You're crazy if you think I'm enjoying that place without you, and I want us to make it our own." There were a million things on Cain's mind, but Emma figured picking furniture would be a good way to clear her head and give her a new perspective. That kind of mental break could trigger something Cain hadn't thought of before.

Cain turned into the loading dock and leaned over the console. "Did you think I was going to make you do it by yourself? That would make me an asshole."

"That's not usually your thing, honey." She laughed too when Cain pressed her lips to the side of her neck.

"Remi's been telling me about their house renovation saga, and it gave me the idea for the new place. Last time there was renovating, I was recovering from Barney's gunshot, and all I got to do was bully the contractor a little."

"He twitches around you, mobster, so I think it was more than a little. This place, though, we should do together." Emma traced Cain's jawline and huffed when the phone rang. "It was too good to be true."

"I told them to make sure it was important, so give me a minute." Cain retrieved her cell and glared at the screen before relaxing. It was Remi. "Hey, everything all right?"

"Are you free for lunch?" Remi was someone she met with regularly, but she wasn't usually this formal when asking for a lunch date.

"We got going early to do just that—you beat me to the invitation. How about we double-date?" Cain mouthed *Remi* and the question made Emma think it'd been a rough night for Remi and Dallas. "Does your new place have a table yet?"

"That and everything we need except food." Remi sounded a bit subdued from what Emma could hear.

"We already took care of that too, we just have an errand to run first, so give me an hour." Cain ended the call and rested her head back.

"Did Dallas tell you anything specific last night?" Emma asked. "You don't have to tell me what—I just want to know if she did." The way people flocked to Cain was something she was proud of, but sometimes it opened her up to more danger. Not that helping her best friend would get her killed, but Cain was stretched too thin, and she wanted to help.

"I can hear your brain humming, and she did." Cain rubbed her back and kissed her forehead. "From experience, I also know there's more to the story."

"Dallas isn't that old, but she's already been through enough hardship for a hundred lifetimes." Her mother had never been June Cleaver, but Dallas's father sounded like a nightmare few would've escaped. She'd never wished death on anyone, yet she was glad he was dead. "She survived it, but she still carries a lot of shame because of it."

"Her past is a series of nightmares that still haunt her, so I told her there's one way to fix that."

Emma lifted her head and gazed at Cain, waiting. "What?"

"You kill and bury it." Cain smiled, and Emma loved that smile. "To be able to do that, I need the whole story. It's the only thing that'll give me a starting place."

"Promise me you'll wait until she's ready. Pushing her might spook her," she said, kissing Cain like they had all day. "Just don't let her run. Remi will lose a big part of herself if Dallas goes, and Muriel won't survive another loss like that if Kristen decides to go with her."

"You have my word that it'll only be a small push to keep her tethered to what and who are important."

"I keep saying it." She smiled and pressed her hand to the side of Cain's neck. "You're a romantic at heart, my love."

CHAPTER SEVEN

Muriel sat in her office on the second floor of Emma's and thought about the teasing she'd gotten from Cain and Remi last night when it came to her and Kristen. She glanced at the picture she kept of her and her father at her law school graduation. He appeared so proud, and all that changed when she fell for Shelby's bullshit.

His death with that animosity between them had come close to making her give up, but then she'd accepted a dinner date with a college student who demanded her attention. Kristen had infused her with hope and hadn't allowed her to backslide into the darkness the loss of her father had left her with. This was the first time she truly believed she was in love and wanted to build on it for a lifetime.

"Muriel." Linda Bender said her name softly as if loath to knock her out of her daydreams. "Do you have a moment?"

"Sorry, I was out of it there." She stood and pointed to the table with four chairs in her office. Sitting behind her desk would be rude, she thought. "What's up?"

Linda sat quietly, like she had from the moment she'd joined them. She seemed to never say anything without careful consideration first—a trait you wanted when someone kept your secrets. "Right before Yury Antakov—David Eaton, as the world knew him—died, he had me working on the ledgers as always, but he gave his go-to guy the job of finding Abigail and her children. Boris St. John wasn't someone I particularly cared for, but Yury trusted him."

"Was he the guy who came after Abigail and her kids?" The family had heard what happened from both Finley and Abigail, and Cain was ready to annihilate everyone in Nicola's orbit. As the family attorney, Muriel was hard-pressed to talk Cain out of it. Their family wasn't what most thought respectable, but they were nothing like the monsters the Antakovs were, especially when it came to going after women and children.

Linda nodded slowly. "It was the guys who worked for Boris who took the shots at her, but it was Boris himself who Yury sent to New Orleans to get the kids back."

"Minus Abigail, I'm guessing." She'd never met anyone in the Antakov family, and she hoped they'd be taken care of before she had the pleasure. Her main concern was for Finley and her new family. Nicola's death would mean they'd be safe.

"Their whole agenda was to have the next generation waiting in the wings to grow the business." The way Linda said that made Muriel want to laugh. "In some families it's not necessarily a bad thing, but Yury's addition to what his father-in-law gave him was the trailer operation. That, and the Hell Fire Clubs. Neither one is something you want to be your family's legacy."

"From what I've heard, Sacha is continuing the low end of the operation that takes place in those trailers, but the high-end clubs are out." She wanted to keep the conversation going without spooking Linda. Since her arrival, Linda had only talked to Cain at length. "We believe in family too, but nothing like that will be associated with our business."

"I know that, if not I would've run by now." Linda laced her fingers together and stared at them as if trying to find a way to go on. "Boris called me from here all those months ago to tell me he'd lost Abigail's parents. When Abigail didn't come back to her house, Boris was smart enough to sit on her parents' place, since they were his last chance. Losing them, though, was one too many mistakes, and he knew Yury would've killed him if he'd gone back to New York."

"Was Boris important to you?" Muriel was confused as to where this was going.

"Boris has never been a favorite of mine, but in the end, he was a scared little boy begging me for help." Linda, in a way, reminded her of Dallas and Kristen. All of them had survived lives they wanted to escape and were strong enough to do that. "He calls me every week, but he doesn't tell me where he is. That's been our rule."

"There's nothing wrong with that."

"Muriel, I'm not sharing anything about your family or anything else with Boris, of all people," Linda said, as if reading her mind. "I'm talking to you because it occurred to me how many jobs Yury had Boris do for him."

"You think the missing link to finding Nicola is in Boris's head?"

"I doubt he knows where Nicola went—Yury did a good job of keeping her a secret. As far as the family knew, she and Fredrick died in a crash. We had no reason to doubt his word."

She nodded and tried to think why they were having this conversation. "So, Nicola went back to where she was hiding before?"

"I doubt that, but if Yury lied about Nicola—"

"He lied about Fredrick," she finished for Linda. "Cain thought that could be a possibility, but if Fredrick's alive, Yury hid him well."

"Would Cain agree to talk to Boris?" Linda flattened her hands and made eye contact. "I won't ask if you think she'd be upset. Being here is my best chance of giving my brothers a good life. I don't want to mess that up."

"Cain wants this problem behind us, so ask. Any clue that gets us to our targets will get you a bonus, not thrown in the street." She stood and glanced at her watch. "I'll call Cain and have her and Finley set aside some time."

"Thank you, and I owe your family so much. I live in fear my mother and the family will find us. My mother believes in our right to exploit those women. Living well off the misery of someone else was perfectly okay with her." Linda stood as well, and Muriel had to admire her for what she'd done for her siblings.

"Cain will take care of you and the boys, as will the rest of us." She accepted Linda's hand and saw her out. Cain's phone went to voicemail, so she and Finley would have to wait until she resurfaced with Emma. After trying Cain again, she decided to leave early and head to Tulane. Kristen would be finished in forty minutes, and she wanted to surprise her. She walked along the part of campus with the oldest buildings, and the scenery brought back her time there with Cain. Most of Kristen's classes were there, and once she graduated, Muriel was going to miss picking her up, even if she worried about their age differences.

"Are you lost or trying to butter me up for something?" Kristen walked up behind her and put her arms around her. "You're a nice surprise, babe."

Cute names were never her thing, and Kristen knew that, which was why she went through a variety of them. "I was going to ask you to lunch, but only if I'm not luring you to play hooky."

"You've been dying to say that, haven't you?" Kristen pulled her down by the lapels and kissed her. "The truth is you're way sexier than anyone on this campus, and I don't have that much longer, so you'll have nothing to tease me about."

"You go at whatever pace you want—I got you." The way Kristen looked at her made her hold her breath at times. She'd watched Cain and Remi fall in love, but it'd proved elusive when it came to her, until it was right there gazing at her with an openness that swamped her. Kristen was young, but she was in love with her, and it was something she couldn't hide.

"What?" The softness of Kristen's voice made her blink. "You are the sweetest thing, but you need to learn to relax."

"I was thinking about how much I love you." She took Kristen's bag and held her hand for the walk to the car. "And I'm plenty relaxed, thank you." Kristen shook her head at that when she opened the door for her. "I'll prove it to you."

They drove to the lake and the spot Cain had told her about. Her conversation with Linda was a reminder of how special Kristen was, and she needed to be better about letting Kristen know that. Life was too short to hide her feelings, due to their age difference or anything else her pea brain came up with. That's how Kristen liked to explain it at times. She parked and opened Kristen's door again, getting her to laugh when a waiter from Blanchard's was waiting by one of their catering vans and handed her a picnic basket.

"You're an idiot, but you're the sweetest one I know, and you're mine." Kristen waited for her to sit on the blanket before taking the spot in front so she could lean against her. "Tell me what's wrong."

"There's not a thing wrong—I was simply reminded of something today." The trees gave sufficient shade, and the breeze coming off the lake was nice enough to make her drowsy.

Kristen pulled on her fingers before placing them under the loose blouse she wore. "Are you going to share, or do I stop that hand from going any higher now *and* when we get home."

"Linda came by the office this morning, and she's so skittish." That was the best word she could think of.

"Did that remind you of me or my sister?" Kristen sounded not her usual sarcastic self.

"She reminded me of *me*." She scratched along Kristen's waist, and she squirmed when she hit a ticklish spot. "I'm used to having to hold back because of what I do. Not overshare anything about myself,

I mean. The one time I decided to step out of the firm rules I set for myself, I really screwed up, and my father died thinking I was a fucking idiot."

"Don't talk about yourself like that, I hate it. Someone played you, sweetheart. You're not the one to blame, so I doubt your dad stopped loving you."

"That's what Cain keeps telling me, but my real fear is holding me back from you." She waited for Kristen to turn around before going on. "I love you," she said with her hand on Kristen's cheek. "You're who I want to build a life with, and I don't want to hide any part of myself from you."

"Are you…are you proposing?" Kristen's expression was hard to decipher.

"No," she said, and Kristen's disappointment was clear. That prompted her to grab her jacket. The ring box was in her pocket and had been since they'd come home from Wisconsin. "*Now* I'm proposing. Kristen, I love you, I want a life with you and a future we both make for each other. Will you marry me?"

Kristen watched her open the box and exhaled when she glanced down. The ring had been something she'd gone back and forth on, wanting to get it right. Her final choice had been a simple square diamond she thought Kristen would wear since she wasn't a jewelry kind of person. Muriel held the ring and waited what seemed like a decade.

"Yes," Kristen said incredulously. "On one condition," she added, snatching her hand back.

Of course, Kristen would want to negotiate. "Name it." She slid the ring all the way on when Kristen moved her hand back, and kissed her knuckles.

"You mention our age difference again, and I want a divorce." Kristen kissed her, then went back to staring at the ring. "Thank you for asking, and I love this." Kristen held her hand up, and it made her understand what Cain and Remi had been saying.

"You're hard to shop for, so I'm glad." Her phone rang as Kristen pressed their lips together.

"Go ahead, but the only place you're going is home since we'll get arrested getting naked out here." Kristen reached for Muriel's phone, and Muriel hesitated when she saw a couple of guys she didn't recognize walking slowly toward them. "It's okay," Kristen said. "They're some of Remi's guys."

"Casey," she said when the phone rang again.

"Muriel?" She recognized Emma's voice.

"What's wrong?" The last time Emma had called her sounding like this, Cain was in the hospital.

"There's been an incident at the house. Did you meet with Linda today?"

"We talked this morning, and she wanted to have a sit-down with Cain and Finley." It couldn't be that someone had breached the house again. Linda had told her she was going straight back, so she hoped she was okay, and if she wasn't, her brothers had to be frantic. "Is she okay?"

"She was leaving to pick up the boys and someone shot her. Don't worry, she's alive."

"Where is she? I'll go if you're taking care of the kids. Keep them home if you can. This might've been a drive-by or it could've been something else. Like someone finding her—and she'll give up if someone takes Tim and Joshua." She nodded when Kristen put her shoes back on and started gathering their things. "Where exactly did this happen?" The memory of a group of guys shooting up the house was still fresh in her mind, and she wanted no repeat of that.

"Come to the house first, and the boys are fine. Mook takes a few guys every day since Tim and Joshua are with Hayden. Cain sent people to the hospital with Linda to make sure she's okay while Cain checks on what happened."

There was no need to elaborate on what Cain was doing. Someone attacked someone under her protection, so she wanted answers. "We're on our way."

The two guys flanked them to the car and followed them out of the parking lot, and she couldn't take her eyes off them. There was something not right, and she couldn't pinpoint what it was. "I don't think—"

Muriel didn't get a chance to finish. She threw herself over Kristen when the spray of bullets hit the front of her SUV before taking out the windshield. It stopped as fast as it started, and she grunted as she sat up.

"Muriel!" Kristen screamed.

"Are you all right?" she asked and saw the terror on Kristen's face.

"Muriel…baby, stay with me." Muriel felt the wetness at her side and the pain was intense once she noticed it. "Open your eyes. Honey, open your eyes."

Kristen's command came more than once, but she was too tired to comply. The darkness was welcoming, and she gave in to it.

❖

Nicola wiped the sweat from her eyes but strained to finish the reps the physical therapist set out for her. She was walking with a cane, and every day it got a little easier to go farther, but her stamina was a joke. The fatigue from pushing herself as well as the headaches and the pain in her side were the only ill effects health-wise, and she was starting to think this was as good as she was going to get. The headaches made her want to put a gun in her mouth and pull the trigger, but the medication was starting to take the edge off. Another couple of weeks and she'd be ready to start getting back what she lost. There was no other choice, no matter how she felt.

"You are a tough bitch," Kira said as she dropped the weights on the bench.

"Why are you still here?" She wanted to stay seated, not anxious to show all her weaknesses at once. Her fucking aunt didn't give her that out when she walked out to the patio, expecting her to follow. One of the women Fredrick kept came out and poured them each a glass of the juice the PT woman insisted on. "I would've thought you'd be out proving the Volkov name's something to fear."

"I don't have to continuously prove something people already know about my family. Tell me why you hate your mother so much." Kira sat and turned her face to the sun. There were remnants of her good looks there, but her face held more of a cold hardness than she remembered. Her mother had been the same. "She was proud of you both, and when you gave her grandchildren, she was hopeful for the future."

"That letter you gave me should tell you why." The pride both Kira and her mother had for her grandfather, Ivan, was a joke that was in no way funny. "Ivan has had years to crush what my father built, and still he hides behind his whores. He's too old now to become something other than a pimp."

"Wake up to the real world, Nicola." Kira sounded like the need to be a happy family had bypassed everyone on the Volkov side of the family. "Your father and his top lieutenants are dead. He traded his place at the head of his family for the women we put to work, instead of keeping his family whole. In our world, that makes you a stupid fuck."

"My mother had to always be right," Nicola said, "and after years of ridicule and threats, my father went to someone else for what he needed. That's not something I blame him for since I can tell you it's the only way to stay sane." Marriage was a trap not meant for people like her and her father.

"I'll excuse it in you because of who you picked."

Nicola barked out a laugh when she sat with no grace or control. "You think Abigail was my choice?" She laughed again. "Abigail was someone easily manipulated and even easier to bed. My mother pushed me to marry so it'd be simpler to get what we wanted from her once the kids came. I was bored after a month, but Valerie got what she wanted until she didn't. Abigail and a lot of other things were anything but my choice."

"So you're okay with your children growing up not knowing who they really are?" Kira was staring at her with the same intensity her mother had perfected.

"I'll deal with my family."

"How do you plan to do that?" Kira had drained the emotion from her voice, so her question was more curious than anything else. "You rose from the dead—and your loving family tried to send you right back to the grave. If your father was as powerful as you say, that would've never happened."

"What do you want?" That's what she couldn't figure out. Kira and the others had been absent from their lives until now. "You haven't shown any interest in us, and Ivan even less."

"Your grandfather stayed away because Yury asked him to. None of us lived up to the image he was building, and he was quick to tell us all what scum he thought we were. He did that only after asking Papa for the money to start his business."

"He had to maintain an image, but if Ivan was as powerful as you say, it shouldn't have mattered what my father wanted. My mother was, after all, his daughter."

"Your mother didn't agree, but she wanted to keep the peace. She saw the family often but abided by what Yury wanted when it came to you and Fredrick." Kira rubbed her knee with the palm of her hand, but Nicola didn't think it was a nervous tic. "You should know that we've started our move into New Orleans, Vegas, and here."

"Just because my father's dead doesn't mean the agreements we put in place go away." Her headache was coming back, and she wanted Kira out. She had to get all the information she could first, though, since it was the only way to undo whatever her grandfather was planning and putting into place. "Moving into all those spots is a breach of what Ivan promised."

"There's plenty for all of us, but think about what a partnership could get us."

That was the simplest answer to surviving, but Nicola'd never stoop to that no matter how desperate their situation was. Her father had known a partnership with Ivan would be the equivalent of scraping the bottom of a dumpster. "We appreciate the offer, but we're not going to partner in anything."

"You're turning down a meeting with Papa?"

"Once I'm on my feet, I'll be happy to sit with him and talk about old times, but no business." She had to circle back to one thing. "What moves did you make in New Orleans?" That's where her children were, so it was the only place she cared about. Anywhere else, she'd clean the streets of Volkov people in a way they'd never be found.

"He ordered a hit against Casey. To get anything done in that town goes through her, so Papa wanted to distract her." Kira shrugged and smiled as if daring her to say anything.

This was the first time since the shooting that she resented being this weak. It pissed her off daily, but having Kira there talking to her like an asshole made her sorry she couldn't put her hands on her. Beating Kira until she was dead would be a perfect lesson to both sides of her family. Making stupid moves was going to make what she wanted that much harder to accomplish. The element of surprise was the only way she'd win against Casey's forces.

"What kind of hit?"

"Don't worry about that now, and I'll let you know when Papa gets here. He's looking forward to seeing you. You and Fredrick concentrate on getting better." Kira walked out as if she'd agreed to everything she wanted.

Svetlana joined her a few minutes later. "She's gone."

It was times like this that she missed Nina. Her head of security aggravated the hell out of her, but she was meticulous in how she dealt with situations like they were facing. She was left with Svetlana, and she'd hopefully grow into the role. All she could hope for now was Svetlana following orders.

"Where's she staying?"

"She's at the Eden Roc on Miami Beach. My contact said she has a block of rooms until next week. The only people there now are a few flunkies, so no one from your family."

She was impressed. What Svetlana reported took more steps than what she'd ordered, and she'd gotten it right. "Can you move on her without it coming back on us?"

"She runs every morning at six, so we could do a drive-by if you want." Svetlana never relaxed around her and acted as if she needed to be ready to run out if Nicola ordered it.

"Keep someone on her and tell me immediately if anyone joins her."

"Sure, do you need anything else?"

She had to think like she was the head of her family again. It was time to stop with the self-pity. "Do you trust the people watching Kira?"

"They're the first people we got from Oleg and Larissa. These guys have been at the club over a year and have taken care of every problem perfectly. They're ready to prove themselves."

"We'll see, but I'll take you at your word." She smiled when Svetlana swallowed with force. "This is what I need you to do."

CHAPTER EIGHT

Cain sat in the waiting room of the emergency room, holding Kristen's hand. They didn't know each other that well, but Kristen was tethering her to reality. She and Emma had been on their way to meet Remi and Dallas when Remi called. The news that followed narrowed her vision to Emma's face and Remi's voice. Déjà vu was all she could think about as the memory of all those calls she gotten that'd taken her family one at a time. Muriel, Finley, and the other cousins were all she had left of the family she'd grown up with.

She'd stared at Emma, and it was the slap she needed to concentrate. She needed to find who attacked Muriel before they touched anyone else in the family. It hadn't been easy, but she talked Emma into going home and staying with the kids. She wanted to sit with Kristen and get as much of the story as Kristen was willing to share.

"Any word?" Emma asked when Cain answered the phone.

"She's in surgery, and the last update was positive." Kristen squeezed her hand when she said that. "I'll call you as soon as I know anything."

"She'll be okay, right?" Kristen wiped her face and seemed agitated because of the bloody shirt she was wearing. It was a chilling sight that defined mortality better than anything else.

"Muriel's a great attorney because she's a fighter. Nothing in life is a sure thing except for that. She'll fight for everything and everyone she loves." She noticed the ring on Kristen's finger and smiled. "She has plenty to fight for, so she'll come back to you even if she has to negotiate with God. Giving up isn't in her makeup. Can you tell me what happened?"

Kristen told her about the call Muriel had gotten from Emma about Linda and that they were leaving the park when someone shot up the car. Muriel had met with Linda that morning, so she'd been worried about her. The two guards she'd thought were Remi's had disappeared.

The call about Linda had come from Emma, so it wasn't a story to lure Muriel out. What Cain couldn't figure out was why anyone would've targeted Muriel and Kristen, or why they'd waited until they were in the car. If their intent was a hit, out in the open would've finished the job. She started making a list in her head and lost her train of thought when Remi and Dallas arrived.

"Any news?" Dallas asked moving quickly to her sister.

"She's in surgery," Kristen said and started crying. "She asked me to marry her, and then this. It's so unfair." Kristen leaned against Dallas, so Cain waited out of respect.

"Do you have any idea?" Remi asked.

"I don't know, but I have Lou's guys pouring money on the street. What happened to your people? Kristen said you sent some guys, but they weren't there anymore when the ambulance showed up."

"What guys?" Remi glanced at Kristen but appeared confused. "I didn't send anyone. The guy that follows Kristen to school took off when Kristen said she was leaving with Muriel. He thought they'd be fine."

"Kristen," Cain said placing her hand on her knee to get her attention, "are you sure you recognized the two guards?"

"They looked like the guys you send to campus with me. Muriel had just proposed, so I didn't pay that close attention." Kristen seemed mortified all of a sudden. "Was this my fault? Oh my God, I could've gotten us killed by dismissing Oliver."

"This is in no way your fault," she said, holding Kristen when she started crying again. "An attack on you or Muriel makes no sense, so it shouldn't have mattered if you had security or not."

"The police are questioning witnesses, according to my contacts, but those are slim. Muriel picked a secluded spot," Remi said.

She nodded, knowing they'd never find these guys if they concentrated on the lakefront. "Kristen, did Muriel pack a lunch for you two?"

Remi's expression changed as if picking up on where she was headed.

"She had a picnic basket delivered from Blanchard's," Kristen said. "We were laughing about it as we walked to the trees she picked."

"Muriel Casey's family?" A man in scrubs stood at the door in the corner.

They all stood, and Cain put Kristen at the front. The surgeon explained the bullet had nicked Muriel's liver, and she had taken one to the shoulder, but she'd make a full recovery. He wanted Muriel to take it easy for a few weeks after her stay in hospital. Kristen followed him to the holding area so she could sit with Muriel as they waited for a hospital room.

"I'll see if Blanchard's will share their surveillance footage," Remi said.

"Let Fin take care of that, and I'll check with Tulane. If I'm right, they targeted Muriel for some reason, and we'll have to tighten security on everyone. Let your father and Mano know, and have them call Vincent." She stopped when Shelby ran in, almost frantic. "If whoever this is has started at the edges, they'll eventually move to the center, so none of us should let our guard down."

"Is she all right?" Shelby's tears and obvious emotion moved Cain to get her out before Kristen came back. "Please, Cain, tell me."

"Come on." She took Shelby's hand, and Dallas appeared grateful. "Let's get everyone some coffee." Once they were in the hall, Cain gave Shelby the only kindness she could think of and held her as she cried. "It'll take some time, but she'll be okay." The explanation of Muriel's injuries made Shelby's tears build into sobs, and she offered the space for Shelby's emotions to play out. Whatever relationship Muriel had shared with Shelby, it'd been a mixture of the job and affection. "She's also engaged, so what I just shared is between friends."

"I know you hated what I did, but I care about her. You're never going to believe me about that." Shelby wiped her face and gazed at her with an expression of determination. "I love her."

She shook her head. "I do believe you, and more importantly *she* believed you. She loved you too. What I hated was what you did made her question her father's love for her. He's in the family crypt, so there's no making up for it, no matter how much you care." She exhaled and took a big breath. "You took a call about work, about what you'd found at Muriel's house, at his funeral. I'm no angel, but that was low. She was distracted because of her father, and you took full advantage of that."

"It would've never worked—you were right about that."

"I didn't want to be, and I speak from experience when I tell you it's hard to let go. You still love her or you wouldn't be here, and she feels the same. The difference is she's moved on, and she's happy."

Shelby smiled when Cain put her hand on her shoulder and squeezed. "You should try it."

"I'm not here to mess anything up, Cain." Shelby took a step back and accepted a tissue to blow her nose. "The call came through, and I had to know."

"The prognosis is good, but if you want, I'll keep you updated." Shelby nodded at her offer, and she walked her to the front of the hospital. "I'm sure your pals are working the emergency room, so head out through the clinic."

"Who did this, Cain?" Shelby sounded almost like when she'd asked for help finding the people who'd killed her parents.

She heard Emma's voice in her head telling her not to trust Shelby or any of her friends. "I really don't know. Muriel's an attorney and that's it. She's a Casey and part of my family, but she swore an oath to uphold the law. That's what she's done."

"Is that your way of telling me I screwed up?" Shelby finally smiled.

"Louisiana, at least south Louisiana, isn't a place for weak foundations. Houses collapse in this sandy, swampy soil along with the streets unless we maintain them. The same can be said of relationships. Muriel has found her place, and so will you."

Shelby gave her a sad smile and took her hand. "You're becoming a good philosopher, and thank you for keeping me in the loop."

Cain started walking back toward the waiting room and stopped at the chapel. A prayer never hurt anyone, her mum always said, so she sat in the last pew and closed her eyes. She prayed for her family to watch over Muriel and took a moment to call Emma.

"She's out of surgery and will be fine. The ring she put on Kristen's finger should be incentive enough to wake her up." The memory of the morning popped into her head, and it felt like months ago.

"The boys are back from practice, and Merrick's locked the house up, so I'm coming to join you. No arguments."

"I'll send Lou out to get you."

There was something about the way Muriel had been attacked. There was no finesse or planning, but they meant business. The blitzkrieg was thuggish and didn't fit anyone she figured was upset with her. Enemies who wanted to exact revenge would be more surgical, or at least she would be. Maybe she was giving them too much credit.

Killing, to her, was always the last resort no matter the situation, and when she gave those orders, it was very seldom so public. Flashy was not the way to go when you had such dedicated watchers. This reminded her in a way of Juan Luis's mother, Gracelia. She killed the people in her orbit who were innocent because those were the only people she could get to. It proved her point that Gracelia was a thug, and that's what she was facing again.

The walk back to the waiting room gave her more time to think, but her gut said it was tied to Nicola and what was left of her crew. The Antakov family seemed to treat every problem with a sledgehammer approach. Nicola had needed to eliminate the one girl who'd successfully gotten in touch with Finley when she was an agent, so she killed an entire busload of women. She'd done that next to The Plaza in New York, one of the most iconic places in the city. It'd been not only over the top, but stupid. Acting like a murderer was never without consequence.

"Did you think of anything?" Remi was alone when she got back, saying Dallas had joined Kristen sitting with Muriel. "I had Simon check with everyone to make sure, and whoever was out there wasn't with us."

"This doesn't make sense," she said, not really focused. "Unless whoever planned this is an idiot—then I guess it was a genius plan."

"I don't follow." Remi appeared confused but did smile.

"You remember Juan and his mother, right?" Remi nodded and they brought their heads together. "She killed people on our periphery. Our innocents who worked for us but made no decisions. Her reasoning was to show us she could get to anyone."

"But she couldn't. No one really close to us was killed."

She nodded and hated to relegate Muriel to that category. Her cousin was important to her, and she loved her. Losing her would hurt as much as Dallas would be devastated losing her sister. Family was off-limits, but she had sanctioned the killing of Nicola's parents. Payback would be more than Muriel and Kristen before Nicola was satisfied. It didn't matter that Nicola's parents had targeted the mother of Nicola's children. Abigail was expendable because she'd completed her part in Nicola's world. But Nicola's parents were not, so there would be a price to pay for that—if Cain didn't get to Nicola first.

"It was an amateur move, I agree, but sometimes the rage beats out the smart play. I hear you had to repeat that lesson to my son, so thank you. Nicola is not only enraged, she's in survival mode. It'll take some time to prove it, but this might be a way of finding her."

"If it is her, we're in for whatever needs to be done. It wasn't just Muriel she shot at, so I don't really care who it is, we'll take care of this."

She stood when Emma entered followed by Merrick, and it reminded her of Linda. Muriel had been attacked after Linda had been hit outside the house. She called Lou over, but before she could ask him to do what she needed, Dallas came out and told them Muriel was awake and they could all go back.

The room was quiet, and Kristen was sitting on the edge of the bed, while Dallas took the only chair. Muriel was indeed awake, but her eyes were glassy from whatever drugs they had her on. Cain waved Kristen to stay in place, and she moved to the other side with Emma.

"Take care of Kristen," Muriel said, "and promise me you're going to kick someone's ass. This hurts like a bitch."

"Don't worry about that—it's a given." She placed her free hand on Muriel's chest, happy that her heart was still beating and she hadn't lost someone so important to her. "Do you promise to be good? You're going to look like crap in the wedding photos if you don't. Congratulations to both of you."

Emma leaned over the rail and kissed Muriel's cheek. "We'll be right outside if you need anything, but you need to get some rest. We love you."

"Dallas, would you join us?" Cain asked. It was time to do things differently to get some answers.

❖

Remi sat with Simon and thought about what Muriel had done. The police dispatched to the scene had filled in the holes in Kristen's story, and it made her want to hit something. This had been way too close, and it would've changed Dallas in ways she couldn't imagine. Muriel had gotten them to the car, though, and had shielded Kristen with her body. That act had made her sure they'd never have to worry about Kristen's choice.

"Honey," Dallas said when they were back in the waiting room.

"Lou swept a spot for us, so how about that talk we were going to have at lunch?" Cain would've helped Dallas, no question, but she had extra motivation to put all her wife's nightmares to rest now. Remi could see it from the intensity on Cain's face.

They stepped into Linda's room while Lou and Simon stayed

outside. Lou assured them the room was clean and the jammers were in place. All she could hope for was for Dallas to talk about what was causing her so much pain. They needed to eliminate it before Dallas's emotions made her too hard to reach.

"Linda," Cain said getting her to turn her head from the window, "I'm sorry it took so long, but I wanted to make sure the boys were okay, and then Muriel got shot."

"What?" Linda seemed shocked. "I'm sorry, Cain. This is my fault." Linda ran her hand over her leg with what appeared to be a soft touch. Whoever had shot her had hit her thigh, but it hadn't broken the bone from what the doctors had told Simon.

"I'm sorry. You didn't want protection, and I gave in. Now I'm going to insist." Cain placed her hand on Linda's shoulder and squeezed.

Linda smiled, and it made her appear sadder. "Promise me that you'll raise my brothers if they're a better shot next time."

"That's your job, and mine is to watch over all of you." Cain sat in one of the chairs Lou had found, and Emma sat next to her. She and Dallas took the small sofa. "I think we all can agree that what we've been doing isn't working. Nicola was in New York, was shot, and now has crawled in a hole so deep, we'll only find her when she makes another move."

"Do you think Nicola did all this?" Linda asked.

"We'll work backward on that before we can answer it with certainty," Remi said, glad she didn't have to explain in more detail. Linda grew up understanding what had to be done and that it wasn't often them pulling the trigger. Finding the shooters or the lowest man on the totem pole would lead them up the chain. "We will, but we need to change our approach to finding her."

"How?" Linda asked.

Cain gazed in Dallas's direction. "Do you feel okay sharing what you started to tell me?"

Remi put her arm around Dallas's shoulders and kissed her cheek. She whispered in her ear, wanting her to feel safe. "You know Cain and Emma—they love you. Whatever you need to say, it's okay. No one is going to hurt you."

Dallas nodded and turned her attention to Linda. "We don't know each other well, and I started to worry when you began to work for Cain and Remi." Dallas didn't seem to be able to control her tears but she didn't stop to wipe them. "I wasn't always Dallas Montgomery."

"You probably don't trust me," Linda said, looking at Dallas first and then the rest of them. "All of you know my story. My job was to keep my family secrets—until I didn't. I'm smart enough to know in any other situation, the fact that I allowed the feds in would be the one thing that'd seal my fate with Nicola and make you wary."

"I think I speak for all of us when I say I'm glad you didn't. Keep those secrets, I mean," Remi said. She agreed with Cain that it had to be done. If Linda hurt Dallas, though, there'd be hell to pay. "I love Dallas, so please don't betray that." The best option was to be nice for now.

"That night you came for me and my brothers…you saved our lives. Nicola sent those people to kill all of us because I exposed the Antakov family for who they are. We deserved death because of what I did, and I'd bet my life my mother agrees with them." Linda's hand touched her bandage again, and Remi got the impression of a haunted soul. "You're the only people I've spent time with who agree with me that exploitation of women isn't something to build a life on."

Dallas started speaking softly and told Linda the story of her life. Her words and demeanor were detached as if she was reading a script, and it sounded like the only way she could get through it. "Like you, I did plenty of disgusting things for the sake of my sister." Dallas talked about the adult films she'd made and where. "The guys in charge of those productions were Russian. I just don't know who."

Cain leaned forward when Dallas stopped abruptly. "Did Yury have any of those in his ledgers?" she asked Linda.

"The adult entertainment industry," Linda said, being kind. It was something Remi appreciated. "It's a part of the business that's lucrative. The family owns a slice, a big slice—Yury insisted, since the industry makes over twelve billion a year. That's billion with a *B*."

"Is the studio in one location, or did he spread the productions around?" Cain was talking fast, but not fast enough in Remi's opinion.

"There's a studio in New York, and the Miami location opened two years ago." Linda was quick to answer, but Remi could tell she was as confused as Emma and Dallas as to what Cain was talking about.

"Where are the master copies kept?"

Remi understood where Cain was headed by her question. Destroying the masters wouldn't work unless they got all the copies—all of them. The digital age they lived in would make that impossible. She was set to fail Dallas again. If the master copies were the key, they had to be in New York close to Yury. Linda hadn't lied about the numbers. Getting his girls to perform kept the money rolling in.

"They were in New York until the Miami place opened. I didn't ask questions, but I thought it was strange." Linda glanced at Dallas before giving Cain her full attention. "The masters aren't important, though, or as important, any longer. All the information is on servers maintained by a crew in Miami. Boris told me the guys working to produce that stuff work for chump change since Yury always gave them access to the girls."

That made Dallas drop her head and blush. Cain wasn't going to ask anything else—she'd give Dallas her secrets that shouldn't be talked about again unless Dallas needed to. "Querida," Remi said, placing her fingers under her chin, and gently encouraged Dallas to look at her. "None of this will ever touch us. I'm here, and I'm yours."

"Remember what I said," Cain said to Dallas. "Your past deserves to have a bullet put through it and be buried permanently."

"You're never going to destroy them all." Even Dallas understood that. Once it was on the web, it'd exist forever.

"Let's let Linda and Fin take a look at what we're facing, and I might prove you wrong." Cain tapped Dallas's knee with her fingers. "My mum always told all of us to have faith, and with that came the hope to change what needed changing. Have faith in me and Remi to set you free of what haunts you, because you're family. There is nothing else more important to fight for."

"Thank you." Dallas faced Remi and gave her a brief kiss. "I know you love me, and you'll be faithful no matter what. I also know you all will fight for me." Dallas closed her eyes and flattened her hand over Remi's chest. "My head believes all those things. My heart, though, has kept score of everything that's happened to me, and the one lesson it's taught me is disappointment."

"Hopefully Remi has told you some of the stories about your new house. I've known your wife for most of my life, and we have plenty in common. The most important thing is our belief in marriage and the women we love. Once we're committed, only one thing will sever that bond."

"That is if we leave—something I foolishly did. I ran and hid a child from her," Emma said. "Those were the most miserable years of my life, and I thought I'd never get back to where I am now. She forgave all of it because I'm her wife. To Cain that means everything, and Remi is cut from that same tightly woven cloth. Listen to her, and believe she'll be the most steadfast person in your life."

"If I'm right, then not only do you get what you want, so will the rest of us." Cain took Emma's hand and pressed it to her lips. "Linda, when you get discharged, you're coming to stay in the house with us. No one can guarantee complete safety, but I'll do my best."

"They said I can go today, so let Fin know I'll be ready to begin."

"I'll have some guys come and escort you home to make sure you're safe. I also want to introduce you to someone," Cain said, tapping her finger on her chin.

"Who?" she asked Cain.

"Remember Bryce, my first IT guy?" Cain's fury over Gracelia killing the young man was hard to forget. Bryce had met Cain right out of college and offered to work for free if she helped him with his brother who was in jail at the time. He was responsible for the security measures they all used, so she missed him as well.

"Shame what happened to that kid," she said, still not sure why Cain had brought him up.

"His brother Charlie got out and worked with him until he was killed. The kid's got skills even if he's on his own now." Cain took Emma's hand and intertwined their fingers. "He needed some space after what happened to Bryce, but he's still on my payroll."

"What kind of skills?" Emma asked.

"Same as Bryce, but Charlie always had more edge to him, so he expanded on what his little brother did for us. Let me work it out in my head, and I can explain it better."

"Can we finish our meeting? Maybe drinks before dinner?" Remi asked.

"Come to the house and I'll block off the sunroom for us. You two can stay and eat with us, and we'll come back here to check on Muriel and Kristen. I'm sure Kristen will want to stay, but we'll keep a heavy guard on their room."

"Thanks, Cain," Dallas said. "And thank you, Linda. I'm sorry I mistrusted you."

"We were both in a bad place, and now we're not. You can trust I'll do what I can to erase both our pasts." Linda smiled at Dallas and accepted Cain's help to sit on the side of the bed when the nurse came back in with her discharge papers.

"Go and check on Muriel and Kristen," Emma said. "We'll bring Linda home. Meet you guys there."

"Thank you, my friends." Remi loved her family and her wife, but Cain was someone she was glad to have in her corner. When she formally took over for her father, this would be the partnership that'd keep her on top. The bonus would be that Emma would be there for Dallas no matter what came her way.

Dylan Gardner stood in front of Annabel's desk and tried to keep her temper from erupting. The mall incident with Cain had been investigated, and the findings had been finalized, so Hicks had asked her to report to her office. It was her bad luck to engage the asshole in the one place in the city that had wall-to-wall cameras and plenty of concerned citizens with phones at the ready.

"The internal investigation is done, and I'd like you to speak up for yourself and tell me what the hell you were thinking. Casey didn't take a step toward you, so your self-defense argument won't hold." The file Hicks was holding seemed to be thicker than the one they had on Casey. "Well?"

"I thought I was in danger, and I acted. You and the team you stuck me with seem to be more interested in giving Casey a pass than backing me up. Go ahead and toss me out so I can contact my attorney."

"A three-month suspension is not tossing you out. Once you get back, there'll be some steps you'll have to take before you're back on the street. Call whoever you like, but this information will back us up. You might need to make that call anyway if Muriel Casey decides to press charges or decides to take legal action against you."

"We'll see." She turned and put her hand on the knob. "Anything else?"

"Use your time wisely, and maybe take a breather. You need to figure out why you're so angry."

She left and waited in the stairwell. After checking and rechecking, it was one of the only places in the building that wasn't covered by CCTV cameras. This was where she'd met her contact when she'd taken the offer to come to New Orleans, and then they'd moved to her apartment once she had one so no one would ever see them together.

"Did you have no influence over this shit?" she asked Angus Covington III, which had to be the stupidest name in the history of names. "I'm out for three months. That's not going to look too good in my file if I decide to go elsewhere."

"Look"—Angus swept the thick lock of hair at the front of his head back and sighed—"I tried, but the boss said it's better you take the suspension and lie low. The time off gives you the chance to work on what's important, and that's not in the back of the van."

"So I take the hit? What kind of bullshit is that?" She'd followed orders up to now, and this was the only thing it'd gotten her.

"That's all he told me, but he thinks this is the opening we need to finally nail that bitch," Angus said, and his phone sounded loud in the enclosed space. "Covington," he answered and listened for a bit. "Give me five minutes—I'm in the bathroom, man." He ended the call and squeezed the phone in his hand. "I have to go, we're rolling out, but I'll be at your place tonight. Once we finish, your record will be spotless. He gave me his word."

She sped out of the parking lot. Her actions had cost her three months, but seeing Casey bleeding on the floor made every single day worth it. The real laugh would come when Hicks, Shelby, and the rest of them would be exposed. None of them were smart enough to figure out they were the ones being investigated.

The drive uptown took fifteen minutes, and she slowed when she passed the Casey house. They'd been watching for months and had nothing to show for it. That was getting ready to change because of all the traps they'd put in place. There was parking off the street, and she used the back door to check into her real job. Special Agents Barry Knight and Christina Brewer had leased this place a year before and had worked from here, since it had a better vantage point for surveillance. The Casey family knew them as Drew and Taylor Kennison and Lucy, their only child.

"What's going on?" The couple were on their phones and sounded agitated.

"Muriel Casey was shot today," a man said from behind her. "And we have nothing."

Dylan turned, not appreciating anyone sneaking up on her. "Who are you?"

"Special Agent in Charge Ronald Chapman." He held his hand out and waited for her to take it. "You must be Dylan. You've done some good work for us. I'm glad you accepted my offer to work on this."

"Agent Chapman." She noticed how unusually soft his hands were, wanting to wipe hers on her pants when he let go. "Good to meet you. Barry and Christina wouldn't share your name, and my transfer came from my old boss."

"I want to keep a low profile." He smiled, and it made her uncomfortable. "I'm responsible for getting you here. You're an excellent addition to our team, but we're still no closer to bringing Casey in on something that'll stick."

"When do I get to meet the rest of the team?"

He laughed, and it somehow ratcheted it up her anxiety. "You already have. This has to be a small operation for it to work. I had you and Covington working from the inside, but he'll hold everything together until you're reinstated. When you talk to him, I'd appreciate you not mentioning you met me."

Barry finished his call and joined them. "All our contacts at the hospital can get is that Muriel Casey's out of surgery and listed in stable but critical condition. The NOPD is nowhere as far as suspects are concerned."

"Of course not, these locals usually can't find their mothers. Do any of you have a clue as to what Casey's been working on?" Ronald seemed agitated, and in a way his displeasure made him more effeminate. That wasn't something she'd run across much in her time with the bureau, especially when you swam up the food chain. The FBI wasn't the most evolved organization, and change would be slow if it came at all when it came to anything but alpha males with egos that could choke a herd of cows. "You've been at this for months, and you've gotten nowhere."

"Cain Casey isn't your average person involved in organized crime, sir." That Barry and Christina had become mute was a red flag, but there was no way she was kowtowing to someone else. Having Hicks on her ass was bad enough. "You were here, from what the team told me, so you have to know what it's like."

The way Ronald's face twisted into something ugly was hard to miss. Cain Casey had stymied him from what Joe had told her, and he ran from a field in Wisconsin so fast he'd left skid marks. Someone that terrified of the suspect he was investigating was telling. Ronald had something to hide, and Casey had guessed what it was. If she was right, this endgame wasn't going to be cut-and-dried. Casey would muddy the waters so much they'd never make headway.

"Casey is a common bootlegger and murderer. Don't let all the nice clothes, big house, and family fool you about that truth. No one has come close to an indictment because they've been afraid to take risks. I am not." Ronald turned with military precision and left. The slamming of the back door left her staring at Barry and Christina with a lot of questions.

"Let's sit." These guys were either going to answer questions, or she was going to find a hobby for her three-month suspension. The anger management and sensitivity courses she'd have to complete afterward were going to be an added special bonus.

"You need to cool it," Barry said. "Agent Chapman doesn't tolerate dissension well."

"Explain to me what you've done so far," Dylan said. "I don't have a total grasp on how you plan to get to Casey in a way that will hold up in court. You mentioned traps, but if I'm one, that didn't work out well." Her father had been a state patrolman, staying on the highway until he'd been retired early when a gangbanger shot him in the leg during a traffic stop. He'd told her any law-enforcement individual's best weapon in the line of duty was their gut. "Start talking or I go to Hicks, even if it means my job."

Right now, her gut was screaming for her to get out of there. She needed to not only leave but to erase her name from anything having to do with whatever the hell this was. Barry started spilling the story, starting with Detective Newsome of the NOPD who'd recruited Emma's mother, Carol Verde, to work with them. Newsome was now dead, and Carol had been arrested, making that whole scenario beyond fucked up.

"Newsome and Verde did more damage than good, which is why they're no longer part of the team."

"How did Newsome die?"

Christina told that story, then she and Barry exchanged a weird look, and the back of Dylan's neck got cold. Barry's explanation didn't warm it up. He told her it was an open investigation, and they'd only heard about it after coming back from returning Lucy. There was no more elaboration on that, but disappearing a kid deserved some explanation. It wasn't like returning a pair of pants that didn't fit when you got them home.

"Where is Lucy now?" She slid her hands into her pockets to hide her unease, but she could feel the sweat on her upper lip.

"Back in foster care. That'd been the arrangement all along," Christina said.

She nodded and acted as if this was acceptable procedure, when it was anything but. This was the kind of operation that got you jail time, which would be ironic since that's what she was after when it came to Casey. She had to try to remember if she'd put anything in writing. Casey had winked at her, and it had set her off. When she'd offered to follow her instead of Emma, that's what she'd been after, and Cain had turned on her without much effort.

"Let me know what our next steps should be." She gripped her keys, finding the pain in her palm comforting somehow. "I threatened Hicks with legal action for my suspension, and I want to follow through."

"Sure," Barry said. "Just remember to keep quiet about this. The only way this works is if we have the element of surprise. Don't disappoint us." He held her by the arm, and she stared at his hand until he let go.

Elton Newsome had learned that lesson well, she thought. She smiled and looked him in the eye. "I have skin in this game too, Barry, so I understand. We all want the same things, so worry about yourself."

"We'll be watching." Christina's inflection was the same as always, and Dylan just gazed at her not knowing what the correct response should be.

She took it as a threat because there was no other way to take it. She'd deal with that the same as the mound of crap she was facing, and that was head-on. The only thing on her mind was how to extract herself from the situation without imploding her career. Ronald didn't seem the forgiving type, and the rules he'd broken were hard to think about.

"Gardner," she answered the phone, and she drove by the Casey house again.

"What punishment does someone deserve when they use a child who has been removed from an abusive household and placed in foster care, Agent Gardner?" There was a pause, and she could hear her blood rushing in her ear. "What happens when the world finds out you threw her in a pit because you're done with her? She's five."

The questions made her grip the steering wheel and pull over. She couldn't concentrate on the road she was so freaked out, and whoever this was didn't disguise their voice. She just couldn't place it. That could be a problem.

"I asked you a question, Agent."

"They deserve whatever the law will throw at them. Who is this?" The question was the stupidest fucking thing she could say, but her nervousness overrode her brain.

"I'm what's left of your conscience, and I'm fading fast. Think about today when you're on the other side of what you do. The spotlight can burn you if you let it."

"I haven't used anyone, so your threats don't mean shit." The cloak-and-dagger was getting tedious, so it was time to turn it around. "All I've done is my job."

"I'm glad you're so confident, Agent. Just remember one thing. We'll be watching."

"Wait," she yelled, but the line was dead. The same words Christina had used chilled her more than anything Ronald could throw at her.

CHAPTER NINE

It was still dark outside when Finley opened her eyes. It'd been two weeks of working with Linda, and she'd been a good partner, getting through all the information she'd been slogging through. Whatever process the Antakovs had in place when Linda kept their ledgers was now different. The move was smart, and what they'd discovered was Nicola was as good as Cain when it came to hiding what she didn't want found.

"Is there some reason you're thinking this hard so early in the morning?" Abigail sounded groggy. "It's not even five. I'm having flashbacks to my residency days."

"Sorry." She kissed Abigail's forehead and took a deep breath. "Go back to sleep."

"No such luck, sunshine." Abigail rose on her elbow, and Fin could feel the stare she was getting, even in the dark. "Spill it."

"I need to find that one needle that'll get us somewhere, but sometimes I think it's impossible. You're all in danger until I do, though." She put her arms around Abigail when she lay back down. "Muriel and what happened to Linda only ramped up the stress."

"Listen to me, okay." Abigail flattened her hand over her abdomen and kissed the side of her neck. "The danger we're facing isn't your fault. I'm sure of one thing and that's you. You're going to keep us safe."

"I can't even bring you home." They were still with Cain and Emma.

"Trust me, the day we move, our kids will have a fit. They're in love with the Casey kids, and leaving them behind is going to be painful." Abigail's touch went from soothing to a hard pinch. "Tell me what's really bothering you."

"Are you channeling my mother?" The way her fiancée and her mother had bonded surprised her, but her mom had finally gotten grandchildren, so it wasn't a total shock. Three at once had sent her into overdrive when it came to spoiling.

"I have her on speed dial, so answer me."

"It's embarrassing," she said, trying her best to keep her voice even. That got her another pinch. "I'm good at my job, but she's always ahead of me. How am I supposed to keep you all safe?"

"You're an adorable idiot." Abigail moved on top of her and kissed her. "My big mistake doesn't play by the rules, and never has. She's not a step ahead of you, it's just that you two think differently, and I'm thankful for that. That she was such a sick bitch was something I didn't know in the years we were married, so give yourself a break. You're my choice, and this time I got it right."

Abigail rarely said Nicola's name out loud, so Fin followed her lead. "I'd bet our house she's in Miami, and the problem with that is, it's Miami. It's a lot of area to cover."

"The people Cain sent haven't gotten anywhere?"

Her cousin had sent two of her people to the city, and Sabana called weekly, but there'd been nothing. "It doesn't make any sense, but no. A sex club, even there, you'd think would be on someone's radar. So far, they've found nothing."

"Maybe she's asking in the wrong places, or the wrong way." The softness of Abigail's voice had a way of wrapping around her brain like a warm bath that loosened every muscle in her frame.

"What do you mean?" The suggestion didn't register right away since she was getting sleepy again.

"How long did the Hell Fire Club take to hit Cain's radar? The truth of the club, I mean." Abigail rested her head against her chest and didn't sound agitated at all. They'd never had a long conversation about what Abigail thought of what Nicola and her family did. From snippets here and there, she knew she was disgusted, but at times she wondered what was really in Abigail's head.

"I'm not sure. When I arrived with you guys and met with her, Cain knew about it." She rubbed her hands in small circles on Abigail's back and tried to figure out what she was trying to say.

"Did she know *exactly* what was going on?"

She stopped her hand and stared down at the top of Abigail's head. "She did, but she didn't share how she knew."

"Maybe try what Cain did here, in Miami. How did she figure out what Nicola's family's business was?"

Sometimes it was the simplest move that broke a stalemate. "She didn't tell me, but I have a good guess. It had to be the Red Door."

"That's real?" Abigail sat up again and squinted in her direction. "If it is and you go there for a bachelor party, you can't imagine the trouble you're going to be in."

"That's the last place I'd go, and my cousin would be the first one to give me a black eye if I tried." She was always careful with Abigail because of her history with Nicola. "You have no problem when it comes to me being faithful to you."

"You're all I want, Fin." Abigail put her head back down on her chest, the comfort of their talk gone.

"Honey, you're it for me. I'm going to make a living working for Cain, and I'm going to make a life with you and the kids." They had another few weeks before the adoption went through, and the only way to stop it was for Nicola to rise from the dead. That wasn't a trick Fin thought Nicola could afford to pull off.

"You are the best thing to happen to me, so don't listen to me and my insecurities. I know you, and I know how you are with us. We wouldn't have survived without you."

"I listen to you all the time, and it's a little flattering that you're jealous. There's no need to be, since I belong to you." She rolled them over so she could kiss Abigail soft and long. "I promise, as soon as we get through this, all we'll have to worry about is getting our kids to school and finding time alone so I can ravish you."

"They love you, and it's maddening that she's not gone. Wishing death probably isn't the best thing to hope for since I took an oath to do no harm, but I want to stop looking over my shoulder."

"Hopefully what you mentioned will be the answer to finding her. Let me worry about what'll happen once I do." She glanced at Abigail when her hands landed on her butt. "The best thing is to stop talking about it right now."

"Good thinking," Abigail said and laughed.

How they'd met was unusual, but winning Abigail's love was the best thing to happen to her. The kids were a great happy extra, and she loved them all. Having the honor of touching this gorgeous, smart woman wasn't something she'd ever take for granted. She kissed Abigail, and she ran her hand down her side, smiling when Abigail spread her legs.

"You're going way too slow," Abigail said as she ran her fingers through Fin's hair and pulled gently.

"Sometimes I want it to last." She slid her hand between them, stopping when she felt how wet Abigail was. "You're so gorgeous that you can't blame me for that." The light knock on the door was like getting an unexpected ice bath, and she considered ignoring it.

"Mommy." She recognized Victoria's voice, so ignoring it was out, and she dropped her head to Abigail's shoulder.

"Later, I promise, honey." Abigail stood when she rolled off her and put her nightgown back on before tossing Fin's sleep pants at her head. "Thankfully you remembered to lock the door."

She got up and made it to the knob first, opening the door to Victoria, Liam, and for some reason Hannah. "You guys okay?"

"Liam had a bad dream, Mama." Victoria was Liam's protector and had been his interpreter until the little guy had started talking.

She squatted down to his level, and Liam put his arms around her neck. He didn't cry often, but nightmares set him off, and he sniffled against her shoulder. Liam was sharing Hannah's room with Victoria, which should've made him feel safe, but there was something lurking in the back of his mind since this was the third nightmare in a week.

She sat on the bed with him wrapped around her as Abigail walked the girls back to their room. Liam reminded her of her brother at this age, if Neil had light brown hair. They were both kind and a joy to be around, and Liam seemed to have become attached to her and had been from the very beginning. The girls loved her, but Liam wanted to be around her all the time and talked to her in a constant stream of words and babble as if he had plenty to say.

"Are you okay, buddy?" She rubbed his back and kissed the top of his head.

"No go away, Mama." He gripped her T-shirt and cried a little more. "No go away."

"I'm not going anywhere." She leaned back against the headboard and kissed the top of his head again. "I can't go anywhere, and there's a good reason. Do you know what happens in two weeks?" She saw Abigail standing in the doorway, and she was smiling.

"What?" Liam gazed up at her with total trust, and she felt lucky all over again. Damn Nicola for all the things she'd thrown away like they meant nothing to her.

"We're going to the court, and I'll be your mom forever. You'll be Liam Abbott forever too, and once the house is finished, we're going to live there once Mommy marries me." His big smile was a sign that whatever was worrying him was a memory for now. "Are you ready to go back, or do you want a story?"

"You're a soft touch, my love," Abigail said, heading for bed.

"That's true." She held Liam against her and started telling the story of Rosin Casey and her voyage to America from Ireland. It'd been her and Neil's nightly ritual with their mother, who was proud of the long-ago grandmother who built the empire Cain ran today. There could be only one clan leader in each generation, but their responsibility was to take care of them all. Liam and the girls weren't ready for the whole story, but she wanted to share with them the tale they'd all learned from an early age.

She'd told Abigail about where the money for the big house on the lake and the renovations had come from. The trusts Cain had set up for all the cousins were buried in the Caymans and added to monthly, even when she was with the bureau. She had enough to retire now if she wanted a leisurely life, but that wasn't in her DNA from either the Casey or the Abbott side of the equation.

"He's asleep," Abigail said in a whisper. It was starting to get light outside, so the commotion of six children would begin again, and no one would sleep through it. "What do you think he's worried about?"

"He's worried I'm going to go away, which doesn't make any sense. Do you think someone told him something?" They were under threat, but they tried to keep the kids' lives as normal as possible. Sadie and Victoria were thriving in their new schools, and Liam was happy at daycare for a few hours a day. It was important for his development, Abigail had told her.

"The girls are okay with the people Cain has watching over them and Hannah, and you know everything about everyone with a child at the daycare center after your background checks. I doubt it would've come from there." Abigail combed Fin's hair back and scratched behind her neck. "If some of those Karens knew about the extensive research you did on them, you might come home with the BMW emblem tattooed on your ass when one of them hit you with their car. It's amazing what people are capable of while judging others."

"Hey, I wanted to know who my kids are being exposed to."

"Why in the world didn't I find you wandering around Tulane when I was young and impressionable?" Abigail moved closer when she lifted her arm. "My kids would've been Abbotts, and none of this crap would be happening."

"Your kids are Abbotts, and that means my parents will indulge them until we own a pony that'll keep the grass down in the yard. The rest will work itself out like it did when your ex-in-laws tried their plan." She kissed the side of Abigail's head and put her arm around her. "That didn't work out too well for them."

"So, what's your plan, Abbott?"

"A visit to the Red Door with Neil." She hissed when Abigail pinched her side. "It was your idea."

"I know, and it wasn't my brightest moment." Abigail laughed and pinched her again. "It's a good move, but you'd better behave and keep your hands to yourself. I doubt any of those women have stretch marks."

"Brandi Parrish doesn't push her girls on anyone, according to Cain, and that's who I'm going to have make the call. Cain left some guys over there to make sure nothing happens to any of the women who work for Brandi. I've also been blinded by your gorgeous body, so no worries." She gently laid Liam next to her so she could get closer to Abigail. "Are you working today?"

"Just half a day. Mom and Dad will help Carmen and Ross keep an eye on these guys."

Fin placed her hand over Abigail's heart and bit her bottom lip. "Since you're not in clinic all day, how about a lunch date?"

"I'd love to, and if you're stealthy now, you can join me in the shower." She smiled when Abigail wiggled her eyebrows and gladly followed her to the bathroom after putting some pillows around Liam.

She carried Liam down after she got dressed to have coffee with Abigail before she left. That Cain and Emma were already in the dining room didn't surprise her. If she needed role models for a successful marriage, there they were. They'd all grown up learning from their parents, but her mother was right. The secret was finding the right person.

"You two are up early," Emma said. She smiled when she spotted Liam and seemed to understand. "They eventually outgrow it."

"Hannah and Victoria dropped him off early this morning."

"Did we make a mistake putting them all together?" Cain seemed happy to take the little boy when Liam reached for her. "I remember what we were like, so I think our kids might be the same."

"Liam and the girls will be fine, and he helps me think when the house is still quiet. The little guy is a great conversationalist."

Cain listened to her plan and nodded. The problem would be that

Brandi didn't work outside the city. Her business wasn't something easily replicated, so branching out wouldn't be smart. "I check in with her every couple of weeks, and she hasn't mentioned any problems. She's guided plenty of young women through those doors, so with any luck, some of them ended up in South Florida."

"Do you think it's a bad idea? To ask her, I mean," Abigail asked.

"There's no such thing as a bad idea when it comes to stuff like this. Brandi's a good source of information, but I try to keep her insulated. She had a hard life before she was able to lock that infamous red door to keep her girls safe from the horrors she survived. It's why I offered our protection when our Russian friends reappeared." Cain rubbed Liam's back like he enjoyed, and it made both Fin and Abigail smile. Her cousin was a natural when it came to children. "The children are at the top of what they want, but Brandi's is going to be a close second."

"What do you mean?" Abigail asked.

"The business needs a future, and in this case that means heirs, but it also needs what's most important to it."

Fin appreciated Cain not saying Nicola's name out loud since their kids never talked about her, and she hoped it was because they'd forgotten her existence. "You mind calling her? There are more clubs in Miami than any of us thought. We're going through them, but no red flags yet."

"Thank you, Cain, and you," Abigail said to Fin, "call me once you're done, and make sure Mom and Dad are up and ready before you run off. I think Dad's going by the house later to oversee the new wiring going in. Do not let any of the kids talk him into cutting school to go with him." Abigail kissed her on the lips and Liam on the head before following the two guys Cain assigned to her out the door.

"I'm meeting Dallas for lunch, so let me know if you need me to do anything," Emma said to her. The noise from upstairs started, and Emma shook her head. "Good luck, Fin."

"This is making me crazy," she said when it was just her and Cain. Liam had followed Emma to join the frenzy going on upstairs, if she had to guess. "Where's this bitch?"

"Calm, Fin. Keep your head, or she wins." Cain and her mother preached the same thing, and it was annoying.

"I'm worried about Abigail and my kids." She didn't raise her voice, but she was certain Cain heard her frustration.

"You might not believe me, but so am I. The difference is, I have to worry about your family, Linda's family, mine, and everyone else's." Cain tapped her index finger on the dining table as if to get her to focus. "Trust that as soon as Nicola lifts her head out of whatever hole she's hiding in, I'm going to lop it off."

"I know that, so sorry. Liam keeps having nightmares, and I'm not sure why. I probably worry too much whenever they're all out of my sight."

"Let's try something different today." Cain rose and poured her a cup of coffee. "You concentrate on the house across the street, and I'll call Brandi. Maybe if we both break our patterns something might break in our favor."

"What exactly do you have in mind for across the street?" She was beginning to question the people Annabel Hicks had in place, considering what she'd seen after her retirement. Cain had assured her whatever the hell was going on in the house across the street had nothing to do with Hicks or any of her people.

"I'm not sure yet, but cockroaches don't like it when you flip the lights on and expose their cockroach ways." Cain's smile was relaxed and somewhat mischievous. She doubted the outcome of that for whoever was hiding in the dark in that house. "We're waiting for a clue from the head bug to find Lucy, and then there'll be lessons taught. I did give a strong warning, so he can't say what happens will come as a surprise."

"Are you sure about that? It's hard to believe anyone in the bureau would've done that."

"Someone like you or the crew that follows me around wasting taxpayer money would never contemplate what's happened because you have integrity. These guys are different animals."

"You told me about Drew and Taylor Kennison, and you were right—they don't exist. But a kid they plucked from somewhere then ditched isn't FBI protocol." She twisted her cup around, trying not to spill any coffee on the tablecloth. "Doing something like that actually is illegal as hell and will get you front and center on every news outlet in the country before they bury you in federal prison."

Cain laughed and snapped her fingers. "The world is made of two different kinds of people, no matter what side of the law you're on, Fin. There's the scum who do stupid shit to get what they want, and there's the rest of us who live by a code. They've talked themselves into justifying what they did because it'll bring me down, but children aren't pawns in any game I play."

"Damn straight. I'm not sure who told them that'd be kosher in an operation, but we'll do what it takes to make sure they never do it again."

"Let's regroup tonight, and we'll discuss what I haven't told you yet when it comes to our friends across the way."

"Sure, and please let me know what Brandi tells you."

"You'll be the first to know."

She laughed when Cain slapped her on the back, and she headed out. Life had changed so much in the last year, but she was happy despite the drama and the danger they were in. The children and Abigail were the center of everything she believed and held dear, and she'd take a bullet for any of them. They'd be spared all Nicola's depravity even if it came with her own death. "That I can promise you all."

CHAPTER TEN

Cain rode with Emma and the younger kids to school, since Hayden, Tim, and Joshua were being dropped off by Mook and the crew he was heading up.

"Mom, can I invite *all* my friends to my birthday party?" Hannah put her hand on Cain's knee and smiled up at her.

"We already invited half the school, Hannah Marie, and that's enough." Emma jumped in before the puppy eyes did her soft-hearted spouse in and they'd have to add another thirty to the long list they had for a party that was still a couple of months away.

"Mama has spoken, so you'll have to be happy with a gazillion people in the yard." Cain picked Hannah up and kissed her on the nose before doing the same with Victoria. Sadie had been dropped off first at Cain's old alma mater, five miles away. "So let's go before Mama starts taking people off the list, including me and Victoria," Cain said as a joke, and the girls screamed and laughed. Each child held one of Cain's hands to the school's front door and kissed her cheek before running through the door, waving at Cain.

The few car horns drew Emma's attention away from how happy Hannah and Victoria appeared before she lost sight of them. Seeing the guns sticking out of the passenger side windows made her instantly nauseous because she knew who they were aiming for.

"Cain!" Emma screamed right before they started firing. She was scrambling to get out of the car when a bullet hit the side of Cain's upper chest when she spun around.

The force of the shot knocked her back against the thick wooden doors, but the bullets were still coming. Cain went down, which saved her from the other shots that ricocheted off the brick of the building and splintered doors where the kids had entered. All Emma could see was

Cain lying there, and all she could hear were the hysterical screams of children freaked out by the attack.

Lou barred her from getting out as Hannah and Victoria's detail dragged Cain inside, and the sound of squealing tires erased the echo of the shots and everything else. This was her greatest nightmare, and she'd be damned if anyone would keep her from Cain.

"Lou, open the goddamn door or I swear I'll have Merrick shoot you." The locks clicked open, and a wall of people surrounded her as she ran to the entrance. "Cain," she yelled again when she entered, and Cain was still on the ground. Teachers were holding the kids back, but she could hear both Hannah and Victoria crying at the front of the line. The girls were fine, so she didn't waste time comforting them. That'd come later. "Honey, open your eyes." The white shirt and tan linen suit had a red bloom that was spreading, so she pressed her hand over the wound.

"The ambulance is on its way, Miss Emma," Dino Romero, Lou's nephew, said. He took off his jacket and took over applying pressure.

"Honey, please open your eyes." She waited an eternity before Cain did as she asked and gazed up at her and groaned. "Stay with me. Don't go to sleep." She wanted to shake her to get her to stay alive, to stay with her, but all she could do was hold her hand and try not to die of despair herself.

"I love you, lass." The declaration came out in a wheeze, and Cain's eyelids blinked as if they weighed a thousand pounds.

"No, no, no." She raised her voice. "Keep your eyes open. Don't freak out your kids and me."

The school nurse dropped to the other side and replaced the jacket with a wad of bandages. "Ms. Casey, open your eyes and take a deep breath for me." The woman pointed to one of the teachers and placed both their hands on the wound. "Keep pressure on that." Her next move was to get behind Cain and lift her up so Emma could hold her.

"Mama!"

Emma's panicked fog lifted enough to hear Hannah's fear. She couldn't see her, but Hannah could be loud when she wanted to be. She glanced up at Lou, and he nodded as he moved toward Hannah and Victoria. "Have them brought home, Lou, and make sure there's a wall around them." The big man appeared somber, and she had a feeling he'd blame himself later even if this wasn't on him.

"Cain, please." She held Cain's hand, hoping to keep her tethered to life. They didn't talk about this often, but with what happened to

Cain's family, she knew Cain's wishes. Her wife was good at what she did because she was a planner. She left very little to chance. Death couldn't be planned, but her and the children's welfare was if an enemy ever got lucky.

She jumped when the doors crashed open to allow the EMTs in. The nurse thankfully gave them all the information on Cain's injury so she didn't have to talk. All she could concentrate on for the entire ride to the emergency room was the warmth of Cain's hand and the rise and fall of her chest.

The way Cain seemed to struggle with each breath, though, made her chest ice cold and her mind numb. This couldn't be it. She could not lose the one person who made everything make sense in such a senseless act. They'd made love that morning before the baby was up, laughed together, made dinner plans, and taken tomorrow for granted. All of it was in jeopardy now, and she wanted to curse the heavens for what could so easily be taken away.

"The doctor will be out as soon as possible, but please allow the staff to show you to the waiting room." The nurse held her back, and her instinct was to protest. Being separated might equate to Cain giving up. Didn't these people understand that? She needed to stay close to remind Cain of all she had to fight for. "We promise we'll take good care of her."

She followed another woman to a private space, but there was no dissuading Lou from standing guard outside Cain's room. "Remi," she said into the phone, "Cain's been shot." The words unleashed her tears and gave her permission to lose control, which she hadn't wanted to do in front of Cain or the children. "I don't know what this is yet, so be vigilant. Can you call the others and give them the same message."

"What hospital?" Remi sounded as if she was already running.

"Mercy," she said as Merrick and a few guys gave her space. "Be careful if you're coming." She didn't have the strength to hold the phone, but there were other calls to make. "Let me go so I can talk to my father and everyone else who needs to know."

"Let me worry about that," Remi said. "Trust me to keep you and your family safe."

"Okay, thank you." She pressed her fists into her eyes for a moment, but all she could see was Cain falling back, the expression on her face, her bleeding on that drab beige floor. The memory made her get up, pace the room, and stare at the second hand of the clock over the door. It seemed way too slow, but she couldn't take her eyes off it, praying the damn thing would speed up so she could see Cain. She needed to remind Cain to keep all those promises she'd made—a life, grandchildren, years. They had too many years ahead of them for Cain to give up now.

"Mrs. Casey," a young man said. He appeared too young to work in a hospital, but he had on navy scrubs and blood-spattered athletic shoes. It looked fresh, and she wanted to throw up thinking it was Cain's. How much could Cain lose before she lost her? "I'm Dr. Joseph."

"Where's Cain?" The fear coursing through her made the question louder than she'd intended.

"She's being prepped for surgery, but I didn't want to make you wait that long for an update." He sat and gazed at her until she joined him. "There's some paperwork we'd like you to sign, but Ms. Casey's stable for the moment. From my initial assessment, the bullet nicked her lung, so she's in stable but critical condition. She's also young, healthy, and—from what Sam Casey told me—has plenty to live for."

Sam came in and hugged her once Dr. Joseph said her name. "She's in good hands, Emma. Matt looks like he's late for his high school classes, but he's an excellent surgeon. I was in there when she came in, so we'll get her fixed up."

Matt smiled at that before placing his hand on her knee and squeezing. "All I need is your okay to get her into surgery. I promise we'll keep you updated until she's in recovery." His hand went higher, and Emma put hers down to stop it.

She nodded and wiped her face. "Don't let anything happen to her. Sam"—she turned to her old friend—"please take care of her."

"You have my word—she'll get our best."

Matt Joseph walked out with three nurses trailing after him down the wide hall. Emma hated the smell of this place and that she had to trust Cain to someone she didn't know, someone who had no idea what Cain meant not only to her but to her children and the rest of their family.

"Come on," Sam said, holding her hand out. They walked away and stood by the doors that led to the surgery suites, and the transporter stopped when Sam held her hand up.

Cain's eyes were closed, but she was warm when Emma kissed her. "Listen to me, mobster," she whispered in Cain's ear. "Do what you have to, but you come back to me. The kids need you, and I love you more than anything in this life. Don't leave me here alone." She kissed

Cain again, glad to get the chance, but hating the slackness in Cain's lips. "I love you, so you fight to stay with us."

The transporter at the head of the stretcher handed her a bag with Cain's phone and wallet, and the other guy handed over Cain's wide wedding band. There was a prominent tan line on Cain's finger, but holding something Cain cherished from the moment she'd slid it on her finger made fresh tears fall. She stood there until the double doors closed, and the loneliness came close to swamping her.

"Let's sit," Sam said, taking the bag. There was another private waiting room where the guards were waiting, along with her father and Carmen. "Let me make a few calls, and I'll be right back."

Sam Casey and her partner Ellie were the fertility specialists who'd helped them conceive all their children. From that first appointment, Sam had kidded around with Cain like very few people could get away with, and Cain had told her it was because of her sainted last name. Her concern for her and Cain now was genuine, and Emma was happy she'd been close by when they'd arrived. If she couldn't be in the room, it was good that her friend had the seniority to keep her posted.

"Mama," Hayden said when he ran in. "What happened?"

The way he hugged her was something he'd learned from Cain. She could see her lover in every inch of his face and mannerisms. He'd been a blessing from his birth, but God, staring at him, all her children really, without Cain would be harsh reality going forward if something happened. They needed Cain, especially Hayden, so their clan would survive.

"We were dropping off your sister and someone shot her." He was mature for his age, but hearing that made his head drop to her shoulder and he started crying.

She'd carried all three of them, and her children loved her, but Cain was who held them all together. Cain loved her, and when they met, she'd fallen hard, but seeing Cain the day Hayden was born had blinded her to anyone else. The way Cain loved all of them made that possible.

"The doctor said she'll be fine, buddy." She held him and kissed the side of his head. "It's going to be okay, my love."

"Don't make me leave, Mama. I need to be here." He squeezed her tighter, as if clinging to her in an effort to not be sent away.

"No, you're not going anywhere, but we need to get your sister and brother here." It was getting time to feed Billy, and Hannah had to be a mess by now. "You need to take care of Hannah when she arrives. She didn't see what happened but she did see a little bit of the aftermath." All that blood had to have scared both little girls, and it was time to start the healing process.

"Was it that bitch?" His emotions went to anger in an instant, and she couldn't blame him.

"We need to wait to hear, but keep your head, please. If something happens to you while Mom's in surgery, I'm not going to be able to handle it." He nodded when she squeezed his shoulders. "Promise me."

"You don't have to worry, Mama. I'll be okay, but can you send some of the guys to get them?" Hayden glanced at Lou. "Mom's going to want them close by when she wakes up."

"Dino," Lou ordered, "make sure the house is secure, and have someone bring Hannah and the baby."

The room filled with Dallas, Remi, Vinny, Mano, and Ramon. They all gave her support but stayed quiet. That was a blessing since she was incapable of making conversation. Hannah ran to her when she arrived with Abigail, Finley, and their children. Her father held Billy until he started to cry, and she wanted to join him when Hayden sat with Hannah and whispered in her ear. The two of them had bonded from their first day together, and Hayden took his job as Hannah's big brother seriously.

She covered her chest with a blanket and fed the baby, splitting her time watching him and the clock. It was easy to understand now what the definition of being mired down meant. Billy kept spitting her nipple out, so she took a deep breath and tried her best to relax.

Carmen took Billy to burp him when the surgeon came in and sat next to her. "She's stable and in recovery." Everyone in the room seemed relieved, but no one more than her. The news knocked off the blinders that had given her tunnel vision to a world without Cain. She put her hand to her chest as her heart rate returned to normal, and the nausea finally dissipated. The ground finally stabilized under her feet, and she could breathe again. "The bullet pierced her left lung, collapsing it. She'll have a chest tube for a couple of days while she's in the ICU."

"Is that necessary?" Intensive care didn't scream *stable and fine* to her.

Matt's hand hung in the air but didn't make it to her knee when Hayden moved to sit next to her and put his arm around her shoulders. "Answer my mom's question."

"The chest tube is protocol due to the nature of the injury. She did well in surgery, but we need to monitor her closely for infection and keep that lung from collapsing again. That means she'll be with us for at least a week." He glanced at Hayden and Hannah as if trying to work out a puzzle in his head since he seemed confused. "Your mom is going to be fine, and we'll take good care of her so she makes it home as fast as possible."

"Can we see her?" Hayden asked. "Mama needs to talk to her, and Mom needs to know we're here and love her."

"I'll take care of that, Matt," Sam said, staring at Matt like he wasn't handling the issue of comforting the family as well as he could be. Both Sam and Ellie had been sitting with them the whole time and had gotten information on Cain's surgery as it progressed. "These guys are some of our best patients, and Hayden's right. It doesn't matter if she's not awake—Cain needs to hear these guys."

Emma held Hannah and followed Sam to the recovery area. It took Hayden holding her up when she saw how much equipment was hooked to Cain. The chest tube the surgeon had mentioned made what happened real, and her fear of loss shocked her system. Hayden took Hannah from her so she could take Cain's still hand. If she'd been given a wish, she'd have asked for Cain to open her eyes not only for her but for their kids, but she settled for the steady movement of Cain's chest.

"Honey, we love you so much, and you need to know we're okay. The kids and I will be right here when you wake up." She lowered her head until her forehead rested against Cain's right shoulder. This had always been her safe place. "You scared the hell out of me, mobster," she whispered in Cain's ear before she kissed her neck. "So you have plenty to make up for when you wake up."

"Mom," Hannah said softly. "Wake up." Hayden had moved to Cain's other side and lifted Cain's other hand so he and his sister could touch Cain.

"She will, but she needs to rest first," Hayden said. The way he stared at his mother made Emma think there was so much going through his mind. This proved Cain wasn't invincible, but she doubted her kids would totally believe that. "Do you want to go and draw her a get-well picture?" Emma was glad Hannah loved Hayden the way she did. With all of them talking to the little girl and trying to cheer her up, she doubted their daughter would be scarred by this.

"I'll be right back, love." She leaned in and kissed Cain's cheek. The day had been horrible, but that she still had Cain with her made it bearable. She ushered the kids back to the waiting room and gave everyone an update so they could go home. "You two be good, and you can come back later to say good night." Both kids kissed her, and her father stood with Billy. Her boy was wide-awake and smiling like he knew better than all of them that Cain would be fine.

"Lou, please get them home and get some sleep. I'll need you to stay with me tonight." She looked at Katlin and Merrick, and they both nodded, not needing to be told they should stay.

"Between our families, we'll cover security," Remi said. "And we're also taking care of finding these people. I'll put them on ice if I have to until Cain's up and around."

She nodded and took a deep breath. "Make sure they live long enough to tell us who sent them. If you can prove they shot Cain, then don't let them go." Remi hugged her and held her. "They put her in there, and I want them dead." That she meant with her whole heart.

❖

The rub of Nicola's shirt against her side was driving her crazy. She'd had no choice but to get back to work, so the nurse had padded the site of her worst wound as best as possible. There'd been enough time for the damn thing to heal, but it was still oozing and painful to the touch. She needed a new doctor, but that would come only after she wrestled back the power that'd been stolen from her.

She leaned against the car window and closed her eyes. Her grandfather hadn't arrived yet, so this was the opportunity to deal with Kira alone. Svetlana's people had been watching the block of rooms at the Eden Roc, and her loving aunt didn't have the muscle she'd alluded to, and she was going to take advantage of that. Once Ivan arrived, there'd be a pack of morons roaming around dying to prove themselves, since Ivan needed plenty of propping up. She and her father had laughed about it every time they'd had to deal with Ivan.

"Our guys are already inside," Svetlana said from the front seat. She was starting to grow into her new role, but she had plenty of things to learn.

That gave Nicola no comfort, and her thoughts went again to Nina and where she ended up. Not that she was sentimental about the loss, but she wanted to plant Casey in the same dark hole because she'd bet her children's lives that's who'd killed Nina. She opened her eyes when the car stopped, and the line of vehicles outside the iconic hotel made her concentrate on controlling her expression. No matter the pain, she couldn't show any weakness.

A small teal-colored BMW cut them off, and she shook her head when Svetlana reached for her gun. "Calm down before you get us all killed." They moved forward slowly as the idiots in the small flashy car were now boxed in. The lesson here was if you were going to do stupid shit, drive a car that blended in. These idiots hadn't learned that, obviously.

"Wait," she ordered when they started moving forward but only moved two feet. The woman and the muscular young man with her standing on the curb that led to the front entrance—they caught her attention, since they were staring intently at the small BMW. "Have you seen these guys before?"

"Who?" Svetlana asked like a simpleton.

"Them." She pointed to the couple. They appeared to be biding their time, but they had the teal car in their sights. The BMW tried to cut someone else off, but a big man in a black SUV that'd slammed its brakes got out and banged on the window hard enough that Nicola heard it.

"Get out, motherfucker," the big blond said. The two passengers in the car didn't notice the people she'd spotted moving in on them. Nicola brought her window down to hear what was going down. "Get out or I'm going to fucking break it." He banged on the window again, hard enough to rock the small car.

The standoff had traffic snarled, but Nicola couldn't take her eyes off the hothead with road rage. There was something about him, and it made her wonder if this was only a case of good timing or good planning.

"Do you want to walk from here?" Svetlana asked, her hands on the door handle.

"Don't fucking move."

The driver of the BMW opened the door, and as soon as he began to stand, the blond hit him hard enough to knock him back into his seat. The guy's mistake was getting out because it unlocked all the BMW's doors, giving the blond's woman partner the opportunity to open the passenger side. The blond and another guy picked up the driver and put him in another SUV waiting on the street, and the passenger went along with the woman like a tame puppy. Nicola couldn't see the gun, but it had to be the reason for the passenger's cooperation.

She laughed at how smoothly that had gone, and she was sure

she'd just watched Kira's plan go up in smoke. It ended as quickly as it'd begun, and no one got out to demand an explanation of what was going on. No, everyone just moved up when one of the valet drivers took the BMW away like what'd happened was a common occurrence.

Nicola ordered everyone to stay in the car and walked through the lobby out to the pool bar. Kira was going to have to come down if she wanted to talk to her, and if she declined, she'd never see her or Fredrick again. The table she requested overlooked the water that matched the color of the BMW, and it reminded her of Abigail, since they'd stayed here more than once. She'd never brought Abigail to the house, though, and now she realized what a brilliant move that'd been.

No, they'd stayed here, and the memory of Abigail in a bikini relaxing in the sun was as vivid as the day it happened. They'd been married ten months, and they'd just found out Abigail was pregnant with Sadie. On that beach, though, her stomach had still been flat, and she'd smiled at her as if Nicola was her whole world.

"Papa isn't here yet." Kira sat down and waved a waiter over, knocking her out of her head. She ordered vodka on the rocks for both of them, but Nicola had no interest in drinking with her. "You're not thinking of blowing him off, are you?"

"What did the two guys in the BMW do for you?"

Kira stared at her as if trying to figure out how she knew enough to even ask the question. That proved that her mother's family wasn't capable of getting more than they had already. To rule, you had to be aware of everything happening in your orbit. "Why are you asking me that?"

She tried her best not to smile at the bull's-eye she'd hit. "Because someone picked them up easier than one of your whores. Since I didn't see anyone flash a badge, it's my guess they'll be dead by tonight, but not before they give up everything they know about you. Everything." Her smile made Kira's eye twitch, and she wanted to laugh. "Depending on what you had them do, you might want to take care of the fallout. If you went after a big fish and you didn't get a kill shot, there will be consequences."

Kira didn't say anything for a full minute, then got up and made a call. Her conversation seemed intense, and she appeared furious. That made Nicola add a few things to her own list, since if what Kira had ordered was bad enough, it could blow back on them. They were in no position to fight off anyone with enough muscle to choke them all to death. The incompetence Kira and Ivan had displayed was the reason they'd never be partners in anything.

Nicola stood and left, not interested in Kira's fuckups aside from how they might affect her and Fredrick. She'd accomplished what she needed and was certain Kira would be too busy cleaning her messes to worry about them. She needed distance between them as she headed back to New York. "This should prove to Ivan and Kira they need to stay in their lane. Only the strong get to wield real power."

CHAPTER ELEVEN

Marisol sat in her hospital room waiting for the police to come and interview her, since gunshot victims couldn't simply say never mind. She would've left by now, but the shot to her leg and the consequent infection made that impossible, and the hospital wouldn't release her unless she had someone to take care of her and bring her home.

She had neither of those things, so she'd been sitting in this fucking room for a couple of weeks, and her only chance of going was if she left under her own steam. The detective came by often, which meant her story of being mugged by someone who stayed behind her the entire time wasn't believed. He visited, and she kept repeating she hadn't seen the guy's face, which prompted another visit every few days. How she'd been dumped at the hospital was what made her story implausible, but talking would only bring more pain.

The detective listened to her every time and took notes, but she could tell from his expression he didn't believe any version of the story. She didn't give a damn if he did or not, but he'd promised to be back after he checked every aspect of her story. She stared out the window and tried to plan her next move. This time, whatever that would be would depend on only her. She doubted even her mother would help her after her mistakes from the moment she'd landed. Her phone had been silent since she woke up from surgery, and it'd stayed quiet while she recovered.

She whipped her head to the door when it started to open, her chest a block of ice since she was defenseless. If Hector had changed his mind about letting her go, this was it. The last person she expected to see was Nicolette Blanc's old lover, Luce Fournier. Luce had gladly gone back to France when Nicolette ordered it after Marisol and

Nicolette had cut a deal to move drugs through the Blanc Winery. The humiliation Nicolette had dropped on Luce had prompted her to leave the Blanc family for another smaller syndicate. The only person who'd been upset over her loss was Nicolette's father Michel.

"What do you want?" From what Nicolette had told her, this was not someone worthy of respect.

"It only took four words"—Luce held up four fingers and laughed—"to see Nic was right about you." The French accent was immediately annoying.

"Are you joking?" She laughed as well. "Nicolette told me about you too. Are you pissed because she landed in my bed, or that she threw you away?"

"I'm so pissed I moved on and got married." Luce lifted her hand to show off the gold band that appeared new. "Nicolette and I were over before we came to make deals here. She kept me around only to scratch that need that crept up every so often. It was nothing more than that."

"Then what are you doing back?" She moved and stopped when pain shot up her arm.

"I might not work for Michel, but I'm still loyal to him and care for him a great deal. The loss of his only child is slowly killing him, so I'm here as a favor to him." Luce crossed her legs and sat back like they were old friends. "As you said, you and Nic spent time together, so you're my first stop. Do you know what happened to her?"

"Why would I tell you?"

"You're smarter than to believe Nic loved you. She wasn't going to stay with you, and there were only two reasons she was with you." Luce smiled again but this time she figured it was from pity. "You were plan B when Casey fell through, and you hated Casey as much as she did. The night she disappeared, she'd already found a replacement when it came to doing business with you and your family. If it had worked out, you would've never seen her again."

"You're full of shit." It was how straightforwardly Luce told the story of what'd happened that fueled her anger, but it was the truth.

Luce put her hands up. "I have no idea what happened or why. The last time I spoke to Nic was before I left for the airport, and then briefly when she called to ask about Nunzio Luca. I gave her the information, and that was the last time we spoke. I was already moving to Paris for my new job, so I didn't fall for Nic's bullshit any longer. Had I known it was our last conversation, I would've asked more questions."

"You didn't love her?" The scar on Nicolette's face had been jarring at first, but after sleeping with her, she'd found her beautiful.

"In Nic's mind there was only one prize for her love. It'd never be me or you, so if you feel guilt over her death, don't. Cain Casey was who Nicolette loved, and she never wanted to hear that it was untenable. Casey was out of her reach, and from what I learned always had been."

"How do you know she was doing business with someone else?"

"Michel told me everything he remembered about their last talk, and Nic told him she was on to something big. That was the last he heard from her."

"So, he blames me and you're here to kill me?" She shrugged, even though it hurt. "Go ahead, I made it easy."

"Accept that Nic only loved and cared about one person when she came to hate Casey, and that was her father. When she was with you, she made you feel like there wasn't anything or anyone else you needed because she made it seem like you were the center of her world." Luce spoke with an almost detachment that had to have come from finding someone to fill the hole Nicolette had left. She envied her that. "All she was doing was climbing one more rung to help Michel, and that's all it was. Feelings for anyone in her bed would never compete with her devotion to her father."

"Why did you stay so long?" She was more curious than sarcastic, and she wanted the conversation to continue.

"I started working for Michel when I was seventeen, and I hoped eventually I'd share the responsibility of running the operation with Nic as more than her employee. She made me believe that, as I did whatever Michel wanted to advance his business." The way Luce stared at her made her believe what she was saying. "Our trip to New Orleans was to seal the deal with Casey that would've saved what Nic and Michel loved most. Their vineyard had been in the family for generations and their shared obsession. Casey killed that deal because of me."

"She told me, and it was the reason she came to me. I doubt she considered drugs before, but she seemed desperate."

"What she didn't tell you was her history with Casey started in college," Luce said and brushed something off her knee. "Nic wanted much more than a deal, but Casey turned her down *again*, and it pissed Nic off that Emma Casey won what she'd wanted for so long. She met Emma and found her weak and lacking. In Nic's mind, Cain needed a true partner, specifically *her*."

"She never told me anything about Casey except that she wanted her dead. I wanted the same thing, so I didn't ask too many questions."

"Nic never did like talking about her failures, but she deserves being buried with her mother and ancestors. What happened to her?" Luce repeated the question, but she didn't appear to be in a rush.

Not knowing—and she didn't—would make her sound like an uninformed punk, but it was the truth. Hector would've laughed at that since it proved everything he believed about her. "She left one morning, and a few days later she was gone. I tried finding her, but my father had me doing damage control for the problems we were having. Trust me, she would've been my priority if Hector had allowed it."

"Do you suspect Cain Casey?"

She chuckled at that. It'd be way easier to blame Casey, but Hector was right about that too. Not all roads led to her, and thinking that they did gave Casey too much credit. "You're right about how much she hated Casey, so there was no chance they were going to do business together. Whatever happened, it did because Nicolette chose what she thought was a better deal. I really don't know who she cut that deal with."

"If she was alive, she'd crawl through glass to talk to her father, so it's my conclusion she's dead. My job is to find out why."

She nodded, admitting to herself she'd lost something important when she lost Nicolette. "I don't know, and while Casey wouldn't do business with her, she would know what happened to her." It hurt more admitting that than getting shot, but Casey knew the streets better than anyone. "She's who you need to ask."

"What happened to you?" It was humorous that it had taken Luce this long to ask.

"My father's men shot me on his order." Saying it out loud made the proverbial weight on her shoulders fall away. Why had it taken this long to figure out what a piece of shit Hector was?

The truth was her life, from the moment she took her first breath, had been a mistake. Her mother had tried to trap Hector in order to coax him into giving her a better life, and her mother's punishment had been Hector taking her away. He hadn't done it because he loved her, but because he hated the whore who'd played him. If she was honest with herself, Hector had always looked at her as something shameful and dirty. She was a daily reminder not to be so fucking stupid again.

"That's harsh," Luce said taking her phone out and speaking

to someone in French. "You were my first stop, but can I drop you somewhere?"

"There's nowhere for me to go." Why she was being so honest was a mystery to her, but there was no reason to lie. "Good luck on your search. She might not have loved either of us, but Nicolette was special. I hope you can give her father peace."

"Come with me to New Orleans," Luce offered. "Michel is meeting me at the end of the week, and I'm sure he'd like to talk to you."

"How did you know I was here?" The question should've occurred to her earlier. Now that it did, the fear was back.

"Michel's had someone watching you since you were the last person in Nicolette's life. He figured you'd be safe here until you heal, but you might be better off with us. You can help me navigate the landscape of people and problems in New Orleans."

"I didn't kill her." The words came out in a rush, making her more pathetic by the second.

Luce raised her hands again and shook her head. "He knows that. She found another avenue for a deal, but that's as far as he's gotten. Not only is Nicolette gone, but so are her security people. They followed her to their deaths as well. So will you come?"

This was a way to put distance between her and the problems she was facing. Deadly problems. New Orleans, though, was like running right into Hector's bullets. "Sure," she said. Going back was the last thing Hector was expecting. "I'll talk to him and help however I can." What did she have to lose?

Emma put her head down on Cain's open palm and had a conversation with Therese Casey in her head. It was more of a plea to Cain's mom to watch over her child and make everything okay. Therese had been the kind of mother she'd always dreamed of having, and she'd mourned her death with the same devotion as Cain. Her loss robbed her of all the things she wanted to learn from her, but there were times she could still hear Therese in her memories.

"When we were kids"—Katlin's voice made her lift her head—"she used to treat us to candy and ice cream when our fathers were talking business. Things weren't as dangerous then, it seemed, so we'd ride our bikes to a neighborhood place and sit on the sidewalk to enjoy whatever she got us."

"She loves doing that with the kids in the backyard and makes them promise to keep it a secret from me when it's right before dinner." She loved watching them through their bedroom window as Hannah and Hayden laughed with Cain. Seeing Cain spoil her kids was a side of her very few got to witness.

"Cain was everyone's favorite then, and still is. We all come to her with our problems, and she never says no, just like she didn't back then when we ordered whatever we wanted." Katlin wiped her face almost like she didn't know she was crying. "She's done that always, and we all failed her today."

"Don't say that again. No one failed today, and the only way that'll be remotely true is if we stop looking for who did this." She stood and walked to Katlin. "Are you planning to do that?"

"No, and we might have something on that." Katlin sat when she pointed to the other chair.

"Tell me," she demanded. The anger of watching Cain go down had been brewing from the moment she'd watched it, and it'd been replaced with worry.

"The guys in the car behind you took off after the shooters, but we had to hang back because the feds did the same thing. Your shadows caught up with them and turned them over to the NOPD." Katlin spoke softly and kept her eyes on Cain. "They're in central lockup, but our friends told us who they were, and Finley's working on why this happened."

"Who are they?" She couldn't believe she had to prompt Katlin.

"They're Russian," Katlin said, and Emma closed her eyes. "Wait," Katlin knelt next to her. "It's not what you think."

"This isn't Nicola?" That couldn't be true. Nicola was the only Russian on their radar. If there were more, they might not survive this.

"Finley's still digging, but these guys don't have a connection to the Antakov family from what Fin's been able to find." Katlin moved back to her chair when Emma nodded.

"Save the rest," she said, ready to be alone again. "I'm sure she'll want to hear it. The orders for what comes next can only come from her."

"For now, they might have to come from you, Emma. You're the only one she'd trust."

"Let's give it a few days."

The nurse came in to take Cain's vitals and change the bag of fluid. "We're ready to move her, Mrs. Casey, if you'd like to follow." She glanced at Katlin and shook her head. "Sorry, only Mrs. Casey."

"The big guy outside is nonnegotiable, as are the guys with him. Someone shot my cousin, and we aren't going to give someone a chance to do it again." Katlin stared the woman down, and she nodded, saving her the trouble of having to contact hospital administration. "I'll go once you're settled."

Lou and Katlin flanked her on the way to the ICU, and seeing the rise and fall of Cain's chest prompted her to smile. The heart she loved still beating gave them the chance at the future they both wanted. She and Katlin stayed to the side as the staff situated Cain and all the equipment she needed. According to Matt, the chest tube would stay for a couple of days minimum, and then Cain would be fine and able to recover at home.

Matt came in and supervised before typing into Cain's chart and injecting something directly into Cain's IV. "Ms. Casey," he said, holding Cain's wrist as if monitoring her pulse, "there are a couple of people waiting to see you, so wake up."

Emma almost tripped over her feet to get to the bed, and she held her hands to her mouth when she stared into those beautiful blue eyes that had captivated her from the beginning. "Hi, love."

"You okay?" Cain asked, sounding breathless. "Hannah and Victoria?"

"We're all fine, honey. Hannah and Victoria were upset, but they're fine." She lifted Cain's hand and kissed the back of it. "You're going to be okay too, your surgeon here promised."

Cain's eyes cut to Matt and then back to her. It was hard to read her expression, but there was something there. "The bullet nicked your lung," Matt said, giving Cain the entire explanation of what he'd done and the need for the chest tube. "It'll keep your lung from collapsing, but we should be able to remove it in a few days. Emma was on board with everything we did."

"Mrs. Casey," Cain said, her eyes still on Matt.

"I'm sorry?" Matt said.

"Her name is Mrs. Casey," Cain repeated, and Emma almost laughed. Cain had been shot, had surgery, but still had enough energy to be jealous.

"Of course, sorry." Matt didn't seem to get the message when he put his hand on her shoulder. "If you have any questions have the nurse page me, *Mrs. Casey*. You have my number," he said to her as if they were old friends. "I'll see you in the morning."

She shrugged his hand off and placed her free hand on Cain's chest. "How do you feel?" she asked when they were alone. "You scared the hell out of me today."

"Was I unconscious so long that you started dating?" The way Cain smiled made her laugh.

"You're injured, so I'll let that go." She leaned in and kissed Cain, losing the battle with her tears when Cain kissed her back. It was something she thought she'd never get the chance to do again. "I love you so much."

"And I love you too much to leave you." Cain kissed her again and squeezed her hand. "Is Hannah really okay?"

"She was upset, and she came in to see you before Hayden took her home. Seeing you sleeping made her feel better, and Hayden did a good job of talking to her." She combed Cain's hair back and enjoyed the spark in those beautiful eyes. "Everyone is fine and working, so concentrate on getting better."

"I'll be up in no time." Cain pulled on her hand a little so she moved closer. "Our story has years of chapters left, lass."

"You promise?"

"On my word as your Casey." She lowered her head and pressed their lips together at those words. "Now go home, take a shower, feed the baby, and put our brood to bed."

"No." She still had on the clothes she'd been wearing when she'd held Cain, but the blood had dried. It hadn't occurred to her until just that minute. Neither of them needed the reminder.

"Lass, they need to see you, and I'm sure Lou or someone is right outside. Bring them in the morning, and try to get some sleep."

"I don't want to let you out of my sight." Cain falling after that shot was playing on a loop in her head.

"At least a shower and a change of clothes, then. Come back after the kids go to sleep. It'll make you feel better, and it'll assure the kids that we'll be fine." The way Cain spoke to her proved what a gift she was.

"I don't want to be away from you." That need to be with Cain and watch over her for a change was overwhelming, so leaving wasn't something she wanted to do.

"I want you here, so hurry back." Cain smiled and closed her eyes.

"I'll take a nap while you're gone, so try not to worry, and kiss our kids for me."

She stepped out, and Katlin motioned for Dino and the two other guys to guard the door. That Matt was at the nurses' station surprised her, but not as much as when he walked toward her. There was something about him that she couldn't put her finger on, but she'd let it go because of what he'd done for Cain.

"I want to apologize if I overstepped," Matt said. The way he cocked his head slightly and smiled must've worked on more than one woman, she guessed, but she wasn't just any woman. "I recognized Cain when she came in, and I have to say…" He stopped, and his smile widened.

"You had to say what exactly?" Matt seemed like a man used to getting his own way, and it made her want to get him as far away from them as possible. She wanted him off Cain's case no matter how great the surgery had gone.

"It's none of my business, but you deserve better. Someone who lives like she does isn't capable of giving you the life you want." He lifted his hand to take hers, and she stepped back after slapping it away. "Maybe we can build on the connection we made earlier."

It was like she was in the twilight zone. "Are you delusional or stupid?" She spoke loud enough that some of the nurses stared in their direction. "I'm not sure what you're talking about, but I'm not interested in anything with you. There was no *connection*, and you know nothing about my life, much less what I want out of it. Don't bother to show up in the morning, or ever. I'll have a new doctor for Cain by then, and I'll be brutally honest if admin asks me why. Cain and I are married. Whatever our life is or anything else about it is none of your business."

"Come on. You needed me today." Matt lowered his voice and waved his hands in a shushing motion. "I'm sorry I got the wrong impression, but you were leading me on. How else did you want me to take it?"

"I needed you to bring Cain back to me, and that was your job. It didn't matter if it was us or someone else who'd been hurt—that's your job. That's it, and thank you for your service, but now you're no longer needed for anything to do with us." She glanced at Dino, and he stepped closer to her. "Don't go back in that room, and don't talk to me ever again. Whatever this is you're trying is bizarre and unprofessional."

"Dr. Joseph," Cain's nurse said, "it's time to say good night."

"Has he tried this before?" she asked when Matt left the unit.

"I'll be happy to back you up if you file a complaint," the older woman said. "Between you and me, it's only certain cases that bring out that side of him. A few of the nurses get the same treatment, but stuff like that is hard to prove."

"Thank you, and I'll be back in a few hours. Please keep him out of Cain's room." Great, some idiot with a crush wasn't what she needed on top of everything else she had to worry about. "Katlin," she said.

"Don't worry. She's going to be pissed when you tell her, but she'll be alone when you get back."

"Thanks." She strode out and cried in the car the way she'd never do in front of Cain. Therese told her a long time ago that tears washed away bad days and proved you loved. "Today was a bad day, Therese, but we'll go on tomorrow, and so will the love I have for her."

❖

Dylan had given up cigarettes in college, but after that phone call she'd gotten about her secrets, she'd stopped at the first convenience store she'd found and picked up a couple of packs. The caller hadn't hidden their voice, so if she could get Cain Casey on the phone, she could prove that's who it was. If that was true, she and the small group she'd been working with were screwed. Casey played to win, and if she knew what they'd done with Lucy, a kid in the system, she was going to fuck them all over.

"She's not going to care that I didn't know anything about that shit." She was sitting in her car outside Mercy waiting for news about the shooting and what condition Casey was in. The safest way out of this was death—Casey's death. Talking to herself was something she'd learned when she was little and had no one to talk to her because her father was never home because of his job. Her mom took advantage of that and partied with any man who'd pay for drinks.

She slipped down in her seat when she saw the black vehicles stop at the entrance. Emma Casey was at the center of Cain's world, but without the head of the snake, the body would become impotent. Without Casey, it wouldn't matter how many little bastards Emma had brought into the world. No one left to train a new crop of psychopaths meant the end would come in Cain's generation. The bureau should give her a medal for that alone.

Emma appeared upset, so maybe all her wishes were coming true. She didn't take her attention from the entrance when the passenger side door opened. Her graduation from Quantico seemed like a lifetime ago, and her plans for her career were at the opposite end of the spectrum from that day. She'd gone from a bright young agent ready to take down as many scumbags as possible to fighting to keep her place in the world.

"I think you underestimated the queen, Gardner." Matt Joseph laughed and grabbed the cigarette out of her hand. "The little bitch has claws, and this favor you asked me for is going to bite me in the ass. I still have a shitload of student loans left, so think about that before you get any more bright ideas."

"You had a fast solution, so how about that?" The entourage pulled away, so she turned and stared at Matt. Their time at Yale had been fueled by alcohol and parties before they decided to buckle down, as her father was fond of saying.

"Oh yeah," he said pointing at her with the cigarette. "I'm going to kill the head of a mob family in a crowded surgery suite with another doctor watching my every move. Why don't I go in there high on meth, smoking a joint too? That comment was too black ops, even for you. If that's where your plans are headed, count me out. There's no fucking way I'm doing anything like that."

She hated that he always went straight to sarcasm when anyone suggested any mistake on his part. "All right, it was only a thought."

"I did what you wanted and put the moves on the bitchy little blonde. If I end up not being able to work because my hands are broken, I'm going to be pissed." He flipped the cigarette out and laid his head back. "Did you want me to do anything else?"

"Do you think you can get back on the case?" If Casey was going to live, she needed her to react to a threat against her partner in the way she knew Casey always took care of problems. Entrapment was only thrown out of court when you could prove it.

"I was planning to show up in the morning." He smiled wide enough to show off his dimples. "Emma should be over the trauma by then and more open to what I have to offer."

She almost laughed at Matt's ego. "Let me know how it goes."

They shared another cigarette and talked about what had brought them both to New Orleans. It took another hour before the cars came back, and Emma returned on the arm of a really big guy. She noticed how Matt's eyes stayed glued to the pretty woman. This might be easier than she thought.

"Just your type," she said, slapping Matt's arm. "Too bad she's not interested in you."

"She will be." He waved over his shoulder as he crossed the street, as if unable to resist Emma's appeal.

"This will be over soon." Of all the things they could put Casey away for, this would be the most hilarious. Having her attack Matt for touching Emma would stick like it did when she'd done it to one of the cartel guys when she was in California. Now all she had to do was erase herself from Ronald's clusterfuck before that hit the fan. "Then Annabel and her misfits can kiss my ass."

CHAPTER TWELVE

Cain concentrated on her breathing and willing away the pain. The shot had been like a hot poker slicing through her, and as much as it'd hurt, she was thankful it wasn't the type of bullet that did maximum damage on the way out. Being gunned down like that in front of Emma and their daughter was the worst-case scenario, and someone was going to pay.

The area outside her room was quiet, and she noticed Katlin and Merrick standing close by. The new nurse on shift for the night had her hands up when the doors opened, as if to stop them from coming any closer. It didn't take long for Emma to win that battle of wills and enter with the kids. She had a chance to take one more deep breath before Hannah came in with that smile Cain loved so much.

"Hey, Hannah girl," she said with her right hand up.

"Mom, are you better?" Hannah stood next to the bed and held her index and pinkie fingers with her little hands. "You're talking."

"I am talking, and in a few days, I'll be tickling." She smiled when Hannah let her go and put a card an inch from her face. "That's beautiful, lassie. Did you do that by yourself?"

"Hay helped me. He made one too." Hannah sat still next to her and told her about how she felt and how scared she and Victoria were when they heard the shots. "Mama told us we didn't have to be scared no more, and I won't, even if you sleep a lot. I promise."

"You're right that I might sleep a lot, but you can nap with me if I am," she said, winking at Emma. "Mama said I have to rest, so I'm trying not to get into trouble."

"You have to learn how to duck, bud," Hayden said and slapped hands with her. "Don't worry, I'm taking care of Mama and everyone."

Their son was the kind of kid anyone would be happy to have, and she'd been proud of him even when all he could do was sleep and spit up. Her da was existing somewhere with a puffed-up chest because of the kids who'd continue their family line.

"I know that, buddy, and let Hannah stay with you if she needs to. Stick with Mook and the guys. Tell your friends the same thing," she said of Linda's brothers. "We need to do some homework before you guys can go out alone, so don't make your mama worry."

"We'll be good, so concentrate on getting better."

"You two kiss Mom good night," Emma said, placing the baby on Cain's uninjured side. "Katlin and Merrick are going to bring you home and stay with you. I'll be here with Mom, and with any luck we'll be home in a few days."

"Can we come back tomorrow?" Hannah asked.

"You could come and eat my Jell-O." Cain smiled at their daughter and laughed when she clapped her hands.

Emma got them ready to go, and Merrick smiled as she took the sleeping baby from her. Her family was safe and whole, but this wasn't at all in her window of possibilities. She could remember Emma screaming her name but had no image in her head of who'd pulled the trigger. All she could think of was Nicola because of what she blamed Cain and her family for.

She lifted her right arm and welcomed Emma to lean against her. "You saved my life today, love."

"That was the worst thing I've ever seen. I've seen you get shot before, but today terrified me beyond anything I've ever felt." Emma cried, and she let her get all that emotion and terror out. It hurt that she couldn't do more to comfort her wife than lie there, but it seemed to be enough when Emma's tears slowed. "I can't lose you."

"I don't know what today was, but it was a learning experience." She'd been thinking since she'd regained consciousness, and it made no sense. "We'll change a few things so it doesn't happen again, but I don't want to make you and the kids miserable with too much security."

"Katlin said whoever did this was Russian, and they're in central lockup." Emma spoke into her ear because no one had swept the room. "There's something else." That came with more hesitation.

"Wait on all of it, and get Lou in here." Injury or no, this was no time to get sloppy.

Lou joined them and placed a jammer on her chest as he swept with the detector and held up six fingers. That prompted Emma to head to the nurses' station. Emma talked the staff into changing her room, and that took more time than she thought necessary.

It was all for nothing when Lou found five bugs around the new room and one under the bed. The assholes who followed her liked to cover their bases, but insulating them from the danger was not in their job description. Bugging someone's hospital room didn't seem like something legal, but she was used to people cutting corners when it came to her and her business.

That the new room was bugged meant they'd planned ahead. She shook her head when Emma went to flush them. Lou laughed when she finished the note she'd written. Dino and another young guy stood post while Lou left to carry out what she wanted. Emma got back on the bed and put her mouth next to her ear and told her about Dr. Matt Joseph. What he'd tried only rounded out the strangeness of the day.

The way Emma looked at her when she finished made her want to deal with him right then, but her usual short fuse when it came to all things that upset her wife was going to have to wait. "Give Muriel a call, and let her know what's going on—let's see what happens in the morning. I wanted to give her a few more weeks to recover, but we might need her on this."

"I want someone new taking care of you," Emma said. "Not for me, but for you. I don't trust him not to do something to you. All these people injecting things into you without us knowing what they are is making me twitchy."

When you were on your back and weak, someone like Joseph could do more harm than the idiots who shot her. Emma was right about that. She nodded and pointed to the phone. She motioned for the pad again and wrote for Emma to bring Hayden in the morning.

"Why?" Emma asked but from her expression she guessed.

He was still young, but like her and Billy, he'd grown to a point where he was stronger than he knew what to do with. When Gardner had pushed her down and Remi talked him down, she knew the anger was still there. He'd had no outlet for it.

Now after this, she knew Hayden needed to be useful—she'd give him that in a way she could control and sanction. Her note was the conversation Emma had to have with him and what he needed to do when it came to protecting his mother. Hayden was a few years from being introduced slowly into the business, but teaching him to protect his mother and his siblings had started early. He'd know what to do—she was sure of it.

"Let him step up, but only if you need him to."

Emma surprised her when she nodded. A good leader had to know when the satisfaction of smashing your fist into a smug face was better than any other course. Their son was young, but old enough to know what was expected of him. It took another fifteen minutes for Fin to show up with Lou and set up what she wanted. Fin finished the job without saying a word, and Lou went back outside.

"You need to get some sleep," Emma said, moving back to the recliner.

"Are you sure you wouldn't be more comfortable at home?" She yawned as the pain medication kicked in.

"I'm not leaving you." They kissed, and Emma stood again and fixed her blankets. "I love you, so go to sleep and dream about getting out of here."

"Do you remember the weekend we spent at the beach house when we were dating?" That first year together laid a foundation strong enough that they'd survived Emma's leaving. "I know you asked me about it not that long ago."

"It was my first time in a float plane and seeing you in shorts. I loved both experiences," Emma said and laughed. "You probably thought I was such a dork, but God, I was so in love with you."

"Hey," Cain said pulling on Emma's fingers. "Don't call my wife a dork. I don't think I've ever told you that was the weekend I knew for sure I'd never be able to let you go without losing a part of myself. I told Mum I'd found what'd always be the most precious to me."

Emma smiled and leaned in to kiss her. "Sometimes I still have to convince myself you chose me. You've been everything I could want even when you drive me nuts, and I love when you're shmaltzy." They stared at each other until Cain couldn't keep her eyes open. If she'd forgotten anything, she trusted Emma to take care of it. "Go to sleep, my love, and let me watch over you."

"You truly walk with the angels, Derby," her mother said when she entered her dreamscape. Her mom had believed how you lived your life equated to how much luck you were given. Emma had given her a family and a good life, so hopefully their bounty of luck wouldn't ever diminish.

"I miss you," she said when Marie and Billy joined her and put their arms around her. She loved these visits, but this place was nowhere to linger. There were too many important people to stay behind and live for.

❖

Nicola went back to the house to pack for her trip to New York and to make sure Fredrick would be fine in her absence. After the crash that left him in the wheelchair, both she and her father tried to refocus Fredrick's life to keep him engaged in living. Before he'd become a prisoner in his own body, her brother had been an important part of the operation as well as one of their best recruiters. There were plenty of girls willing to pay to end up in the United States, and Fredrick had a talent for finding them and introducing them to the business.

Once they arrived, Fredrick got them hooked on various drugs they were starting to dabble in as a sideline, but nothing that would take away from the beauty that the rich were willing to pay for if you gave them free rein. The girls who overindulged ended up at the trailers they moved around the city, since the men there could've cared less if they were conscious or what they looked like. She'd worked with both Fredrick and her father to expand the network of clubs they owned around the country and had pushed her father into films. She'd counted on her brother to continue doing his part after she took over, but now the burden of running the business and the family fell to her.

When Fredrick had been hurt, their father had given him a new project he could run from the house in Miami, and her brother had grown their erotic film productions to the point even she was impressed. The money the studio was making would be the fuel she'd need to rebuild their security forces to where they'd been before her parents were killed and she'd gotten hurt.

"I have a group waiting for you at the airport," Fredrick said as she placed her clothes in her bag. "It took us some work, but Svetlana and I have found what was left of the guys who are loyal to us."

"I did the same thing here with the new guys." She sat next to him and took his hand. The scars that started at his fingers and ran up his arms were a testament to how broken he'd been and how strong he was to have lived. "You are a true Antakov," she said, taking a deep breath. "I'm glad you survived and are with me."

"Don't get sentimental now," he said and laughed. "None of this is your fault, and you're the true head of our family. It's time for you to reclaim what's rightfully ours."

"You have my word on that, and that you'll share the throne with me."

"I have some plans to talk to you about when you get back." She liked his smile since it had been missing for so long. "It can wait, but it might speed up our timeline when we're ready."

"Let's talk as soon as I get back, and maybe consider looking for a new place. I want us to stay in the city, but we need a more secure location with room for the children." They both needed the hope of a future, and the kids would give Fredrick a new project. He could start to mentor Sadie to be ready to eventually take over the business. The final lessons would come from her, but Fredrick could start her education. "Start hunting for that while I'm gone, and we'll decide together later."

Her reality was Fredrick and her children. They were all the family she had left, and it'd have to be enough. She'd been thinking since Kira's arrival and the best ways to move forward without too many entanglements from the past. To survive meant letting New York go. The other families were too strong to wrestle for what they'd taken like vultures when they'd thought she was dead. With no one of consequence to stop them, they'd picked the businesses apart and absorbed them into their own operations. There was no getting them back.

Her cousin Sacha, though, had to pay for the failed hit on her. Without Nina, she'd never prove it was Sacha, but she knew he was the only one with something to gain from her true death. He'd sworn allegiance the day they'd met, but he was the type of scum with no character. There was no way he'd ever keep his word. Sacha's death would start a war others would fight, and she'd leave them to it and come back to Miami and start over.

"Talk to the studio in New York, and have them transfer everything to you. We'll keep it open, but everything runs through us." She put her other hand on his chest and brought her head closer. "We're weak, but we're not dead. In a few years we'll remember today and laugh."

"We will because you're the strongest of us all." He leaned in as well and kissed her cheek. "Call me when you land, and hurry back."

"This shouldn't take long. Sacha isn't the brightest star in our orbit, and the family can fight over the scraps once he's gone."

She left with only Svetlana and glanced back at Fredrick before the door closed. Superstition had never been in her wheelhouse, but something stopped her cold. It was irrational, but she had to take a few deep breaths to calm her fear. Their parents were dead, but losing Fredrick, no matter how broken he was, would be like losing a part of herself. He was her twin and the keeper of all her secrets.

"What?" he asked, his smile still in place. "Did you forget something?"

Maybe she should stay and not open any more fronts against them. "No," she said and lifted her hand in farewell before closing the door.

If she didn't go and deal with Sacha, it'd only prove Kira right. Sacha was her family, but he'd tried to kill her without hesitation. Kira and Ivan, though, would never move against them. They might push them to do business with them, but death was not on their agenda. Ivan at least respected that they were family in the truest sense, no matter how distant they were.

She boarded the plane three hours later and stared out the window as Miami disappeared from view. The pain in her side was constant now, as if her body hadn't acclimated to losing a kidney, but she did her best to try to sleep without painkillers. Between her side and headaches from the plane crash, she'd become an addict if she tried to deal with it through pills.

"What was all that with Kira?" Svetlana asked.

"Something I'll deal with after Sacha. Did you leave someone at the hotel?" The problem with Svetlana was she needed to make small talk, and to ask questions about things that didn't concern her. She'd tolerate it for now out of necessity, but she'd replace her as soon as she could.

"You know," Svetlana said, stopping to take a sip of her drink, "if you wanted someone else with you, I would've stayed and helped Fredrick. I'm loyal to both of you, but you don't think I'm ready. The last thing I want is to hold you back."

"I doubt you'd be happy with Fredrick, and if I didn't want you, I'd have left you." Stroking someone's ego wasn't her strong suit either. "You're here because of your loyalty, and going forward we'll see. I'm not sure how you'll fit in the business, but you'll always have a place with me."

Svetlana nodded and didn't say anything else for the rest of the flight. When they landed, a group of four guys embraced her before driving her to her old apartment. The feds had seized everything owned by the Antakovs and Eatons, but the Trump Tower apartment was still listed under Crista Belchex, the name her father had given her after the crash to convince the authorities she was dead.

Everyone else was waiting inside, and it was nice to regain some of the people she knew and trusted. These men and women had taken an oath to her and the family, and they stood waiting for an order. Their readiness convinced her what she wanted was possible.

"Sit and we'll begin."

CHAPTER THIRTEEN

Cain woke first and watched Emma sleep as she listened to the hushed conversations outside. She was in pain, but it was worth it when she considered a very ugly alternative. Bishop Andy told her there was no pain in death, but to find that kind of relief wasn't worth the dead part. She'd been lucky, but to stay that way she needed to start piecing some of this together and find a solution. A very permanent solution.

"You have that thinking face on before you've had coffee." Emma came to a sitting position, then stood to lean over her. "Are you in pain?"

"I'm in a little pain, but I'm also breathing in a room with you." She winked when Emma snorted. "It's not too bad, so maybe they'll move me out of here today."

"One more day, honey, so don't start complaining." Emma kissed her before going to the bathroom.

Lou was still outside, but someone had gotten him a chair. He stood when Shaun entered and spoke to him with their heads close together. The young guy had been in Miami for a while, and before that he'd backed Lou up when they were out. She trusted him, along with Sabana, to find something on Nicola in Florida. Seeing him here surprised her, but asking why was going to have to wait.

"The kids should be up, so let me get them over here," Emma said, setting everything out for her to brush her teeth. "If I do that, you have to promise me you won't let them talk you out of going to school, soft touch."

They heard the older nurse order Finley to stop, but her cousin ignored her and walked to her door. Any more of this and she'd get her wish to get moved out of ICU if only to give the staff back their strict rules. Emma went out and Cain watched her whisper in Fin's ear, and she stared at her before going in. It wouldn't take a psychic to know Finley was twisting herself into a knot, taking the blame for this because of the problems she'd brought to their door.

"Lass, wait on that call." She wrote something out and handed it to Fin. It was the name of a local sheriff's deputy who enjoyed betting on all sporting events, even some she'd never heard of. The guy got lucky every so often, but that luck came from whoever he had in custody she needed information on. Right now, she needed access to the triggermen who put her in here and had most probably shot Muriel as well.

Fin put the paper in her pocket and handed her a file. She skimmed it and sighed. Life would be easier if everyone stuck to their lanes, but then people who colored outside the lines were fun too. The other life lesson was that shitheads had a way of finding other shitheads so they could pretend to be the smartest people in any room.

"Keep Hannah and Victoria home today," she said, and Emma seemed to understand her. "Hayden has baseball practice today, so if he can spare some time, have him come, but talk to him first."

"About?" Emma asked.

"The virtue of moderation. Too much of a good thing isn't good for anyone."

"Do you need anything from me?" Fin asked.

"Plenty, but that can wait." It couldn't really, but she couldn't chance removing the bugs yet. "I should be home soon."

Emma helped her clean up and went down to meet Hayden when Mook called. The plan Cain had in mind would only work if she'd guessed right about everyone involved with the limited information she had. Her da always told her being smart didn't always have anything to do with a high IQ. It came from learning things like not sticking your feet in a roaring fire because it'd burn you every time.

The other important thing was not to put your hands on a woman who didn't ask it of you because she had every right to say no. Anyone pawing at Emma would learn the same lesson as that fire thing—they'd burn until it hurt enough that they'd wish for death.

She closed her eyes when Emma entered alone and steadied the rhythm of her breathing. The eye of the storm was only quiet and safe if you stayed inside the circle and did what you were supposed to. Step outside that safe zone, and the storm would rip you to shreds along with the life you'd built for yourself. Staying out of harm's way had mostly to do with listening to that little voice in your head that said *Careful, this is dangerous.*

"Good morning, sweetheart," Matt Joseph said to Emma. "Did you have a good night?"

"What are you doing here?" Emma sounded angry, and it was in no way an act.

Matt laughed, and it made Cain open her eyes. The idiot had moved close to Emma, and there was jack she could do about it. "You know you didn't mean that last night. You also can admit that you want me." He grabbed Emma's arms and pulled her in. "You put out enough hints that you can't deny it now."

"What are you doing?" Emma was struggling but he was stronger. "Cain."

"You can forget her." He moved to kiss her silent when Emma yelled for him to stop again. "Keep it down." Before he could get his lips on Emma's, Hayden came in and pulled him off. Matt laughed at what he probably saw was a kid in a school uniform complete with neat tie.

Hayden hauled back and let his fist fly into the center of Matt's face, knocking him into her legs. He didn't stay long when Hayden pulled him up and hit him again. Matt screamed with his hands on his face, and Emma held Hayden back from hitting him again.

"You little son of a bitch," Matt said, bleeding through his fingers.

"Don't ever touch my mother again," Hayden said, standing in front of Emma. He stayed there until Lou came in, followed by the nurse.

"Get security," Matt screamed, his hands still over his nose. "You're going to pay for this, you bastard."

"You're a smug little bug, aren't you?" Pain was relative, she thought, as she stood and opened her arms to her family. "And you're going to pay for putting your hands on her."

Sam Casey came in with an older guy, and she could see both of them trying to figure out why there was a crowd in an ICU room. That one of their surgeons was bleeding had to have added to the mystery.

"Get him some help," the older guy said.

"No, I want the kid arrested," Matt said starting to sound nasal.

"Cain, are you okay?" Sam asked, helping Emma get her back on the bed.

"I'm the one bleeding," Matt said.

"Again," the old man shouted, "get him some help, and call security." He offered Cain his hand. "Ms. Casey, I'm Dr. Norris Belanger, the hospital administrator. Are you hurt?"

"I'm fine, but I would like you to call the police."

"We might want to wait on involving the authorities until we're finished investigating." Norris sounded like a guy who tended to believe anyone who had an MD behind their name, so whatever Matt Joseph told him was going to be the story they were going with. "Violence is never tolerated on my campus."

"Would it change your mind if I tell you the room is wired for sound and video?" She enjoyed the way his back straightened. "Your talented surgeon touched my wife inappropriately. She told him no last night, fired him, and was trying to fight him off this morning. Investigate all you want, but our son was defending his mother, and your response to something you know nothing about will play well in court."

"HIPAA doesn't allow taping in any room, so I highly doubt that." Norris shook his head as if he could make it all go away.

"Lou, call the police," she said, and Lou stepped outside. "Sam, could you arrange for a transfer? If you can't get involved, I'll take care of it."

"Where do you want to go?" Sam asked and Norris appeared ready to hit her. "I understand you're upset, but you do need medical care for a few more days."

"Let me see the recording?" Norris blurted out.

"We wouldn't want to ruin the surprise for you," Emma said. She was typing something into her phone. "Our attorney will be in touch."

"Whenever I'm in the hospital, I never have this many visitors," Sanders Riggole said when he walked in and placed his briefcase on the chair Emma had been using. He worked for Muriel and had a talent for sarcasm. He'd been standing in for Muriel while she was healing, but Cain had confidence in him. "You'll be hearing from our firm, as Ms. Casey said, but I'd like to confer with my clients, please. Before we leave this room, though, let's collect our property."

Lou and Shaun removed the cameras and the bugs that didn't belong to them. She agreed to stay when Sam offered the maternity ward, and they'd have her original surgeon take over her case. Mark Summers had taken care of her the first time she'd gotten shot.

"Good job, you two," she said when it was just Emma and Hayden. The next part of what she was thinking would hopefully close one avenue of attack.

"Lou sent Shaun up to get your room ready," Emma said pointing at her as if warning her not to complain.

"I think our privacy will be important until I get to go home. We should do them a favor and make sure everyone's privacy is respected." She pointed outside and made a circle with her finger. Bugs were a given, considering how relentless the agents were, but there was a slim chance they would've known what room she was going to be in. "Can you call the nurse for me?"

"We're almost finished with your transfer," the older woman said when she came in with a few syringes for her IV.

"Take your time—I just have a question. When are patients assigned to a room?" The nurse appeared confused by what she was asking. "What I mean is, does the doctor assign them?"

"We moved you last night because you requested it, but we assign rooms when you arrive from surgery. Whatever's open is where we put you."

"One more weird question," she said, and the woman nodded. "Did anyone recently do any work or maintenance on all the rooms? When I say recently, I mean while I was in surgery."

"A young woman from respiratory was here yesterday checking and recalibrating all the oxygen gauges, but only the empty rooms."

"Sam, let Lou check the others." She cocked her head toward Lou, and he stepped out with the equipment he'd need. The bugs they'd found in this room were in the envelope he handed her. "Something else you allowed someone to put in my room," she said to Norris when he stepped back in with two men in nice suits. Legal had arrived and the negations weren't far behind. "This isn't going to improve my review."

It took Lou forty minutes, and he came back with five other labeled envelopes with the room numbers on them. The good thing about the government was they were sticklers for keeping inventory of their little gadgets, at least the ones she'd found so far.

"Thank you, and thank you for moving us." Emma stood by the glass door and waved Sam and Norris out. "Please keep Dr. Joseph away from us."

"It's time to call Annabel and Shelby." She closed her eyes again and shifted to get comfortable. Standing had shifted the damn chest tube, and she was in so much pain she was nauseous. "Get the nurse and ask her for a pain shot, please."

She felt the warmth in her arm as the woman pushed the medication. For once she welcomed the bliss of darkness. Her last thought was about Dylan Gardner and what the best course of action was. Whatever she decided, it was going to be a lesson in pain worse than what she was in right now.

❖

Finley sat in the dining room and went through the files she'd edited from across the street. That the people who leased the property were active federal agents still surprised her. She'd been part of operations where they'd tried to surveil from as close as possible, but only after running an extensive background check on where they were going to set up. Granted, in this case it would've taken a deep dive because of Muriel's talents, but the layering should've raised red flags.

The truth was Cain knew her neighbors because she owned the house, like she did five others on the street. Her elderly tenants who took turns calling the police on the surveillance van rented from her at a very reasonable rate because of their limited incomes. These tenants, though, had as much layering as Cain, so she'd leased it for the full market value after wiring the place like she was conducting her own reality show.

"So, what exactly is over there?" Abigail asked. She was having lunch at home and wanted to sit with Fin.

"Before we returned to the city, Hannah befriended a little girl in her class, Lucy Kennison. Her parents were in the middle of some over-the-top arguments that were leading to divorce, so Lucy spent plenty of time with Hannah."

"Sounds like the kid I know." Abigail tapped on Fin's plate so she'd take a bite.

"The mom came for a visit after Billy's birth to thank Emma for all they'd done, which was nice until they found the bug in the family room." She stopped to eat and now Abigail was prompting her to go on. "Hannah and Lucy had a falling-out right before we got here, and Cain finally got the story out of Hannah."

"Babe, you're killing me."

"Lucy wanted Hannah to bug Cain's office, and if she didn't, they couldn't be friends. The kid told Hannah that if she wouldn't go along with it, she'd have to go back to bad people."

"What does that mean?" No matter what, above all else, Abigail loved children. It's what made her a good at her job, and why their three little humans were so great.

"That's what I've been trying to figure out." She turned her laptop so Abigail could see the various rooms of the house. "Lucy, Drew, and Taylor Kennison disappeared after Hannah's confession."

"You said Drew works in the oil field, so he could've been transferred."

"True," she said and tapped the square for the kitchen. The feed cut to only that spot and showed a man and a woman fixing sandwiches. "The problem is, the Kennison family is fictional, and these are agents Barry Knight and Christina Brewer."

"That's the Kennison couple?" Abigail put her fork down as reality dawned. "Please tell me one of them has a kid named Lucy."

"Lucy, I think, was prophetic in what she'd said. She went back to bad people, and in this case that means the system." She didn't have a lot of leads, but the clue of Mississippi narrowed her very large scope.

"I'd ask you to lie and tell me you're kidding, but that's horrible." The way Abigail pushed her plate away and sat back made her want to comfort her, but sometimes Abigail did better on her own. "What Nicola did was horrible, but the one blessing I hang on to was there'd been no children involved that I know of. That a federal agent would exploit the most vulnerable in our society is almost worse."

"I agree, and it's driving me crazy that I can't find her." Her problem was that Barry Knight had done a masterful job of covering their tracks. If he left any clues, the new player Ronald Chapman had buried them.

"If you give me what you have, I'll find her." Abigail sounded so sure.

"How?"

Abigail kissed her and laughed. "To find what's hidden in a social service web, you need the right treasure hunter. My friend Jane Corri's been working in the system for thirty years and knows where all the skeletons are buried. She's a social worker who calls whenever she needs a medical consult."

"We need to find Lucy, but not tip anyone off that we're looking for her, much less that we found her."

"You can trust her, Fin. The only thing she cares about is the kids."

"Can you make us an appointment?" She needed the kid somewhere safe before they could go to Annabel Hicks.

Abigail made the call, then drove them to the beigest office she'd ever been in, but the dull color couldn't hide the big emotion running through the place. The kids trapped here made her plan to consult with Muriel for more than the adoption. Her children would never have to face this, even if she had to pay with her life.

"We need a plan in case something happens to us. Our kids need to go to someone who'll love them and keep them safe."

Abigail squeezed her hand and leaned against her. "Thank God we found you, Fin."

"And I better be invited to the wedding," a woman said from behind them. To Fin she looked like she'd just come from Woodstock and didn't get a chance to take the flowers out of her hair before coming to work. "You got good taste, Dr. Abigail."

"Jane, meet Finley Abbott, my fiancée."

Fin coughed when Jane hugged her like someone told her she was choking and the Heimlich maneuver was necessary. "Come on, Finley. Let's go to the one place in here that doesn't scream depression as a paint color." Jane's cubicle was like being inside a rainbow, so she was right about that. "What can I do for you?"

"I need to find a kid." She gave Jane part of the story, as Abigail nodded, and hoped this wasn't a mistake. Tipping off the agents would drive them out of their reach.

"Stop frowning," Jane said. "We just met, but you look smart enough to know there's ways of doing things that's under the radar. Let's see where the initial inquiry gets us. If this child was shipped to Mississippi, there had to be a relative willing to take her involved. We wouldn't have sent her otherwise."

"Our problem is, we don't know her last name." Finding someone by only the first name was like finding a man named John in the United States and expecting to find a specific one.

Jane typed for a few minutes, glancing at the information she'd provided. "There's one Lucy in the system, but she's fifteen living with a family in New Orleans East."

"I already found that Lucy and checked to make sure it hadn't been entered wrong to throw us off." If Lucy was a foster kid, the operation the agents were running had buried her so deep, they'd never be able to prove what they'd done. That's what they were probably hoping for, but she'd keep digging until she found her. This was a dead end. "Thanks anyway."

"Lord, girl," Jane said with heat. "You give up that easy?" She typed in more information and scrolled through what she'd found. "We deal with kids put into the system from neglect, abuse, or the death of a parent. Those true orphans are rare, and our goal for the others is to have the parents get their shit together so they can take the kids back."

"When it comes to this kid, I have no clue. If my family hadn't met her, I'd testify Lucy isn't real."

"She might not be if you didn't have access to the backup files. The state implemented a strict policy after we were hacked, so let's go back to where Lucy Kennison first showed up." Jane put in a good date range based on what Cain and Emma had told her. "Here," Jane said, pointing to the screen.

Lucy Antill was put into the system when her mother was sentenced to life for killing her pimp. There was no father listed, which made sense, and the mother had listed no other relatives, so her one-year-old became a ward of the state. She'd been bounced from a few homes until the Kennison couple took over her care. To get that much information took five different searches, since as of four months ago she'd been erased from the system.

"Someone with higher clearance than me deleted her out, but I doubt she's dead," Jane said as she tapped her monitor.

"They replaced her in the system—at least her name." That was smart. It was like hiding someone in plain sight. You just had to know where to look, and the only way to do that was knowing the system like Jane did. "You can compare what happened to Lucy to being put into the witness protection program."

"True, and lucky for you there were only thirteen females in the age range you're looking into, and only three of those were moved out of our jurisdiction." Jane printed what she was looking at and handed it over. "Those three are in Mississippi, and all of their records were altered in the system." Jane typed something else and stared at the screen. "That's really bizarre since it's not standard procedure for us."

"Depends on why it was done, and how many times it's been done." Jane cut through the frustration she'd been battling for weeks as far as finding Lucy, but not why Lucy was involved at all. Well, she knew why, but it was still hard to wrap her head around. "Do you mind me hiding your search?"

"Trust her, Jane," Abigail said. "You don't want these people coming after you."

She went through Jane's system and wiped out what she'd found. "Do you mind me hunting for one more thing?"

"If it's another child, no," Jane said, moving as if to take her chair back.

"I wouldn't take advantage like that, but you've made me curious about who would've done this. Moving children so they can't be found easily isn't standard procedure either, I'm guessing."

Jane hesitated but nodded. She and Abigail talked while she worked as fast as she could. The location wasn't as private as she'd like since Jane was in a cubicle that looked like a psychedelic ice cream cone. One name seemed to have driven what happened with the three different cases. What some midlevel supervisor was doing manipulating records was worth following up on.

"Who's Lawrence Alexander?" she asked, going back to her original seat.

"He's our boss, but his office is by the courthouse. Larry's a closet pervert if you ask anyone, and you never want to meet with him alone, but he's never been reprimanded. It's like he's bulletproof." Jane lowered her voice, but Fin could tell she was pissed. "His office has been charged with digitizing all the records, so he's got free rein."

"Thank you," she said, and Abigail took her hand. "We were never here, and leave Alexander to me." She returned Jane's hug before they left, and her FBI brain was humming.

"What?" Abigail placed her hand over hers when they got in the vehicle she'd borrowed from the garage at the house. "You're too quiet."

"Do you find it odd that Alexander was able to disappear three kids? I mean, no one asked any questions."

"That we know of. What's going to happen to Jane if she starts?"

Perhaps she was jaded because of what she had done for the bureau, but children no one was going to miss were the easiest to exploit. "Call her and tell her to leave it alone. It might be my brain skittering off to one of the dark holes I know exist, but if it's what I think, she doesn't want to draw attention to herself."

Abigail did as she asked, and Jane didn't ask too many questions. "Do you think Lucy's endangered?"

"With some luck we'll find her by tonight." She started the car and drove to the house. "Thanks for introducing me to Jane, but I have a bad feeling about this."

"The kids she calls me about are horrible cases. I can help them heal from the physical wounds, but Jane and the counselors on staff help them with the nightmares." Abigail leaned across the console and kissed her cheek. "Trafficking children is something I'll never understand."

"We'll check it out, and it starts with that supervisor. I'll ask Cain—she might already know something about him." Her cousin skirted plenty of rules, but exploiting women, much less children, was never going to be on the tally against her. "If he's done what I think he has, he's going to pray for a fast death."

❖

The sling the orthopedist ordered Muriel to wear was a pain in the ass, but the ache in her shoulder and abdomen was something out of a horror movie. Her hospital stay had put her way behind, and now that she was home, Kristen didn't let her work too much.

"You just got up, so you can't be in a bad mood already." Kristen handed her a cup of coffee when she walked into the kitchen. Her fiancée had been at the hospital the whole time and had moved in after she'd come home to assure herself she was following the doctor's orders. "You're brooding—I can tell."

"This pain in my side makes me want to start drinking at dawn," she said, taking a sip of the dark brew, and accepted a mild painkiller. "I owe you an apology."

"For what?" Kristen buttered a bagel and put that in front of her. Neither of them ate much in the morning, but Kristen wouldn't allow the pill unless she had something. "If it's the age thing again, I should warn you that Remi gave me a gun."

She had to laugh. Kristen's sense of humor was firmly rooted in sarcasm. "I asked you to marry me."

"You had the ring and everything, so if you've changed your mind, remember I'm armed."

"No, I just thought we'd be celebrating that, and all you've been doing is playing nursemaid." She wanted to stop talking, knowing her personality when she didn't feel well, but she couldn't stop herself.

"It's a good thing you're so cute because I could strangle you sometimes. Marriage, Counselor, isn't always romance and flowers. I hate to break it to you, but getting shot is someone else's fault." Kristen stood between her legs and kissed her like she was trying to prove something. "You aren't going to take care of me if I'm sick or hurt?"

"Of course I am, and ignore my bad mood. It's the pain talking."

She shared the bagel with Kristen and walked her to the car. "Be careful and don't freak out if you call later and I'm not here. I'm going to the hospital for a staff meeting."

"Do you want me to go with you?"

The news of Cain being shot surprised them, and she'd panicked when Emma had called her. She came close to ignoring her order to stay home, but Lou and Katlin had convinced her to stay put. They were under attack, and they didn't need to be such enticing targets until they figured it all out. From Merrick's cryptic call that morning, there might be something new to shed light on the who of all this.

"Go to school, love, and I'll come over later and meet you. All the cousins will be there, so I think this will be all about business." She loved Kristen and trusted her, but there were things she wanted to shield her from.

"You'll be careful, right?" Kristen fixed the strap of the sling and flattened her hand over Muriel's heart. "I love taking care of you, but you're almost healed and I'd like to keep you from getting any new holes."

"That's a given."

She had to laugh a half hour later when she followed Katlin to the maternity ward. It hadn't been that long since they'd been here because of Billy. "This has to be more comfortable than the ICU." They'd put Cain in the same birthing suite Emma had been in, and it was like a nice hotel room. "When are you due?"

"How are you feeling, comedian?" Cain held her hand up and waved her closer.

"I'm like one big ache, but Kristen keeps telling me I'm getting better." She laughed, thinking about Kristen's hovering. "She gets mad at me when I mention the age gap, but the last couple of weeks should be good practice for when I'm old and gumming my food."

"We might have something to make you feel better," Emma said as Lou closed the door and set up a large jammer.

"I'm more worried about Cain and what all this means." Her shooting wasn't something she understood in a general sense. She was important to Cain, but killing her would only bring the pain from losing a family member. The business would go on.

"Like you, I'll be good once this damn thing gets better," Cain said. "What we need is to figure out who did this and why. We are in a war we didn't know we were fighting until these two idiots came close to killing both of us."

"The guys in lockup are Russian," Katlin said.

"Does that mean Nicola?" Emma asked.

When Cain had let Emma back into her life, she'd let her all the way back in. She hid nothing from her wife, and Emma sat in on these meetings when she had plenty to worry about. The threat Finley had brought with her had them all worried. Nicola wanted her children back, and she'd kill them one at a time to get them.

"You'd think so, but there are more Russians in the world than the Antakovs," Cain said.

"So not Nicola?" Muriel asked.

"If it was, she's more desperate than I thought." Cain was always thinking like a chess grand master in a world full of checkers players. "I met her a few times, and she was a different kind of asshole."

Emma threaded her fingers with Cain's. "What do you mean by that?"

"Nicola thought of herself as the top of the food chain. Her family were the czars of whatever city they were in, and she crushed whoever went against any of them. She wouldn't do this because she'll want me to see it coming. That means burying a knife in my chest while telling me what's going to happen to my family."

"That's quite literal," Muriel said.

"What happened to us isn't something she'd do."

Emma seemed to be thinking the same thing she had on her mind. Certainty without proof would bring chaos. "Are you sure about that? I trust your gut, honey, but in some cases a duck is just that, if it quacks and swims."

"There are some Russians in jail, and I'd like them to be on Nicola's payroll, but I don't think they are." Cain glanced around the room. "If they are, then this will be easily finished because they're going to tell us where she is. They're going to do that to make the pain stop."

"Good, and until then, I'll meet with Remi about security. Nicola's looking for an opening, and wherever that comes, she'll take it." She wanted to prove to everyone her shooting hadn't slowed her down.

"I'll take care of that," Lou said, and he left with Katlin and Merrick.

"Muriel," Cain said, pointing to the closest chair. "Emma's got a story to tell you."

Emma told her what happened and how they landed here, out of all the wards in the hospital. Muriel shook her head as she listened to the threats this guy had made in front of witnesses. All Emma cared about was Hayden. Cain had let him work out some of his frustrations, and she doubted someone like Matt Joseph would let it go.

"Is this a guy with a crush?" Muriel tried her best to remember everything since she couldn't take notes. Once they were done, she'd have to meet with her associate Sanders, considering he'd already talked to Joseph and the hospital administrator.

"Not quite," Finley said and showed her the pictures of Joseph and Agent Gardner together. "We've been watching the watchers, and found the Kennison couple."

"Lucy's parents?"

"Actually, they're agents," Finley said, and she should've known. How Cain was always right should be annoying, but it really was a blessing.

"What'd they do with Lucy?" She knew the answer wasn't going to be good.

"Abigail gave me a lead, so I sent Neil and some of the guys to check it out. We might have another issue, though."

"We're trying to clear our plate, Fin, not add to it." She made Cain and Emma laugh, but hell if she was ready for a string of normal days.

"I know that, but we met with someone who works for Children and Family Services, and she brought this guy to my attention." She took the file Fin had put together and skimmed it. "Lawrence Alexander isn't following the rules when it comes to these kids. He's erased three of them from the system so far."

"Is Lucy one of those three?" Emma asked.

"Yes, but she's not like the other two, who are both fifteen. Lucy might've been a favor to the agents working with Gardner."

Cain skimmed the file as well and made a face. "Does the state not do any background checks before they put someone like Lawrence in charge of children?" The question of Cain knowing this guy was answered, but she didn't know why she was so pissed.

"Have we run across this guy?" She has no memory of him.

"Do you remember the place Bracato opened to compete with Brandi?" She tried not to think of the horror show that was. "He went by Larry back then, but I never forget a slimy face. How well does Abigail know this woman Jane?"

"Sounds like they've known each other for a while," Fin said. "She gets in touch when she needs a doctor for one of the kids, but I take it that doesn't happen too often."

"Do you think there's a problem with this woman?" She'd been wanting to come back to work, but this right out of the gate was going to suck up all her time.

Cain put her hand on Emma's back and didn't give anything away by her expression. "Fin, can you get more information?"

"I erased Jane's research from the system and gave myself a back door in." Fin's answer made Cain smile.

"To answer your question," Cain said to her, "it's going to take what Fin can find. What I can guess is that this is a puzzle that's missing some pieces. We have some of the players, though, and I'm going to do whatever we can to make them choke on all of this."

"So how do you want to deal with it?" There were rules the family followed, and Cain never let Muriel get her hands dirty. She was the attorney and always aboveboard.

"What's your suggestion?" Emma asked Cain.

"We serve Matt Joseph and the hospital with legal action for what happened to you. We'll go hard after Joseph," Cain said, and there was no humor in the order. "That bitch Gardner did this to get a rise out of me."

She could tell how angry Cain was from the use of the curse word. "You're serving them, so that's kind of a rise."

"More of a mobster rise, cousin. She's drowning in shit right now, and trapping me is her best way out."

"And you know this how?" She stared at Cain to see what she was missing.

"You know that house across the street?" Katlin said.

That a small group of agents set up in one of their houses was, in a word, hilarious, but there were laws against recording people without their knowledge. It was pure luck that Cain knew their game plan, and how they'd capitalized on the attempt on Cain's life. All they needed was a way to take the information they gathered and use it in the arena she controlled.

"Do you have a video of what happened in the ICU?" She watched what Fin cued up and was as angry as Cain and Emma when it was done. "Don't talk to anyone from the hospital—I know you won't, but we need to flip Joseph. We're going to do that by going after everything he owns, including his license."

"That's what I was thinking," Cain said and winked. "Fin, I need you to dig into Larry and Jane, but find Lucy first."

"Why Jane?" Fin asked.

"Because she could use the excuse of not knowing what happened to those kids before today," Muriel said and Cain nodded. "Now she does, and three kids have been disappeared. If she's legit, she's working right now to find them."

"Exactly," Cain said. "Right now, what I am most looking forward to is posting bail for two comrades sitting in jail. If this tube comes out soon, I'll need a short field trip while I'm still checked in here."

"I'll coordinate with Lou, Katlin, and Dino to put something together." Muriel stood and hugged Emma before taking Cain's hand. "This is some wild shit, but we have your back."

"I know that, and it's what sets us apart. These guys line up for the glory."

Muriel squeezed Cain's hand and glanced up at Fin when she moved closer. "We do it for family. Clan."

CHAPTER FOURTEEN

Two days later, Dr. Mark Summers visited Cain and removed the chest tube. "The damn thing hurt more coming out than the bullet did going in." Cain grimaced as Mark placed a bandage and seemed to smile at the grumbling.

"If you're good, I'll send you home in four days or so," Mark said as he checked the bullet wound. "I want to make sure your lung doesn't collapse again. Trust me when I say you want this fully healed before you leave."

"She'll be the perfect patient," Emma said as she pinched Cain's hand.

They chatted for a bit, and Mark gave her the good news that her wound was healing, and the lung repair should hold. He promised to stop by in the morning, and to give him a call if she needed him before then.

The room Sam had put them in was perfect, since it was the last one down the hall and closest to the stairwell. "Can you tell the nurses to give us a whole night of sleep?" Emma asked. The way Emma had stepped up and taken care of her as well, as what was happening around them, made Cain sure her wife would be fine if something really did happen to her. Emma didn't want to hear it, but this proved even she wasn't completely bulletproof, but Hayden would have Emma to mentor him if she was no longer around. "I want Cain to get some rest."

"I'll put in an order to give you a break until the shift change in the morning. If she's in pain or struggling in any way, just call and they'll come," he said, shaking Emma's hand then hers. "See you both tomorrow."

The phone rang when they were alone, and Emma answered.

"Hold on." She handed the phone over as she got a bag out of the small closet.

"Yes," Cain said, and Deputy Sheriff Brandon Hebert started talking.

"The ponies are running tonight, and I'm looking forward to the action," Brandon said, talking about one of his favorite subjects. "Sounds like the field will be crowded, but your favorite horses will be in the action."

"That'll be a nice outing. Have fun, and remember to leave some aside for rent," she said, laughing as she swung her legs over the side of the bed. The pain in her side was still acute, and her energy level was nil, but she couldn't put this off any longer. "Sorry I'll miss it."

"See you around." Brandon was a smart guy with a bad habit, but in this case he'd start with a clean slate.

Coordinating the young attorney who got the two Russians bail in night court was a helpful move on his part. The two geniuses in lockup would run as soon as they got out, but she had Shaun waiting to give them a ride. Her shooters would be joining the two guys from Florida he and Sabana had shaken loose. There'd be a bonus for Sabana and Shaun as well as the backup Vinny had sent to help them out.

"Are you sure it's a good idea for you to leave?" Emma stood between her legs and combed her hair back. "I don't want to take any chances with you, and you heard what Mark said."

"We need answers, lass." She stood up and came close to moaning when the pain in her chest ratcheted up enough to double her over if she gave in to it. "Damn," she said pressing her hand to the wound.

"Sit down," Emma said, helping her. "You're not in any condition to go anywhere."

"I'd like the satisfaction of shooting at least one of these guys," she said and laughed. That only made the pain worse.

"How about this?" Emma held her as she lay back, then got in after her so Emma could put her head on the shoulder of Cain's uninjured side. "Let Remi take care of this one for you. She was with you the night you met with the Antakov couple, which puts her family in as much danger as we are when it comes to Nicola. Maybe that's why they went after Muriel and Kristen."

"I never thought of that," she said, being truthful. All she could think about was Muriel and if she'd make it. She didn't think she could stay completely sane if she lost any more family. "That's an interesting thought."

"We'll never be sure unless we ask," Emma said, rubbing circles on her abdomen. "So how about your aunt comes tonight and sits with you, and I go with Remi."

"Lass," she said, not wanting to shoot Emma down, but needing to shoot Emma down. "These types of meetings—"

"I know what the agenda is, honey. If you remember, I lost my mind once because of one of those meetings, and it wasn't even the type I'd like to attend tonight." Emma sat up so they could face each other. "There are questions I'd like answered so this doesn't happen again. These idiots shot you and came close to stealing what I need to live." She pressed her hand over Cain's heart. "Do you understand that? I'm not going to run back to my mother if Remi or one of our people puts bullets in their foreheads, mobster. We need answers, and I can get them for us."

"Things like this change you, lass. I won't have you suffering from nightmares if I can help it." Her job was to protect Emma and the family, not send them to do things that were her responsibility. Right now, though, she couldn't protect them from Nicola if she mounted an attack. "I love you and would never do that to you."

"Derby Cain Casey, I am your wife—your partner—your lover. You made vows when you put this ring on my finger and swore to me we were equals." Emma appeared pissed. "Have I ever done anything like this? No, but I faced that moron Bracato when he took our son. You were in the hospital like you are now, and I would've shot him without remorse if he'd hurt our family."

"I know that, and you did things perfectly, but this will be different. To get someone to talk takes more than punching them in the face." She had no idea how Emma would handle Remi and her very special cigar cutter that took off fingers faster than a meat cleaver.

"Let me go, and if it gets to be too much, I'll wait in the car and let Remi take care of it. I'll have Lou and Merrick with me, and you know neither of them will let anything happen to me."

"Okay, but promise me you'll leave if you need to." She reached up and cupped Emma's cheek. "It's not that I doubt you, lassie, but I'd like to keep you away from things like this. You're my salvation because your heart and soul are pure, and I'd damn myself to hell before I changed that about you."

"Don't worry, and my job is to take care of you—this is the best way to do that right now. Once you're back on your feet and healed, you can take that job back and burn the world to the ground if that's what it takes to keep us safe." Emma leaned down and kissed her. "I love that you're strong, noble, and mine. You always have been, but I need to do this for us."

"Call Lou in, and we'll make some plans."

"Are you upset I want to do this?" Emma took her hand and appeared not as sure of herself as she had been.

"Lass, you are the person I trust most in this life. You go, and don't take anything from anyone."

Nicola woke with a start after taking a pill for the headache that'd made her vomit, it was so violent. It was dark outside, but New York City never really slept. She stood at the window that overlooked Fifth Avenue. The iconic facade of The Plaza was lit up in the early evening, and the park was right beyond that. This was one of her favorite spots in the world, and she'd enjoyed sitting with her father while she healed from the plane crash, talking about whatever came to mind.

They'd discussed so many things, and made plans for how they'd move forward so she could take the reins from him when the time came. Her mother didn't know she and Fredrick had survived, but her father had complained about her constant demands to do something to get her custody of the children. Valerie'd had a warped memory when it came to her talent in parenting. She wanted to raise Nicola's children, but when it had been her and Fredrick, Valerie hadn't been as interested.

Her phone rang, and she stared at the view, not wanting to talk to anyone. It stopped and started ringing again immediately. The only person she could think would do that was Fredrick, so she walked to the main room where she'd left her cell. "Fredrick," she said when she pressed redial.

"You didn't call," Fredrick said, and now that he wasn't right in front of her, she found him annoying. "Did the people I called show up?"

"They did, and they're out trying to find a window to get to Sacha." She pinched the middle of her brow as the residual pain still made it uncomfortable to concentrate. "From what they told me the business is growing, but Sacha's still far behind."

"Be careful. He's still a butcher, and he's already taken a shot at you. I don't want anything happening to you." Fredrick was breathing harder than usual, and she had a twinge of guilt. "I'll see you soon, I hope. The files from the studio arrived, so I'll be busy with that."

"Take care, and make sure the guards stay vigilant." She sat and closed her eyes. "I don't think this will take more than a couple of days. Call me if you see anything out of the ordinary."

"You do the same."

She dropped her arms to the side and took a few deep breaths, opening her eyes when she heard the door open and close quietly. Her gun was in the bedroom, but she wasn't worried when she watched Svetlana navigate closer in the dark. There were guards next door and one right outside, so Svetlana had gone to her own place while they were in the city. She wondered where the woman who was so eager to jump into bed with her had gone because Svetlana showed no interest in her now.

"We've put people in all the places Sacha likes to go, and we haven't found him yet. The word on the street is he's not in the city, and actually out of the country."

She pointed to the chair across from her, tired of talking to Svetlana while she stood. "Where did he go?"

"The bartender at the Russian club in the Meatpacking District said he's in Moscow trying to reestablish the pipeline of girls Fredrick set up for the Hell Fire Club. That means he's most likely going to revive that part of the business."

"No shit," she said, louder than she should've because of her head. "The bartender at that club is a bauble who's bought by the highest bidder." Of course Svetlana would tip her cousin off the first chance she got.

"He's dead and in the river. After he spilled his guts, we got our money back and put a bullet in his head instead. If you'd like to do something else until Sacha returns, I'll have our people start on it, whenever you're ready."

"I have a headache," she said with no intention of apologizing.

"You should relax and get some sleep. I'll see you in the morning." Svetlana turned and walked out before Nicola could say anything else. She could order her back, but her patience was nonexistent tonight, so sleep won out. It didn't surprise her that Sacha was trying to copy what they'd done. The man had never had an original thought because he was one step above a simpleton.

Her phone rang again, and she didn't recognize the number. "Hello," she said, not needing another problem to deal with.

"Where are you?" Kira asked.

"Not in Miami." Why Kira thought she deserved answers from her was a question she didn't have time to answer. "What do you want?"

"I need you to deal with something for me."

She chuckled softly to not jar her head. "I thought you and Ivan had everything under control."

"Nicola, remember that there'll be a day when the only thing that'll keep you and Fredrick alive will be your family. Since every member of your father's family is dead, aside from you and your brother, that leaves us." Kira didn't sound angry, but her words enraged her. "Forget about the meeting with Papa—we don't need you. All I was trying to do was honor something my sister wanted."

"Are you threatening me?" she screamed, despite her headache. Kira had already hung up, and the silence only made her angrier. Her fingers shook as she called Fredrick, and he sounded as if she'd woken him from a deep sleep.

"What's wrong?" he asked, groggy and disoriented.

"Call everyone we have and get them to the house. I'm coming back." She stood and had to take a moment when she came close to falling back. The damn headaches were more than just pain and nausea. They also made her dizzy, and all those symptoms together made it hard to function.

"Wait, tell me what's going on." Fredrick sounded totally awake now, and it allowed her to rein in her emotions.

"Kira just called me," she said and explained what they'd talked about. "You need to put as much security in place as you can find."

"Come back if you want, but I'll be fine. Ivan isn't the smartest man we've dealt with, but he's our grandfather. There's no way he moves against us." What Fredrick was saying sounded so reasonable, but he'd lost not only the ability to walk in their crash. He'd lost his cunning and the talent to see danger when it was right in front of him.

Ivan was their grandfather, but the man was also cruel and easily offended. People like that were petty by nature, and that pettiness led them down roads that there was no coming back from. There was that, and the fact that Kira had seen Fredrick. Given the wheelchair, the women he surrounded himself with, and his weakness, ending him would be seen as doing both him and her a favor. Kira would kill what she'd seen as a tumor on their family tree.

"Fredrick, listen to what I'm saying. Call for more security even if we close the club until I get back. Don't take any chances, and you can tell me I'm overreacting when I see you again."

Fredrick laughed, and she wanted to scream. "Nicky, finish what you started there. I've been here since that damn plane went down, and I've been okay. Hardly anyone knows where this place is, and the people who do will never move against us." He paused and there was something he wasn't saying. That was new.

"Tell me."

"My lot in life was always to back you up to keep our family strong. That has always been my honor, but when this happened to us and I came out of that plane this broken hideous thing, I lost that spot in your life." He took a deep breath, and she wanted to cry for the first time since their father had been killed.

"You're my brother, Fredrick, and that will always be your job. Not having the ability to walk or be strong doesn't matter to me." She sat and took some deep breaths herself.

"Face it," Fredrick said, sounding so resigned. "The responsibility of the family is yours now. I'll never not help you, but my role will be different. You need to finish what you started and then come back. Don't use me as an excuse to not kill the people who've moved against us."

"Sacha isn't here, so there's no reason to stay." She wanted to go, but would going make Fredrick think her weak?

"Then move against some of his people. Come on, Nicky, think. If you kill and disrupt his business, that'll draw him back sooner."

She had to laugh. She was wrong. He might have lost his legs, but his mind was still sharp. "I blame the headache I'm having today."

"Good," Fredrick said. "I'll be fine, so call me in a few days. Larissa's coming tomorrow to talk about the studio expansion, and I'm going to start training her on how to add to our numbers. It's a lesson Sacha never learned."

"Have a good night and I'll be in touch." She hung up and sighed before she stood and started stripping to go to bed. It'd been forever since she'd had the urge to have sex, which was something she'd have to take care of soon. The sooner she got back to normal, the faster she could get back in the mindset she'd need going forward.

"Fuck," she said softly as she tried to get comfortable. A visit to the club in Miami would have to take care of that because she was moving Svetlana to a new role. Her attitude tonight wasn't something she was going to put up with, and if Nicola let it go on, it'd only get worse.

"You'll be lucky if you don't end up with Nina—only this time it won't be Casey putting the bullet in your head."

CHAPTER FIFTEEN

Emma sat with Cain the next afternoon as the kids told them about school and everything happening with the activities they were involved in. She had to laugh at how riveted Cain was when Hannah explained all the things she'd done in soccer. To Emma it looked like chaos as twenty little kids ran from one end of the field to the other with or without the ball, but it bled Hannah of some of her excess energy. For that alone she was in love with soccer.

"Mom, I ran faster than everybody," Hannah said, pumping her arms to add to her story. "Can you come to my game next week?"

"If I'm home, I promise I'll try my best to be there. I want to see you run, and I'm sure your mama would love that too. She's your biggest fan after me." Cain sat in one of the recliners in the room and had her arm round Hannah's back so she wouldn't fall off the arm. "Have you been good for your grandparents?"

"Abuela made us waffles this morning, and Liam got syrup in his hair." That made Hannah laugh and clap her hands. This kid was someone who could make her wife smile like no one else.

"Come on, funny girl," Emma said, picking Hannah up. "It's Mom's bedtime. She needs the sleep if she's going to watch soccer next week. First your game and then Hayden's."

"Can we come back tomorrow?" Hannah asked, and Hayden took her from Emma. "Hay and me can bring a game we can play."

"You bring the Go Fish cards, and we'll play for cookies," Cain said, and Hannah did a happy dance in Hayden's arms.

"She's really good, so you'd better get more than one pack of cookies," Hayden said as they both kissed Cain good night. "Do you want anything, Mom?"

"Just for you guys to be safe, so listen to your mama, and I'll see you tomorrow." Cain stood and put her arms around Hayden so she could whisper in his ear. Whatever she said, Hayden nodded and smiled. "And you," she said to Emma.

"What about me?" she asked and smiled.

"Remember everything I told you." Cain held her like she wanted to keep her in the room. "There's no problem in coming back."

"You take a nap, and I'll be fine." She kissed Cain and pressed her hand to Cain's cheek. They looked at each other and said so much more in their silence than they ever could with words. "I love you, and I'll see you in a little bit. If you nap, I promise I'll bring you a snack later."

She took the kids home and put them to bed as Finley and her brother Neil prepared to leave with a few guys. They were all headed out to meet Remi, and hopefully after tonight they would have enough answers to make headway. Lou was waiting for her in the yard, and she took his arm to the gate and the path Cain used when she wanted to leave without a tail. The car they stopped at, parked a block away, wasn't like anything they had in the garage behind them. It was small, rusted in more than one spot, had a dented front bumper, and overall appeared tired, as if a car could actually feel exhaustion.

"It belongs to a car dealership from the Westbank, and we'll have it back before they miss it," Lou said and laughed. She was surprised the groan of the passenger side door opening didn't get their neighbors to come to their windows. "Two hundred bucks and it's all yours."

They didn't talk much as they drove in a random pattern for thirty minutes until Lou was convinced they weren't being followed. That's when he pulled into a parking lot, and they changed vehicles to one driven by Simon, with Remi in the back seat. The four-door truck had tinted windows and a few stickers on the back windshield, so it must've been something else they'd borrowed.

"Has Finley found anything on these guys aside from that they're Russian?" Remi asked as Simon started driving.

"You're not going to try to talk me into not going?" She'd been proud of Cain and how she'd held back saying anything else about this.

Remi laughed and shook her head. "I believe you and Dallas have plenty in common. It'd be easier to French-kiss a lioness than to change your mind about something you really want to do." She laughed at that because it was true. "I'm glad you decided to do this because I think these guys are expecting a wounded Cain, and not her wife. They'll see that as insulting, so it might speed this up a little but the end isn't going to change. Taking a shot at Cain sealed their fate."

"I'm still so angry they did this, but Cain is convinced they don't work for Nicola. When we're done tonight, I'd like to know if that's true or not. If she's right, I'm not sure what that means." They drove across the river and into one of the low-income housing complexes that'd been abandoned to make room for the much nicer single-family homes that now sat close by. Remi told her the place they were entering was set for demolition in a year. That was good because there was no one in screaming distance, which was perfect for what they had in mind.

The apartment they entered had a dining table with six chairs, and none of them matched. Not that it was important, but it was the first thing she noticed after glancing at the four large men, each tied to their own unique seat. They were gagged, but they seemed to stare at each other as if trying to send some kind of message, or maybe to give each other courage for what they were facing.

"Which two came from central lockup?" Remi asked. Those were the men who'd shot Cain. All of them appeared imposing, but none of them wore what she'd call the face of evil, but to her that's exactly what they represented.

Katlin stood behind the two on the right side and placed her hands on their shoulders. "Right here, and over there"—she pointed to the other two—"are the two who gave the order."

"Then we don't really need these two, do we?" Remi sat and crossed her legs so she could tap on the heel of her boot. She did that as all the men widened their eyes and tried their best to get the gags off. "Simon," she said, and her guard moved the man closest to her and farthest away from Emma.

Emma watched as Lou joined Simon. They held the man's hand on the table, and Simon pulled a switchblade out of her pocket. In one swift move, she pinned the guy's hand to the table, and it wasn't hard to hear the scream that was muffed by the gag. Remi nodded, and Lou held the guy's other hand in place, and it didn't matter when the guy made a fist to prevent Simon from repeating her actions when Lou handed over his knife. The man who'd been in the car with him was in the same position, and if they thought it was over, Remi put down another two knives.

She thought it'd be harder, watching something that was basically horrific—it wasn't, though. These men took an order from the other two, and they'd come close to gutting the life she had. They didn't know them, had probably never met Cain, but they'd done it because these other two men told them to. Now she knew what vengeance looked like, and it wasn't enough. For once she wanted these people dead, but it wasn't her place to ask for that.

Maybe her mother was right, and she'd changed something fundamental about herself. She'd been taught in all those Sunday school classes every week that it wasn't her job to judge anyone no matter their sin. It was best left up to God, but right now that wasn't good enough. She not only wanted to judge, but to find them guilty and mete out punishment.

"Do you know who this is?" Remi pointed at Emma, and they all turned to face her. "This is Cain Casey's wife. You shot her a few days ago, and I know you're going to tell me it was only business. Someone paid you to do that, so you did."

Simon released the gag of the oldest man who was one of the pair who'd given the order. The man said to Remi, "You've given a thousand of those orders, so don't fucking act like you're innocent." The accent was Russian, but he didn't sound sarcastic.

"I have," Remi said, taking a cigar out of the leather case with her initials along the top, Emma knew, because Remi had given Cain one just like it and also kept it full of the smokes Cain liked to indulge in every so often. Cain had warned her that this wasn't the usual cigar case Remi kept in her pocket. "What I've never done, though, is order something like this in front of a school. Not where children were present, and certainly not in front of someone's child. *You did that*," Remi screamed, pointing at the two men sweating, they seemed to be in so much pain, as blood bloomed on the table around their hands, but there was no pulling those knives out. "Cain and Emma's daughter has nightmares because of you."

"I didn't ask them to do that," the man said. "Casey is just well-guarded, so they took the shot when they had the opportunity."

"What are the deaths of a few children, including my own? Right?" she asked. "Their lives aren't important because you had a job to do."

"Mrs. Casey," the man said—only now he did sound a bit condescending. "Your partner understands the dangers of the world we live in. Yet she brought children into the world."

"Do you have children, you bastard?" She wanted to ask Remi for another knife so she could drive it into this guy's chest.

"I have a son, but he will never know this life. You should've thought of that before you brought little bastards into the world."

"Lou," she said, and the big man nodded. "His wallet, please." Lou handed it over, and she started taking things out of it. His license, money, and credit cards all fell to the ground as she tossed them away. Men who had sons were often very proud of them, and there was always proof. "You have a *junior*, how very manly of you."

"You'll never find him, so don't bother trying to threaten me," Rurik said, it was the name on the license. "The truth is women never can be as ruthless as men, so the job is never finished."

"Junior is in a condo on Miami Beach with the prostitute who gave birth to him," Shaun said. "I left four men on the building before we brought you two assholes back, so not only do we know where he is, Mrs. Casey is going to treat him with the same respect you have her family."

"Look," Rurik said, still sounding somewhat in control, but the panic was starting to bleed through. Cain told her there came a moment in these meetings that at times had nothing to do with bullets, knives, or anything else she thought to punish someone with. If it'd ever be her tied to a chair, she'd give them whatever they wanted to keep her and the children from harm, and Rurik seemed no different. "I was doing a job, and I'm sorry Casey got killed, but it's no reason to kill an innocent child."

"I'm glad you have such morals when it comes to your own child and not mine," she said. "So I'm going to let Cain decide what I do with you."

"Casey's dead," Rurik said with such finality.

"Cain's in the hospital taking a nap. You endangered all those children in front of that school for nothing. You didn't kill her or anyone else, thank God." She tapped the edge of the picture on the table and smiled at him. "The difference between us, aside from the obvious, is that we're Caseys. Our clan has a rich history, and when we do a job, it's finished. There is no rising from the dead to haunt us, so the truth is you will die a painful death here, and your son will die with his mother in a nice condo on the beach."

"What do you want?" Rurik asked, and the guy next to him shook his head and moaned through his gag.

"Lou," Remi said, and Lou held the gagged man's hand flat on the table while Simon gagged Rurik and undid the other guy's. "Let's see how much you don't want to talk." The cigar cutter sliced through the cigar with ease, and Remi sat forward after lighting it. "My mother's family grew tobacco in Cuba and made cigars. They were so good, my father still talks about them, and he taught me all I needed to know about the vice. A good cutter is key."

"Your threats aren't very scary," the guy said and laughed.

"I'm not threatening you," Remi said and laughed with him. "That would be a waste of both our time, but I am making small talk about cigar cutters." She grabbed his hand and pried his index finger straight. With little effort, the cutter went through it above the knuckle, and his finger was lying on the table.

The sight reminded Emma of the toys the kids had during Halloween. It was lifeless and didn't look real at first, but the scream the guy let out shook her from that notion. Remi pried his middle finger next, and the begging began. That didn't work when it dropped next to the lump on the table. Rurik started straining against the ropes tethering him to the chair, but that was of no use as well.

"You have eight more chances to tell me who hired you, and then we'll have to get more inventive about what I lop off next." Remi put the guy's thumb in the cutter and snipped. "Make that seven."

"We can't tell you what we don't know," the guy said.

"Simon, does he have a wallet on him?" Emma asked. She went through the same process of dropping all the useless things, finding no pictures. "How about a phone?" Simon held it in front of the man's face and unlocked the latest model iPhone. There were dozens of pictures of a woman with two little boys enjoying their day on the beach. From the date stamp, that day was less than a week ago. "Shaun, do we know where Makari lives?"

"Small house in Coral Gables," Shaun said, as if he'd memorized everything about these guys.

"Peel two guys off Rurik's place and send them over there. Tell them no survivors."

"What? No…wait," Makari said, sounding more pained by her order than from what Remi had done to him. "You can't do that."

"I can and I will. Remember, you ordered the same for my family." She turned the phone so he could see the picture she'd been staring at. "Here is where the saying *karma's a bitch* should mean something to you. When you throw bad things into the universe, sometimes the universe takes the lives of your whole family as punishment."

"We don't know who hired us," Makari said, crying.

Emma scrolled down and found a few more pictures of a young man and an older woman. "Your family?" She didn't need an answer when he cried harder. "When I'm done, your family, the entirety of it, will not exist. No one will be left to mourn for them because of what you've done. Is your boss worth that kind of loyalty? Do you think if she was in the same position, she wouldn't give you up in a second to save herself?"

"Kira," Makari screamed. "Call them back and leave my family alone, and I'll tell you."

The name was as foreign to her as all of this, and Remi glanced at her as if in question. She shook her head and went into the phone's settings to take the locks off. They'd need to mine it for all the information it could give them.

"Kira?" she asked. "Don't stop now. Shaun, how much time?"

"The guys can be there in forty minutes. I had them check it out when Sabana and I were on our way back, so this won't be a hard job."

"The clock is ticking, and when you're in hell, you can think of how you could've saved your little girl. Can you bear the weight of all that regret?" She tapped the phone against her palm and shrugged before glancing at her watch. "Trust me, Makari, you're going to tell us everything you know if only to make the pain stop."

"You talk big for a woman," he said and inhaled deeply as if to control his tears. "Have you ever killed anyone?"

"To be honest, no," she said, glancing at Remi. Makari's ring finger joined the others, and he screamed again, straining against Lou to try to free his hand. He'd have better luck chewing through his ropes. "That's Cain's job, and she's good at it. She's also less forgiving than I am, so when she's done, trust me, your next family reunion will not be necessary. Getting shot is something she's planned for, but someone pointing a gun that could harm our daughter is never going to be forgiven."

"Traffic wasn't that bad, so they're down the street," Shaun said. "Do you want them to go?"

"I don't know," Emma said. "Do you want them to go, Makari?"

"I told you, *Kira.*"

"There's so much more, so don't say I didn't give you fair warning. Once they're done, Shaun, send in the guys for Rurik's family. I have to get back to Cain." She saw Remi glance at her and smile. Who knew she had a talent for threats?

"Wait," Makari said. "Kira Volkov is who hired us. We work for her and her father, and they wanted Casey dead."

"Okay," she said, still confused. "Who the hell is Kira Volkov?"

Simon removed Rurik's gag and he coughed and spit on the floor. "She's Valerie Antakov's sister. You should remember her since Casey killed her and her husband."

"It's the family who keeps on giving," Remi said as she removed her gun. "So this is nothing more than revenge?"

"Yes," Rurik said.

"No," Makari added. "Do you promise to spare my family?"

"Rurik, did you think this was a good time to lie?" Emma asked, and Simon put a bullet in his knee. "Put the gag back." The screaming was unnerving. "Makari, this is your last chance. My wife tells me there's only so much pain the body can take before the heart gives out."

"Kill me, then." Makari watched as Rurik twisted in the chair as if he was trying to move to keep from passing out.

"Trust me, that's coming." Remi tapped the cutter on the table and slipped Makari's pinkie into the hole. "You can handle a little bit of pain, but what happens when we sit with your wife and your daughter? The one thing we've gotten good at is making it last. There's plenty of ways to keep them conscious until we get tired of inflicting what you were going to do to the Casey family."

"My daughter's nine," Makari screamed.

"Mine is five, and yet you opened fire where she was walking," Emma screamed back. "If you don't give a crap about my family, I'll give even less about yours. No, you'll get a bullet to the head, and you leave your family to take your punishment for you even if I have to do it myself."

"Kira wanted Casey dead because her family is moving into the South. From everything Valerie told her, Casey runs the city, and killing her without heirs old enough to take over gives them the freedom to do whatever they want here." Makari had snot running down his nose, and Rurik was nodding. "This place is easy."

"Why?" Remi asked.

"Of the top four families, two are run by women, and there's already a high-end place Kira has in mind." Makari stared at Emma, and she could guess what was going through his mind. It was either killing her if he had the chance, or what was going to happen to his family.

"I almost believe you," she said, and Remi nodded. "Now tell me who shot my wife."

"Him," he said, nodding his head in the direction of the guy on the right.

Before she could say anything, Lou pulled his gun and shot the guy in the head. The splatter of brain and blood behind him made her take a deep breath to keep from being violently ill, but she wasn't sorry.

Lou loved Cain, and it was mutual. They'd come up together, and what he'd just done was his way of making up for what he'd seen as his mistake. Cain had gotten shot on his watch, and she knew how upset it had made him.

While she was trying to recover from the horror of what she'd seen, the man next to the dead guy was struggling so much he'd knocked himself over. "Sit him back up." She pointed at Shaun and one of Remi's guys.

"I agree with Mrs. Casey that you're telling the truth. But not all of it," Remi said, snicking the cutter open and closed a few times. "Do you have anything to add? Before you say anything, remember what Mrs. Casey said about your family. Lie now, and you won't live to see what happens to your daughter."

"That's all I know. We work for the Volkov family, and that's all Kira told me. If her father, Ivan, has something else in mind, I don't know what it is." Makari stared at her. "If you have a soul, you will not only leave them alone, but you'll warn them. Kira is an animal, and our failure will have to be paid for. If you don't kill my family, she will."

"We'll check what you said, and I can promise you I'll keep my word if you lied. My wife lives by a code—she won't move against you if you leave her in peace. Break that peace and she's relentless."

"Simon," Remi said and held her hand out to Emma, "you and Lou finish here."

"Thank you." Emma stood and put her hand through Remi's bent elbow. "Lou, I'll wait for you at home." He nodded, and she saw the weight he'd been carrying had visibly fallen off his shoulders.

"Wait," Makari said, his voice carrying through the room. "I beg you to save my family."

"That is up to you and what you said. I'm taking you at your word, so whatever happens, it's on your head. I'll leave here and sleep fine that you and your men are dead." She walked out with Remi after that, not needing to see what came next, but glad at least this part was done.

❖

"Tell me why I should believe you." Sacha Oblonsky stared at the phone, wondering what kind of game this was. He was the undisputed head of the family now, and he owed the success he'd achieved in part to Cain Casey. The woman was straightforward in asking for what she wanted and laid out what needed to be done. He was the one who'd insisted on doing it himself, and he'd failed. Nicola was alive somewhere, waiting and planning.

She might've been injured but she was still the same snake Yury had raised, so he'd been vigilant, awaiting her next move. He'd had two of his best men do the hit, and all they managed to do was kill the valet. They'd paid for that by guarding trailers in empty parking lots out in Jersey. He'd had Nicola in his sights and missed, and it made him want to kick his own ass he hadn't taken Casey up on her offer to do the job for him.

"You're related to Nicola, so you should know how she treats people. I'm tired of constantly being bitched at. If you want me to work for you, I will, but if you don't, I'll move on."

He recognized Svetlana's voice since she'd been the bitch who'd killed the old man who'd taken care of him coming up. She'd gifted him an ice chest with his friend's head inside and smiled while doing it. The only reason she was still alive was because his guards had also gotten killed at a meeting where Nicola had promised protection. He'd learned that not only did Nicola's word mean nothing, but she was also full of shit. That went for everyone who worked for her, so this sudden change of heart was something not to be trusted.

"Where are you?" He motioned for his man, Vadik, and put the phone on speaker.

"I'm in New York, but I'm not telling you anything until we meet." Svetlana sounded angry and, for the hour, very alert.

"Take a cab and go to the bar on Eighth and wait."

"Kill me if you want, I wouldn't blame you. I know how hard the loss of your man was."

He grunted. His mother was Yury's sister, and once Yury'd made it to the top, the only favor he'd gifted her was giving Sacha a job as a grunt. The day he'd found out Yury and Valerie had been shot, he'd laughed. Yury had always come off as a man who was not only untouchable, but someone to be feared. Whoever put a thousand bullets in him obviously hadn't gotten that memo.

"Just get a cab, and we'll see what to do with you," he ordered and hung up. "Get someone over there and pick her up and throw her in the trunk so we can have a talk. Bring her to the trailer at the warehouse, so she can get an idea of what her future holds if she tries to fuck me."

"Do you think this is Nicola?" Vadik asked. He was with Sacha every day and was the son of a man who'd lost his life to Nicola's vindictiveness. If anyone was ready to kill his cousin with as much pain as he could manage, it was Vadik.

He nodded but slowly. "I'm not sure, but I'm not falling for any shit. Whoever you send, make sure they aren't followed."

Once he was alone, he pulled out his wallet and took out the card Cain had given him. He'd never used it and doubted it would be Cain who answered, but she'd gotten him in this, and he wanted her help to stay in control of the family. Nicola hated Cain, but he'd liked her right off, and she'd convinced him killing Nicola was the right move.

"Hello, may I help you?" Whoever the man was who answered had a deep voice, but it was soft.

"I need to talk to Cain Casey," he said, wondering how he was going to reach her with a New York City area code.

"Can we use this number?" the man asked.

"Yeah, and if it could be in the next hour or so that'd be great." Sacha hung up and rubbed his face with both hands. He'd hoped Nicola had run off to die somewhere less humiliating than in front of a restaurant in a town she owned. It startled him when the phone rang before he stood to leave. "Hello."

"Sacha, how are you?"

He laughed, recognizing the voice and the slight humor it always held. "Cain, it's been too long. It seems our problem is still alive and making interesting moves." The city was laid out before him, but he hadn't been able to enjoy the success he'd made after taking the reins. Looking over his shoulder wasn't something he wanted to do for the rest of his life.

"Did something happen?" Cain asked and told him where she was calling from. "Two guys took shots at me in front of my daughter's school. Our friends in the police department tell me they're Russian. Have you heard any chatter on your end?"

"I just got a call from the guard closest to Nicola. She wants to meet and come to work for me because my cousin's a bitch." He and Cain wanted different things out of life, so he told her about what had happened to his protector at the hands of Svetlana. "We all give orders, but that one cut deep."

"I understand that kind of pain. On my end, I don't think it was her. I don't know who these guys work for, and I could be wrong, but in my gut, I don't think that's who ordered this." Cain paused and coughed a bit. "If her guard is calling you, I'd be wary. I'm not telling you what to do, but if it were me, I wouldn't trust blindly."

"I'm going to meet with this skinny bitch, and I'll let you know how it goes." He hung up and took one last glance out the window of his apartment that overlooked the park on one side and the city from the balcony. There was no way in hell he was giving this up. Nicola was going to have to pry it away, and he wasn't an easy target.

The trailer in one of his warehouses was getting cleaned since these places started smelling like cesspools after a month. He'd inherited this nightmare from Fredrick, and he was letting it run its course, but not adding women. Yury always bragged about how much money they brought in, but it wasn't enough to put up with the constant misery of replacing girls who'd rather die than work there.

There was a lot more cash in opioids and places like the Hell Fire Club if you offered not only beautiful escorts but gambling. Angelo Giordano, the head of the East Coast mob, wasn't thrilled with the gambling part, but they'd come to an agreement eventually. Hell, if Nicola wanted to come back and run the trailer operation, he'd let her have it. There was no way she'd make any headway back into power with only that.

He was sitting at the small table where the security guys set up and waited. The headlights of a car cut through the dark outside, and he placed his gun right in front of him. When the door opened, he had to stop himself from reaching for it and shooting Svetlana before she said anything. He pointed to the empty chair and shrugged.

"It's your show, start talking."

"It's good to see you, Sacha," Svetlana said, and she showed courage by uttering those words. "I know you hate me, but I'm tired of doing Nicola's bidding. The truth is, I want out, but out to try to find something closer to home. You may not like me, but you know me, and that means if I pledge my loyalties to you, I'm going to be loyal to only you."

"Where is she?" He wasn't interested in the pretty words coming out of that beautiful mouth. "Let's start there."

"Miami," Svetlana said with no hesitation. "She and Fredrick are planning to start over there. You know that's where Yury sent Fredrick before the accident."

He put his hand up, and she stopped. "Fredrick is alive?" He sounded like a punk asking that, but damn. Yury might've been a piece of shit, but he knew how to keep his secrets.

"He's not well and is in a wheelchair, but he's alive," Svetlana said. She described how he was living, and that Sacha could believe.

Fredrick might've been part of the royal Antakov family, but the little fucker was nothing more than a pervert. "They have another club there, and he's moving the main studio to Miami."

"You're full of information, but why are you really doing this?" How they went forward rested on how she answered that question.

"Tonight, Nicola planned to find you and kill you. When I told her you weren't in town, she dismissed me like trash. I've killed for her, taken care of her when she was shot, and put up with Fredrick's strange habits." Svetlana got louder with each thing on her list. "All that, and she still doesn't respect me."

"My problem is I don't trust you," he said and placed his hand on his gun. "I have no idea if you're telling me the truth, so we're going to try to build a bridge between us. If you're not lying, then I give you a job, and if you are, I'm going to send you back to my cousin like she gave my friend back to me."

"What do you need to know?"

"Write down the address, and we'll start there. If you lead me to Fredrick, eventually Nicola will follow."

He left three of his men with her and locked them all in. If Svetlana was still working for Nicola, she'd never be found, and there was no way to get a message out. She'd die if she tried to do that. The address Svetlana wrote down was in Miami, and according to her it was on the beach. If Fredrick was really alive, he was alone because his sister cared more about revenge than she did the only true family she had left.

"Vadik," he said into his phone. To stay under the radar, he'd come alone. "Get us a plane for Miami. I feel like a vacation. Call our crew leaders and tell them I want a meeting tonight before we go. Put a team together of about five, and be ready to leave in about two hours if you can find something."

With a plan in his head, he was ready to make a move and take charge of it this time. "Can you call Cain back and tell her I need another call. Right now if she can swing it."

"Sacha, what happened?" Cain asked, not bothering with any greeting, which was fine with him.

"Fredrick is alive," he said, still not believing it.

"I thought that might be a possibility," Cain said and stopped as if she was thinking. "What are you going to do?"

"I'm going to check out Svetlana's story, and if he survived the crash, he won't survive me. If he's dead, that might draw Nicola out."

"Good, but can you do me a favor?" she asked and told him what she wanted.

He wasn't sure why, but it seemed reasonable, so he agreed. "Can they move tonight?"

"They'll beat you there and check out what you're walking into. Thank you, Sacha, and when this is done, I'll be happy to arrange a meeting between you and Angelo. I'm not making any promises, but there doesn't need to be any more bloodshed."

"Feel better, and I'll wait on your people." He laughed, looking forward to this. "You have my number even if I don't have yours."

CHAPTER SIXTEEN

Cain hung up and stared out the window. It was dark outside, and she was starting to think of ways to leave the hospital and find Emma. There were dumb mistakes, and then there were real fuckups, and sending Emma with Remi fell into the latter category. Her job was to shield Emma from things like this, and she'd sent her right into the teeth of it.

"You can stop worrying," Katlin said. "When I met Emma, I could tell she was the woman you needed because she'd never be afraid to stand up to you. Maybe there was a time when she was—afraid, I mean—but that time is over. Whatever happened tonight, you'll talk her through it without making her feel weak."

"She was never supposed to be in that situation, cousin. She's not like Merrick." She hated to say that, but in her heart she knew it was true.

"No, she isn't. Emma's her own woman, your woman, and tonight she proved that to you better than when she stood pregnant with your son and promised herself to you." Katlin looked at her and smiled. "She's yours, cousin, but not only for a time. She's yours forever, and her love for you is fierce."

"That is true," Emma said from the door. She was dressed in yoga pants and a loose shirt as if she was ready to go to bed. "You can relax that worry line in the middle of your forehead—I'm fine." Katlin stepped out as Emma walked to the bed, and Cain opened her arms when she lay down. It felt like a blessing when Emma pressed against her and kissed the side of her neck.

"I'm sorry for agreeing to let you do that," she said, and her throat closed from emotion. For once in her life she was so weak she was useless. It had nothing to do with the bullets that hit her or the fact she could barely walk to the door. No, she'd opened Emma to the uglier side of their life, and there was no erasing it now.

"Listen to me." Emma rose on her elbow and gazed down on her. "Do you remember the vows you said to me?"

"Every word," she said, her tears dropping into her ears.

"Then live up to them. You're my partner, my wife, my lover, and most importantly, mine. You are mine, and your promise to me was a long and happy life. The first step of that was to live, and you've done that. My promise to you from the beginning of us was to always take care of you and the family we share. That's all tonight was about."

She nodded, but her heart could only see the shadow across Emma's face. The shadow that she'd seen only once when she'd stepped out of a room after beating her cousin Danny Baxter until he was bloody. That night had cost her Emma, the birth of their daughter, and years of misery. It wasn't something she wanted to repeat in her lifetime.

"Honey," Emma said, pressing her hand to her cheek. "I'm not going anywhere." The vow made it seem like Emma understood what she was thinking. "The only way I leave is in death, there's no more running in me no matter what happens." She pressed down, and Cain didn't care about the pain in her chest. "Not ever again, and I need you to believe that."

"I never wanted this for you." That confession cost her a bit of her pride. "Tonight was my job."

"Tonight was me standing in for you, and finding out if this threat at least is behind us. Lou made sure of that, so don't give him any grief about it." Emma kissed her and threaded her fingers through her hair. "I'm not going to lie and say it wasn't horrific, because it was, but it was also cathartic. The man who shot you paid with the most valuable thing he had, and that was his life. Does it make me a bad person that I'm glad?"

"Would it make me a bad person if I tell you I wished it was me pulling the trigger?" She held Emma against her and listened to Katlin's advice. "All you need to know is what you saw isn't the norm of our lives. Remi, Lou, Simon, and the others were doing a job none of us relishes. The other thing is—I love you for going."

"I think Lou got what you wanted when it came to making the guy pay. He seemed less stressed, and we did get some answers." Emma touched her face in a way that made her heart rate slow, and she smiled. "You're hurt, and in here, but you were right."

"About what?" She combed Emma's hair and slid her hand down to her neck.

"It wasn't Nicola. A guy with a bunch of missing fingers told me so," Emma said and shuddered. "I'll never look at you smoking a cigar the same way for a long time to come."

"Are you okay to tell me what you found out?" She didn't want to push, but some of this stuff needed resolution so she could work her way back to peace.

"Shaun and Sabana were watching a club on the beach that was a Russian hangout. A lot of those guys are tourists, but last week some of the regulars seemed like people who were connected to someone." Emma lay back down and put her hand on Cain's chest. "They took their chance and brought two of the guys back. After dropping plenty of money on the bartender, Shaun and Sabana learned that the two they snatched were the ones who ordered the hit on you."

"Did the money they spent get us any information on Nicola?" How many Russians living in Florida could be after them?

"We need to call Finley and see if she has something in her files."

Cain shook her head. "Let's wait until tomorrow for that since she's running an errand for us."

"I'm not going to make you wait that long. The two guys in charge work for Kira Volkov. He didn't give me anything except the fact that Volkov is Valerie Eaton's maiden name. Kira's her sister."

"So this was revenge from another angle?"

Emma moved her hand from Cain's chest down to her thigh. "I don't think so. From what Makari told us, Kira and her father are expanding into New Orleans because there was an easy in."

Cain was about to ask what that was when the door opened, and she smiled at the owner of the Red Door, Brandi Parish, standing there with a bouquet of flowers. "I doubt she's that easy, but she's got good taste in flowers."

Emma sat up and finger combed her hair. Her expression wasn't one Cain saw often, and it made her smile but not as much as Brandi. "Look at you," Brandi said and winked at her. "Damaged but still handsome as hell."

"Emma, this is Brandi Parrish," Cain said, squeezing the side of Emma's hip. "Brandi, my wife, Emma."

"Nice to meet you." Emma stood and held out her hand. "Cain's told me so much about you."

"I bet she has, but she's unfortunately only a good friend.

Good enough that she's kept me safe when it's not really in her job description." Brandi held Emma's hand for a moment before handing over the flowers. "These are for you, Mrs. Casey. Married to Cain and three kids makes you superwoman."

"Please, it's Emma, and they're all a joy when they're not driving me crazy." Emma placed the vase on the windowsill and went back to sit with Cain on the bed. "Have you been okay?"

Emma asked because the easy way in for Kira and her family led through Brandi's red door. "Any problems at the house?" Cain followed up.

"Sounds like both of you are expecting there to be problems." Brandi took the chair and crossed her legs. Her dress was designer and the heels were impressive. She'd always found Brandi beautiful, but she'd never been interested. "Remember what I said, Cain. I don't do well acting as bait."

"If I only found out a minute ago, you can't blame me for not telling you yet." She opened her hand when Emma took it. "We have Russian problems in common, and that means the guys will stay as long as they're not in the way."

"Why do these people think they can come in here and we'll roll over?"

"Because it's easier to steal than to put in the work yourself," Emma said. "I hope you take Cain up on her offer. From what she's told me, you've saved a lot of girls from fates I don't want to think about, so please let her take care of you and your people."

"She was right about you too. You're a remarkable woman wrapped in a very beautiful package," Brandi said with a large smile.

"I don't think I put it quite like that, but she's right." Cain laughed when Emma pinched her. "So you haven't heard anything? You're usually the one with all the gossip."

"It's called *tea* now, stud, and I have nothing to spill. I'm here because Wilson heard you got hurt, and I wanted to make sure you were okay." Brandi wasn't one for too much sentimentally, but they'd known each other a long time, so she believed in the concern she was showing. "Do you know who this person is that's trying to make a move?"

"Not yet, but you know how much I like to be the welcoming committee. Keep your eyes open, and tell Wilson I'd like to talk to him whenever he gets a chance. Remember the name Kira Volkov, at least the family name. That's all I have for now."

"What about the club near Emma's? Madame Laveau's is still

operational, and someone has to be behind it." Brandi also knew how best to cut out the competition, but she must have read the expression on Cain's face when she shook her finger at her. "I'm not advocating for a fire sale, Cain, but if they come recruiting like when the Hell Fire Club was open, I'm going to lose people. If it's for a better life, I'm all for it, but not for animals like that."

"I am advocating for a fire sale," Emma said. "That place is too close for my comfort, and I want it gone."

"What's the one thing I always preach?" Cain asked, and Emma pinched the top of her hand again.

"Patience," Emma said when Brandi appeared confused.

"Exactly. Neither of you can think I've forgotten about those places and what they're about, but I like doing my homework before I ruffle my feathers a bit." Her burner phone rang, and she glanced at the number before answering. Finley was someone she definitely wanted to talk to, only without an audience.

"Brandi, how about some bad coffee?" Emma asked.

"I'd love some." Brandi stood and came to kiss her on the cheek. "Don't forget about me and my people."

"You know that's impossible, and I'll be in touch." She glanced at Emma and gave her a grateful smile. "Well?" she asked when the door closed. When Fin started talking fast, she knew it'd be an interesting story. Her cousin had been the same since they were little kids. "Tell me."

❖

Finley stood in the woods in rural Mississippi behind the big house that appeared to predate the Civil War and stared at the back porch they'd been watching since the sun went down. The thick woods where they were seemed to go on for miles in three directions, and whoever owned it had very few neighbors. That was strange since the front yard was now full of cars like the party inside was too good to pass up. They'd left one of their guys in the front in case there were any surprises.

"What's your plan?" Neil asked. Her brother was more of a doer than a sit-and-watch kind of guy, but this was going to take some finesse. From what they'd seen that afternoon, Lucy wasn't the only kid in the house, and she didn't want to think about what was going on in there. If there was a way to go in guns blazing and not hurt any of the children, they'd have been on the road by now.

Most of the cars belonged to older white men who'd worked on their beer bellies diligently for years. This was either a GOP rally or something out of a horror movie. "My plan should be arriving in a few minutes." Her phone buzzed, and she walked farther away from the house before she answered it. Sound carried in places like this, and she wanted the element of surprise.

Russell Welch was the supervising agent she'd worked under for three years while she was in New York, and he'd been a good friend as well as her mentor. He'd partnered her with Peter Stanley, and their jobs had been mostly surveillance. Russell had finally let her out of the van to go undercover in the police precinct where they'd traced some communications from Yury Antakov, and that had been the best thing to happen to her. If she'd stayed behind the scenes, she'd have never met Abigail.

"Abbott, where the fuck am I?" Russell said, and she could tell he was in a car.

"Deep in the heart of Dixie, sir. Once you get a load of this place, you'll see what I mean." She stopped talking when a guy with a shotgun stepped outside and scanned the woods. "Hold on," she whispered. The headlights from a police cruiser lit up the area where they were standing, so they took cover behind the trees. Dino was with them, and the kid was resourceful.

"What's happening? We're still ten minutes out," Peter said.

"They let you out of the van, or did you escape?" She peeked her head out a little and watched shotgun guy hand the deputy a thick envelope of cash.

"Give a report before Russell has a coronary," Peter said, laughing.

"Run the plate—Tango, Alfa, Lima," she said, followed by three numbers. "If you have the roads covered in both directions when they get to the state highway, pull the deputy over and make a withdrawal. Don't worry, he can watch it on candid camera." She glanced at her watch and noticed four more cars pull in. "Tell me you guys are close. This is getting hinky."

"Is the deputy still there?" Russell asked.

"He's chatting with the armed guy at the back, so watch it when you arrive. How many units did you bring?"

"Enough that we'll make the national news," Russell said. "You know how good I look in the windbreaker with the big yellow letters."

"We're turning in, Fin, so keep your head down and cover the back," Peter said. "If they shoot and you shoot back, remember that you were never here." Peter gave that reminder because Russell officially couldn't.

"Did anyone from the local office join you?" she asked, curious if Annabel wanted in on this action if Russell had clued her in.

"We have a team from Gulfport backing us up, but it's our operation," Russell said. "What do you want me to do with the kid if she's in there?"

"Clear her through social services here so she can head back to New Orleans. Abigail has a therapist lined up and a foster family who's willing to adopt if Lucy is interested in that." She saw the deputy turn his head and swing his door open when the line of SUVs turned into the property. The jammers that would make his radio or any cellphone service stop working around the perimeter of the property were on, so he wasn't getting the message out. It also dropped her call with Russell and Peter, but they'd expected it.

"Remember," she said to Dino and Neil, "aim for the feet. We don't want to shoot anyone unless they shoot at us. You brought the ammunition I told you, right?"

"Yes, so stop being such a downer and enjoy this," Neil said as the screaming began.

The last thing she expected was about twenty naked women to run out the back, but the line of fire they put down sent them screaming in the opposite direction. Neil lined up his shot and hit the engine block of the one car that came out of the garage, and that's who she was interested in the most. The guy Cain had mentioned, Larry from child protective services in New Orleans, was responsible for Lucy getting here, but rounding up the people he'd handed her off to would help Russell in the ongoing investigation he led on human trafficking.

It took over an hour to get everyone handcuffed and processed before Russell took a walk in the yard. He headed where she'd told him to, and he wiped his brow when he reached the woods. The sun going down had done little to curb the heat, but the breeze was at least keeping the mosquitos down. He lit a cigarette and inhaled deeply. "I'm not sure how you found this place, but damn."

"Was it what I thought?" In a way she'd wanted to waste everyone's time, to discover that the big old house was a place where

Lucy was happy and loved, but humanity sucked sometimes. At least parts of it.

"The deputy you saw taking the money is actually the sheriff. This is the Hell Fire Club on a more Bubba kind of scale. There's twenty-five women in there, and most of them are undocumented." Russell sounded disgusted, which was his norm for these types of operations. Even after years on the job, he'd never gotten jaded. "The kid Lucy and three others were in there too, but in a room they built in the attic. My guess is they were keeping them here and grooming them, but no sign of trauma other the obvious of being in there at all."

Her knees were weak after hearing that. Cain had told her about the sweet kid who only wanted someone to love her, and Hannah had filled that need. "Thanks, Russell." He nodded, and she waved Neil forward. "I don't believe you've ever met my brother, Neil."

The two men shook hands, and Russell glanced at her. They'd met in New York a month ago, and she'd told him she wasn't coming back no matter what a mistake he thought she was making. She'd also told him who her new job was with, and who Cain was to her. After threatening to arrest her, he'd listened to reason, since her old partner at the NYPD had been found tortured and killed.

"Nice to meet you," Neil said and pointed in the direction Dino had gone. They'd parked on a fire access dirt road about a mile away. "We'll swing by the front and pick you up."

"You can't deny your training, Abbott. Damn fine work, and the door's always open if you change your mind. Thought you might want to know we picked up Brock Howard after your tip and a few months of surveillance. That guy was dirty, so thanks for your help." He kept taking drags of his smoke until he crushed it under his shoe and picked up the butt. "How are Abigail and the kids?"

"A little freaked that Cain got shot in front of the girls' school Hannah and Victoria attend. It happened right after Cain had dropped them off, so I need to find that bitch Nicola."

"I heard about Casey, and that they have two Russians in custody. She still in the hospital?"

"She'll be there for the next week or so. My kid is scared and doesn't understand why someone would do that, so no lectures please." She put her hands up, wanting to stop another round of how she was throwing away her life. "Abigail and I are getting married, so I don't want your life any longer. I want to be home with them, and Cain gives me that."

"She might also give you jail time."

She had to laugh at that. "Come on, boss. My cousin isn't the boogeyman everyone makes her out to be. The government gets plenty from her in tax payments, and she owns a slew of business that aren't this. The important thing is they'll *never* be this."

He put his hands up too. "I know, and I've read her rather extensive file, so there's nothing like this in her past. You also know I care about what happens to you, so come on. The social worker we brought with us should be done with her assessment by now."

It wasn't hard to pick out Lucy when she saw the line of little girls on the porch. Like Cain said, she was small for her age, and she appeared terrified. Cain had anticipated that one as well, so she went over and crouched in front of her, so they'd be at eye level. "Hey Lucy, my name is Finley." The little girl was shaking and silent. "Do you know we have a friend in common?"

Lucy's eyes met hers but only for a moment. "Who?"

"Do you remember Hannah?" That got a positive reaction when Lucy nodded and smiled. "She and my daughter Victoria are waiting to play with you," she said, taking a chance to hold Lucy's hand. That's all it took for Lucy to fly into her chest and start sobbing as she clung to her neck. "It's okay, sweetheart. You're going home, and you'll never have to leave if you don't want to."

"This place is scary," Lucy said through her tears. "Please don't make me stay here. Take me to Miss Emma and Hannah."

The social worker came forward and handed over the papers she'd need to place Lucy as soon as they got back. It had taken some effort, but she'd put everything in place so all she'd have to do was drop Lucy off, and it was a done deal. She hadn't involved Jane or Lawrence, so tonight would go off without a hitch.

"Thank you, Russell, and I'll call so we can debrief in New Orleans. I owe you and Pete a meal and a few drinks."

"Damn straight, Abbott, now get the hell out of here and let me deal with this scum."

Neil drove up, and she headed for the car, not wanting anyone to identify her or Lucy. "Let's go home," she said as Lucy didn't let go of her hand after she'd strapped her into the booster seat. All she had left was to make the call her cousin was waiting on. "Cain," she said and couldn't talk fast enough.

CHAPTER SEVENTEEN

The sun started to rise in Miami, and Sacha sat in the car to admire the orange sky. Nicola and Fredrick's house was in a quiet neighborhood, the kind with tall fences and manicured lawns. The men he'd brought with him had made their way from the beach and were clearing the way for him to drive through the front. All of them looked like early morning joggers who enjoyed running along the sand.

"Whenever you're ready, boss."

He started the car and drove slowly from the parking area a mile away and made it through the now open gate. Every camera outside had a bullet through it, and he took a breath before stepping out. Life gave you a few chances to cement your fate, and this was one of those times.

One of his men opened the door, and he stepped over the two dead men in the foyer. They'd been trying to make a run for the front and died cowards, he guessed. "Which room?"

"The last one down the hall to the left." The man pointed and made a shushing motion with his hand when the women he'd gathered up wouldn't stop crying.

"You always were the little freak, weren't you, Fredrick," he said when he noticed not one of the women wore a stitch of clothing. "Do you want out of here?" he asked the women, and all but one nodded. "Go put something on and wait out here." He pulled the only one who hadn't nodded up by the hair, pushed her down the hall, and had her open the door.

The shotgun blast made the woman fly into the wall behind her and hurtled Fredrick back into the bed. It'd be hilarious if it weren't so pathetic. Fredrick looked like a turtle someone had flipped over and couldn't right himself. He squeezed Fredrick's hand holding the weapon until he let it go, and it fell to his side. All they had to do now was wait to see if anyone else was up and heard it go off.

"What are you doing here, you bastard?" Fredrick said as he struggled to sit up so he could lean against the headboard. The big bed seemed an interesting choice for someone in his condition, but then Sacha thought of all those naked women.

"I came to see you," Sacha said and smiled. "I've missed you, and I'm disappointed you didn't send word that you'd risen from the dead. I would've sent flowers."

"When Nicola finds you, she's going—"

"To what? Kill me?" he said louder. "The bitch can't even keep you safe. She left you all alone here, asshole, and from what I hear, you're in no condition to be left alone. Let's see if those stories are true."

One of his men came in with a large hunting knife, and it was hard to miss the fear that flashed across Fredrick's face when he put it on the bed. The guy sat Fredrick up straighter, close to the side where Sacha had chosen to sit. In the growing light in the room, he could see the damage to Fredrick's body, and it was extensive. How he'd survived was hard to believe, but if it'd been him, Sacha would've rather died in the crash than be this.

"Did you and Nicola sit here and plan how you were going to kill me?" Sacha nodded at his man, and he brought the knife down on Fredrick's foot. Half of it lay on the bed. It was interesting not to hear the scream that should've come with that. "You really can't feel anything, can you?"

"This is beneath even you," Fredrick said. He seemed almost fascinated by seeing a part of himself lying on the bed and the growing bloodstain on the white satin sheets.

"Don't worry, we'll get to the parts you can feel eventually. So tell me," Sacha said, holding his hand out for the knife. He stabbed into the skinny leg closest to him until the blade went all the way through the mattress…and nothing. It was like Fredrick was a talking head and nothing more.

Sacha pulled the sheet covering Fredrick's genitals away and had his man pull the catheter out. It was obvious his dick was as useless as the rest of him. "What the hell were all the women for?" the man Sacha handed the knife back to asked.

"They belong to me, so they had no choice but to come with me when I moved here to heal," Fredrick said. "They love me."

"They do, huh?" Sacha stood and walked around the room, finding the safe behind the large painting on the wall opposite the bed. "The thing about you and your family"—Sacha punched in a series of fifteen numbers—"is you're set in your ways." The safe clicked open. It was the same combination as the safe in Yury's office, and he'd put plenty of money in it when he'd become the top guy after the twins supposedly died in a crash.

"What are you doing?" Fredrick yelled.

The stacks of cash were impressive, and it changed Sacha's mind about how to handle the women in the house. "Bring them in."

"You're going to fucking die for this," Fredrick said when his harem walked in, fully dressed and packed. "You can't run fast or far enough."

"Your choice is stay because of your love for Fredrick, or take your share of the money and go. Where that is I don't give a damn," Sacha said, making equal piles on the bed. It was enough for each of them to start over fresh somewhere else.

The first woman, a brunette with a slim build, surprised him by walking to Fredrick's side and coming close to him. Before Fredrick could gloat, the woman spit in his face and slapped him before taking her stack and walking out. It was repeated by the eight that were left, and Sacha had to laugh at the anger rolling off Fredrick like sweat.

"Tell me where Nicola is, and I'll make this quick."

"Fuck you, and get out of my house." Fredrick turned his head and wiped his face with the sheet.

"Do you really want me to take you a piece at a time and leave you here to rot?" He nodded to his man again, and Fredrick's genitals came off in one clean swipe. There was a scream for that but only because it was his dick and balls in the guy's hand, Sacha guessed.

"Mr. Sacha," a young man with a messenger bag said from the door. "Do you mind if I get started?"

"Go ahead and take your time. Fredrick isn't the smartest boy on the block, so this might take some time." Sacha nodded again, and Fredrick's other foot came off, and the man laid it next to the growing pile of useless body parts.

"Who is that?" Fredrick asked showing no signs of pain.

"Charlie's a computer expert like his late brother, and he's been working on a special gift for you and all your customers." The head of the studio Nicola and Fredrick owned now worked for him, and starting tomorrow, whoever wanted to replace the porn they'd downloaded was going to have to shop the few items he had available. "Once that virus he's putting in your system worms its way through your account list, all those titles are going to disappear like you and your sister, once I find her."

"You can't do that," Fredrick said, appearing stricken for the first time.

"Are you going to glue yourself back together and stop me?" He nodded again, and his man got to work. It took until they were at the upper chest level before they had to gag Fredrick, and he never took it out. He was never going to betray Nicola, no matter how much pain they put him through, so this was more about the men Sacha'd lost to these sons of bitches.

Once Fredrick was dead, his man laid him out on the bed, putting him back together like a macabre dismembered mannequin. His men had gone through the house, including Nicola's room, and boxed over five million in cash, and Charlie had given him the customer base from Fredrick's computer. He'd also handed over the security footage from the hidden cameras in the house, which he asked Charlie to delete.

"Did you drive, kid?" Sacha asked Charlie.

"Yes, sir. I didn't want to hit any radar on my way down here, so I drove all night." Charlie was soft-spoken and wore sadness like a badge of honor.

"What's your story?" Sacha asked, curious how Cain knew this kid.

"My brother was the real genius when it came to all this computer stuff, and my dumb ass went to jail. He's the one who got me out, and then he was killed by Gracelia Luis only because he worked for Cain. I learned all this to honor his memory." Charlie held out his hand and smiled. "Thanks for letting me in."

"Here, for gas money home." He took a stack of cash and handed it over. "And I might call if I need you again, but I'll go through Cain. If we don't ever see each other again, it was good working with you."

Charlie smiled and nodded before putting a baseball cap low on his head. "There's plenty of cameras in this neighborhood, so here's the license plate that came with your rental," he said, handing over a plate. "The one on your car now I changed before you picked up the car. If you change it back at the parking lot you used before, you should be fine, but for security wait until you're closer to the return place. The cell lot two blocks away is having camera issues for the next two days."

"Thanks," he said, impressed by the kid's attention to every little detail.

They cleaned the house and sprayed Fredrick down with enough bleach that it made his eyes burn. There'd be nothing left here for the police to find, but the one thing they would find was that both Fredrick and Nicola hadn't died two years before. Fredrick was dead now, but his sister would now be the subject of a massive manhunt from not only Cain, the feds, and the NYPD, but his entire family.

"Who's the idiot now, Nicola? Enjoy what's left of your life."

Mark Summers stood by the bed and studied the healing wound on Cain's chest before bandaging it again. "I see you have the ability to listen to your wife," Mark said as he typed something into her file. "You're ready to go home, but please take at least a week, preferably two, and try not to overexert yourself, and I'll see you in three days."

"You're still hilarious in your own mind," Cain said, and Emma cleared her throat in what she assumed was a reprimand.

"We'll be there, and she'll be at home for two weeks," Emma said. "She might be hog-tied in the bedroom, but she'll be there."

"Emma, I'm sure Mark doesn't want to know all our secrets." Cain teased her, loving the blush coloring Emma's cheeks and neck. "Thanks for everything, Mark, and there's nothing I can't do from home, so no worries."

"Good, and thanks for the suite tickets to the Saints games last year. My wife and son think you're the greatest." Mark kissed Emma's cheek and held her hand a moment. "If you need any help with Matt Joseph or that ninny Norris, please let me know. You've been the talk of the hospital for days, and the nurses want to wash your car for you since you've gotten rid of that creep."

"Thanks, Mark, and I'm leaving it up to Cain's cousin Muriel." Emma didn't like talking about what happened, but they'd been left alone after the ICU incident. "It's a good thing we're going home today, since I believe Norris, the hospital, and Joseph are being served this morning."

"Take care, you two, and I'll see you in a few days."

Mark left, and there was a knock on the door. Lou had let whoever it was pass, which meant they were okay. She had to laugh when she saw Detective Sept Savoie and her partner in the doorway. They'd seen the news that morning and the bodies found on the levee. She doubted even the best forensics people in the world would pull one clue from any of the four.

"Come to see if I'm dying?" she asked, and Sept shook her head.

"Come on, you ass. I came because my mother's worried sick about you. I'm beginning to think she likes you better than me." Sept came in and hugged Emma before taking her hand. "Are you okay? This isn't our case, but the brass thought you might talk to me since I'm charming and way better looking than you."

"No wonder your mother likes me better. I'm less delusional." She held her hand up to Nathan Blackman and smiled. "I can't remember if you've met Emma, my wife. Emma, Detective Nathan Blackman."

"It's been hectic since I partnered with Sept, but it's nice to meet you." Nathan had an angelic look about him.

"I apologize in advance since you're about to curse me out, but I have to talk to you about four dead guys a dockworker found this morning." Sept sat and took out her notebook. "Three days ago, the two men accused of the shooting that put you in here were released on bail. Did you know who they were?"

"I did hear you guys made an arrest," Cain said, not elaborating.

"Actually, the feds made the arrest and turned them over. They had American passports, fake of course, but they were Russian." Sept read off the names Emma had told her, along with everything else they'd said. "Do you know these guys?"

"I know plenty of people, old friend, but not one is Russian." She never lost eye contact with Sept, wanting her to believe what she was saying. It wasn't a lie per se, since she didn't really know Nicola or anyone in her family. They'd met once but they didn't know each other. "I'm not sure what this was about, but I can tell you it's upset my family, especially Hannah. Whatever you do, make this one stick. I didn't see them, but if Shelby and company caught them, I'd believe they're guilty."

"They were found today along with two other men, also Russian, dead on a part of the levee with no camera pointed at it. Whoever dumped them knew what they were doing."

She smiled and put her hands up. "You got me, Detective. I snuck out of here and killed four guys and carried them to the levee. I'm shocked no one saw me in my hospital gown. Arrest me."

"You're such a pain in the ass. I'm asking if you know of anyone who would go after these guys." Sept sounded as exasperated as she always did when she had to deal with Cain on a professional level. "Do you have any idea why they'd try to kill you? I assume they were trying to kill you."

"If I knew that, I'd play the lottery. I realize you think I know everything that happens in the city, but I'm stumped on this one. Right now, all I know is that they're Russian, and one of the guys in jail shot me. If I don't have names, how in the world can I know who sent them?" She grimaced when her voice rose, and it pulled at the stitches.

"Okay, take it easy." Sept put her hand on the bed and waited to make sure she could go on. She also gave her the names of the guys in jail, and she had no clue who they were because she'd never heard of Kira Volkov. Nicola and her whole family had a weird sense of things, so there was no telling why this woman would take a shot at her.

"Emma, could you buy the detective here a coffee? I'd like to talk to Sept for a moment." When they were alone, she sighed. "Look, I didn't lie. I really don't know anyone who's Russian, but I do have some people in my house who do."

"This should be good," Sept said, shaking her head.

"Dr. Abigail Eaton was married to Nicola Eaton. While she was in New York a year ago, someone shot her and tried to take her kids. Turns out, Valerie and David Eaton thought they wouldn't win a custody trial, so they tried something different." She explained the relationship between Abigail and Finley and exactly who Finley was. When she was done, Sept fell back in her chair and cocked her head toward the ceiling.

"You have an FBI agent and Nicola Antakov's widow living with you?"

"Finley's my cousin, and don't try to pin anything on her because of me. She went as far from the family as she could to get started in her career. Fin concentrated on sex trafficking and was the one responsible for breaking the Antakov family exploits." There was no reason to share everything about how Fin had broken the Antakov family. "She fell in love with those kids and Abigail, and they've become her life."

"The Eaton couple died here on Poydras Street," Sept said, as if she was reporting on the crime for the news.

"When in the world have you ever pinned me with prostitution and trafficking?" She did think those things were disgusting, so there was no acting when she asked that question. "The Eatons were shot here, but they were really the Antakov couple running a sex club in the city. That's illegal, I'm pretty sure, and if you need my alibi, call Shelby and Joe with the FBI. I was home because they tried to pin that on me too."

"Where was your cousin Finley?"

"Protecting her family in New York. Trust me, Sept. I had nothing to do with any of this. If someone in that family blames me somehow, I'm not sure why. I have nothing against them because I didn't want anything to do with them." She waited and Sept nodded. "Buddy, I can barely walk to the door without losing my breath, and most of my people have been here so no one finishes the job. The rest of them are protecting the family. I didn't survive all this for someone to come along and hurt someone I love."

"Can you at least point me in the right direction?"

"I called you before all this happened because I wanted to tell you about Madame Laveau's. It's a block from Emma's."

"I know that place. Never been there, but from what I heard, it's been hopping." Sept wrote that down and glanced back up at her. "Are you saying to try that place first?"

"It's a sex club in line with the Hell Fire Club. Who owns it and is profiting from it, I don't know, but it's too close to my business, and I know Abigail worries about it." She stopped when Emma came back in with Sept's partner. "Abigail married and had three children with that Nicola woman, but she had no idea who she'd shared a life with. I know it's impossible to believe, but if you talk to her, you'd see I'm telling you the truth."

"I know that, since you would've never let her in the house with your kids if she did know and condoned it."

"She and her children have been trying to put all that behind them since she learned the truth of who Nicola and her family were."

"Thanks, and I'll check it out. Once you're home, call Mom and tell her I'm not harassing you. You have my number, so call me if you need anything." Sept hugged Emma again and held Cain's hand. "I also heard what happened with the first surgeon. If this guy bothers you again, call me and I'll take care of it."

"Keep your head down out there, and make sure Nathan's watching your ass," she said to Sept.

"If he's doing that, trust me, he'll be joining you in here."

Finley came in as Sept was leaving, but the two police officers kept walking. The raid on the house in Mississippi was still unfolding, but so far Fin had only given Cain the broad strokes. There was still a lot of information to be gleaned from the operation, but at least Russell was keeping Finley in the loop. She had that to worry about, as well as what had happened in Miami. It was shocking it hadn't hit the national news yet considering the scene, which could only mean it hadn't been discovered yet. All she could do was wait for Sacha to call.

The nurse walked in with a folder and hesitated until Emma waved her on. "Your discharge papers are finished, Cain, and we wanted to thank you for bringing Billy and the kids so we could see them. You two do beautiful work when it comes to cute babies." The nurse took out her IV and rechecked her bandages so Emma could help her get dressed. It was time to get back to work.

"Lass, give Dallas and Remi a call, and ask if they'd like to come to dinner tonight. There's something I'd like to share with them." If she was right, Charlie White was about to become famous, even if no one would ever know his name. Where his little brother had excelled at security and the occasional hacking job, Charlie was a natural at not only hacking, but the creation of viruses.

"How's Lucy?" Emma asked Finley as she got Cain's pajamas and robe ready. "Don't pout. You wear clothes now and they're going to rub against that wound and you're going to be miserable."

So much for complaining. "How is Lucy?"

"She's looking forward to seeing Hannah again and meeting Victoria. I told her about the kids on the way back, and she shared a little of what's happened to her." Fin stood to the side as Emma threaded her arms through the blue pajama top. "Your choice was perfect."

"Levi Layke might be a great principal at Hannah's school now, but he was a nervous little guy when we were growing up and needed constant propping up. He's made a good life for himself and his partner, Leo. The added bonus is Leo's a therapist specializing in childhood trauma, so both of them are what Lucy needs." She'd talked to Levi and Leo like she had Emma's oldest friends when she'd placed the Bracato baby with them. When people who couldn't have children were given that gift, they became extraordinary parents, and she had no doubt that's what would happen when Lucy joined their family.

"The other thing is Levi will be able to look after her during the day when they're in school," Emma said, as she helped with Cain's slippers as the nurse came in with the wheelchair. "You did good on this one, honey."

"I have my moments."

The day was warm, and it felt good after being inside for so long.

She told Shaun to drive by Hannah's school first so they could pick her up a little early. If she could do anything, it would be to erase those memories from Hannah's mind, and Victoria's as well. From the way they came out and jumped in the back of the large SUV, she hoped they were on their way.

Levi came out with them, and he reached for Cain's hand through the door. "You can't know how happy you've made us, and thank you for easing the way for us to adopt her. Leo thinks a few days at home with him talking things out would be good before she starts school again, but we promise to take good care of her."

"I know you will, and as a favor to me, keep her home until I get rid of any obstacle that might come up for you guys." Levi agreed and squeezed her hand before closing the door for them.

Sadie was next, and finally Hayden and Linda's brothers. It'd be good to be home, but she glanced in the direction of the house across the street. Once she was ready, she'd remind Ronald why he should've stayed gone. "You're about to learn how to play hardball, Ronald."

"Did you say something, mobster?" Emma asked as she helped her inside to the den so she could watch the kids.

"Nothing important." She stared at the house a minute longer, hoping the pit vipers inside could see her. "Nothing important at all."

CHAPTER EIGHTEEN

You'd better fucking fix this," Matt Joseph screamed at Dylan while he paced in her apartment. She'd been sleeping when he started banging on the front door until her neighbors piled out and started shouting at him to stop. "I should've fucking known this was a bad idea."

"What do they think they have on you?" She scrubbed her face with her hands and tried to wake up. The night before, she'd written a letter to Annabel accepting her suspension and asking for a transfer once the three months were up. Getting out of here was the only way she was going to escape Ronald Chapman and whatever the hell he was up to. If she had to leave Matt and his issues to make it a clean break, so be it.

"The administrator said they have a recording of me attacking Emma Casey. I don't know how anyone could think that was an attack, but whatever it is, I'm sure that bitch will spin it into me losing everything I have." Matt gave her the explanation like she'd never met him. Their college days were fun, but Matt had racked up enough offenses to land him in jail, and only his daddy's money had kept him free to attend medical school.

Someone else knocked before she could talk Matt down, and she sighed when she saw Angus Covington on the other side of the peephole. "Fuck," she whispered.

"Open the door, Gardner," Angus said with annoyance. "I need to talk to you."

"What do you want?" She waved him in and glanced around the area outside. There were plenty of parked cars, but nothing jumped out at her as being suspicious. That phone call about her conscience was still in the middle of her brain, preventing her from getting any restful sleep. "I'm not due at work until next week."

"Agent Chapman has been trying to get in touch with you." Angus, as he'd mentioned plenty of times, came from old money like Matt. His purpose at the agency was to climb to the top, then retire to his father's firm with plenty of management experience. Clients with big bank accounts loved being represented by a former agent, like that made any difference. "It's not smart to ignore him."

"Did the house burn down?" She got a glass of water from the tap and finished it before staring Angus down. "Did Casey come across the street and shoot everyone?"

"Wait, who is this?" Angus pointed at Matt like he'd suddenly discovered a human-sized cockroach hovering behind him.

"Dr. Matt Joseph," she said. "We went to college together, and he was helping me with a problem I'm having."

"What kind of problem?" The disbelief on Angus's face was funny as hell, but she didn't feel like talking him down. "Gardner, there's plenty in flux right now, so it's not real smart to bring other people into our orbit at the moment."

"I thought of how to at least hold Casey for a bit, so we can all get what we want, but it didn't work out. We've all tried a lot of things that haven't worked out, so don't give me any shit about it."

"Didn't work out?" Matt said loudly and laughed. It sounded like he wanted to strangle her. "I'm about to lose my job, my license, and everything I've worked for. Do you think I give a shit about your orbit, asshole?"

"Tell me what happened," Angus said and sat down after forcing Matt into a chair.

Matt was animated as he repeated everything he'd told her, but again it sounded like he'd been the victim. She remembered what he'd been like the night he'd gotten in the car with her and had seen Emma Casey. He was interested, and Matt wasn't deterred when it came to a woman saying no. If Casey really had recorded what happened, this would blow up in her face as fast as Matt's career. What she had to figure out now was how to get out of this with as little blowback as possible.

"I'm beginning to see bringing you in on this was a mistake," Angus said, appearing shell-shocked. The rich kid was most probably used to getting his way on everything he did because daddy's money was what paved a smooth path for him. "Casey isn't someone to screw around with—I told you that at the beginning, but as usual, you know more than everyone else."

"Casey isn't anything special, but the way you guys treat her, she's going to become citizen of the century instead of getting indicted for any damn thing." She'd had enough of the softball all these agents were playing, and if she continued to go along, she was the one who was going to end up in jail. "Barney Kyle had the right idea, only his aim was bad."

"Kyle was on his way to being convicted on attempted murder, racketeering, and bribery charges before he was killed by the organized crime boss who had him on his payroll. Saying his form of justice is how we should proceed is not only fucking stupid, it also is a fucking clue to your character." Angus stood and buttoned his suit jacket. "My advice to you," he said to Matt, "apologize and hope Mrs. Casey is the forgiving type. From our understanding, the recording she has in her possession doesn't paint you in the best light. I haven't seen her, but listen to what I'm telling you if you want to salvage anything. The other thing is don't listen to anything Agent Gardner has to say on the subject."

"Fucking great," Matt said, throwing his hands in the air.

"Wait, how do you know that?" She suddenly understood the true predicament she was in. Ronald and his little band of bastards were cutting and running and needed a scapegoat if Casey had figured out what they'd been up to.

"We questioned some of the ICU personnel when Casey was moved to the maternity ward, of all places." Angus acted like he couldn't get out of her place fast enough.

"They couldn't have seen anything," Matt said. He was hitting his forehead with his fist hard enough to make the area red.

"There's probably no recording, or she would have shown it already." She wanted to laugh at herself for freaking out over nothing.

"You really need to read up on protocol, Agent. This isn't some game or quest for fame. You're playing with someone who can burn you to the ground."

"She's bluffing you."

"You think so? Agent Hicks ordered the questioning of the hospital staff when their family attorney, Muriel Casey, turned over a large number of listening devices. They'd been placed throughout the unit without anyone's knowledge including ours—which was curious, considering we own all the inventory she gave back." She lost her relief in an instant. That Casey had so easily found what she'd planted made her want to peel her skin off since this was going to be so much worse than she thought. "I'm sure Agent Hicks will review how this happened, so you might want to get your story in order."

"Are you saying that was me? It could've easily been Agent Chapman, Angus. So maybe you and he should get your story straight." She threw the words at him, hoping he choked on them. "Don't deny all of you didn't think to get the advantage when she was shot, and the number one person on that list would be Agent Chapman."

"That would be one mistake too many, Agent. Believe me, it's easier to go through life with friends than alone on an island surrounded by sharks." Angus slammed out after that, and she was convinced she was the one going down. It was time to be proactive.

"Who the fuck was that? And what did you get me into?" Matt asked with his hands covering his face. "I'm not from New Orleans, and even I know who Casey is. If she knows what I did was for you, she's not going to need a gun to kill me over this."

"No one is getting killed, so calm down. All I need to do is think, so get out of here and don't do anything until you hear from me." She got up and opened the door for him. "The best thing you can do is keep quiet. All Casey is doing is testing you. Fall for her games and you're done and I can't help you."

"I'm in this because I tried to help *you*, Dylan. Try to remember that, because I'm never going to forget it."

The door slammed again, and she rested her forehead against it. "Fuck me." She figured that's what Casey was planning to do to her, and she wasn't going to enjoy a moment of it.

❖

The Piquant suite bedroom Marisol was in was comfortable and quiet, but she wanted out. They'd been here for days, and Luce came and went but never shared what she was doing. Luce's promise that Michel, Nicolette's father, was coming hadn't materialized, and she was getting antsy being so close to Hector. She found it humorous that all these people were nursing her back to health only to kill her.

"Ms. Delarosa," the nurse that came every day said from the door, "I think today we can get you out of bed after I remove your stitches."

She watched as the woman did that, and considered the scars the bullet and the surgery to remove it had left. They'd be a permanent reminder of what her father had done to her because she'd dared to speak against him. Hector had four children altogether, and while she'd gotten the same opportunities as the other three as far as schools and gifts, Hector had been different with her. He'd expected more from her and was easily swayed by others' opinions of her. She wasn't what he'd wanted, and it wasn't hard to figure that out.

The nurse was finished, so Marisol sat up on the side of the bed, then stood to test the pain level. Her problem wasn't the wound, but the bone the bullet had embedded itself in. At least the shot to her arm had been a through and through, so while it was sore, it would heal faster. She took a few steps and stopped to take the cane the nurse held up.

"You are improving," Luce said. She'd walked in and stood ten feet in front of her with her hands in her pockets. "Are you having pain?"

"Not too bad, and that's good since I'm tired of sitting on that bed," she said as she took more steps, trying to smooth out her stride.

Luce nodded and moved to the chair by the window. "Michel is arriving within the hour, and he'd like to talk to you if you're up to it."

"Can I take a shower?" she asked the nurse, who nodded. "I'd like to do that before I meet with him."

"Go ahead, and there's some clothes in the closet." Luce walked out with the nurse, and Marisol sat back on the bed.

"What the hell do you want?" One thing Hector taught her was no one gave anything for free. Luce had saved her from the hospital, taken care of her, and now was giving her the opportunity to meet with Nicolette's father. All that would have to be repaid somehow, and she doubted she'd like the choice of coin.

She showered and put on the slacks and white dress shirt Luce had purchased. There'd been enough pieces in the closet to last a week or more, and everything fit perfectly. When she entered the main area of the suite, there was a man sitting having a cup of something hot while staring out at Canal Street. Michel Blanc wasn't a large man, but he was handsome for his age. It was easy to see where Nicolette had gotten her looks.

"Marisol, this is Michel Blanc," Luce said as Michel stood and faced her. "I'll run a few errands so you can talk."

"Please, Ms. Delarosa, sit," Michel said in that same French accent she'd gotten used to, talking to Luce.

"I'm sorry for the loss of Nicolette." Did Michel blame her? Was this meeting the reason Luce had been so nice? Of course he thought she was to blame because they'd been lovers and she hadn't kept Nicolette safe.

"My daughter was someone I raised to be strong and independent. The one thing we both loved aside from each other was the vineyard where she grew up, just like I did." He took a deep breath, and she could see how upset he still was. "Her mother is buried there, as well as all my family, and all I want is the chance to do the same for her. Until I find her, there's no opportunity to do that. That truth has made my grief never-ending."

"Nicolette was special to me, and I tried to keep her with me and safe. She left one day, and I never saw her again. I tried to find her, but my father thought it was a waste of time. He cares only for himself, but I wanted to do whatever we could to find her." She was still emotional about Nicolette's disappearance even though Luce was probably right that Nicolette had never really loved her. "I miss her."

"You have no idea who she was meeting with?" Michel's attention on her became laser-focused.

"All I know was she had a deal with Cain Casey, but it had fallen through. When it did, she spoke only with hate about Casey, and she had to look for something new. You are right about how she felt about your business. It was a passion for her, and she did what she could to save it." She'd answer whatever questions he had, then get out of here. Grief like his had a way of turning to find an outlet, and she was as good a target as anyone when it came to blame.

"I understand what your father's business is, and in truth, I wanted no part of that, but it was me who made the call. I mean no disrespect when I say that, but I was willing to cut a deal with your family." He spread his hands and stopped as if to make sure she understood that part. "Nicolette was fine with that but then found a no-lose opportunity to get us the cash we needed to keep making wine. She did what she wanted even if I did not agree. Drugs, though, no matter where you deal in them, only bring death."

"And she didn't tell you who that deal was with?" The list of who Nicolette was dealing with was small, but she still had no clue.

"All she said was to trust her," he said, punching his palm. "I want her back and for someone to pay for her death."

"Believe me, what I told you is all I know."

"Luce told me you do not blame Cain Casey. Is that true?"

She took a moment to think about her answer. "Casey does not deal in drugs. She and Hector are not enemies but do help each other by sharing information. If she knew anything about Nicolette, she would have shared it with him."

"Luce tells me Jasper Lucas and Vinny Carlotti are under her protection," Michel continued. "She is not in the business but has good friends in the business. Could she have helped those friends by killing my child?"

"I wish I had an answer for you, but I don't know. All you can do is call Casey and ask. She has children, so she will understand your pain."

"We need much more information before I sit with Cain," he said, and she tried to think of what he meant.

"You were going to do business with her," she said as a reminder of what Luce had told her. "That means you know her, and if she's not in a giving mood, she will tell you nothing."

"I understand that, Marisol, and I also understand that if anyone would know, Cain will. All I need is something to leverage her cooperation." Michel finally smiled, but she was still confused. "My daughter wanted so much more than a business relationship with Cain, and no one could tell her it was not going to happen. You are right— Cain, from what I know, is married and has children. A woman throwing herself at her feet might not be something she would put up with."

"I believe she made Nicolette understand when she broke Luce's nose. I'll do whatever you ask of me, but I do not think the answers will lie with Casey."

"You will help me finish what Nicolette started, and we are all going to make Cain tell us what I want to know, so if I ask you to do something, I want you to do it. Is that something you are willing to do?" Michel stood and waved for her to keep her seat. "I'll give you until tomorrow to give me an answer. I will not force you, but you have to understand that this will be all the help I will give you if you refuse."

"I do not need a day. If you want me to work with you, I will."

"Good, we leave for New York tomorrow. The only other person Nicolette might have talked to is Nunzio Luca. He is someone else who hates Cain, so it will up the pressure."

"He is small in the business, but if that is what you want…"

"I want my child, and I am willing to kill to get her back. You are either with me or not. If not, then run before I have Luce finish this for me." He left after that ultimatum, and she had to wonder what she'd done to piss off the universe. Why did other people go through life with relative ease? She'd never had that.

"Fucking Casey," she said, making a fist. Nicolette had wanted Cain dead, and she would've done that for her. It would be easier than what Michel was asking of her. "I'm tired of begging for scraps, but what choice do I have." Dealing with Nunzio would be worse than dealing with Casey. "It's the only way to live to see Hector dead, so I'll give Michel whatever he wants."

Cain sat in her formal living room with Russell Welsh and Finley's old partner, Peter Stanley. She almost laughed since they were staring at her like she was the missing link, and they didn't know what to do with her now that they were in her company and not observing her from a distance. Emma didn't have the same control over her humor, and she laughed with her hand over her mouth.

"I know you probably won't share with me how you found all this stuff, but I had a long talk with Annabel. She told me the story about a rogue agent in her office who shot you." Russell seemed amused by her silence, but she wanted to know what this meeting was about. "When they brought Kyle in, the mountain of evidence against him was impressive, from pictures of him taking money off Bracato, to recordings of him taking orders from the same guy. Money for hire is not in the FBI handbook."

"When I was growing up," Cain said, "my da taught me a long list of valuable lessons. One he repeated over and over was that you had to do your homework. That was important because punching an FBI agent in the face is illegal." She'd agreed to this meeting because of Finley, since her cousin saw Russell as the key to finding Nicola. The family had resources, but not on the scale of the bureau. "I tell my children that all the time. When it comes to me, I research when it's important to me. In this case it's personal because Lucy spent plenty of time here. She was Hannah's best friend, and she vanished one day."

"How did you find her?" Russell asked and Peter nodded.

"I didn't," she said and pointed at Fin. "She did, or at least she thought she had after meeting with a woman from child protective services. Whoever this Jane is, she's a small cog in Larry the sleazeball's wheel."

"What does that mean?" Peter said.

"Lawrence Alexander, a supervisor with child protective services, had a job before he started working for the state. Before they let him loose with kids, he ran a prostitution house for the same Bracato Annabel told you about. It wasn't successful for a lot of reasons, some having to do with Larry and his sense of privilege."

"Still not following," Peter said.

"Larry's the kind of guy who thinks the world owes him because he's Larry. The guy is a loser, but that's who Bracato likes to hire. He put Larry in charge, and he came this close to getting arrested because of the women they found working at this dump." She held her fingers close together. "The women and where they got them were the only things Bracato and the Antakovs have in common. Not one girl had volunteered for the job."

"So more trafficking," Russell said.

"That's right, so in this case, Finley did her part, and I added my knowledge of who the players were, and it led you to rural Mississippi."

"The main coincidence in all this is a lot of people from Russia no one ever heard of doing some shitty things." Russell glanced at Emma after cursing, and Emma waved him off. "The only known is Abigail and her family's problems, but that's the Antakov angle." Russell spoke freely, and that made her more curious. "Do you think it all stems from Nicola Antakov? We thought we were done with them because of the shooting here and the plane crash, but life isn't always rainbows and happy endings."

"True, but not necessarily when it comes to Nicola."

Russell took out a sheet from the folder on his lap. "Can we both agree we've never had this conversation?"

"I'm known for my secret-keeping ability." She held her hand up as if she was testifying. "Whatever we discuss will stay between us. All I want is to stop my family from being a target only because I'm helping Finley and Abigail."

"It might've been a rural spot, but the highest person on the food chain we fished out of that house was Mila Volkov," Russell said, handing over her mug shot.

Cain and Emma stared at the picture, and Cain couldn't help but think this woman bore a resemblance to Valerie Antakov. If this was another of Valerie's sisters, then the story Emma got from the guy they'd interrogated made sense. The Volkov family were cutting out problems to get what they wanted as easily as they could get it, and she fell into that category. It had nothing to do with revenge, or anything to do with the family as a whole.

"I've honestly never heard of this woman," she said, handing the page back. "What I would like to know is why she had four little girls in her attic. I'm not a person who pays for sex, but that doesn't seem normal for a place like this."

"The investigation has just started, and as soon as I find Lawrence Alexander, I might be able to answer that. He's in the wind, so would you consider working together?" Russell stared at her for a long moment again, and she could almost guess what was on his mind.

"I'll do my best to find him, and I promise he'll be breathing when you get to talk to him," she said and laughed when he shrugged. "Just don't forget Jane in all this. Lawrence couldn't find his shadow if he looked for it, so it had to be this woman who found him the girls to cull. That she wasn't feverishly searching for Lucy and the others after her conversation with Finley seals her guilt in my opinion."

"No, she was busier trying to delete things off the system than any searching, so you're right. She's already in custody and talking. Jane keeps telling us she's not built for jail, so we're having a hard time getting her to *stop* talking."

"I hope you have her in protective custody. This is the kind of situation where people like Mila Volkov start killing the little guys who are the only way to getting the big guy." She scratched at her side, and Emma grabbed her hand to get her to stop. "Thanks for coming, and I'll be in touch if I find something."

"Take care and make sure you keep Finley in one piece." Russell stood and shook her hand. "I'm sorry to lose her, but I can see she's in good hands."

"Our family will always protect our own." She waited for Finley to see them out before heading to her office. Merrick and Katlin were waiting, along with Remi and Dallas. "No word on Larry?" she asked Merrick.

"We had a chat with his girlfriend, who just turned sixteen by the way, and she said he's on vacation. Miami seems like a popular spot these days. He's not answering his phone, but the last time she talked to him, he was at the Eden Roc." Merrick would've been a good agent, if agents were allowed to have interesting interviews with suspects that involved drastic measures in the eyes of the law.

"I've heard that's a nice place," Emma said.

"It is," Dallas said. "I was there for a month on a film."

"We'll go on a couples trip after all this is over and no one accuses us of anything. Right now, how about we send Dino and some of his guys. We'll give Shaun and Sabana a break with a bonus for what they got done." She thought about Sacha and what he'd told her before he flew back to New York. It was a ticking bomb ready to blow up, but the fireworks were something she was looking for. The water had been chummed, and all she had to do was wait for the shark she was hunting to show up. "Do you have anything else on the Volkov family?"

"Plenty, but nothing that has to do with this," Katlin said. "They're the Antakovs all over again on a smaller scale. Also, a scale not so high-end."

"Okay, get Dino and his guys ready to go. Make sure Lou talks to them before they leave. He'll let them know everything they need to before they check into the Eden Roc. Have them meet with Sabana and Shaun as well," she said and moved to the sofa when Merrick and Katlin walked out.

"I don't think I've ever seen you in your pajamas," Remi said when Cain sat next to Emma.

"Yes, you have," she said, laughing. "Billy, Marie, and I snuck over to your house, and we talked you and Mano into falling asleep under the old gazebo. We all got grounded in the morning except for Marie since Mum said we were a bad influence on her."

"The way she could take every penny off you playing checkers makes me think Marie was good at being mischievous all by herself," Emma said. "She was such a fun person to have around."

"She was that," Remi agreed. "It's a shame you weren't around to get one of her hugs, Dallas. Marie put her whole body into it."

"That kid was one of a kind for sure," Cain said, "and hopefully you two will give my kids someone to play with and get in trouble with soon. They'll grow up with their moms, Dallas and Remi, and they'll only know one mom likes to make movies, and the other likes games of chance. They'll never know a woman who once lived in Tennessee named Katie Lynn Moores." Cain stared at Dallas, hoping she understood what she was saying.

"How can you be so sure?" Remi asked seeming to have caught on.

"You know the old saying how the world can fit in a thimble sometimes?" Cain asked, and Dallas scooted to the edge of her seat as if she couldn't wait to hear this story. Dallas kept a hand on Remi's knee, but she seemed to want to be closer to her and Emma. "Katie Lynn took a lot of jobs that she didn't want to keep her and her sister alive." She decided to tell it like this to make it easier on Dallas. Now was the time for Dallas to separate herself from who she was then and accept who she was now. "No matter what your feelings about that young woman are, I find her story admirable. She's someone you should be proud of."

"She'll never completely die away—that girl, I mean," Dallas said. "The past can't be changed or forgotten."

"Let me finish, and then you decide." She smiled when Emma took the same position as Dallas had by scooting forward. Her best friend was about to need her, and Emma was ready. "In New York about the same time, there was a man named Peter who made money, lots of it, and no one asked where it came from, especially when he gave to charity and appeared in the social pages. Like Katie Lynn, Peter had plenty of secrets, but the money kept rolling in with very few questions."

"Only Peter's really Yury Antakov. What does he have to do with anything?" Remi asked.

The door opened, and Abigail and Finley walked in and pulled up some more chairs. "Sorry we're late. We were trying to get the kids situated," Abigail said.

"You're just in time, since this next part has to do with you and your children," Cain said, and Abigail immediately gripped Fin's hand. "Peter was Yury, and he and Valerie had twins. One went to Miami to run that part of their business, and the other was here. That twin married, had three children, and was heir to the throne Peter owned."

"Nicola and Fredrick," Abigail said.

"Yes," she said, and Fin seemed agitated.

"This isn't a fairy tale, cousin." Finley put her arm around Abigail's shoulders and pulled her close.

"No, fairy tales have much nicer storylines. In this one the evil twins continue what Yury started and were successful until they were in a plane crash. They both supposedly died, only that wasn't true. Not only did they survive, but they also kept the operation going, which included prostitution and adult films."

"Wait," Abigail said, sitting up. "Fredrick is alive too?"

"Fredrick survived the crash as well, but from what I understand, he wasn't as lucky as Nicola. He was paralyzed, confined to a wheelchair, and living in a beachfront house in Miami." She rubbed Emma's back and glanced between the two couples.

"Has he moved?" Abigail asked, her panic climbing. "You don't know where he is? If Nicola has an ally like Fredrick, my children will never be safe."

"I know exactly where Fredrick is, and he's not getting away," she said. "Sacha Oblonsky found out from one of Nicola's people. Svetlana…"

"Svetlana Dudko," Finley said. "She was allegedly one of Nicola's fixers when I had no idea who exactly Nicola was. I was starting to get a picture of what the operation was, and who was involved, but was having trouble finding anyone to talk." Finley pinched her brow as if trying to remember. "It wasn't until you wandered close to that shooting by the park that I started to narrow it down." She was talking to Abigail, but she sounded apologetic, as if she should've found all this earlier. "When they became the Eatons they hid in plain sight."

"Sacha made it sound like Nicola's cracking up, and Svetlana is getting out before it involves a body dump—hers. She gave Fredrick up, but Nicola's in the wind."

"Where is he?" Abigail said.

"Not to be blunt, but at the moment he's rotting in a beach house in Miami. Sacha tested his paralysis a little bit at a time. A bit dramatic for my tastes, but he's dead." She shook her head at the vivid description Sacha had given her. "Fredrick was in that house with a group of naked women he claimed he owned, and a group of guards."

"If any of them survived and ran, their first stop will be Nicola. Once she knows he's dead, she's going to disappear, and this will never end," Finley said.

"The guards are dead, and the women were compensated and given their freedom. They had quite a bit of money in the house, and now that's gone." She made eye contact with Finley to keep her quiet for a moment so she could finish with Dallas. "Sacha called me before he left for Miami, so I asked for one favor."

"What was that?" Remi said, smiling as if guessing it was good news for them at least.

"Do you all remember Bryce White, the young man who took care of our electronic security? He was killed, and we took care of his brother Charlie," she said, explaining how she'd met the two young men. "Charlie was glad to go to the house and find what I figured was in there."

"Tell me," Dallas said.

"Fredrick had the servers that housed the adult film company they owned. You were right—the master copies aren't important any longer."

"All of them?" Dallas asked and she nodded.

"Fredrick wasn't the same man after the crash, but he did take over what he could to keep the money coming in. He and Nicola took what their father had and built on it, despite the world thinking they were both dead." She turned the laptop on the table next to the sofa so Dallas could see the screen. "Sacha got a lot of information out of Fredrick before he died, and this was something Fredrick thought was a safer topic than his twin sister. She was someone he wouldn't betray no matter how much pain he was in."

"What did Charlie do?" Finley asked staring at the screen as well.

"He did two things for me," she said, handing Dallas the computer. "One was building a worm. Charlie has a freakish talent for them. His creation can either find to retrieve, or find to destroy. This time he did both." The cursor was blinking over a green square with *KLM* at the center. Charlie had used Dallas's birth-name initials as the name of the virus that would erase her past. "This is your gift from my wife."

"Emma," Dallas said as her eyes filled with tears.

"From the day she met you, she saw how haunted you were and told me no one could fake that. She also told me how important you'd be to all of us, especially to my best friend." She made brief eye contact with Remi. "I promised her a while back that I'd do what I could so you could stop running. Click on the square, and lay Katie Lynn to rest once and for all."

"Oh my God," Dallas said as she looked back at Remi.

"Go ahead, love," Remi said, and Dallas did just that.

"The worm in Fredrick's servers was waiting for this. It'll release the virus that will wipe the system, but Charlie's an overachiever. Any visual media on any computer in the world that has the same code as anything on that server will be wiped."

Dallas didn't hesitate to press her finger to the pad, and the square swirled until it turned into an animated worm that was swallowed by a hole that opened on the screen. Whatever Dallas was worried about went with it.

She and Emma stood when Dallas started crying and fell into Remi's arms in what appeared to be relief. When the tears slowed, Dallas turned to Emma and Remi to her. Remi was careful when she put her arms around her and didn't have to say a word. Hopefully it wouldn't take too much more time before she could do the same for Finley and Abigail.

"This one I'll never be able to pay you back for," Remi said.

"Like Da used to say, there are no debts between friends." She bent when Dallas kissed her cheek. "Now all you have to think about—aside from being happy—is that any reporter who digs up anything left, if there's anything left, will not ever go to print. Remi and I are persuasive when it matters to us."

"And Nicola?" Finley asked, and she walked closer to them so she could put her hand on Abigail's shoulder.

"Nicola's in a scary place. They were hoarding money in the house, and it's gone. She was holed up with the only family she has left, and he's dead. There aren't too many moves she can make that won't get her killed, and Sacha is as motivated as we are to get that done." She sat back down and tried to ease Abigail's worry. "To be honest, the only wrinkle I had no clue was out there is the Volkov family."

"They're Nicola's family too," Abigail said. "Even if this is the first I'm hearing about them."

"That's true, but think of it the way I do. The Nicola you knew is dead. That strong, confident, and arrogant woman no longer exists." That was all true, and it changed how she thought Nicola would come at them. "She's frantically trying to find something to hold on to from her old life, but it's all gone. That leads to mistakes, and that'll make it easier to find her."

"You know she'll never stop until she gets to the children. They're all she has left."

"And you know my goal, like Finley's, is to find her. Once I do, I'm going to put a bullet in her head and be done with it." That was her best way of letting Abigail know how she planned to solve their mutual problem. If Abigail had a problem with it, now was the time to speak up.

"Good," Abigail said without hesitation.

"How do we iron out the Volkov problem, then?" Finley asked.

"The same way Sacha dealt with Fredrick, but not as graphic. Damn if the guy doesn't have a talent for going into detail," she said, and Remi laughed. "That's your avenue, Fin, so we need some more information."

"You got it," Fin said, as she and Abigail stood to leave. "We'll see you guys for dinner in a bit."

"I just need to see our kids," Abigail said, leaning down to kiss Cain's cheek. "If I was on my own, I'd have gone insane by now."

"Cain, thank you," Dallas said.

"You're welcome, and I'm glad we found the servers. Charlie tells me this worm would've worked without them, but now it's a guarantee." She stood again and held her hand out to Emma. "You two take a minute to celebrate, and we'll be right down. I have to put on my dinner pajamas, so we'll give you some privacy."

She took her time up the stairs and smiled as Emma led her to their room and locked the door. "I love you more than anything or anyone, but sometimes you leave me in awe. What you did today, I can't tell you how much that means to Dallas."

"I think I do, and she deserves to let go of all that and enjoy the life she's built. She was due." She thought about the people across the street and what they'd done in pursuit of what they defined as justice. There were cardinal rules she lived by, but every so often, rules had to be broken to assure her ghosts were laid to rest. "I think we all are."

CHAPTER NINETEEN

The old Oldsmobile Agent Ronald Chapman had taken from one of the only occupied houses in New Orleans East had bad shocks, but little in the way of security. The rust bucket had been easy to hot-wire and wouldn't be missed, considering it belonged to an eighty-five-year-old widow who drove to the grocery on Wednesdays and bingo on Friday nights. All he needed was a vehicle that was in no way tied to him, and he'd been careful this time that no one was following him.

"Fucking Cain Casey," he said, punching the dash so hard the radio stopped working. That night in that field in Wisconsin she'd handed him an envelope that was a warning she had him by the balls, since it listed everything about his interesting stress reliever. There'd been no pictures or anything else that'd corroborate that she did indeed have proof, so he was going with she was bluffing. The FBI were, after all, the experts in surveillance.

The drive from the east to Airline Highway took him almost an hour, since he went the speed limit the entire way with the windows rolled down. Not only was the car rusting away on the outside, the air conditioner didn't work, which was a sin in south Louisiana. He was taking a chance cruising in the same area as before, but who the hell was going to remember him? There were plenty of women who walked to the edge of the sidewalk as if advertising, but he was looking for a specific type.

He found it two blocks later in the attractive face of the petite young blond man in shorts. There was no problem getting him in the car when he held up three one-hundred-dollar bills before the guy's pimp ran to the car screaming. He'd have plenty to scream about before the night was out. It was a short drive to the construction zone he'd scoped a mile away that had no activity at night and, more importantly, no security.

The blow job was nice and it melted the tension in him, but the guilt over paying for this shit fueled his rage. He got out and went around to the passenger side and opened that door. "Come out here and I'm going to fuck you up." It had to be consensual if he warned the guy, and he got out of the car anyway. That's how he likes to think about it. These assholes knew the risks, yet they still got in every car with anyone with a dollar to spend, so what was about to happen wasn't his fault.

The Taser knocked the guy to his knees, giving him a clean shot with an uppercut to the bottom of his jaw. He swore he heard the jawbone break against his fist, and it made his skin tingle from the excitement of it. No one understood the constraints he had to live his life by, the narrow avenues he had no choice but to follow. The only thing that gave him the sense of being alive was this. All the violence brought him to life and allowed his true nature to run free.

"You're nothing but a dirty little motherfucker." He hit the guy in the mouth, loving the blood that seeped through the golf gloves he'd purchased a week ago. The leather was hot in this weather, but after plenty of testing, it was almost like using his bare hands. "You stand out there and beg for this kind of shit to happen to you, then expect someone like me to clean it up."

"Please," the guy said, two teeth falling from this mouth. "Stop." He held his hand up.

"Stop?" he screamed back and laughed. The only thing better than hitting was hearing the begging. It made him hard in record time, so he picked the guy up and bent him over the hood. The shorts came down fast, and he finished the ritual by taking the spoils due him. It didn't matter at all that the guy was unconscious by the time he was done. In this arena he got to take whatever he wanted.

He zipped his pants, opened the trunk, and got the bag he'd stored there. The wig went in first, then the gloves and fake mustache. That was new to his alter ego. Hiding wasn't something he liked, but it was necessary if he wanted to retain his freedom. He couldn't give this up.

The guy had fallen off the car and lay face down on the shell drive. Those good looks that'd attracted him were gone, along with his front teeth, but he'd promised the three hundred, so he shoved it in his mouth when he checked to make sure he was still breathing. He drove back to the old woman's house, enjoying the air on his face, and dropped off the car after retrieving the bag. His car was three blocks away, and he was looking forward to the walk. It'd give him time to think about Casey and if she was worth his time any longer.

There was a promotion waiting on him in DC—not anything like Annabel's post, but there was always time. He knew it wouldn't take much longer before the guys in Washington replaced not only Annabel but her entire team. To lead effectively he needed people who'd do his bidding with no question, like Covington, Knight, and Brewer.

He stopped half a block from his car and tried to make the person leaning against the passenger side of his rental. They resembled Casey, but he had to be hallucinating. Casey was at home recovering from the shooting. Angus had told him she barely had the strength to pick up a coffee cup, so being out at night alone and facing a seasoned agent wasn't something she would chance.

"Ronald." It was a woman, but he couldn't force himself to take a step forward. If she got ahold of the bag, he was done. "I'm talking to you, Ronald." Casey had a way of making his name sound buffoonish, but still, it could be her cousin.

"It's Special Agent Chapman," he said, digging deep for his courage. If she was alone, no one would suspect him if she died in this crappy part of town.

"Do you remember showing up to my son's baseball game? So much hubris for such a little man," Cain said with plenty of humor. He knew it was her now that she'd stepped into the circle of the streetlight. "I told you then that you were into something freaky, and I warned you what would happen if I found out what it was. Hell, I even warned you what I'd do if you came back."

"You can't prove anything." He gripped the bag, wanting to pretend it was the only real thing about this encounter. "And you're the only person Annabel is going to go after if you kill me."

"I'm not going to kill you, little guy." Cain stood straight and proud, and it irked him that she was at least five inches taller than him. "It's apparent that you didn't believe me the day we met, and I don't need to be a psychic to guess that bag in your hand contains the same list of things as the stuff in my safe deposit box. I have to say, Special Agent, I was only guessing when it came to the spanking. Who knew you were such a freak."

"Shut up," he screamed and stopped to take a breath. Having

people come out of their homes with camera phones set to record would not be in his best interest. "You know nothing about me, and it's going to be my word against yours."

"I don't think that's right." Cain shook her head and tapped her chin with her index finger. "I haven't spent a lot of time thinking about you, Ronald, but I haven't forgotten you, either. You're the kind of little twerp who thinks he can mold the world into something he wants, the rest of us be damned."

"You haven't forgotten me because you know I'm going to lock you up until even your children will forget you." He pointed his finger at her and had a sudden thought. The Taser was in the bag, and all he had to do was get closer to her.

"I've been thinking how to deal with you since Taylor Kennison came to my house. We both know that particular person is a figment of your imagination, but Special Agent Christina Brewer is real. She and Barry Knight used a child to try to bug my office."

The night was hot, but that statement made him stop sweating because a chill had seized him. "I don't know what you're talking about."

"Really, Ronald," Cain said, laughing.

"You can't kill me," he said, and he hated the pleading in his voice.

"I already told you I'm not going to kill you—I'm not going to lay a hand on you."

He laughed too and dropped his shoulders. "That's the smartest thing you've said all night."

"Sometimes satisfaction comes from knowing what will happen to you, Ronald," she said, making his name sound like an insult. "That young man tonight, unlike you, has someone who loves him."

"What are you talking about?"

"Andy O'Donnell is such a good Irish name," Cain said and took a step toward him. "He works the street, and his boyfriend is his manager. Says the term *pimp* is so passé. You laughed as you drove away, and he chased the car. Tiny watches over him, and he's pissed."

"Tiny." He smiled. "Sounds like a small problem."

"What do you think, Tiny?" Cain asked and glanced over his left shoulder. "Just don't kill him, he's got a court date soon, and I need him to make it."

The size of the guy behind him made him wonder how the hell he'd snuck up on him. He ran to his car, slid in, and locked the doors as he dug in his pocket for the key. There was only a click when he turned the key. He didn't have time to figure out what was wrong with it when the driver's side window shattered, and Tiny pulled him out. Cain's SUV pulled away, leaving him to face this mountain of a guy.

He noticed the vehicle stop as Tiny slammed his head into the car, and someone got out and picked up the bag. Whatever his life was an hour ago would never come again. "Stop," he begged as he spit out a tooth. "Please." The world went black after that.

❖

Cain took a breath when the car stopped inside her garage. Breathing painlessly was getting easier to do. "Ready, boss?" Lou asked.

"Let's go, so we get in there before our guests arrive." They entered through the mudroom, and Lou placed the bag in a banker's box. He'd put on surgical gloves to assure the only fingerprints on it were Ronald's.

They walked to the front of the house, and Lou poured them both a small splash of Irish whiskey. "We've been through a lot together, but this is some weird shit," Lou said.

"Takes all kinds to make a world, my friend. How's your romance going?" she asked as she sipped her drink more slowly than he did.

"Strange change of topic, boss." He smiled and loosened his tie. Lou always looked sharp.

"I'm not getting sappy on you, but I want the people I care about to be as happy as I am." She laughed when his smile widened. "Sickening, I know."

"Nah, your softer side is something only Emma gets to see consistently, so it's nice." He sat across from her and brushed his short hair back. "I don't know if I ever thanked you for all the years of friendship."

"We've been together since junior high even if we were at different schools. You know I'd do anything for you," she said, meaning every word. "We raised our share of hell, and now it's time to raise kids." She winked at him, and he laughed again.

"I'm happy, and I think Sabana is too, so give me some time before I'm out shopping for rings." His smile dimmed a little when she scratched her side. "I'm sorry for failing you that day. If you want me to step back, I'll understand."

"We still have a lot to do, Lou, so it's no time to fall on your sword. I'm not blaming you, and neither is anyone else." They both turned when Emma entered and slid the pocket doors open.

"Are you ready? Our guests have arrived," Emma said.

Shelby led Joe and Annabel inside, and they sat when she nodded toward the chairs facing the sofa. This was her month of out-of-psyche experiences since she'd never invited the FBI inside her house more than she had lately. They all stared at her and Emma for a second before their attention seemed to zero in on the box Lou had on the bar.

"Thank you for coming, and for keeping an open mind." These things were always iffy, facing that one of your own was so out of bounds, there was no bringing him back in line. "Last year, for some reason, Ronald Chapman came into all our lives. You allowed him to drag Brent Cehan along with him, even though I'd had your promise that he'd be disciplined for what he'd done to me."

"Cain, sometimes things are out of my control, so I apologize," Annabel said.

"Brent's shown his true colors, so he's old news. Ronald, though…I figured out then that there was something off about him. He was too focused, not that you all aren't, but there was an edge to him that was wrong. I actually teased him about it, and he bit. No one reacts like that unless they have something to hide, and Ronald had plenty to hide." She glanced at Lou, and he brought five more boxes in and lined them up on the folding table she'd had brought in.

"What is all this?" Joe asked. He'd helped Shelby when she'd handed over the information they'd accumulated on Barney Kyle, so he seemed to have an idea of what was coming.

"I'm a bartender by trade," Cain said, "so I've learned to pay attention to people, all types of people. Some of us blow off steam with an ale with a sidecar of whiskey, and others with a variation of other things," she said, taking Emma's hand. "Some people, though, the ones who are wound a bit tight, pick something completely different." She stood and put on a pair of gloves before lifting the top off each box to reveal only a series of black plastic bags. "They're twisted in ways that only come out in rare moments because the rest of the time they're disciplined and controlled. That only slip when they're stressed and need that release."

The agents all stood as well and stared inside each box, seeming confused as to what they were looking at. Ronald had made her capture a priority, so she'd returned the favor. Two of her people had spent months following Ronald whenever he got off work. Most of those nights he spent on the phone with Angus Covington III to make sure his little operation across the street was on target, but four nights in all those months, the pressure had obviously gotten to him.

"I'm sorry, but I'm not sure what I'm looking at," Annabel said.

"You didn't collect this evidence, but Ronald sealed each one perfectly to preserve what's inside. He threw them away in places where he thought they'd disappear, but sometimes our demons come back to haunt us." She reached for the box on the bar, then removed the bag that Ronald hadn't had a chance to knot closed and dumped it on the sheet of butcher paper Lou had set out, so any trace evidence wouldn't be lost.

The gloves caked in blood, the short dreadlock wig, and the belt would all be rich in Ronald's DNA as well as the blood of the guy he'd attacked. "You'll notice the wigs change from bag to bag, so maybe that's part of his ritual. The rest, though, is always the same."

"What kind of ritual?" Shelby said.

Emma turned on the television that'd been set up on the other table. "I owe you an apology, Agent Phillips," Emma said. "I blamed you for approaching Hannah, and I was wrong. This is the man who's to blame, and that no one's figured out all the aspects of his personality is rather mind-boggling."

The video started, and from a distance you could see the bobbing head of the escort as the man in the driver's seat got off. That changed when they got out of the car and the beating started. It ended with the guy having sex up against the car with the limp escort, followed by the money exchange and them leaving.

"You can't tell who that is, and any defense attorney will tear it apart," Joe said.

"That's just the start, Agent Simmons, an overview. You're not the only one with good surveillance equipment." The next clip Emma played was a close-up of the guy's face, from beginning to end. It was Ronald in a series of wigs, his face twisted in a cruel snarl even when someone was doing what he was paying them to do. "Ronald's like a little teapot who blows every so often, and the consequences have led to this. We've only been following him since we met, so I can't say how often he's done this before that date, but box three holds evidence of the one young man who died of his injuries."

"And you've hung on to it all this time?" Shelby said, sounding outraged.

"He isn't any less dead, Shelby, and I wasn't as interested in this as I have been about keeping my children and wife safe. This man came into our lives, surrounded himself with people intent on doing us harm, and you all gave him free rein." She let some of her anger bleed out. "This will convict him, but I want him exposed for more than just this."

"I would think this is enough," Annabel said.

"It is, but there's always more. I remember you coming to my office and telling me that I might come to miss the landscape I looked out on every day. The same goes for you. I'm the devil you know, so you should realize that if you come for my family, I'm going to react."

"It's kind of why we watch you all day long," Joe said, and it made her laugh.

"True, but there's something you should think about," she said, tapping under her eye. "What happens when the person being watched returns the favor?" She pointed to all three of them. "You're so busy hiding in that van across the street that you never bother to look behind you."

"Cain, we're not dirty or doing anything like this," Shelby said, sounding concerned. It most likely had to do with what'd happened to the men who killed her parents.

She nodded and smiled. "I do know that. You're all a nuisance, but you follow a code just like I do. People like Ronald, though, aren't quite as honorable." There was one bag she held back, having learned how these people kept their promises. Brent Cehan, if given a choice, would rather the five-month suspension she'd asked for than the ten years he'd gotten. His years at Angola State Penitentiary would give him plenty of time to think about his bad choices.

"This is not something I could've guessed." Annabel stared at the television and blinked slowly.

"There is film of every one of Ronald's little adventures, but the first one I discovered is one I'm keeping safe until I see how your office deals with this. Trust me this time when I tell you these videos will be on the news stations for months to come." Cain made eye contact with Annabel. "I promise it won't paint you in a negative light, since Ronald's stationed in DC, but the bureau will be sorry if he's saved from serving time."

"Can I ask why you didn't bring this to us when someone died?" Joe asked.

"The young man took two weeks to succumb to his injuries, and like Cain said, he was dead, and we wouldn't stand by and let him do it again," Emma said. "Ronald wasn't directly responsible for what happened with Hannah, but he was the one who ordered what happened. It'll be hard to believe, but that part of the operation is almost worse than this."

"I find that hard to believe, but I'm not going to question it." Shelby started putting the covers on all the boxes as if assuming it wouldn't be a problem to take them.

"Have you found Taylor, Drew, and Lucy Kennison?" Cain asked, and the blank stares meant no.

"We've looked, but you were right—they don't exist," Joe said. "We've exhausted all the leads to these people."

"You should've looked closer," Emma said. "We found them." Lou went to the television and plugged a laptop into it. "A few years back, we purchased some real estate and leased it out. When the last tenant died—at ninety-six, of natural causes, lest you blame Cain—we put it back on the market. The company leased it to a couple from out of town, and we were looking forward to meeting our new neighbors."

"Turns out, they're shy," Cain said.

"If you want me to guess, I'll go with the Kennison couple along with their daughter are now living across the street." Annabel sounded ironic but she did smile. "I keep telling you, you'd make a good agent."

"Maybe in my next life, but that's not who's living across the street. Joe's right, they don't exist." She glanced at Emma, and she changed the feed and a live picture came up. "This is who introduced themselves as the Kennisons, and their best friend Angus."

"I recognize Angus, but who are these people?" Annabel moved closer to the television and studied the couple standing in the kitchen while Angus sat at the table.

"That would be Special Agents Christina Brewer and Barry Knight. They work for Ronald, and they don't have a daughter named Lucy."

Shelby and Joe sat down like someone had pushed them over. "This isn't going to be good," Shelby said. "And where's Ronald?"

"Let's talk about Lucy first," Cain said, moving back to the sofa. "Is there such a thing as an FBI newsletter?"

Joe laughed and shook his head. "We have reports that are sent on, and they are about the operations here."

"You should expand your reach, then," she said and produced the file Russell gave his okay to share. "We found Lucy in a place that in no way should have a child within fifty miles of it. A good old-fashioned whorehouse is where Agent Knight arranged for her to go, along with three other little girls, with the help of two people from child protective services."

"This is Russell Welsh's operation?" Annabel asked.

"He'll be in town as soon as he finishes combing through the house to see what kind of information is hidden there. The other girls the state police rescued from here weren't as lucky as Lucy, and they were trafficked." She pulled out the pictures of the fifteen- and sixteen-year-old girls. "Another strike against Ronald and Knight."

"Is Lucy okay?" Joe asked. "Forgive my language, but this is fucked-up."

"That's a good way to put it," Emma said. "And to answer your question, Lucy is in the best possible place after what happened. The principal at Emma's school and his partner are fostering her with plans to adopt."

"I'm going to have to send agents across the street, and I'm going to need all this surveillance you've done," Annabel said. She made a call and closed her eyes.

"They're not going anywhere, and they've been watching me since Ronald ran off, that night in Wisconsin. Angus was their inside man, and his job was twofold." She remembered Angus and his ridiculous clothes the day he came looking for a job. Once she showed him a picture of his family, he'd run out of the house faster than if she'd been shooting at him. "He was helping Ronald watch us, and he was also watching you."

"Backup is six minutes out," Shelby said, standing.

"They're not going anywhere, Agent Hicks. You all know Muriel will have to get involved, and the star of that litigation won't be any of these people." She got their attention with that and they sat back down. Annabel made a call and told her people to stand down. "Ronald brought one more agent into your fold to help him move things along."

"Dylan Gardner," Shelby said, snapping her fingers. "I knew it."

"Moving things along meant staples in my head and bringing Dr. Matt Joseph into our lives. I think the surgeon was a stroke of luck she took advantage of, but Gardner's main gripe is that you guys have moved too slow." The staples had come out, but Gardner was someone who'd caught her attention. "Here you go." The pictures of Gardner with Joseph outside the hospital backed up her story.

"Son of a bitch," Annabel said, sounding uncharacteristically furious. "Joe, get Lionel and a team over to Gardner's place. I want them all in interrogation tonight." Annabel stood and held her hand out.

"Thank you, Cain. When we met all those months ago, I never thought it would end here. Can we have some help getting this to my car?" She pointed to all the boxes.

"Sure, and I'd like an update on all this. I'm not sure what I've done to become a magnet for all these rogue agents, but let's hope this is the last time we need to do this. For what happened to Lucy, though, they deserve to go down." She shook Annabel's hand and smiled at Emma when all of them ran out the door. "Let's get some air."

They climbed to the catwalk on the wall and watched what was going on across the street. "What do you think will happen to them?" Emma asked as the three agents were brought out in handcuffs.

"I'd like to think the right thing, but they're not great at punishing their own." She put her arm around Emma and kissed the side of her head. "Let's give them their shot."

"And if they do the wrong thing?"

"Then they'll wish, like Brent, they'd taken the FBI up on whatever they had in mind. The alternative will be hellish."

CHAPTER TWENTY

The phone at the Miami house rang for the hundredth time for the third day in a row and still no answer. Last night Nicola had flown home alone, since in that same time she'd woken up the same way—alone. Svetlana wasn't answering her phone, and the guards in the apartment next door were all dead. They'd been killed in their beds, which made her think the same had happened to Svetlana.

If this was a test, it'd be hard to pass if she had to do it alone. She sat on the beach a couple of miles from the house and tried to think of what to do. There'd never been a time in her life she'd been indecisive, but she was stuck trying to decide. The only person she had left to call was Kira, but she wasn't crazy enough to do that. Admitting this kind of weakness would drive Ivan to kill her so she wouldn't pollute his family line.

The sun set, and she gazed in the direction of the house she'd come to hate for all the time she'd spent there healing. The thought of seeing Fredrick every day in the condition he was in made her want to escape, but she owed it to him to see what was wrong. She stood and brushed off her pants and headed for her rental car. The drive didn't take any time, and she drove through the open gate, the first clue there was something off. How dark the house was also was wrong, but she got out and put the key in the lock. It wasn't necessary, as the door swung open, allowing the stench of decomp to slam into her nostrils.

She lifted her shirt over her mouth and nose and stepped in, leaving the lights off. Using the flashlight on her phone, she saw the bloated guards. They'd died with their weapons in hand, but they'd been killed anyway as they ran toward the door to make their escape. The rest of the house was quiet, but she only cared about getting to Fredrick. The lamp by his bed was on, and she had to grip the doorframe when she saw the bed.

The butcher who'd done this would pay for this was her first thought, but she also couldn't help but think about what Fredrick's last moments were like. She sat in the chair the killer had dragged next to where he lay and stared, having a hard time wrapping her mind around what she was looking at. Fredrick had been cut up and put back together once they were done. Only there was a gap between the pieces, so he took up most of the bed like a macabre puzzle.

Her tears fell when she stared at his head. It'd been sliced from his body and stood straight up on the pillow, and his eyelids had been cut off so his eyes were permanently open. This was the last of her family, and the world seemed a scarier place with no one she could really trust. In the end she'd failed Fredrick, and there was no making up for it.

"Fuck," she said and stood. There were things she had to do before she left here.

She walked through the house, and every guard was accounted for, but the women who spent their days with Fredrick were missing along with all the money in the safe. If they'd done this, their lives were over when she did the same to them. They'd missed the safe in her room, and she took her time gathering everything she'd need.

Whoever did this had wiped the security feed along with all of Fredrick's work. The loss of income would hit hard, but the clubs were still in business, so she'd be able to bankroll new people to keep her safe and go to war for her. That'd be the only way forward.

It was late by the time she was done and drove away. Her plan had been to burn the place down, but drawing attention to herself and her resurrection would only complicate things. Having the feds take up the investigation into her and their business would be one too many things to overcome.

She parked close to the Eden Roc, walked back to the bar, and called Kira to come down and meet her. This time around she ordered the round of vodka and slammed two shot glasses back to erase the smell of death from her nose. Fredrick would haunt her dreams for the rest of her life, but she couldn't focus on that if she wanted to stay alive.

"You have time for me now?" Kira sat and picked up a drink. "It might be too late."

"Fredrick is dead." She lifted her hand for a refill and stared at her aunt. "So yes, it's too late."

"What happened?" Kira appeared genuinely shocked.

She told her what she'd found at the house and what had been taken. "You don't know anything?"

"Why would Kira know a thing about you or Fredrick?" The gruff voice with the thick Russian accent was the last thing she wanted to deal with. "You turned your back on your mother when she was alive and have forgotten her in death. You've also made it clear to Kira that we are beneath you."

"This is a waste of my time," she said, standing only to be pushed down by Ivan.

"Your mother's mistake was to give you the sense that you're more important than you really are. You're the daughter of Yury—so fucking what. That means shit now. He's dead, and he was a weak man, which is why he's dead." Ivan brushed down his long beard, showing off the tattoos on his fingers. Her grandfather was old-school and had earned every bit of ink he wore.

"My mother wrote letters full of lies," she said, hoping he picked up on her hatred. "She never acted so victimized when she was with my father, so I think she fooled you to get what she wanted."

"Girl, do you think I didn't know who your father was?" Ivan laughed as if her entire life had been a lie. "To show you my good faith, I won't expect the rest of what Yury owed me. The business god was as big a lie as the ones he told you and Fredrick. He did build a business with the money I gave him, but it took more than he was ever going to admit to you. Yury was nothing but a pit that needed to be constantly fed."

"That's the lie." Her father had always held such contempt for Ivan. He'd laugh about how crude her mother's family was, and how he'd wanted nothing to do with them. "He thought you were a joke."

"And yet he took my money. He kept taking it until someone cut him in two. Believe what you want, but do not brag to me how you are better than all of us because of Yury and the shit he put in your head." Ivan lost his smile and slammed his fist on the table. "You have enjoyed the life you have because of this crude ape. The money came from me and my girls."

That was what her father used to call Ivan. "Why wouldn't he have told me?"

"He told me how brilliant you are, so figure it out. The truth is, he didn't lose the Hell Fire Clubs and the rest because of the feds—*I* lost all that. Yury was more interested in getting fucked than in fucking doing his job." Ivan accepted a file from the man behind him. "The truth is in here, so know that all the clubs you and Fredrick started are mine. The real estate, the money, and everything else you have—it's all mine."

"Keep it. I'll start over somewhere else." This news made her world that much smaller, so it was time to leave the Antakov and Volkov families behind.

"Nicola, I had Kira come to you because it's time to come home. You can hate your mother for speaking the truth, but it's what she wanted for you and your children. Those children are your responsibility. You brought them into the world, and you've given them away." Ivan covered Kira's hand with his. "Who will be strong for you when you are old and at the end of your life?"

"It's too late for my children." Starting over meant much more than a business and a life. "I'll rebuild and make sure, this time, no one can take what's mine."

"Talk like that truly makes you Yury's daughter. Come, Kira, there is no reaching the coward."

"I am no coward, old man," she screamed, wanting to strangle the life out of him.

"Prove it," Ivan taunted.

"What do you want from me?" She was sure this was a trap, but for now she'd gladly step into it.

"If you give me what I want, you get what you want." Ivan offered his other hand.

"I'm not sure you can give me that since my list is long," she said. "Tell me."

"Are you sure?" Ivan asked, his hand still on the table waiting for her to take it.

She stared at it before swallowing her pride and giving in. "I've lost everything important to me, so I have no choice." That was true, and she wouldn't mind dying, but she needed to repay Casey for her parents, and whoever had killed Fredrick. She'd only be able to do that by holding her nose and accepting Ivan's offer. "What do you want?"

❖

Cain sat in her pub and nursed a beer while she waited for Linda, while Lou, Katlin, and Dino sat a few tables over. They were having the meeting here since the news crews were parked in front of the house and would be for the foreseeable future. She'd seen a few people from the national shows giving live updates on the sins Ronald and his minions had committed. Annabel had told her to prepare for a visit from the head of the FBI since she'd been right. The fallout had mostly hit the bureau's DC office.

The only ones they hadn't found were Dylan Gardner and Matt Joseph, but she had enough people out looking that it wouldn't be long before they'd run into their handcuffs. Their running gave Cain permission to find them and dispense her form of justice, and she was looking forward to it. That was especially true of Matt Joseph. She'd gift him his hands for touching Emma before she killed him.

"You're looking good for a gunshot victim," Josh, the pub's manager, said. The place was full, mostly with locals who came for not only the drinks, but for the band who played a long list of Irish drinking songs and ballads. "Those are a bitch to get over."

Josh had been shot as they planned the expansion so they could have a Bourbon Street entrance. The space had doubled, which was great for business, but it'd come with problems like the shooting. That Josh had survived it and was able to return to work was a relief, but she wasn't taking any other chances. The pub now operated as before but with new security.

She remembered finding this place with Billy and talking about all their plans for the bar they'd work together. They'd have fun here with their crews, drinking and singing along with their father on the nights he joined them. She and Billy had also bartended, talking to pretty girls and laughing with each other. This place was a part of her past that she'd treasure until she died since it had brought her the greatest treasure of all. A few feet from where she was sitting was where Emma had dumped a tray of beer on her, and that had brought her nothing but joy ever since.

"They are, but even with the injury, you've done a great job here." She raised her glass and tapped it to his. "The bar alone is a thing of beauty." The new bar had come from the same workshop in Ireland as the old one. Her da had ordered the original one, so she'd gone back to the same place and enjoyed meeting the grandson of the man who'd refurbished her da's gift to them. Tradition was something she believed in because it'd been engrained in her.

"The receipts have been better than we expected." Josh put a fresh beer down and pointed to the door. "Your guests have arrived."

She glanced at Lou, and he sat back as a way to make his jacket flap open. The man with Linda was massive and, in a way, reminded her of Lou, only with a much crueler face. Yury had seemed like the kind of man who needed someone like this backing him up. She had Lou but wasn't afraid to do the dirty work when it needed doing. She doubted Yury had ever gotten his hands dirty.

"Cain, this is Boris St. John," Linda said.

"Boris." She held her hand out and smiled at the strong grip. "Thank you for making the trip."

"I don't know what Linda has told you about me," Boris said, taking a seat at the table she'd moved to.

"I told her you were Yury's fixer until you lost Abigail in New York. Once you did, Yury was going to kill you." The way Linda spoke, Cain could almost feel the hatred she had for this man. "Boris and I have never seen the world the same, but after we both had to run, we've come to a truce. It's not a friendship, but we are in the same situation when it comes to Nicola."

"So you've kept in touch?" Cain asked Boris.

"I talk to Linda every Monday at five in the morning my time. When we were working for Yury, I was a pain in the ass to this woman." Boris smiled and Linda didn't. "She's kept me alive, so I've apologized as many times as she's let me, but I think she still doesn't believe me."

"Let's start with the reality that if you warn anyone in the family that Linda is here and under my protection, your life will end just like Yury was planning, only I'll find you." She smiled now, and Linda did as well. "Her mother wants her sons back to work in that cesspool, and that's not going to happen." She stopped while the waitress took their order. The band wouldn't start up again until she was finished with this.

"There's no reason for me to reach out to anyone from a past that's dead," Boris said, never losing eye contact. "Yury and Valerie are dead, and what's left of the family probably want me dead too."

"Then you can either stay where you are now or join us." She was going to build a road to Nicola a brick at a time, even if it was with people like Boris.

He seemed surprised by her offer. "What do you want me around for?"

"You can start pouring drinks either here or at the other club we own, and then we'll see." She watched him study the room. "We'll get you a place, and my guys in here will make sure you're okay. Think about it before you turn me down, or if you need more reassurance, talk to Linda."

"I'd like to stay," he said, not hesitating. "The truth is I'm tired of being alone. That might make me sound like a coward, but all this has humbled me."

"Just remember that Cain, her wife, and most of her family are women," Linda said. Boris nodded and smiled again. "She rules like Yury, yet they're nothing alike."

"Good," Cain said and leaned forward. Lou caught her attention and pointed to the door. Her watchers had come inside but hadn't spotted them yet. "Let's head to the office so the band can start up."

With the expansion the office was now a spot Josh could use to get away from the crowd, and Emma had come and decorated it herself. They sat at the table Josh let the staff use for breaks. Cain and Emma's own club's upgrade was close to being complete, and she hoped Emma's turned out this well. Linda sat on her side and handed her the sheet of information she'd written up about the Volkov family.

"What can you tell us about Ivan Volkov?" she asked, and Boris shifted in his seat.

"He's Yury's father-in-law, and they hated each other. A month before his death, Yury was planning to kill Ivan and didn't care what Valerie would think. It all came down to the money and how much Yury owed Ivan."

"That's interesting." If that was true, then what income would Nicola use to go forward? The best part of all this would be Nicola's desperation. Desperate people were sloppy. "I thought Yury was successful with the clubs and other businesses he had. What could he possibly owe his father-in-law?"

"The money for everything Yury had came from Ivan. Even after the clubs and the operation had been going for years, Yury still needed Ivan's money to keep it all going. It was a secret he kept quiet, and he hated that Ivan wouldn't let him forget it. I went with him a few times when he met with either Ivan or one of his girls." Boris was a fount of information.

"One of his girls?"

Boris nodded. "Ivan has no sons, but four girls. He's taught them to be vicious, and Valerie learned those lessons well. Her sisters Kira, Mira, and Inga are the same but only more vicious since they're still working for Ivan." He counted off the family on his fingers. "Only Valerie and Mira had children, but Mira's are young. I don't know that much more about them than that, since Yury had as little contact with them as possible."

"I was shot recently, and I know it was Kira who ordered the hit. What did she have to gain by that?"

The way Boris's eyes roamed up and down her body made her think he was trying to figure out where the wound was. "I can't be sure, but it has to be the same reason Yury wanted you dead after you found his grandchildren. Brandi Parrish has a good business here with some of the most exclusive clientele in the city. It's established, making millions, and has very little security. Why work to build your own when you can steal someone else's?"

Damn if she wasn't going to have people at Brandi's until all these bastards were dead. They'd need another meeting so she could convince Brandi to take her help even if she'd rather not. "If they try that, they're going to see Brandi isn't such an easy target. She'd have been under someone's thumb by now if that was true."

"I wish I had more to tell you," Boris said, and Cain found Linda studying him like he was a safe she was trying to crack.

"Start thinking, and we'll talk again. Yury and Valerie are dead, but Nicola is very much alive. I doubt she'll be any more forgiving than Yury."

"And stay, but if you have something else in mind, I'll kill you myself," Linda said, and Cain believed her. "You were given free rein by Yury, so I know how you think, but like I said, Cain and Yury are very different people. She has a family she loves, a wife she adores, and businesses that have nothing to do with selling women."

"I'm not as smart as you," Boris said, "so I know I'll have to earn your trust, but Linda knows I'm loyal."

"Remember what Linda just said, and we'll be fine. When it comes to my family, and Linda and her brothers are now my family, I won't hesitate to keep them safe." She stood and shook Boris's hand. "Josh will set you up and give you the keys to the apartment near here."

"Thank you, Cain, and you too, Linda." Boris lowered his head in what she thought was his way of appearing humble. It was a hard look for him to pull off, considering he could've been the villain in a horror movie. He'd be on probation until she was sure, since she seldom allowed new people into her circle until she was absolutely sure.

"Good, I'll be in touch." She pulled Linda's chair for her and opened the door for Josh. Lou had the car waiting, and Linda got in with her. "Is everything set?"

"I'd love to tell you that he's not full of shit, but I've known Boris too long. If he's working for Ivan, we'll know it soon enough, but I was surprised by what he said about Yury. I started working for him after he'd been established, and he never mentioned he owed Ivan that much." Linda rubbed over the spot on her leg where she'd been shot, and Cain could commiserate. Bullet wounds weren't like anything else that could happen to you. They carved a path through your body, and it took time to heal from the outside all the way to the point where the bullet ended up.

"Boris might be what he's saying, or he might be trying to get back to where he was, after he helps Nicola regain power. There might be a problem with that scenario he hasn't considered." They headed to the office where Finley and Linda now had a dedicated workspace to watch over everything they had in place, and keep Annabel's people out.

"What's that?"

"After what happened at Nicola's house in Miami, she has limited options. The money's gone, her brother is dead, and the things she depended on to make more money are destroyed." She opened the door again once Lou had pulled into the warehouse portion of the building and waited until they were in the securest room to continue. "She really only has two ways she could go."

"To Ivan or make her way alone," Linda said.

"That's the two I'm thinking, so the Volkov family has to become our new priority because I don't think Nicola is wired to go it alone. Nicola might not want Boris back, but he'd be a good foot soldier if she does make a stand. Ivan, though, will welcome him with open arms."

The only lead they had on the Volkov family so far was Mira, and there was no getting to her. The feds had her in custody, and with all the evidence against her, there was no way she was getting bail when you considered what she was accused of. Finding someone involved in trafficking only led to other people involved in the same, and Russell was focused on bringing down the syndicates one at a time.

"Nicola will never get anything done by herself, and we'll be watching Boris, so don't worry about that."

"You're doing a great job, and the boys are doing well, so I hope all of you are home."

Linda nodded and smiled. It was good to see that Linda had lost that expression of suspicion. "Thank you for giving us one. We're not going anywhere. Josh and Tim are happy, and they love Hayden. He's introduced them to all his friends, and they're enjoying being kids. That's all I've ever wanted for them."

"They're good boys, and I think they'll be with Hayden for years to come. That's my hope, anyway," she said, and Linda nodded.

She headed home and laughed softly when she saw the house across the street had crime scene tape around it. Lou stopped in the front drive when she spotted Emma walking along the garden with the children and her father. Emma swayed with the baby in her arms, and after a glance at her watch, she saw it was bedtime for Billy.

"What's on the menu today?" she asked, lifting a running Hannah off the ground.

"Weeding, so let's leave the farmers to it." Emma carefully handed over the baby after Cain put Hannah down. "They're losing daylight, but it's too hot to do it during the day."

They went in and put the baby in the room next to theirs, and Emma took her hand and led her to their bedroom. She took the hint and unzipped the dress Emma was wearing and stopped to admire the beautiful underwear. "Did you have something in mind, Mrs. Casey?"

"This has been a strange few months, don't you think?" Emma turned around and pulled her shirt from her pants so she could unbutton it. "You getting shot, the crazy people across the street, and every other thing that's happened hasn't left a lot of alone time for us. Seeing you in the hospital scared me at first, but you're you, and I knew you'd be okay."

"I *am* okay, and I'm dying to prove myself," she said as her shirt dropped to the ground.

"Not funny, mobster," Emma said, unbuckling her belt. "Dying is way off for you." Emma pressed herself to her and put her hands in the back of her underwear, on her butt. "Living is what's on the agenda tonight."

"You're damn right," she said, unhooking Emma's bra and adding it to the pile of clothes on the floor. "And I'm sorry this has been so long in coming."

"I don't care about that. All I need is for you to touch me and remind me that we're going to be fine," Emma said, squeezing her as if to prove to herself they'd reached this point.

Emma sat on the bed and pulled her panties off before pulling Cain's underwear toward her feet so she could kick them off. She lay back after that and opened her arms and legs in a sign she wanted Cain to lie on top. The touch of Emma against the length of her was a good reminder of how special what they shared was, and how even after years, Emma fueled her passion. She lowered her head and kissed

Emma slow, wanting to savor it after the days they'd had to refrain because of her injury.

"Tell me what you want," she said as Emma hooked her feet at the small of her back. There was only room for her hand between them, and she took the invitation and touched her. "I'll give it to you."

"I want you to show me how much you love and want me," Emma said, pressing her head back, exposing her neck when Cain felt how wet she was.

She moved her lips to the side of Emma's neck and dragged her index and middle fingers through Emma's wetness. "Have you been thinking about this?" she whispered in her ear.

"You had so much to do today." Emma reached up and combed the lock of hair that always came out of place behind her ear. That lazy smile Emma was aiming at her had been what had hooked Cain from the moment she laid eyes on Emma. "I didn't want to derail your appointments, but seeing you move around without pain, looking strong and alive, made me want you."

"I don't have pain, not any longer, but I am hurting," she said, pinching Emma's clit between her fingers.

"Ugh," Emma moaned. "That was mean."

"Mean is not doing anything about it." She kissed Emma again before sliding her fingers all the way in and pressing her thumb to the hard clit. That made Emma drop her feet to the mattress and widen her knees, letting her fingers go deeper. "I love you, lass, and I've missed this."

"Yes," Emma said louder than a whisper, but seeming to remember the thousand people in their house. "Please, honey."

She went slow as she dragged in and out, loving how Emma clung to her, breathing harshly in her ear. Emma's nails raking up her back and the way she squeezed her shoulders were the signs she wanted her to speed up. That was easier when she rose and put all her strength into the strokes.

"Oh my God," Emma said, reaching up and pulling her hair as a way to make her lower her head. "So good."

The way Emma sounded in moments like this did to her what she imagined a hit of crack did to an addict. She'd do anything to have it again because the deeper timbre of Emma's voice had a way of weaving through the pleasure centers of her brain and turning her on. She was about to speed up when Emma pushed her off and had her roll to her back so she could get on top. Emma accomplished the move without moving her hand.

In this position Emma controlled the speed and gave Cain a view that was hers alone. Emma squeezed her own breast and with her other hand reached back between Cain's legs. "Lass, I can't concentrate if you do that." She spread her legs, hoping to hold off the orgasm.

"That's the last thing I want you to do...oh damn," Emma said, moving up and down on Cain's fingers, making her climb with her. "Come...oh yes...come with me."

She lifted her hips every time Emma came down, and Emma responded by putting more pressure between her legs. "Fuck," she said, not able to hold back any longer. When she was this turned-on, she came fast and hard, and when she took a breath, she flipped them over again and gave Emma what she'd wanted.

"Like that, baby," Emma said in an almost stutter. "Oh yes, yes, yes." After one long moan, Emma tensed, so she flipped them again. Emma dropped onto her chest as her sex squeezed her fingers.

She kept her fingers in and held Emma in place, wanting to enjoy the moment of peace. The sudden wetness on her chest made her smile and Emma groan. "Hey, I always take it as a compliment."

Emma rose and there was a bit of breast milk on Cain's chest. It happened every so often when Emma was breastfeeding, and the doctor said the oxytocin released during sex sometimes caused a small milk spurt. "I'm sorry." Emma used the sheet to dry her off.

"Lass, there's nothing to apologize for, and I'm glad I can make you feel that good." She put her arms back around Emma and rolled on top of her. "Hey," she said when she saw Emma's eyes were glassy with tears. "What?"

"Nothing," Emma said, using the sheet to wipe her face this time. "Really, I'm just happy, and I feel a little guilty since Fin and Abigail are still worried about pretty much everything."

"They're not going anywhere, and we're working to find all those people." She rubbed Emma's back and kissed the side of her head. "Da used to say that life comes with joy that's balanced with pain. The pain part is inevitable, but our job as clan leader is to tip the scales toward joy as much as we can." She never stopped thinking of the moving pieces she had on her chessboard. Some she'd removed in a way she found satisfying, and others would keep her busy.

"You are my joy, love," Emma said, kissing her. "And I'm glad you're better. Once we find the rest of these idiots, it's your job to deal with them. I'm retired."

She laughed and stopped when the house phone rang. "Hello."

"Ms. Cain, the FBI is outside and want to talk to you," Carmen said.

"Lock them in the front room, and tell them I'll be down in thirty minutes." It was late for a drop-in, so it had to be something big. They took a shower together, and as if sensing Emma was up and around, Billy started crying.

"Let me see if he'll take a bottle, so I can let Daddy feed him," Emma said, throwing on a pair of jeans and a linen shirt. Carmen was already in the room taking care of it, so Emma took Cain's hand.

They went down together and found Joe, Shelby, and Annabel were back. "I'd think you were off duty by now," she said, standing by the bar. "So how about a drink?"

"We're actually coming from the hospital where we put Ronald in custody. He'll be in for a few days since someone beat him severely, but he'll live," Annabel said. "The first thing out of his mouth was blaming it on you."

"Of course it was me," she said, laughing, pouring whiskies all around. "I also killed Jimmy Hoffa, so I'm not sure if that case is still open. I'll never tell where he is, though, no matter how much you beat me."

Annabel laughed as she accepted the glass. "I did tell him that not everything that happens in town is your fault right after Shelby read him his rights. He'll be coming in as soon as he's released, and tomorrow we'll be arraigning everyone else. I thought you might want to attend since we couldn't have done it without you."

"Thank you, Agent Hicks, and I'd like to know when you catch Gardner. Of all of you, she's the one who reminds me the most of Barney Kyle, in that she's quick on the trigger."

"Gardner's father was a highway patrolman, and we've been in touch with him to explain what a bad idea it'd be to aid her," Annabel said, taking a sip of her drink. "I have to admit that I approached you to save my job—all our jobs really—and you came through. Ronald was obsessed with being stationed here, and he was willing to smash through us if that's what it took."

"Ronald doesn't strike me as a man who'll like his secrets exposed. His mother and sister are still alive and are regular churchgoers. Finding out who Ronald truly is will go against everything they believe." She knew more about Ronald than he knew about himself. "Right now he's like a bear caught in a trap. He'll chew through his arm to get out of it if he can."

"So you think he's going to escape?" Shelby asked.

"I'm saying you should keep an eye on him. Whoever beat him up would've done him a favor if he'd finished the job. If I was a gambler, I'd bet that's all Ronald's thought about since you slapped handcuffs on him. Things that have to be hidden in the dark never do well in the light." She finished her drink and placed her glass on the coffee table. "I'm glad to help, and if there's anything else, you've caught me in a generous mood. Just ask."

"Thank you, and you should know that Ronald keeps insisting on talking to you. We have enough, so skip it if you want," Shelby said.

"Let's see how court goes tomorrow, and we'll decide then. It might make an exciting chapter when I write my memoirs."

CHAPTER TWENTY-ONE

The next morning, Abigail joined Cain and Emma to have breakfast. The meeting with the feds the night before was the end of one of their enemies at the back gate. It freed Cain to concentrate on her Russian problems while also managing their expansion. The hurricane had been devastating to the city, but a boon to their business. With more territory came more risks along with the rewards, so she couldn't ignore it forever.

"What does this mean?" Abigail asked.

Cain placed her cup down and placed her hand over Abigail's. "It means the people who were close and watching all of us with ill intent are being swept out of the way. Not that my attention hasn't been on finding Nicola, but it's easier to concentrate now."

"I'm so tired of being afraid." Abigail sighed, and she could see her frustration.

"I'll tell you what I told Fin. Nicola's world had been diminished as far as choices. I'll work with whoever I need to until we find her. Once she's dead, your problems die with her, since Sacha doesn't see you or the kids as threats." That was as free of her past as Abigail was going to get when it came to her ex. "Your blessing for him to take Nicola's place at the head of the family means he'll work as hard as we will until Nicola's dead."

"But these new people," Abigail said. "I hate that I'm constantly bringing new problems. Hell, you got shot. If they think like Valerie, they'll want the kids too."

"I've been thinking of them myself because they're possibly who Nicola will turn to," she said, and Emma placed her hand on her thigh. "Their problem is they shot *me*. It had nothing to do with Nicola, so don't blame yourself. It had more to do with power."

"What, kill the king and you get the spoils?" The way Abigail asked made her think Abigail thought it was ludicrous.

"Kill the king and get the city and all it has to offer. After a few phone calls, the same thing that happened to me has happened in two other cities. It's not like I'm in a mobster club, but the head of one of the families in Houston is dead. There are no leads, but someone is leaning heavily on their prostitution operations, so I pointed them in the right direction."

"So we wait?"

"No, we live," Emma said. "That's what we've always done no matter what, and it makes the problems not as significant. Trust Cain to keep the children safe, because to the Caseys, there is no greater treasure."

"You and your kids are as important to me as my own. Trust Fin and I will deal with this, so you never have to worry that any of them will ever grow up to be pimps or anything close to it." She stood and helped Emma to her feet. "Today, all you need to concentrate on are the three little happy people in your life. You'll soon share their name, but first Emma and I are heading to federal court. I've built a wall around you, so don't give the men and women trailing around with you a hard time."

They headed downtown, and Katlin and Lou went in with them unarmed, making both guards nervous. If someone shot her here, though, there'd be hell to pay. She wasn't as interested in the agents being charged as she was with Larry and Jane. They were working for Mira Volkov, and she wanted the connection that had gotten them there. Like Ronald, Larry was wild about his mother, and the old woman couldn't be convinced Larry was a terrible guy.

"All rise," the bailiff said. All she needed was for Larry to notice her because her next stop was his mother.

The judge listened to the group of defense attorneys before slamming his gavel down and remanding everyone pending trial. Like Annabel had said, when it came to trafficking, the judge was taking no chances that any defendant would run. The only upside for them was prison would keep them safe from her.

Larry did notice her and yelled for her to come and visit him. The sleazeball was yanked out of the courtroom by the chains he was wearing and came close to losing his balance. The one who did fall was Angus, and it took more than one officer to get him on his feet. Of all the people heading back to lockup, Angus appeared the most fearful.

"This is surreal," Emma said, her hand in the bend of Cain's elbow. "How do these people think they'll never get caught?"

"Ego, and the badge. Law enforcement don't like turning on their own, so it makes room for people to get away with stuff like this. Their defense is going to be they were doing their job trying to catch the boogeyman doing evil deeds." Larry was going to have to wait because she wanted to take Annabel up on her offer to visit Ronald.

She could understand wanting to get her on something that would land her in jail for years, but motivation like this came from somewhere else. Angus never lost eye contact with her as the door closed, and she smiled. There'd never come a day she'd harm a woman and her children for the sins of the father, but Angus didn't know that.

"Please," she heard Angus yell. Their meeting had made an impression.

"Good morning," Annabel said with Shelby at her side. "Have you thought about a visit with Ronald?"

"Emma and I have an appointment this afternoon, so if he's not tied up," she said and laughed. "Is he sticking to the story that I'm the one who attacked him?"

"The problem with that will be that the DNA recovered from his face doesn't belong to you," Shelby said.

"He's at Tulane hospital," Annabel said. "We'll meet you there."

Tulane hospital was next to Big Charity that was now closed because of the damage from Hurricane Katrina, and she glanced at the photos that lined the walls of different spots in the city as she walked holding Emma's hand. The thought that this was her town came to her full force, and it was time to start acting like it. All these assholes who'd tried their best to kill her either literally or figuratively were going to have to accept she wasn't going anywhere.

The agent on Ronald's door nodded at her when he opened it and allowed them to enter. Ronald's face was swollen to the point of her almost not recognizing him. That the room was bugged was a given. Ronald opened the eye not swollen shut and glared at her the best he could, considering the condition he was in.

"I'm sure you have a list, but what's your problem with me?" she asked, curious as to what he'd say. In all the research she'd done on this guy, she couldn't understand what his beef was, aside from making a name for himself. Their paths had never crossed until that day he sought her out at Hayden's baseball game.

"You don't deserve to live," Ronald said, sounding a bit crazed.

"You act like you're innocent, but you're guilty of so many things you should be put in front of a firing squad. The world doesn't need your kind."

"Do my sins equal yours, Ronald?"

"It's Special Agent Chapman to you, bitch."

"Like I've said before, there's not a thing special about you, Ronald. That title is something you gave away when you plucked Lucy out of her foster home and used her. You lost it when you killed Detective Newsome." She laughed when he flinched. "Did you think I'd forget that one? The guy wasn't the sharpest knife in your gut, but he deserved better than he got after he swallowed your bull about the glory he was going to get."

"Since when do you give a shit about Newsome?" Ronald asked, hissing at her. "He hated you more than anyone, including that crazy bitch Carol."

"But I'm not the one who killed him, and don't tell me it wasn't you, because both of us know better." She gave Emma the chair and stood on the other side of the bed to take Ronald's attention off Emma. "You see, Ronald, you had to pretend to be important by walking on a baseball field with the biggest idiot in the FBI. That caught my attention, and I told you what I was going to do in response."

"You're bluffing, and you're also full of shit." Ronald seemed to be in pain as he turned his head in her direction, so she moved even more out of his sight.

"You think I'm bluffing?" She put her hand in her pocket, enjoying the way he flinched. "You were so busy breaking all those rules, you forgot to turn around and see what was behind you. You never saw who was breathing down your neck," she said as she leaned in and held up her phone. "All those nights when you dressed up in your party clothes and got your freak on." She brought up the last session he'd had. "Messing up all that pretty skin really got you going, but who was watching was something you should've asked yourself."

"I'm going to beat this, and I'll be happy to serve time for killing you." Ronald sounded serious, so it was time to push him a little more and give Sept a role in Ronald's tableau.

"Let's see what else I saw." She pressed *play* and it seemed like he couldn't force himself to look away. "What did that bad boy who lives inside you do on the bridge?" The question came as the door opened and Annabel entered with Sept. "Was he going to tell Special Agent Hicks all about your scheme?"

"Stop it," Ronald screamed. "You don't have a right."

"Cain," Sept said in greeting. Cain had texted all the videos to her friend a week ago so she could put her case together. "Thanks for the information. We issued warrants, so we have it all in custody."

"What information?" Annabel asked.

"The bridge cameras captured the type of vehicle that knocked Newsome over the side, and going over the side had nothing to do with his blood alcohol," Cain said.

"Our security followed Ronald from the airport to the rental place, then to Slidell. They recorded every second of his trip across the bridge, including the murder of Newsome and him returning the vehicle. We purchased the Suburban he leased, which has his fingerprints and DNA in it," Emma said. "We also have the lease agreement he signed and the fake ID and stolen credit card he used to acquire it."

"She's lying," Ronald said, grabbing Cain's phone and throwing it across the room. "She did this to me. I'm in here because of her." He was accusing Cain, which didn't surprise her. People like Ronald seldom if ever took responsibility for their actions.

"You're here because you're an idiot who didn't think all of this through, Ronald. Killing an NOPD detective isn't a federal crime, so I'm covering my bases when it comes to you," she said, texting the video to Annabel.

"Newsome called me that night," Annabel said.

"He did because Barry Knight and Christina Brewer double-crossed him. Newsome lost his job and his pension and was threatened to keep quiet by Ronald and his agents. To keep you from investigating, I'm sure Angus pushed the theory he was drunk when his car went into the lake."

"You're right," Annabel said.

"Newsome wasn't important in the grand scheme Ronald came up with, so his death only served to keep the house across the street as well as his secret investigation from you," she said to Annabel. "That's what Ronald was counting on, and it made him sloppy."

"I'm sure you'll get a shot at him, Agent Hicks, but for now," Sept said and read Ronald his rights. "The NOPD officer on the door will be joining the federal agent. The minute you're able to appear in district court, we have a date, Mr. Chapman."

"If he skates on an insanity plea, my reaction will not be something you'll ever forget," Cain said to all the law enforcement in the room. "Ronald knew exactly what he was doing, and he just threatened me."

"What? You're the one who's crazy." Ronald smiled at her, and she saw he was missing at least three teeth.

Emma held up her phone and played the threat Ronald had made. "Crazy is saying it out loud." She stood and waited for Cain to come around and take her hand.

"Next time, Ronald, listen when the devil whispers in your ear that there'd be a price to pay," Cain said and smiled back at him. "That's how most of you see me but let this be a lesson. Sometimes hell is not only of your own making, but you at times run toward it with the fervor of a zealot. Whatever that hell is will have nothing to do with me."

"You're getting poetic in your old age," Sept said, slapping her shoulder.

"I doubt Ronald will ever love my prose."

❖

"How about a trip with just the two of us?" Cain asked Emma when they reached the car.

"I'll go wherever you lead, love," Emma said as they headed to their next appointment. "Where do you want to go?"

"Angelo Giordano owns a house in Sicily with a small staff and no neighbors. When I talked to him a few weeks ago, he offered it and I accepted. Neither of us has been to Sicily, so I thought a couple of weeks once the summer starts where our only plans are to do nothing except have fun."

"I'll agree on one condition," Emma said, sliding her hand in her shirt after undoing a few buttons.

"Whatever you want, lass."

"We try one more time before we go. One more to add to our clan, so Hayden will have the support he'll need when he rules an even bigger empire than we do." They'd talked about another baby, but Cain had waited for Emma to be ready. Children were something she'd never say no to, no matter how many Emma wanted.

"I think that's the best souvenir we can bring home."

"Once we do that, what would you think about donating what's left of Billy's gift?" Emma asked when they came to a stop.

"To who?"

"Muriel and Kristen, if they want it. Muriel's an only child, and Kristen doesn't have a brother, and I'm sure they'll want Casey children when the time comes and they're ready. This way we all win since they'll be related to our brood." Emma stayed quiet when Lou and Katlin stepped out. "Very closely related, so if you think it's a bad idea, forget I said anything."

"He's probably smiling with a drink in his hand somewhere, proud of all these children he's helped bring into the world. We gave him what he wanted when we started our family. My brother wanted to be an uncle to *our* kids so Mum would get off his back about settling down." She kissed Emma and enjoyed the moment of being happy. "You're a kind soul, Emma Casey, and I love you with all my heart."

"Let's go add to our clan, mobster. There's still a lot to be done, but we need to forget all that for a while and celebrate life."

They walked into the courthouse holding hands and headed to Mary Buchanan's court so they could fit all the people in attendance. The kids were all in their school uniforms since Mary had agreed to a late afternoon appointment, and Cain took a moment to enjoy the family that'd not only come together, but come home.

"Father," she said to Bishop Andrew Goodman. Her father's oldest friend was better than a psychiatrist at keeping her grounded.

"Your family is almost complete, Derby, but these are some fine additions. Somewhere in the heavens Therese Casey is a happy woman." Andy kissed Emma's cheeks and waved Mary to begin. He had a part to play but only after Mary was done with hers.

"Finley Abbott and Abigail Eaton," Mary said, bringing them to the front with their children. "Are you sure about what you're here for today?"

"Yes," Liam and Victoria yelled, cutting through any tension. Sadie nodded as well while they all chuckled.

"Let's not keep you waiting then, Mr. Abbott. I see your grandparents are here and have plenty of spoiling to make up for," Mary said of Aunt Siobhan and Uncle Shaun who stood with Finley and her family. "Today we're completing the adoption of Sadie, Victoria, and Liam Eaton by Finley Casey Abbott. All parties are in agreement, and there are no objections, so please sign here." Mary had drawn up the papers like Cain wanted, so the children signed as well.

The day would come when Nicola would rise back up to claim what she'd thrown away. When it did, she wanted Nicola to see that her children had made this decision. If she wanted to perpetuate the business she loved so much, she'd have to find new heirs—these were beyond her reach. And her children had not only decided, they were thrilled with Finley. Victoria was bouncing in Fin's arms and Liam in Abigail's—their happiness and love was as real as what her own children felt for her and Emma.

"You are all now Abbotts," Mary said. "Fin, congratulations, it's a boy and two girls."

Finley and Abigail laughed when Liam threw his arms in the air. "I Abbott forever," he yelled making his new grandmother cry.

"You, Victoria, and Sadie sure are," Finley said.

"The other Abbott business we have is a name change to add to the three we've already done." She put down another page and handed Abigail a pen. "Sign right here."

"Dr. Abigail Abbott," Abigail said, handing Liam over to Siobhan. "This doesn't mean you can forget the wedding part," she said to Fin.

"The booze has already been ordered," Cain said.

"Let's take some pictures." Emma herded everyone around Mary as she pinched Cain's side.

The photographer took plenty of pictures before Andy blessed the children and their parents, giving all of them new godparents. "Derby and Emma, do you accept your responsibility to raise these children in the church and to accept God?"

"We do," they said together.

"God bless you all, then," Andy said, touching each child, including theirs, on the head.

"One more piece of non-Abbott business and we're done," Mary said. "Ross, the papers have been signed and delivered to Carol. Due to her parole stipulations and the restraining order, all you have to do is sign, and you're a free man."

Mary put the divorce papers down and waved Ross forward. For all that had gone wrong, today made up for it. She smiled when Ross's hand shook as he signed, then turned and kissed Carmen. Pretty soon they could go into business as wedding consultants with the impending marriages they'd helped into being. She hugged Carmen when she turned to her in tears, as Emma hugged her father.

"Congratulations, Ross," she said when Ross put his arms around her next. "I expect you to make an honest woman out of Carmen now that you're free to give her what she wants."

"I can't wait for that," he said, taking Carmen's hand. "We thank you both for making the years we have left so happy."

Cain remembered Carmen telling her she'd married young, and her husband died not long after, before they'd had children. Once Cain was on her own, Carmen had taken care of the house and had been loyal through the years. Her romance with Ross had changed Carmen into a woman who smiled all the time, and Cain was thrilled to see it.

"Thank you, Ms. Cain," Carmen said, smiling and placing her hand on Cain's arm.

"Carmen, you're about to be my mother-in-law, so it's Cain and Emma to you," she said as Emma hugged Carmen again. "We'll talk about everything later, but right now it's time to celebrate all this good stuff."

The staff had the barbecue pits going when they got home, so the kids changed and headed for the pool. There was more screaming when Levi and Leo showed up with Lucy, who was overjoyed to see Hannah again. It took less than twenty minutes for Hannah, Lucy, Victoria, and Liam to be the best of friends, and Leo said that'd go a long way in Lucy's recovery. Before the meal her Aunt Siobhan brought out the bottle of Irish whiskey and asked Cain to do the honors in making her grandchildren true members of their family.

Carmen and Ross brought out all the glasses and poured the adults a drink. "Once Da was gone, it fell to me to welcome all the Casey children into our clan. Today it'll be up to Fin and Aunt Siobhan to tell them the rich history of our family, but I'll get them started." She told the Abbott kids how the whiskey was now part of their history, and going forward they had a family who'd love and protect them always.

"Fin did tell you about this next part right?" Emma asked Abigail.

"She did, and it's been a long time coming," Abigail said, holding her drink and stepping behind her children.

Cain dipped her finger in her glass and put it in Sadie's mouth. "Let this be a reminder of who you are now, and where your people come from. You're a Casey and an Abbott, and you're ours, but only for a time. When your moms set you out in the world, you'll go with our rich history not only in your head, but in your heart. There will never be another day where you question your place in our lives." She repeated it with Victoria and Liam, getting a tight hug from each child.

"You're not done, Derby," Siobhan said.

"Dr. Abigail Abbott"—Cain raised her glass—"welcome to our clan. Your worries and troubles are now mine, and it'll take death for me not to protect what's mine. And as my wife likes to say, death is a long way off for all of us. You're mine until your father hands you to Finley at an altar, and even then, you're my family for all time. Rest easy knowing you're not alone."

Muriel raised her glass, prompting everyone else to do the same.

"To Sadie, Victoria, Liam, and Abigail. May those who came before us watch over them, may God bless them, and may they always know how loved they are."

"Clan," everyone offered up in toast.

The kids headed back to the pool, and Fin and Abigail came and sat with her and Emma. "Cain, thank you," Abigail said. "We would've never made it this far on our own."

"I meant every word I said. We're not done with Nicola, but we will be, and hopefully that'll be one day soon. What you need to remember is to be happy, love your kids, and let Fin share your load. We won't let anything happen to you or those kids, so stay with us until that finale comes."

"Thank you for giving me my family back," Fin said, taking her hand. "Mum found a place close to us, and they're closing on it at the end of the month. She said she can't babysit as much as she'd like from Florida."

"Perfect," Emma said. "I've missed her."

The large table filled up when the staff started serving dinner, and Emma held her back. "I love you, mobster."

"You, my little hayseed, are the center of my world, and what a world you've given me." She kissed Emma and loved the feel of her pressed against her. "Are you happy?"

"Strange question, but yes. You, my love, are relentless in how you protect us, and in how you love all of us. Look at this family you've built and know how proud your parents as well as all that family before them must be of you. The best part is we have so much more to add."

She kissed Emma again and slapped her gently on the butt. "Then let's get to it, Mrs. Casey. The now is perfect, and the future is something I look forward to with you at my side."

About the Author

Ali Vali is the author of the long-running Cain Casey "Devil" series and the Genesis Clan "Forces" series, as well as numerous standalone romances. The newest, *The Devil You Know*, continues the story of Cain and Emma Casey's family and those who wish to destroy it.

Originally from Cuba, Ali has retained much of her family's traditions and language and uses them frequently in her stories. Having her father read her stories and poetry before bed every night as a child infused her with a love of reading, which she carries till today. Ali currently lives outside New Orleans, where she cuts grass, cheers on LSU in all things, and is always on the hunt for the perfect old-fashioned. The best part, she says, is writing about the people and places around the city.

Books Available From Bold Strokes Books

A Wolf in Stone by Jane Fletcher. Though Cassilania is an experienced player in the dirty, dangerous game of imperial Kavillian politics, even she is caught out when a murderer raises the stakes. (978-1-63679-640-6)

The Devil You Know by Ali Vali. As threats come at the Casey family from both the feds and enemies set to destroy them, Cain Casey does whatever is necessary with Emma at her side to bury every single one. (978-1-63679-471-6)

The Meaning of Liberty by Sage Donnell. When TJ and Bailey get caught in the political crossfire of the ultraconservative Crusade of the Redeemer Church, escape is the only plan. On the run and fighting for their lives is not the time to be falling for each other. (978-1-63679-624-6)

One Last Summer by Kristin Keppler. Emerson Fields didn't think anything could keep her from her dream of interning at Bardot Design Studio in Paris, until an unexpected choice at a North Carolina beach has her questioning what it is she really wants. (978-1-63679-638-3)

StreamLine by Lauren Melissa Ellzey. When Lune crosses paths with the legendary girl gamer Nocht, she may have found the key that will boost her to the upper echelon of streamers and unravel all Lune thought she knew about gaming, friendship, and love. (978-1-63679-655-0)

Undercurrent by Patricia Evans. Can Tala and Wilder catch a serial killer in Salem before another body washes up on the shore? (978-1-636790669-7)

And Then There Was One by Michele Castleman. Plagued by strange memories and drowning in the guilt she tried to leave behind, Lyla Smith escapes her small Ohio town to work as a nanny and becomes trapped with an unknown killer. (978-1-63679-688-8)

Digging for Destiny by Jenna Jarvis. The war between nations forces Litz to make a choice. Her country, career, and family, or the chance of making a better world with the woman she can't forget. (978-1-63679-575-1)

Hot Hires by Nan Campbell, Alaina Erdell, and Jesse J. Thoma. In these three romance novellas, when business turns to pleasure, romance ignites. (978-1-63679-651-2)

The Land of Death and Devil's Club by Bailey Bridgewater. Special Liaison to the FBI Louisa Linebach may have defied all odds by identifying the bodies of three missing men in the Kenai Peninsula, but she won't be satisfied until the man she's sure is responsible for their murders is behind bars. (978-1-63679-659-8)

McCall by Patricia Evans. Sam and Sara found love on the water, but can they build a future amid the ghosts of the past that surround them on dry land? (978-1-63679-769-4)

Promises to Protect by Jo Hemmingwood. Park ranger Maxine Ward's commitment to protect Tree City is put to the test when social worker Skylar Austen takes a special interest in the commune and in Max. (978-1-63679-626-0)

Sacred Ground by Missouri Vaun. Jordan Price, a conflicted demon hunter, falls for Grace Jameson, who has no idea she's been bitten by a vampire. (978-1-63679-485-3)

When You Smile by Melissa Brayden. Taryn Ross never thought the babysitter she once crushed on would show up as a grad student at the same university she attends. (978-1-63679-671-0)

A Heart Divided by Angie Williams. Emmaline is the most beautiful woman Jack has ever seen, but being a veteran of the Confederate army that killed her husband isn't the only thing keeping them apart. (978-1-63679-537-9)

Adrift by Sam Ledel. Two women whose lives are anchored by guilt and obligation find romance amidst the tumultuous Prohibition movement in 1920s California. (978-1-63679-577-5)

Cabin Fever by Tagan Shepard. The longer Morgan and Shelby are stranded together, the more their feelings grow, but is it real, or just cabin fever? (978-1-63679-632-1)

Clean Kill by Anne Laughlin. When someone starts killing people she knows in the recovery world, former detective Nicky Sullivan must race to stop the killer and keep herself from being arrested for the crimes. (978-1-63679-634-5)

Only a Bridesmaid by Haley Donnell. A fake bridesmaid, a socially anxious bride, and an unexpected love—what could go wrong? (978-1-63679-642-0)

Primal Hunt by L.L. Raand. Anya, a young wolf warrior, finds herself paired with Rafe, one of the most powerful Vampires in the Americas, in an erotic union of blood and sex.(978-1-63679-561-4)

Snake Charming by Genevieve McCluer. Playgirl vampire Freddie is on the run and a chance encounter with lamia Phoebe makes them both realize that they may have found the love they'd given up on. (978-1-63679-628-4)

Spirits and Sirens by Kelly and Tana Fireside. When rumored ghost whisperer Elena Murphy and very skeptical assistant fire chief Allison Jones have to work together to solve a 70-year old mystery, sparks fly—will it be enough to melt the ice between them and let love ignite? (978-1-63679-607-9)

Aubrey McFadden Is Never Getting Married by Georgia Beers. Aubrey McFadden is never getting married, but she does have five weddings to attend, and she'll be avoiding Monica Wallace, the woman who ruined her happily ever after, at every single one. (978-1-63679-613-0)

Flowers for Dead Girls by Abigail Collins. Isla might be just the right kind of girl to bring Astra out of her shell—and maybe more. The only problem? She's dead. (978-1-63679-584-3)

Rainbow Overalls by Maggie Fortuna. Arriving in Vermont for her first year of college, an introverted bookworm forms a friendship with an outgoing artist and finds what comes after the classic coming out story: a being out story. (978-1-63679-606-2)